Sky Blue

Also by Alexander M. Grace

Coup!

Crisis

Sky Blue

ALEXANDER M. GRACE

BRASSEY'S
Washington • London

Library of Congress Cataloging-in-Publication Data

Grace, Alexander M., 1951–
   Sky blue/Alexander M. Grace
     p.   cm.
   ISBN 1-57488-019-5
   1. Kazakhstan—Politics and government—1991–   —Fiction.
  2. United Nations—Armed Forces—Fiction.   I. Title.
PS3557.R1164S57   1995
813'.54—dc20   95-17039

10 9 8 7 6 5 4 3 2 1

Printed in the United States of America

To my parents, who gave me room to grow.
It is only now that I am a father myself that
I realize how difficult a job they had.

An AUSA Book

The Association of the United States Army (AUSA) was founded in 1950 as a not-for-profit organization dedicated to education concerning the role of the U.S. Army, to providing material for military professional development, and to the promotion of proper recognition and appreciation of the profession of arms. Its constituencies include those who serve in the Army today, including Army National Guard, Army Reserve, and Army civilians, the retirees and veterans who have served in the past, and all their families. A large number of public-minded citizens and business leaders are also an important constituency. The association seeks to educate the public, elected and appointed officials, and leaders of the defense industry on crucial issues involving the adequacy of our national defense, particularly those issues affecting land warfare.

In 1988 the AUSA established within its existing organization a new entity known as the Institute of Land Warfare. Its purpose is to extend the educational work of the AUSA by sponsoring scholarly publications, to include books, monographs, and essays on key defense issues, as well as workshops and symposia. Among the volumes chosen for designation as "An AUSA Institute of Land Warfare Book" are both new texts and reprints of titles of enduring value that are no longer in print. Topics include history, policy issues, strategy, and tactics. Publication as an AUSA book does not necessarily indicate that the Association of the United States Army and the publisher agree with everything in the book, but does suggest that the AUSA and the publisher believe it will stimulate the thinking of AUSA members and others concerned about important issues.

PREFACE

As of this writing, many of the Central Asian republics of the former Soviet Union are at war. Fitful civil wars smolder in Georgia, Tajikistan, and Azerbaijan, another looms in Moldova, and there is the ongoing Armenia-Azerbaijan dispute.

No such conflict now exists in Kazakhstan. The events described in the book are purely imaginary, as are the characters involved. However, there is a long-standing animosity between the Kazakhs and the millions of Russian immigrants who have forcibly altered the way of life of the original steppe dwellers since their arrival in the area in the nineteenth century. There is living memory of the tens of thousands of Kazakhs who were starved to death by the Stalinist government during the collectivization drive of the 1930s. That such antagonisms might boil over into open conflict now that the central government in Moscow has lost the power to prevent it is well within the realm of possibility, given the events of the past few years. Add to this the fact that Kazakhstan, along with the Ukraine, was one of the primary basing areas for the Soviet nuclear arsenal outside of the Russian Republic itself, and you have the formula for a potential disaster of tremendous proportions.

I have taken pains to make the military operations and setting as accurate as possible. I have drawn on extensive research into the events surrounding the commitment of UN peacekeeping forces in Somalia, the former Yugoslavia, and elsewhere as the basis for assumptions about how events might progress *if* a scenario such as this one were to progress in the heart of Central Asia. For the setting, I must express my gratitude to several individuals who have taken the time to correct some of my sillier mistakes in geography and topography, and who gave me insights that provided much-needed local color. John Ranck-Christman and others gave me access to photos and maps and their personal knowledge of the city of Almaty (Alma-Ata in Russian) and of the Kazakh people. I probably should add that Almaty is a much larger city than the book's simplified map would suggest. All times given are local time.

I must also thank Lieutenant Colonel John F. Antal, USA, for his expert advice on the latest advances in military technology, Patrick Roach for an astute first-draft critique, and Lieutenant Colonel Clayton Davis, USA (Ret.), for his kind words and encouragement on my previous writings. A number of other friends in the U.S. Army, the Department of State, and elsewhere in the government gave me valuable guidance and advice. While discretion prohibits the disclosure of their names, I owe them a debt of gratitude for their help and support.

—ALEXANDER M. GRACE
McLean, Virginia

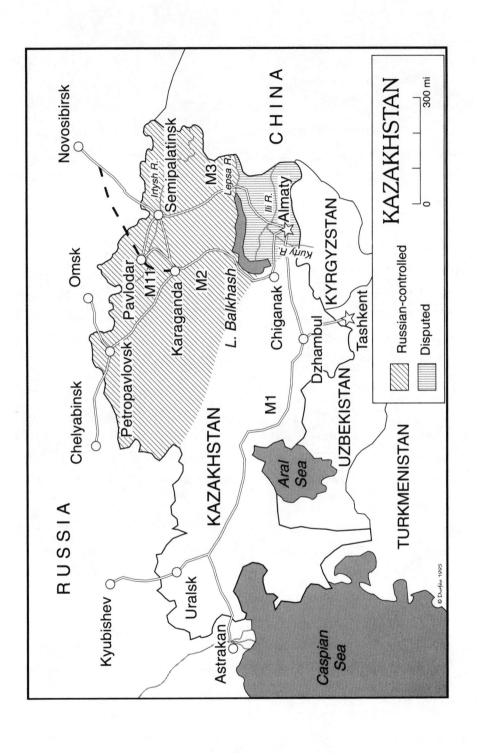

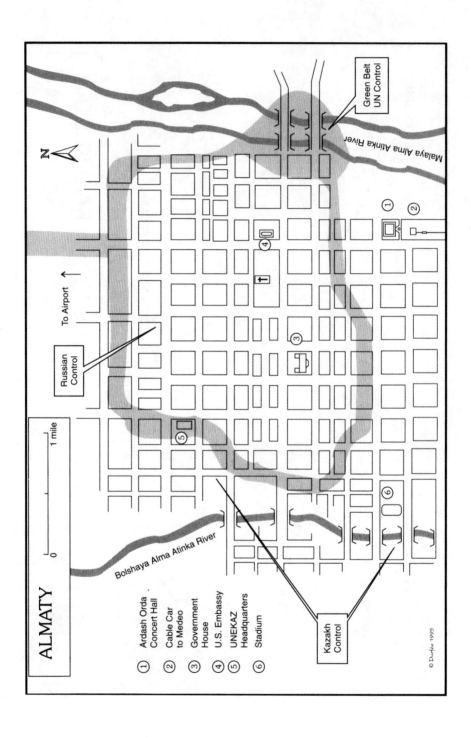

Sky Blue

PROLOGUE

NEAR ZHANGIZ-TOBE, NORTHEASTERN KAZAKHSTAN
15 November, 0345 Hours

Major Yuri Kurilenko sipped his coffee as he stared out the window of the guardroom office into the darkness and swirling rain. This was the perfect weather for it, he thought. The real Siberian winter, with its deep snow, which might inhibit movement for everyone, had not yet set in, but snow would also make it easier to track people and vehicles afterward and would not hinder aircraft overflights. After winter settled in, people became accustomed to the cold, even in Siberia, and the men would be out on patrol regularly once their full winter kit had been issued. The weather now was just bad enough, and irregular enough, to keep men indoors where it was dry and warm, and not so bad that local military commanders would think of it as "toughening" to send men out in it. That was just what he wanted.

The lights were turned off in the guardroom, partly to enable Kurilenko to see better outside, and partly so that he wouldn't need to stare at the bloody bodies of the three fellow duty officers he had already dispatched with the silenced AKM rifle now slung over his shoulder. Kurilenko's night-vision goggles made him look rather like a six-foot insect, and he had to be careful that the steam from his coffee did not cloud up the lenses.

He could just make out the inner security fence of the former Soviet missile base, the main gate, and two of the tall watchtowers. The powerful perimeter lights were no match for the gloom, rain, and great drifts of fog that reached toward the base from the surrounding woods. They would be coming from those woods, Kurilenko knew, using the dead ground off to the right of the main gate for their approach, their camouflaged uniforms making them invisible against the black, white, and gray backdrop.

Of course, the infrared scopes in the towers and thermal imagers on the vehicles of the reaction platoon would see right through all of that and would pick up the body heat of the men. Or *would* have—if only that last shipment of nicad batteries had not proved defective. A new shipment had been rushed out from Moscow, since the security of the base was obviously a high priority, but the cases were now sitting in a closet in Kurilenko's office: he had not found time to do the paperwork on these valuable supplies and could hardly be faulted for not issuing them without it. As it happened, Kurilenko could be sure that the only functioning night-vision equipment on the base at the moment was the pair of goggles he wore—and whatever *they* brought with them tonight.

There would be no alarm when they came through the first fences. The circuits for the electric security fence had been cut, as the red light that flashed forlornly on one of the control panels next to Kurilenko testified. There would be no canine detection either, since a load of infected meat had either killed or disabled all of the animals in the kennel, and replacements had not yet been provided. There were the minefields, of course, but the maps he had provided were up-to-date, and the men should have no trouble avoiding them.

Unless, of course, they made a simple mistake. They could misread the map. The thought struck Kurilenko like a physical blow. How many times had it happened that he was out on a field exercise with his elite border-guard security troops, and some poor lieutenant had misread his map, in conditions not nearly as bad as these. It could happen. He had been assured that the men were the very best, all former Spetsnaz commandos, and all native to this part of the country, but it would be so easy to mistake one fold of the ground in this largely featureless mixture of steppe and woods for another, and a mistake of twenty meters in any direction could lead them right into the middle of a minefield. The resulting explosions, apart from killing or wounding most of the force, would alert the entire base, and then how would Kurilenko explain the deaths of his erstwhile colleagues? So many of the little "coincidences" that had compromised the security of the base could easily be traced to him and him alone.

The possibility that the attack might not go off as planned had not occurred to him. The plan was for him to do his part and then simply fade away with the attackers when they were finished. In the destruction and confusion that would engulf the base, it would be weeks before anyone could be certain that his body was not among the charred remains of the others, if ever. Even then, it would be assumed that he had merely been taken prisoner—but it really wouldn't matter in any case. His "reward" for his contribution to the plan would be more than enough for him to start life anew in another part of the world, not that he was doing it for the money.

Kurilenko's parents were Ukrainian, but he had been born in Central Asia, a child of the mass deportations of Ukrainian peasants by Stalin during the 1930s. He owed his loyalty to his fellow Slavs who were trying to make a life for themselves among the backward Muslims on the steppe. It was the Slavs who had made this formerly barren land bloom under the Soviets' Virgin Lands program of the 1950s. Starting in the nineteenth century, first with Cossack explorers and stolid Russian settlers, they had populated and developed the region just as the Americans had in their own West. They had built Kazakhstan's cities, later the factories, and even the massive space center at Baikonur. Now that the former Soviet Union had collapsed, these medieval mullahs and their flea-ridden followers, illiterate and ignorant, were trying to seize both the land and everything that the Slavs had made of it. There was nothing Kurilenko could do about Tajikistan, Kyrgyzstan, Uzbekistan, and the other republics that had already fallen to the Muslims, but he now had a chance to make a difference in Kazakhstan, and he would do it. He had thrown in his lot with the Russian Provisional Government, which was challenging the mullahs' right to rule the country. The Russians would carve out their own country in the northeast of Kazakhstan where they could live in peace, leaving two thirds of the country to the Muslims. Fair enough.

An ear-shattering horn began blaring in the guardroom, snapping Kurilenko out of his reverie.

"Penetration of the inner perimeter in Sector Two. Multiple contacts. Men on foot," a metallic voice rasped over the public address system.

Kurilenko glanced again at the control panel. None of the electronic motion sensors were functioning. He had seen to that. And the video cameras—he now could just make out the shadowy forms of men darting across one of the screens—only transmitted to this room. It must have been some damned keen-eyed lookout in one of the towers who had bothered to stick his nose out on a night like this. Kurilenko had intentionally assigned the laziest troopers to that side of the perimeter tonight. One of them just *had* to pick tonight to mend his ways.

He snapped the transmit switch of his hand-held radio and called the reaction platoon.

"Hedgehog, this is Castle," he shouted, not having to feign excitement. "Did you copy?"

"Roger," the platoon leader replied immediately.

"Don't wait for backup. Hit them from the east. Keep your men mounted and drive right through them to the main gate. Then regroup and hold there for reinforcements."

A motor rifle battalion half an hour away to the north, in Charsk, would be alerted automatically when the alarm at the base sounded. However, they would find that the batteries of their armored vehicles had mysteriously lost their charge, and these would take time to replace. Even if the unit commander displayed incredible initiative and mobilized ad hoc transport, they would still not arrive for a couple of hours at the very least; Kurilenko had been promised that another ambush force had been dispatched to the highway to intercept them if they did.

Kurilenko zipped up the front of his camouflage jacket and left the office, carefully spinning the dial of the combination lock on the door as he did so. He had just changed the combination himself, so the bodies would not be discovered until it was too late.

He dashed out of the low, squat building into the driving rain, running toward the long, rounded concrete form of the nearest storage bunker. He paused at the crest of a small knoll and turned to watch as the three BMP-2 armored infantry fighting vehicles of the base's quick reaction platoon emerged from the small woods where they were kept hidden. He could hear the squealing of their tracks over the dull patter of the rain and howling wind. Their 30mm cannon and machine guns reached out fiery green fingers toward the perimeter fence, firing blind, he knew, in the general direction of the intruders.

Pinpoints of light now appeared from a dozen places in the rolling, open ground near the fence, and a machine gun from one of the towers joined in. The bullets bounced harmlessly off the sloped sides of the BMPs, sending up sparks that flickered in the rain.

The platoon was maneuvering well, Kurilenko couldn't help but notice with pride. They were echeloned right, so that none of the vehicles masked the fire of the others. The commanders were standing up in their open hatches, readily taking the risk to themselves in exchange for the improved visibility—for they didn't have any working thermal imaging blocks.

Then, suddenly, a bright plume of flame leaped from behind some trees perhaps a kilometer beyond the fences, then another and another. The BMP commanders saw the anti-armor missiles at the same instant that Kurilenko did, and immediately shifted the fire of all their weapons to the sources of the new threat. Since the missiles needed to be guided all the way to impact, the only hope for survival of the targets would be to get the firer to flinch, sending his missile off course for a vital second or two.

One missile did corkscrew into the ground, exploding in a brilliant display of fireworks, but the other two bore in on their targets. One struck the farthest BMP broadside, but merely detonated one of the reactive armor boxes, the explosion of which dispersed the penetrating force of the missile's shaped charge warhead, although the flying debris decapitated the unprotected commander, leaving his mutilated body dangling from the open hatch. The other apparently found a soft spot in the armor of the second BMP and literally blew the vehicle apart, along with its crew and infantry squad.

The one unscathed BMP had stopped momentarily, and infantrymen were piling out of its rear doors. Kurilenko had hoped to eliminate all of the infantrymen along with their vehicles, thus his order to keep the men mounted in the BMPs, rather than having them roaming around individually, making them much harder to round up in the dark. However, these men immediately came under deadly fire from all directions, as the intruders had already infiltrated well into the base defenses, and they began to drop quickly. Also, several rocket-propelled grenades tore through the night toward the stationary vehicles from less than a hundred meters, and several more missiles were already on the way from the trees.

One of the towers disappeared in a ball of flame when a missile struck it, as did one of the BMPs, leaving only the one with the mangled commander's body on top; it backed frantically toward its original covered position, twisting and turning in an attempt to dodge the incoming missiles. But the effort was futile. An RPG round shredded one of the vehicle's tracks, forcing it to spin helplessly in the mud, and then another missile finally found its mark, turning the vehicle and its crew into a small bonfire.

Kurilenko could hear the crump of mortar shells falling on the far side of the base now as the attackers sought to keep the surviving defenders pinned in their positions to prevent them from blocking the breach they had created. He pulled off his night-vision goggles, stuffing them down inside his jacket, sprinted the remaining few meters to the bunker, and punched in the identity code on the cipher lock on the door.

He found himself face-to-face with a wide-eyed young lieutenant, holding an AKM aimed straight at his chest.

"My God, sir, it's you!" the lieutenant sighed in relief. "Their mortar barrage caught a lot of men coming out of the barracks, and we've taken heavy losses. I just heard it on the radio."

"And they just wiped out the reaction platoon," Kurilenko added, pushing past him. "Any word on reinforcements from the motor rifle division yet?"

"They reported that their fucking tracks won't start," the lieutenant almost screamed in despair. "They said it will take at least an hour to put in new batteries and get a company down here."

"It will all be over by then, one way or another," Kurilenko said. "We'll have to hold on with what we've got. How many men do you have in here?"

"Only half a dozen of our men, plus about forty Strategic Rocket Force crewmen, but they're not even armed."

"I want all of your men in their fighting positions at this end of the bunker. This is where they'll hit first," Kurilenko ordered. "We need to give them a bloody nose so that they'll have to regroup. That will buy us time, and we can't accomplish that unless we concentrate our forces."

"But what if they swing around behind us?"

"I'll take a couple of the crewmen and set them up in observation positions at the back end of the bunker and cover them with my weapon. That will give us all the warning we can hope for. Now put the rest of the crewmen in the equipment storage room. If they can't fight, at least we can try to keep them from getting killed. They may not do us much good now, but they've had valuable training and can't be wasted."

"Exactly so, Major," the lieutenant said, snapping a salute and rushing off, shouting orders at the top of his lungs.

Kurilenko strolled to the far end of the bunker, past the small side workshops and offices, which opened onto the central bay. In these rooms were huddled several dozen bewildered, frightened technicians, and he motioned to two of them to follow him, which they did reluctantly.

"Get a move on," he growled. "You may think you're some kind of scientists, but you're just soldiers, and today you're going to have to do a soldier's job." Right, he thought to himself, to die for your country.

It was dark in the bay, with only widely spaced emergency lights casting an eery glow onto the shiny green of the huge transporter-erector-launcher (TEL) vehicle that occupied the center of the bay. In time of war, the roof of the bunker would slide open on hinges and the 18.5-meter-long SS-25 missile, which now lay horizontally on top of its twelve-wheeled TEL, would be raised to the vertical position and sent roaring off into the stratosphere. In an emergency, or to confuse the enemy, the TEL could also haul the missile to one of several previously surveyed launch sites within fifty kilometers of the base and fire from there. The warhead could then travel some ten thousand kilometers, splitting up en route into three independently targeted reentry vehicles, each with a capacity of some 250 kilotons. Properly spaced, the warheads from a single missile could easily do for a city the size of, say, Chicago or Paris. But despite this immense destructive capacity, the huge weapon was essentially a helpless piece of inventory now, its fate to be decided by the actions of a few hundred infantrymen with rifles and hand grenades. Kurilenko found the thought strangely amusing.

When he reached the far end of the bunker, he looked leisurely back down the bay and watched as the lieutenant hustled the remaining technicians into a large side room before scurrying back to the main entrance of the bunker with his handful of defenders.

"What do we do now, Major?" one of the men finally got up the nerve to ask.

"This way." Kurilenko smiled, pointing to a pair of vision blocks mounted in the bunker wall behind a stack of shipping crates.

The two men shuffled off in that direction and were beginning to peer out through the slots when Kurilenko's AKM coughed quietly twice. Of course, no one would question why the commander of the base security detachment did anything, and no one had thought to ask why he would have a long black silencer on his assault rifle. The sound of Kurilenko's weapon would hardly be noticed in any case, because the bunker was already echoing with the clatter of firing from the far end. The bodies were now crumpled in a pile behind the packing crates, out of sight.

Kurilenko sprinted to the rear door of the bunker and punched in the cipher code to open it. Holding the door open only a crack, he held out a red-filtered flashlight and blinked a coded signal, three short, three long, two short. He waited a moment and repeated it. Through the narrow opening, he finally saw a green light blink four times in response. With a sigh of relief he pushed the heavy metal door fully open.

In an instant, a dozen men in dark camouflage fatigues and night-vision goggles like Kurilenko's rushed through the doorway, darting past him and quickly taking up covered positions inside the bunker. A moment later, a short, stocky man with long, drooping mustaches strolled through into the bunker like an inspecting general, flanked by two immense commandos carrying automatic weapons and radio packs. He, too, wore the camouflage fatigues, but Kurilenko could see the small triangle of a striped T-shirt visible at his neck, the symbol of the Russian Naval Infantry, Russia's marines.

Kurilenko executed a smart salute. "Good to see you, General Shchernikov," he whispered. It was an honor for Kurilenko to be in the presence of the leader of the Russian separatist movement, the "George Washington" of his people.

The shorter man's already narrow eyes disappeared in a sea of crinkles as his florid face beamed with a warm smile.

"You have done very well, Major," he said without pretending to lower his own voice. "Now what do we have here?"

"Six or seven armed men up at the other end," Kurilenko explained, pointing with the barrel of his rifle, "and about forty unarmed technicians in that one room with a light on the left-hand side."

The other man nodded and simply looked to one of the commandos, jerking his chin in the direction that Kurilenko had indicated. The men moved carefully, silently down the bay, dodging from cover to cover, some crawling low under the belly of the TEL itself, a couple of them climbing to a catwalk that ran the length of the bunker about ten meters up.

"I appreciate your taking the risk to hand over this one bunker personally, Major," the general said, drawing Kurilenko casually over to one side, behind a couple of oil drums. "The door codes you gave us for the other two bunkers should permit my men to gain easy access there as well. In fact, they are probably storming them now, but it was vital that we absolutely guarantee the capture of one of the missiles, and that you have done for us here."

One of the bodyguards, a tall blond man with a hard-looking face, had been talking in a low voice on his radio, and he silently signaled to the general, first one finger, then two, then the thumbs up sign.

"There, you see?" the general went on. "The other teams have already accomplished their missions. . . ."

A sudden flurry of firing echoed with deafening loudness in the confines of the bunker, coupled with the crunch of grenades and the screams of wounded men. But the general continued his conversation as if merely pausing for the noise of a passing bus.

"And your maps of the minefields were flawless, and the information on the reaction platoon permitted us to neutralize them without suffering so much as a single man lost . . . not that your men didn't put up a valiant fight," the general added hastily, noting a dark cloud of concern that had passed across Kurilenko's face. "They were good men and, in other circumstances, I would have loved to have had them on my side—*our* side—but you know that such was not possible."

"I understood what needed to be done when I agreed to cooperate," Kurilenko said, waving his hand weakly. "It's not *our* fault that good Russians have had to die to save their brothers, even if they didn't know they were doing it. If the weak sisters in Moscow were willing to let the Soviet Union dissolve into a bunch of third-rate, Third World countries and then sell our own people, *Russians*, who live in the other republics, down the river to be ruled by a bunch of stinking raghead goat farmers, let the sin lie on their heads, not ours."

"Exactly, Major. You understand the situation perfectly. We are only patriots, fighting for the *rodina*, the Motherland, the way Russians have always done. If they want to play at being democrats and capitalists in Moscow, let them. But they didn't have to destroy the work of centuries of nation building. They did that just because they were weak, but we are strong, and we will see that Russian children are not slaughtered by pagans or that Russian women are not raped by the bearded 'sons of the Prophet.' We know how to protect our people, even if they don't. We know that the Kazakhs intend to seize control of the government in Alma Ata by force soon. Russia won't help us, but we will fight on our own, and you have just given us our most powerful weapon."

The firing ended with a long burst by several weapons. Kurilenko knew that this kind of firing was not typical of a battle, where short bursts or single rounds were the rule. It was the kind of shooting you did to get rid of large numbers of men in a short space of time. He had done it himself often enough in Afghanistan. He purposefully kept his eyes on the general so that he would not have to look at what was going on farther down the bay.

"Now, my friend," the general said softly. "Those *special* devices?"

"Yes, of course," Kurilenko stammered. He grabbed a mechanic's tool chest off a nearby cart, clambered up onto the TEL, and opened up an access panel in the side of the missile fuselage. He reached inside with a screwdriver and began removing something.

While he worked, the other commandos began returning from the other end of the bunker. There were fewer of them now, Kurilenko noted as he selected a socket wrench, and two of them were badly wounded, supported by their comrades. Kurilenko roughly wiped at his eyes with the sleeve of his jacket and buried himself in his work. One of the bodyguards crouched next to him, carefully watching the procedure.

"Here it is, General," Kurilenko said, hopping off the back of the TEL. He was holding a small black box in his greasy hands, about the size of a packet of cigarettes. "I think your man saw enough to be able to find the ones on the other missiles."

"Perfect," the general boomed. He nodded to the bodyguard, who led several men out into the night.

An hour later, Kurilenko stood with the general outside the bunker. The snow had stopped now, but the bitter wind still whistled around them, causing Kurilenko to try to hunch up his shoulders to protect his ears from the biting cold. The general, however, appeared unaware of the weather.

"This is a great day, Major," he declared.

The three huge TEL vehicles were lined up on the road in a convoy headed and flanked by small armored cars belonging to the attackers. Three large ZIL trucks were also lined up nearby, pointed toward the main gate of the base. The general handed three small black boxes to one of his men, who ran to distribute one to each of the drivers of the ZILs. Then they revved the trucks' engines and pulled slowly out of the gate.

"We'd better be moving out ourselves, General," Kurilenko said nervously, glancing at his watch. "The alert battalion was due on the road from Charsk ten minutes ago, even with the delays we made for them, and they could be here in less than an hour."

"Don't worry, Major," the general continued. "I still have troops waiting for them with an anti-armor ambush well north of here. By the time they punch through them, *if* they've got the balls to do that at all, we'll be fifty miles away. In this weather, aircraft won't be able to help in the search, and we'll reach the place I've prepared to hide our booty long before it clears. It's all over. We've won!"

The general climbed into the front seat of the GAZ jeep that skidded to a halt in front of them, spewing gravel onto Kurilenko's boots.

"Shall I ride with—" Kurilenko started to ask when he saw one of the bodyguards, the tall blond one, swing his machine gun around to point it directly at his chest. "Wait. What's this?"

The general's face sank in an exaggerated expression of sorrow. "I know we had planned for you to come with us, Major, but it occurred to me that, in the remote chance that they did notice that your body was missing, they just might investigate your background, your family connections, and everything, and they then just might put two and two together and figure out who really took these missiles. Then all of our careful planning and deception would have been for nothing. All of your men here would have died for nothing. And we couldn't have that, now could we?" He paused and then called out, "Lushkin!"

Kurilenko didn't answer. He just looked around at the bunkers and support buildings, all of which were now spouting flame from every opening, and at the bodies that lay strewn across the barren ground between them. He didn't hear the machine gun open fire.

MOSCOW
15 November, 2200 Hours

"How many dead?"

President Balinsky sat at the conference table holding his bald, pink head in his hands. The ministers of defense, foreign affairs, internal affairs, and atomic power and the commanders of the several branches of the armed forces and of the strategic rocket forces occupied about half of the other high-backed gilt chairs, their collars undone and their ties hanging at crooked angles in testimony to the late hour and the stress their wearers were under. The table was strewn with stacks of papers, notepads, and maps. A nervous colonel of the GRU military intelligence service stood at attention near the tall double doors.

"We don't have a precise number yet, Mr. President," the colonel stammered. "It seems that all of the men at the missile installation were killed, about four hundred altogether. Then there were at least a hundred more from the troops from the 19th Motor Rifle Division in fighting through to the base. We estimate that at least fifty of the attackers were also killed."

"Not much of a show," Marshal Malyshev, the chief of staff of the combined Russian armed forces, grumbled.

"That's not important, Marshal," Balinsky snapped. "What is important is that some very evil people have stolen three SS-25 missiles with nine nuclear warheads. I want to know how that could have happened and what the hell your people are doing to get them back."

Malyshev sneered at the president and vigorously rubbed his close-cropped head as if trying to clear his thoughts after a night of drinking. "Considering the defense budget, we were lucky to find enough tanks and armored personnel carriers in running order with enough fuel to get to the base at all."

"You're getting hundreds of billions of rubles a year," Foreign Minister Gostev said, hooking his thumbs in the pockets of his absurdly professorial tweed waistcoat, "money that we desperately need for other things. If you people can't even guard our nuclear weapons, what good is all that money going for?"

"Gentlemen," President Balinsky groaned without raising his head, "this is not being very productive. The attack happened. The missiles have been stolen. There will be plenty of time for recriminations later, but there might not be if the scum that stole the missiles have in mind actually *using* them at some point. What we need to know right now is where the missiles are and how we can get them back."

The marshal turned to the colonel by the door, and the eyes of the other ministers followed his.

The colonel shifted his feet uneasily. "The ground search has been hampered by the stay-behind teams left by the attackers. They ambushed our main force, as you know, and inflicted serious losses before disappearing into the steppe. There have been smaller ambushes set on all roads leading away from the base, in all directions, sometimes just mines, sometimes snipers, and sometimes squad-sized units with antitank missiles firing from hidden positions. This has necessitated our units moving out in tactical formations across country, rather than straight up the roads, and this has cost us time."

Marshal Malyshev raised his hand, anticipating comment from the others. "We have already changed those orders and instructed the Army units to proceed at full speed and to accept any losses that result."

"Good," Balinsky said. "Go on, Colonel."

"We estimate that the defenders of the base were defeated some nine hours before our lead elements reached the base." He paused while Malyshev snorted contemptuously. "Even at the slow rate of movement of the SS-25 TELs, that means that they could have been some two hundred miles or more away at that time. And a further ten hours have now passed, about doubling that area. Severe weather has prevented most of our aircraft from participating in the search. We have lost four helicopters and two fixed-wing aircraft thus far in the attempt, but without results."

"But," Malyshev interjected, raising his finger in victory, "fortunately there were locator beacons placed on the missiles, so that even if we cannot track them on the ground, we at least have a very good idea of where they went."

"And where, might I ask, is that?" Gostev queried.

"East," Malyshev replied, stretching his corpulent frame without rising from his chair and pointing with a pencil to a large map mounted on an easel behind him. "Right about here, we estimate."

All heads turned to focus on the spot indicated by the general's pencil.

"But that's inside China, holy Mother of God!" Gostev exclaimed.

"So we're certain that the attackers were Chinese?" Balinsky asked.

"The attackers were very careful to take all of their dead and wounded with them," the colonel went on. "Not a single body has been found, but a preliminary analysis of the shell casings, boot prints, and other evidence all indicate equipment of Chinese manufacture. That, taken with the beacon signal from within China, certainly points in that direction."

"But the Chinese already have nuclear weapons," Gostev argued. "Why would they risk a war to pick up three more missiles?"

"They don't have anything remotely like the SS-25," Malyshev countered, "self-contained, mobile, but with an intercontinental range and multiple warheads. They're twenty years behind us, but you know how those monkeys are about reverse engineering. Now that they have several of these state-of-the-art mobile missiles, they can produce their own. It will improve their nuclear deterrent fifty percent without costing them a penny of R and D funds."

"That's not the worst of it," Alekseyev, director of the SVRR, the heir of the old KGB's foreign intelligence service, added, shaking his head of bushy gray hair. "As you know, central rule in China has been breaking down for months, with local warlords winning control over the People's Liberation Army units in their territories and setting up what amount to independent countries. There is a possibility that one of these warlords has taken it into his head to make himself into a nuclear power without the knowledge or approval of the government in Beijing. We'll need to look into that before we go thinking about any kind of massive retaliation against China proper. I recommend a "hot pursuit" into Chinese territory, if necessary, by Spetsnaz units. We can either get the missiles back or destroy them without escalating the level of conflict that already exists. If the Chinese central government is directly involved, well, we're at war in any case. If they're not, I don't think that they'll object seriously to our discreetly preventing an internal rival from getting his hands on ICBMs. They might even thank us for it."

"Get right on it, Marshal Malyshev," Balinsky ordered. "We're not going to wait for the weather to clear. Send out a dozen teams if you have to, with enough firepower in each to get the job done. If we wait for the aerial or satellite photographs and target studies that you military men are so fond of, it will be too late."

"I have taken the liberty of already dispatching units just as you describe," the marshal said, leaning back contentedly in his chair.

"You sent troops to invade a foreign country without discussing it with the cabinet, without the president's authorization?" Gostev almost shrieked, pulling himself up to his full five-foot, four-inch height and pressing his fists on the table, glaring at the general opposite him.

"For God's sake!" Balinsky shouted, standing up and walking over to the marshal's map. "There's no time for this. Ordinarily, what Marshal Malyshev has done would be worth a court-martial, but in these circumstances, it was precisely the right thing. You, Gostev, should understand better than anyone how important this whole issue is to the question of Western economic aid. If the Americans or Western Europeans get the idea that we don't have full control over the old Soviet nuclear arsenal, their aid will dry up like the steppe in summer. The only reason they've been willing to help us at all is to keep our government stable so that all of those missiles won't fall into undisciplined hands."

"But these are technically Kazakh missiles, not ours," Gostev argued.

"Bullshit," Alekseyev grunted. "Even though Kazakhstan is technically an independent republic now, the West knows that we maintained operational control over the missiles *and* that we were responsible for their security. After all, Russian troops were guarding them, and we even still have regular army units stationed in Kazakhstan. The missiles were all either to be repatriated to Russia or dismantled on site, the same as the deal we finally struck with the Ukrainians, so in six more months these very missiles would not have existed. But the West will know exactly whom to blame for this fiasco."

"Well, what if these Spetsnaz commandos can't get them back?" Gostev asked, unconvinced.

"Don't worry about that," Malyshev chuckled. "Our satellite tracking can locate the missiles' position to within a few hundred meters, and the troops are the best in the world. I have additional conventional troops on call to back them up if there's a chance that they can recover the missiles, which would be the best course. If not, they have the training and equipment to destroy the missiles completely, including the on-board guidance systems, which is what the Chinese are probably after in any case. And if *that* fails, I have a regiment of SU-25 ground-attack aircraft already on station to flatten the entire area, with two more regiments of MiG-29s to cover them, just in case this is a plot by the Chinese government itself. There is no way the Chinese will get possession of those missiles."

"You mean you'd 'flatten' the area with our own troops still in it?" Gostev asked. The animosity and cynicism had gone out of his voice now and had been replaced by simple shock.

The marshal smiled at the transformation in his opponent and spread his hands. "For the good of the Motherland, those troops are prepared to die."

"And what will happen, Marshal Malyshev," Alekseyev went on, "if we can't find the missiles in time?"

"There is absolutely no chance of that, sir," Malyshev stated, wagging a finger confidently in the air.

"Sounds like famous last words to me," Gostev observed.

"Regardless, gentlemen," Balinsky said, the tone of his voice rising quickly, "let it be understood by every man in this room that, no matter what the results of our efforts to recover the missiles—and we *will* make every effort to recover or destroy them—no one will ever breathe a word of their loss."

"But what about all of those casualties?" Gostev asked. "Several hundred dead men. Their wives and mothers are going to be asking some embarrassing questions. It's not like the old days when we could just order people to shut up when we sent them a little note saying that their son 'gave his life fulfilling his international revolutionary mission.' And there is the press, which we don't control anymore either. What about that?"

Balinsky frowned, lost in thought.

"We could just bill it as a terrorist attempt to capture the weapons," Alekseyev suggested, "which our soldiers, with superb efficiency," he emphasized, casting a critical look at Malyshev, "defeated, albeit at great loss. Even the strongest of our critics in the West, to say nothing of their intelligence services, underestimated our missile stockpiles considerably, so we can parade around some other SS-25s as the recovered ones, and everyone's happy."

The men were silent for a moment, and then Balinsky said, "I guess that that's the best we can do for the present. But remember that our credibility with the West would be destroyed forever if word of this got out, their economic aid would disappear like that!" He snapped his fingers. "And even the conservative oppositionists would be able to use that against us. They could say to the people, 'Say what you want about the old regime, but at least you always knew who was holding our nuclear weapons. Time to put things back in order before the democrats get the whole world incinerated.' They came close enough to overthrowing the democratic government in '90 and again in '93, and a piece of ammunition like this would be all it would take to put them back in power. You understand? This incident *never happened!*"

The men around the table nodded solemnly.

OVER THE KHREBET TARBAGATAY MOUNTAINS, NORTHEAST OF T'A-CH'ENG, CHINA
16 November, 0335 Hours

Senior Lieutenant Sergei Brodyagin pulled on the risers of his directional parachute to angle himself a little to the left. He was no longer on oxygen since he had dropped below ten thousand feet, but he kept the oxygen mask over his mouth to help protect his face from the icy wind. The high-altitude, high opening technique was useful in that it permitted Brodyagin and his men to jump from a plane well within Russian territory and then "fly" their parachutes for miles across the border, but it was cold on the ground in Central Asia at this time of year, and at this altitude the wind cut right through your body, no matter how much clothing you wore.

The sky had cleared somewhat, and he could see clusters of stars in the breaks in the cloud cover overhead, but that was nearly all that could be seen. His own slate gray parachute and his combat fatigues of the same color made him and the other members of his Spetsnaz platoon virtually invisible in the darkness.

He held up his satellite navigational system to confirm his location. The fix they'd had on the position of the missiles from the beacon tracking equipment on their IL-76 aircraft before they jumped had verified that the targets hadn't moved for over two hours, and the constant stream of advice he was receiving over his radio earpiece indicated no change. The good news was that they weren't going to have to chase the missiles down on the open road. The bad news was that the Chinese must have planned this in advance and might well have strong defenses in position to protect their prize.

Brodyagin had practiced doing just this sort of operation for years. Of course, his original target had been a NATO nuclear-weapons storage facility near Aachen in West Germany. He had always thought of it as mildly amusing that, in the event of a world war, the capitalist leaders would be agonizing over whether or not to escalate the conflict with the use of tactical nuclear weapons, and when they finally decided to do it, they wouldn't be able to because Brodyagin and his men would have blown up all the weapons in their storage bunkers.

But that was when there was a chance of war, when there was a West Germany—hell, when there was a difference between Russia and the capitalists. How long ago had that been? Three or four years? A lifetime. Now he was gliding into his first real war, heading in the opposite direction.

They had been regularly briefed on the Chinese political situation and the status of the Chinese armed forces since his unit had been transferred to Siberia the year before, and Brodyagin did not expect a walkover. The PLA, if that was who really had the missiles, was tough, professional, well armed, and very, very numerous, but Brodyagin was still confident. There were his own 30 platoon members dropping silently around him in the night, plus the 115-man Spetsnaz company loaded in Hip-8 helicopters hovering just north of the border, ready to come in once a landing zone had been secured. Behind them, a full battalion of the 106th Guards Airborne Division with its BMD airborne armored vehicles were also in aircraft circling within Russian territory, and further ground forces were moving toward the border as fast as possible. There would also be a full regiment of

Mi-35 helicopter gunships on call, and all the air support they wanted. That should do it, he thought.

Brodyagin's night-vision goggles magnified even the faintest starlight and enabled him to make out the dark contours of the ridge-line that loomed up below him. He angled to the left once more and steered toward the narrow draw, braking his descent just before touching down, which enabled him to make one of his trademark perfect stand-up landings, of which he was justifiably proud. He quickly collapsed his long rectangular parachute and bundled it up, piling a few rocks atop it, since time did not permit him to bury it as was standard Spetsnaz practice. If things went well, and the helicopter extraction proceeded as planned, they would stop and pick up the chutes, since Spetsnaz considered the leaving of any trace of their presence to be an unacceptable breach of professional standards.

He could hear the muffled crunch of other bodies hitting the ground nearby, accompanied by the occasional grunt or cursing when a man came down too hard. In a matter of minutes, the entire platoon was present and ready for assignment.

"There's no time for a reconnaissance," Brodyagin said as the section leaders huddled around him. "Our sensors indicate that the missiles are all parked in a draw just opposite this one on the other side of the ridgeline. The reconnaissance aircraft scanned with infrared and could spot the engines, although they were cooling down, and only about a dozen human forms scattered around, nothing else."

"How certain are they that these are the missiles?" Brodyagin's senior sergeant asked. Brodyagin might have resented such a question on a training mission, but this was for real, and Misha had been in Afghanistan and wouldn't just be trying to "sharpshoot" the commander. If he asked a question, it was for a damn good reason.

"They've got the beacon signals clear as a bell," he replied. "Also, the recon bird has sensors for radiation emissions, and there is definitely nuclear material on the target."

There was a long silence while these words sank in. Spetsnaz didn't bother with such niceties as radiation protection gear. They needed to move quickly and efficiently or a 5.56 round would put an end to their lives a lot quicker than cancer, but it was food for thought just the same.

Brodyagin sent one section of seven men out along each of the ridges that would flank the valley where the missiles were located, to take any defenders under a cross fire. He took a third section with him once the first two were in position, leaving the fourth to act as a reserve and to guard their line of retreat.

Once over the ridgeline with its sparse covering of scrub and stunted trees, Brodyagin could see that a gravel road led up the narrow gully toward him, terminating in a small flat clearing where two small huts stood. Just beyond the huts he could see the dark shapes of several large vehicles covered with camouflage netting. He scanned the scene with his infrared scope and could see the eerie green images of two or three men loitering near one of the huts.

His section advanced at a dead, silent run. Spetsnaz had determined that this was the most efficient form of surprise attack, no crawling, no wild yelling, just getting across the open ground before the enemy has time to react and bring the firepower of his emplaced weapons to bear. Then, when you were inside his defenses, you could cut him up at close range while he was still disoriented by the attack.

And it worked this time as well. As he ran forward in a low crouch, his rifle clutched close to his body, Brodyagin could hear two men standing next to the nearest hut talking in Chinese and saw the red tip of a cigarette rising and falling from the mouth of one of them. The red dot of the cigarette stopped moving suddenly and then dropped to the ground. Brodyagin opened fire.

His men were all around him, firing short, controlled bursts and tossing grenades into the huts. The men up on the high ground were firing single shots at selected targets, taking care not to hit their own men down below, and within thirty seconds, it was over.

Brodyagin ran to the nearest of the camouflage nets and began to rip up the edges from where they were pegged to the ground. Something was not right. He had been shown photos and schematics of the SS-25 missile during the premission briefing, and the TELs should have been at least twenty meters long and maybe seven or eight wide. The vehicles here were large, certainly, but not that large.

With the help of two of his men, he scrambled under the netting and found himself standing next to a large ZIL truck. Shit! Brodyagin thought to himself, and he pulled out of the breast pocket of his fatigues the small black receiver of the beacon signal. The tiny red light was flickering at about three pulses per second, which indicated if the beacon were a snake, it would be poised to bite you. He moved around to the cab door, for want of anything better to do, and climbed up. There on the driver's seat was a small, greasy black box, and the red light on his receiver shone solidly.

Cursing, he hopped down from the cab and found the senior sergeant waiting for him.

"They're all just trucks, sir," the sergeant said flatly, "and no tire tracks of any other kind of vehicle having come up this road. The Chinese looked to have been just regular border policemen from their papers. Could we have been mistaken?"

Brodyagin held up the beacon and waggled it in the sergeant's face. "Whoever drove these trucks here was part of the raid on the missile base. That's for certain, but they're gone now. I'll bet anything we'll find foot tracks heading back over the border to Kazakhstan. These Chinese probably just found the trucks themselves and were wondering where they'd come from."

"What about the radioactivity readings?"

"Follow me," Brodyagin said, making his way back along the side of the truck, swatting impatiently at the sagging netting.

He hauled himself up over the tailgate of the truck and helped the sergeant up behind him. Then he turned on his flashlight. The back of the truck was filled with metal drums.

Brodyagin grabbed the sergeant by his shoulders and spun him around roughly. He dug into the man's rucksack, pulled out a device shaped like a small microphone and flicked on its switch. The device began to crackle like frying bacon.

"Well?" the sergeant demanded.

"Well, it looks like we've all been screwed. This is just radioactive waste material, just enough to fool our sensors, and the beacon on the front seat was supposed to be hidden in the missile control housing."

"What does that mean?"

"It means that the missiles are somewhere else. I hope you weren't planning to have any kids soon."

CHAPTER 1

A report from Central Asia indicates that two more UN Spanish peacekeepers have been killed and a third wounded by sniper fire while escorting a relief convoy northeast of Almaty, formerly called Alma-Ata, the capital of Kazakhstan. As a result of this latest attack, for which no group has claimed responsibility, the Spanish government has decided to withdraw its contingent from the UN forces there immediately. This announcement came in response to massive demonstrations in Barcelona and Seville protesting the stationing of Spanish troops with the UN overseas.

CNN

If the leaders of the warring factions in Kazakhstan think they can intimidate me by the killing of UN peacekeepers, they are sadly mistaken. Our humanitarian effort to prevent famine in the region and to help in the establishment of democracy and a market economy will not be obstructed by megalomaniacal little Napoleons and their feeble efforts. I will meet force with force and will send as many troops as I deem necessary to accomplish this mission.

UN Secretary General Justus Muli of Kenya

APPROACHING ALMATY
29 October, 0800 Hours

Only with an act of pure will was Brigadier General Julian Chandler able to avoid wincing as another jab of pain pierced his stomach. It was an ulcer, he was certain, like a long needle, both searingly hot and freezing cold at once, that seemed to stab through his entire body for a long moment before once again subsiding to a dull ache. Perhaps it was just a product of age, he thought, since he had noticed a whole panoply of kinks and twinges in his body during this past year that he had been stationed at the Pentagon, but this new pain was unlike anything he had ever felt before, and it had come about very suddenly, almost exactly at the same moment that he had received his new assignment.

The pain came back again a few minutes later, yet Chandler willed the muscles around his eyes to relax and his jaw not to clench, so that his face remained stoic and unperturbed. He glanced down at his hands, which still held the unopened cardboard box of his MRE lunch on his lap, and he forced the fingers to loosen their grip until the white spots around his knuckles disappeared. He would not tell the medics about his symptoms upon his arrival, because that would mean the end of his command—perhaps of his career if the problem proved serious enough—but it was more important that he keep up appearances right now.

Chandler stared across the dimly lit cargo bay of the C-130 aircraft at the unconscionably young journalist who lounged in the strap harness seat opposite him. Was there some rule that all reporters had to buy khaki safari suits at Banana Republic when they went on assignment to a war zone? Chandler wondered. And was the perpetual sneering smile just another part of the obligatory uniform? In any event, Chandler wasn't about to display any discomfort in front of this puppy, which the reporter would undoubtedly attribute to an inability to handle the jerky banking, climbing, and diving that the C-130 performed as it came in for its final approach into Almaty airport. An Italian support flight had been shot down the week before, and these evasive maneuvers were now SOP to limit the chances of a recurrence, even though the commanders of both the rival militias had assured the UN, first, that their forces were not responsible for the previous incident and, second, that they had taken measures to ensure that it would never happen again.

Chandler had certainly spent enough time in bobbing and weaving helicopters and in the back of bucking armored personnel carriers not to have much of a problem with motion sickness, but there would be no convincing what's-his-name of this. Chandler had forgotten the reporter's name after their brief introduction at the start of the flight eight hours before, in Moscow. He had strained to read the name on the plasticized identity card clipped to the reporter's shirt pocket, but he found that he couldn't make it out without his glasses, which he preferred not to wear when he could avoid it. He wasn't about to make an obvious show of putting them on for the purpose now.

No, the pain had nothing to do with the aircraft. It had hit him back in Washington when his superior, Major General Alvarez, the new commander of the Army Central Command, CENTCOM, which controlled the U.S. Rapid Deployment Force, among other things, had appeared in Chandler's office in the "D" ring at the Pentagon. Chandler started to his feet when the stocky Latino charged through the doorway, peremptorily rapping on the frame as he did so, but Alvarez motioned him back into his seat with a wave of the hand.

"Endicott's been wounded in Almaty, Julian," Alvarez said in a low voice.

Thinking back, Chandler thought he could remember the first little twinge in his stomach at that moment. Endicott had been a classmate of his at the Point, but they had never been close. It was because Chandler knew what was coming next.

"Is it bad?" was all he could respond.

"Lost a leg. Mortar round," Alvarez replied with all of the emotion of a logistics officer reciting the problems of broken-down supply trucks. "He's through, and you've been picked to take his place."

Chandler's brain screamed out, "Why me?" but he said nothing. He knew why. Apart from being the right rank, of which there was an overabundance in the Army in any case, he had all the right tickets punched. He'd had his combat time in two tours in Vietnam and then again nearly twenty years later in the Gulf, but so had dozens of others. What the brass was thinking of was his year-long tour in Mogadishu as liaison between the 10th Mountain Division and the UN command, a longer stretch than just about any American in the zone. And what better experience for an assignment like Almaty? Chandler was a veteran "peacekeeper," used to dealing with disparate UN forces in a hot area as well as with the ragtag gunmen who made it hot. He was the perfect choice.

"But don't they know?" his brain kept screaming. "Don't they know I *can't*?" But still he said nothing, because there was no way that anyone could know. His mind went back further in time.

Didn't they see that boy's face? Chandler thought. Didn't they see the way his body had been all cut up and burned? Couldn't they tell that he hadn't been dead yet when it happened? Of course they did. Everybody did. It was on CNN, and then on every news broadcast for days and days afterward. It was still being aired when Chandler accompanied the body back to the States and delivered it to his mother.

Naturally, the casualty people had fixed the boy's body up a bit, so his mother wouldn't have to see him that way. Chandler, though, could still see him as he lay, sprawled across the hood of the "technical" armed Land Rover at the dusty traffic circle where he had gone to take delivery on the body from the Somalis. Someone told him later that he had stood at the crossroads for nearly an hour, negotiating with the local warlord. The American and Norwegian soldiers of Chandler's escort, in their camouflage fatigues and sky blue helmets, were faced off with the gunmen of the warlord's militia, in their assorted tribal robes and USA-Africa T-shirts, while Chandler and the Somali haggled over the price. Chandler had finally turned over a briefcase with U.S. $100,000, nodding his understanding that the price would have been much higher if the young American soldier had not, unfortunately, expired of his wounds.

Chandler had then lifted the boy in his own arms and carried him to his APC, ignoring offers of help from his men. At that moment Chandler had felt something go out of him, like the pilot light on a stove. He could have sworn that he heard it snuff out.

He assumed that his superiors recognized the change. A few weeks later he had been quietly withdrawn from Somalia, although they called it a normal rotation, and had been given a very undemanding job on the Joint Staff at the Pentagon. They had been very polite about it, of course. They had even promoted him to brigadier, at a time of severe cutbacks in the defense budget, and given him several nice decorations for his service in Somalia. But he was certain that they talked about him the minute he left an office, or quickly changed the subject the minute he walked in.

Not that he blamed them. He had always been a line officer, seeking out troop commands, sleeping out in the field with the men and avoiding the staff jobs that were the accepted ticket to higher rank. He had taken the least appealing assignments just to avoid paper-pushing jobs, much to his wife's dismay, and he had used the threat of retirement more than once when faced with the danger of a soft headquarters job with a guaranteed promotion.

He swore that he could see it in his face when he shaved in the mornings. He was still outwardly the same, tall, muscular, with impeccably short-cropped hair with just enough white to make him distinguished, although the amount of white seemed to be increasing almost measurably from one day to the next now. He still stood straight as a ramrod, but there was something about his eyes, something about his expression that had just . . . lost it.

So much had the fire gone out of him that he had taken the staff job without question or comment, and now he took his new assignment just the same way.

"How much time do I have?" he had asked Alvarez.

"There's a flight leaving for Frankfurt at 2100 hours tonight," Alvarez said dryly. "You can have a car and driver right now. Call home and have your wife start packing for you—oh, sorry," he stammered.

Laura had left him only about two months before, having found it even harder to take Chandler's silences when he was finally home every evening and weekend than she had found it to take his prolonged absences in war zones around the world in earlier days. Alvarez had never been one to pry into the personal lives of his staff, even to the extent of knowing who was married, divorced, single, expecting a baby, etc.

"No problem," Chandler said slowly, and he looked distractedly around his desk.

"Don't worry about your work here," Alvarez said, anticipating him. "That's the word. We'll make do."

Chandler just sighed. It was all too true that the world would not be any the worse if none of his work was ever picked up at all.

"You'll have a twenty-four-hour layover in Frankfurt, so you can hook up with Endicott. He's at the hospital at Ramstein. He can brief you on the lay of the land out there."

Chandler supposed the Alvarez must have shaken his hand at some point, but he frankly couldn't remember it.

When Chandler bounded up the steps of his modest two-bedroom brick cottage in Alexandria, his mind was full of the immediate requirements of packing for the trip. As he opened the front door, his thoughts instantly shifted to how he would break the news to Laura and how she would take it. Then the silence hit him like a blow. Of course, she was no longer there. The bills and preapproved offers for new credit cards crumpled under the door as he swung it open, since no one was there to pick them up after the mailman dropped them through the slot. An empty soft-drink can sat on the coffee table where he had left it, and it would stay there forever unless he moved it himself.

Her half of the closet was still bare, and the handful of twisted hangers jangled against each other forlornly as he lifted out his uniforms and threw them onto the bed. Something about that sound made him stop. He wandered dumbly over to his side of the bed and sat down, staring back at the closet. This was just where he had been while he watched her pack.

"But why do you have to leave now?" he had asked lamely. "You were worried about me being in danger, and now I'm not. You always hated me traveling, and now I'm home by five-thirty every afternoon."

"That's the worst of it," she had told him. "At least when you were on the other side of the world I didn't expect to be able to reach you. Now you're on the other side of the dinner table, and I still can't." She had been talking while she neatly folded her blouses and skirts away, but now she fixed him with her dark blue eyes, leaning across the bed. "Julian, I'm not mad, I'm just too tired to go on."

"You just don't understand—"

"I know I don't, Julian, and I sure as hell never will if you won't talk to me about it. I don't pretend to know what happened to you, to everyone, in Somalia. I know all those boys got killed, and it wasn't your fault, but it wasn't my damn fault either, and I'm tired of paying for it."

"Is it kids? Do you want to have kids? We could try now. We're not too old, and we wouldn't have to be dragging them all over—"

"Idiot!"

It was the last word she said to him.

Half an hour later, the staff car driver who would take Chandler to the airport found him sitting on the edge of the bed, staring at the half-empty closet.

"It's time we were hitting the road, General," the man said in a quiet voice. The driver finished his packing for him and then helped him down to the car, carrying Chandler's duffel bag over one shoulder, and guiding him with a hand on his elbow, the way you'd help an elderly aunt down the steps of the rest home.

"So, Gen'ral," the journalist shouted over the racket in the cargo bay. "This your first visit to Central Asia?"

Chandler suspected that this reporter called all military officers "Gen'ral" as a term of contempt for the idea of rank, and that it was the purest coincidence that he happened to be right this time. Chandler had seen his kind often enough before, vultures trying to get as much of what they called "bang-bang" time as they could so they could later get themselves a talk show on daytime TV. He understood that the picture of himself, sitting in the back of his APC holding that poor dead boy and staring at the camera with sunken eyes, had won the photographer the Pulitzer Prize. It was just as well that Chandler didn't know who the photographer was, because he honestly believed that, even after all this time, he could easily shoot the man in cold blood.

"Yes," he replied, making no special effort to speak over the engine noise. "We didn't used to be welcome in these parts, you know."

The reporter leaned forward and cackled. "From what I hear, you're not all that welcome here now. I just picked it up off the wire before we boarded that they waxed six Irish in an ambush on a truck convoy up near Karaganda. That makes over three hundred dead UN-ies so far."

"Who did it?" Chandler asked absently. "Russians or Kazakhs?"

"Didn't catch that part, but I don't suppose it matters all that much to the Irish, does it?"

"No, I guess not."

"So, what's your plan, Gen'ral?" the reporter asked, leaning even farther forward. "Kick ass and take names? I hear you're a great warrior. Count many coup. Kick many ass."

The reporter made some clumsy chopping motions with his hands, probably in imitation of Indian sign language, and stuck out his lower lip. He was young, perhaps thirty. He was tall and lanky, and his bony legs jutted out from the ends of his pants, exposing several inches of pale, hairy skin above his sagging argyle socks and banana boat shoes. His hair was wildly curly, sticking out in random directions for some distance and framing an angular face in which outsized features had been scattered without any apparent purpose. He wore the kind of three-day stubble that Chandler suspected young men intentionally cultivated these days, although he never could understand how they managed not to let their beards get any longer without shaving them completely on occasion. Perhaps they just remained hidden for a couple of days after each shave, he thought to himself.

"Without divulging any classified information," Chandler answered, "I don't suppose you'll be surprised to hear that there are very few verbs in my orders, and 'kick' isn't one of them."

"Oh, but I'll bet it really toasts your buns not to be able to call in a B-52 strike like in Vietnam or some cruise missiles like in the Gulf War. Now you've got ragheads taking potshots at you from the rooftops, and you might even have to go up after them, mano-a-mano, so to speak."

Time was when Chandler wouldn't have taken this kind of provocation. He could see his former self putting a couple of new bends in the reporter's already impressive nose, but even that kind of fire had gone out of him.

"Actually, we're much more likely to try to open a channel of communications, to engage in a frank exchange of views, and attempt to find a mutually beneficial solution to what might simply be a failure to express ourselves across cultural boundaries."

"Shit!" the reporter snorted, hurling himself back into his seat, and banging his head with a most satisfying thump against the unforgiving fuselage wall. He grimaced and rubbed his head vigorously, and Chandler suppressed a smile, taking the opportunity to give his stomach a surreptitious rub. He leaned back and closed his eyes.

Endicott had lost more than his leg, Chandler had noticed immediately as he was escorted into the brilliantly white hospital room in Ramstein by a gracious and matronly German nurse who excused herself discreetly and closed the door. Endicott's bed was raised to a sitting position, and a magazine lay open in his lap, but he had been staring out the window at the nearly bare branches of the dark trees and the leaden sky. He had lost weight since they had last met in Saudi a few years before, but there was more to it than that. Endicott had been a ranger, a real snake-eater, hyper as a mongoose, but now it took several seconds for him to notice that Chandler had entered the room. He merely turned his head in Chandler's direction without changing his blank expression.

"I'm truly sorry to see you here, Jules," he said flatly.

"I'm sorry too, Bob."

"Oh, I don't mean about this," Endicott said, gesturing languidly down at the spot where the white sheet lay flat on the mattress below his knee. "You throw the dice often enough, and it's bound to come up craps sooner or later. I mean about this fucking job."

Chandler nodded and pulled up a gray metal, U.S. government–issue chair up close to the bed. Endicott was lying, of course, but he wasn't even doing that very well. He was an outdoorsman, one of those guys who truly would prefer to be dead than crippled.

"What can you tell me, Bob?" Chandler said in a low voice, leaning lightly on the edge of the bed and tightening his stomach muscles against a stab of pain. "I read the briefing material on the flight coming over, but I'm going to need some *real* skinny before I stumble off the plane in Almaty."

"To put it simply, old pal," Endicott continued, "we're being screwed, and I don't think anybody's even going to buy us dinner and flowers for our trouble."

"I've been there before, you know," Chandler mumbled.

"Oh, yeah, Somalia," Endicott grunted. "That was bad enough, Jules, but this is worse, much worse. At least in Somalia you had some of the people on your side some of the time and only one really bad bunch out to get you. In the 'Kaz' *everybody* hates our guts, and the only thing they like better than scragging each other is scragging us. They're all sure that, if we'd only get the hell out of the way, they could win it all, so they sometimes shoot their way right through us to get at the other guys. Then, if things go badly, they come squealing to us for protection, until next week when they try it all over again."

Chandler had been trying to focus on his orders, on the disposition of his forces, the intelligence reports on the military and political maneuvering of both the Muslim Kazakhs and their ethnic Russian enemies during the eight sleepless hours of his flight to Germany, but the words had all run together before his eyes, and he had hoped Endicott could summarize it in a few pithy phrases. But it now looked like Endicott's version would be even more unfathomable than the official one.

"Look," Endicott said, seeing Chandler's dismay. "It's really *very* simple. You've got about a brigade equivalent of UN troops including Brits, French, Japanese, Israelis, Senegalese, Argentines, and Ukrainians, with the Americans as the biggest single contingent. Your job is to patrol the Green Belt around the city of Almaty to keep the Russians, who are sitting inside it, from getting at the Kazakhs, who are surrounding it, or vice versa, and tearing each other's fucking hearts out.

"You've got the airport about ten kilometers north of the city under your control, although either side can close it in five minutes with artillery fire. You've got supply convoys coming in by land from Semipalatinsk, northeast of Almaty in Russian-held territory, where there's another UN garrison. But to get there you have to go through about five hundred miles of Kazakh-controlled desert and mountains. Either or both sides can stop that route whenever they want. You've got China to the east, which is in the middle of its own civil war, and the Islamic fundamentalist republics of Uzbekistan, Tajikistan, and I-forget-what-istan, to the south, and you're about a thousand miles from anything remotely resembling friendly territory, and *that's* Russia. So what's the big deal?"

Chandler just sighed. Endicott's bitterness was obviously going to prevent him from being much help.

"How are the men?" he asked.

Endicott paused for a moment and then reached out and touched Chandler's arm lightly. "They're better than we deserve in a place like that. Most of the foreign troops are real pros, and our guys are doing their best. The trouble is that we just don't know what the hell we're supposed to be doing. The only ones you need to watch out for are the Ukrainians."

"Why? What have they done?"

"Nothing yet. I just get the feeling that they take their orders from somewhere else, you know?"

Chandler rose to leave, taking Endicott's frighteningly limp hand in his.

"Oh, and Jules," Endicott called as Chandler reached the door. "If you should ever find yourself in a situation where Shchernikov's life is in your hands . . . kill him for me, will you?"

Suddenly Chandler felt himself suspended in the air, weightless, as the C-130 dropped vertically toward the runway. Across the bay, the reporter was clutching frantically at the hanging straps near him, his feet flailing helplessly in the air. There would be no illuminated FASTEN SEAT BELT sign on this flight, no stewardess to make sure you were buckled in. Then the plane slammed onto the runway hard, the engines screaming to reverse thrust as the aircraft almost simultaneously spun around, and the huge rear exit ramp began to lower, filling the gloomy cargo bay with bright sunlight.

Chandler quickly unstrapped himself, grabbed his duffel bag, and squeezed past the white-painted Hummer vehicles and palletized cargo that filled the rear end of the plane, shouldering his way between the scrambling ground crewmen who were already swarming over the equipment to off-load it. While he was in no particular hurry to start his new assignment, Chandler did very much want to avoid any further contact with the reporter, if he could.

The propellers of the C-130 were still spinning as Chandler emerged onto the tarmac. He shaded his eyes and scanned the horizon. There was a line of snow-capped mountains off to what must be the south, he thought, quickly orienting himself. A cluster of drab white and gray buildings surrounded the airport control tower nearer at hand, with sandbagged machine-gun positions huddled up near the doorways. American Blackhawk helicopters were lined up off to one side, their rotor blades drooping, and a pair of Apaches hovered menacingly off to the west, their pilots' attention apparently focused on some activity invisible to Chandler. Near the control tower, Chandler could see a pile of wreckage, apparently parts of several charred Russian cargo planes that were probably remnants of one of the battles for the airport during the anti-Russian revolution late in the previous year. A cold wind was whipping across the flatland from the north, raising dust devils on the runway and causing a pale brown layer of dust that obscured the horizon in all directions, merging sky and ground.

As he stood there, a column of several white Hummers roared up to the aircraft, trailed by a wheeled armored car with a large UN insignia painted in black on its turret. They slid to a halt in front of him, taking care, he noticed, to fan out in a tactical dispersal, the machine-gunners who manned weapons on the roof of each vehicle taking up a preassigned sector of a quick defensive perimeter. And this was the "secure" area of the airport. He wondered what the "disputed" zones were like.

Out of the first vehicle sprang a rather short, slender man in the uniform of the UNEKAZ, the United Nations Expedition, Kazakhstan, and Chandler could see from the national flag patch on his shoulder that he was British. He had light, sandy hair and mustache, pink skin that was peeling in spots from exposure to the sun and wind, and an aristocratic, aquiline nose. He bounded up to Chandler and snapped an impressive British open-palmed salute.

"General Chandler, Colonel Randolph Morgan, late of the Grenadier Guards, now your executive officer, at your service, sir," he rattled off in what sounded to Chandler like a single, multisyllabic word. Chandler barely had time to return the salute before he found his hand gripped in a bone-crushing handshake of which Morgan's size gave no prior warning.

"I must say that I'm damned glad to see you, sir," he continued, glancing back over his shoulder nervously at the rest of the entourage, which was slowly dismounting from the other Hummers. "I hate to burden you with this so soon after your arrival, but I'm afraid we have something of a *situation* here."

Chandler knew from prior dealings with the British in the Gulf War that the use of such an emotion-packed word as "situation" signified nothing short of a disaster of biblical proportions.

"And I'm afraid that you can't say that this is 'after' my arrival," Chandler chuckled self-consciously. "This *is* my arrival, but I'm very pleased to meet you all the same. May I call you Randy?"

"All the girls do, sir," Morgan beamed. Chandler smiled.

"Great, and I'm Julian. Now what's the problem?"

Morgan had just opened his mouth to reply, when a tall, stocky man in a rumpled dark suit shouldered his way between them.

"General, this is absolutely intolerable! My government is not about to sit by and permit the United Nations to support the genocidal, antinational, hegemonic activities of rebel elements in Almaty. We have scrupulously observed cease-fire for nearly a week, despite repeated violations and provocations by rebels, but if you permit this breach of the agreement, we will have no option but to reply with massive force!"

The man was nearly as tall as Chandler, and about fifty pounds heavier, with a roll of flesh surging over the dingy white collar of his shirt. His strongly Mongol features were set in an expression of determination, his feet planted well apart, and his pudgy fists balled at his sides as if he were bracing to accept a blow from the American.

"Permit me to introduce," Morgan interjected smoothly, "the Honorable Bakyt Qasimbekai, representative of the Kazakh Revolutionary Islamic Provisional Government to UNEKAZ. Mr. Qasimbekai, General Chandler. General Chandler, Mr. Qasimbekai."

Chandler extended his hand but discreetly turned it into a slow shoulder scratch when it became apparent that Qasimbekai had no intention of responding.

"I'm pleased to meet you, sir," Chandler said slowly, trying to watch Morgan's eyes for any hints of how to proceed. "I'm sure that there are many problems which remain for us to work out, but I'm sure that you can see that I've only just arrived and will need to rely on you as well as the members of my UN team to help me understand the complexities of the local situation."

"Of course there are many problems," the stocky Kazakh said. "Russians have been massacring my people for many years and turned our land into a dump for nuclear waste, but now we have stood up like men to defend ourselves, *now* your United Nations wants to come here and 'keep the peace.' *That* is a problem. Moscow pretends to recognize our independence and even pulls Russian Army out of Kazakhstan, but they give guns by the thousands to Russian people still living in my country to help them set up a puppet state. *That* is a problem. And here, in the very capital of my own country, most of the city is occupied by aggressor forces under the butcher Shchernikov, and your United Nations tells us we do not have the right to throw him out. *That* is a problem, but those are *my* problems."

Qasimbekai turned and pointed back toward the collection of crippled, maimed buildings that had once been Almaty International Airport. Chandler could see that some of the huge Cyrillic letters spelling "airport" that were mounted above the roof had been shot away, and most of the huge plate-glass windows had been shattered, leaving a gray concrete skeleton, another relic of the revolution. Nearby, the graceful old terminal building, constructed in the style of a mosque complete with minaret, which functioned as a control tower, was still largely intact, having been built during the Stalinist era with materials more durable than the regime that designed it.

"Right this minute," the Kazakh went on, "several thousand Russians are beginning a march from the Central Market on the north edge of town, heading this way. They will reach Green Line in very few minutes. They want to come to airport and board these Russian airplanes." He gestured toward a pair of white Aeroflot cargo planes that were unloading relief supplies at the far end of the runway. "They claim they only want to evacuate women and children from fighting in the city."

"But what possible harm could that do?" Chandler asked. He could see Morgan shaking his head discreetly behind the Kazakh's back, but there was no time for a briefing now.

"I tell you what harm that can do, General," Qasimbekai snapped. "We, the Kazakh people, held this airport through worst of the fighting. We took it from the Russians and paid for it in blood. Then your United Nations insists on coming in, saying that there will be no food for our women and children from the outside unless we agree to their terms. Your United Nations demands to occupy airport and set up 'protective' ring around Almaty, where the Russian butchers have holed up. They say that United Nations will 'monitor' the arrival of relief supplies at the airport and distribute them to civilian women, children, and sick on both sides. Your United Nations also promises that the Russians will not be able to advance out of their sector while negotiations go on.

"Well," he continued, planting a meaty fist on each hip, "you have been very good about seeing that the Kazakhs don't advance their positions, but the Russians cross your lines whenever they like, and you don't move one hair to stop them. Maybe we're just not white enough for you."

"Now that isn't quite fair, Mr. Qasimbekai," a tall, rather frail man in a dark business suit said, stepping up next to Chandler. He had thinning blond hair, almost white, and his pale blue eyes were fringed with brilliant yellow eyelashes, which fluttered nervously as he spoke. "Excuse me, but I'm Nathan Elders, chargé d'affaires at the

American Embassy, General." Chandler nodded to him but let him speak. "There have been accusations of truce violations, from both sides I might add, but the lines have remained unchanged."

Qasimbekai waved away the objection like a bothersome fly. "That will not matter anymore if those Russians reach the airport. They really plan to take it back from us with their women as shields. There are men with the marchers, men with guns. We know it, and we will not permit it. The agreement with your United Nations was for neither side to change positions during negotiations, and we expect that word to be kept or all truce will be off. We fought for this airport, and we will not give it up now. And what is more, we don't want the Russians to be sending out women and children, leaving only their fighting men behind in the city. That will only make the siege longer, put off the time when the Kazakh people can reclaim their capital."

"But just a few women and children—" Chandler tried to say.

"Nothing, no one!" Qasimbekai shouted. "My instructions for you are that, if your United Nations will not turn back marchers, *we* will do it. We will shell their column with our artillery from the hills, and then we will come down and retake the airport ourselves from whoever stands in our way. Those are my orders, and there will be no further communication on this. That is *your* problem, and you must deal with it."

Despite blurted protests from Chandler, Elders, and Morgan, the Kazakh turned smartly on his heel and stomped back to the nearest vehicle, climbing in and snapping some orders to the driver. The driver, a black soldier in UN garb, looked uncertainly, first to Morgan, then to Chandler. Morgan paused and then nodded, and the Hummer roared off toward the city.

"Bastard!" Elders muttered. "I don't know who that damn Mongol thinks he is—"

"He's the official representative of the Kazakh government, sir, and I think that, if he says that they'll shell the city, they'll do just that," Morgan interrupted. He grabbed Chandler's duffel bag, tossing it onto his shoulder with surprising ease, and took Chandler's elbow with his free hand. "He's right about the march. I know that you're having to jump in at the deep end here, sir, but we absolutely have to get to the checkpoint and see if we can defuse the situation."

"Right," Chandler said, following the two men to the waiting vehicles. "Brief me on the way."

"Thanks, General," a voice called from behind them, and Chandler turned to see the reporter sitting on his luggage and furiously scribbling on a notepad. "Big news, film at eleven." Chandler cursed himself for forgetting the man was there and letting him witness that scene, but there was nothing for it now.

The little convoy sped off down a broad highway toward the city. As he, Morgan, and Elders made themselves as comfortable as possible in the back of one of the Hummers, Chandler peered out the windows to get his first look at Almaty. Neighborhoods of old, squat houses with elaborately carved and painted window frames gave way to cheerless concrete apartment blocks. The city swept upward from the airport into the foothills of the Tien Shan mountain range and seemed, from a distance, deceptively peaceful. But Chandler could recognize a city at war from the deserted streets, the dilapidated buildings, and the occasional burned-out shell of a truck or a house.

"I'm sorry we couldn't give you any warning of this, General," Elders was saying over the grumbling of the engine, "but it was all got up very suddenly, just a few hours ago."

Chandler glanced idly at his watch. For him, still on Washington time, it was nearly midnight of the previous day, but here it was just before eleven in the morning. He had managed to sleep on the flight to Frankfurt and then fitfully on the Moscow leg of his trip. It had been a long haul but he'd made longer ones. There had been a time when he could have gone two or three days without sleep before it began to take his edge away. Now, he felt a deep burning ache behind his eyes and a general heaviness that made it difficult for him to concentrate on what the others were saying.

"I'm afraid this is quite as serious as Qasimbekai was saying, whatever we might think of him personally," Elders continued. "I'm ready to believe that Shchernikov has sent these people out here to try to set a precedent, and he certainly wouldn't be above using women and children as shields if he could manage to seize the airport."

"I tend to think that he's just trying to get rid of a few useless mouths," Morgan interjected. "Besides which, if he can get a few hundred wives and children out of the city, their menfolk who stay behind will fight to the death for him. That's what it's come to here. Blood feuds and blood ties, just like the Dark Ages."

"So what can we do about it?" Chandler asked.

"You've got troops positioned across the airport road," Elders said. "You'll have to use them to turn the crowd back. Our directions from Washington and, more specifically, yours from the Secretary General of the UN, are quite clear. The negotiations between the Kazakhs and their Russian enemies are very tenuous, but they're progressing, and we can't allow this grandstand play by Shchernikov to sabotage the talks by implicating us in a clear truce violation. We can't give the impression that we're taking sides."

"And what if they won't *go* back?" Morgan said tersely. Chandler suspected that this was not the first time that these two had been at cross purposes. "These people were beginning to suffer from malnutrition weeks ago, and I don't think that the word 'starvation' would be an exaggeration now, despite what relief supplies we've managed to get through. Also, winter's coming on, and there's virtually no heating oil left in the city, and they chopped down nearly all the beautiful trees in their parks and along the boulevards last winter. These people don't have many options, and if Shchernikov tells them that Russian planes are waiting for them at the airport, they're going to get there or die trying. Are we going to *shoot* them?"

"The Secretary General has ordered that force be met with force and that any force be used which is required to comply with our mission," Elders quoted dryly.

"It's not as simple as that," Morgan said, pointedly turning away from Elders and toward Chandler. "*Someone's* got to give the order, and then *someone's* got to carry it out."

"The orders have already been given," Elders insisted. "If there's any responsibility here, it lies with the Secretary General."

"I'm not talking about bureaucratic ass covering," Morgan answered back, his voice rising well above the level necessary to be heard over the road noise. "I'm talking about a *man* ordering other *men* to shoot women and children, face to face. And what if the men won't do it? I hate to admit it, sir," Morgan added, turning again to Chandler. "I mean, the men have done a super job here under very difficult and dangerous conditions, really super, but the pressure is getting too much for them. They don't know what's wanted of them, and the only sure thing seems to be that they'd better damn well wear their Kevlar vests if they want an even chance of getting back from a patrol alive. The only good thing so far has been that they haven't really been called on to do more than police the Green Belt between the two warring camps. Both sides had pulled back pretty much voluntarily when we moved in, but, after months of this wear and tear on their nerves, I don't think it would be fair to ask them to deal with something like this."

"Fair or not, it has to be done," Elders snapped. "I thought that discipline was supposed to be the specialty of the military."

Chandler could see both men casting sidelong looks his way throughout the conversation, waiting for him to step in and settle things one way or another. Their eyes were almost pleading for him to do so, even as their argument rose in pitch, but Chandler just couldn't focus on the problem. He would see what was available to him when they arrived on the scene, and maybe a course of action would suggest itself. If he were lucky, maybe there wouldn't be any options at all, and all he would have to do would be to make the best of a bad job and see that his men remained as safe as possible. Yes, he could do that.

"What kind of troops do we have on hand, Colonel?" Chandler asked.

"Our men are spread pretty thin," Morgan replied, and Chandler could see in his face that he knew that Chandler was just playing for time. "The unit manning the position along the airport road is a troop from your American 11th Armored Cavalry, but we've ordered up a platoon of American military police, just for the occasion. I understand that the 11th Armored Cavalry was reconstituted from a training unit for this deployment, so they don't have much practice doing much but playing 'aggressor' during war games. The military policemen have the full outfit for riot control, shields, helmets, batons, and all of that, but there will only be about thirty of them, so the regular troops will have to back them up."

"And the regular troops have nothing but automatic weapons and bayonets," Chandler grunted.

"Exactly."

"I don't suppose I need to point out, General," Elders joined in, "just how closely Washington is monitoring our actions here."

"I'm more concerned about the Kazakh forward artillery observers monitoring our actions, Mr. Elders," Chandler was surprised to hear himself say.

The Hummer lurched to one side of the road in an open area where the relatively sparse houses and workshops they had seen on the road from the airport suddenly gave way to the tall apartment blocks of the city proper, and the vehicles took up defensive positions near where several American M-3 Bradley armored fighting vehicles, painted UN white, were parked. Chandler and Morgan got out of the vehicle, although Elders chose to remain inside.

A double line of military policemen in riot gear stretched across the airport road, just on the near side of another road that ran perpendicular to it. Chandler looked past the troopers to where the airport road widened into a broad, divided boulevard running into the heart of the city. It was now lined with only tree stumps, but it must have been very attractive at one time. Of course, the apartment buildings on either side were typically Stalinesque rectangular concrete blocks, six or eight stories tall, without even a pretense of architectural style, certainly nothing to hint at the cultural richness of this city in Central Asia. To make matters worse, many of the walls bore scars of weapons fire and had been largely abandoned as the population had fled the fighting or been consumed by it. A fragment of white curtain hung out of a shattered window, flapping helplessly in the chill breeze like a flag of surrender. But nearly every window and balcony still held a flower box, now choked with brown, tangled stems, which at least hinted at the little efforts people had once made to brighten their world.

About five blocks away, he could just make out an advancing body of people, some carrying signs written in Cyrillic letters, some carrying luggage or small children hoisted on their shoulders. There was the dull buzz of chanted slogans, but he couldn't have made them out, even if he had been able to speak Russian at more than the minimal level. Another bunch of troops were huddled in the lee of the Bradleys, and from this group strode a determined-looking black officer with the body of a football linebacker.

"Captain Isaiah Greene, sir," the man stated as he saluted Chandler. "Glad you could make it. This doesn't look like it's going to be pretty."

Chandler returned the salute. "I just got off the plane myself, Captain, but from what I'm told, we've got to hold those people back somehow. Do you think you can do it?"

The captain just shook his head. "Take a look at those men, General," he said, jerking his chin in the direction of the men milling about near the vehicles. "I've heard stories about the attitude men had back in 'Nam, but I've never seen anything like it in the eight years since I left the Point. I've overheard a lot of nasty talk about not wanting to crack heads with a bunch of women and kids. I know how this must sound for a unit commander to say this of his men, but I wouldn't want to bet a lot of money on their doing it if we order them to."

"There's more than money on the line here, Captain," Chandler said, and even as it came out he realized how hollow clichés like this would seem to a man who was looking for leadership from his superior.

"If I might suggest, sir," Morgan broke in. "I've spent some time in Belfast, and the situation there is sometimes not all that different from this one. What we need is to get some more 'meat on the street,' as it were. If we can intimidate the people at the head of the crowd with numbers, it might not come to blows at all. With a little carefully dispensed tear gas, it might just disillusion them and send them back home, which is all we want for the moment."

"It's worth a try," Chandler said gratefully. "I know what you're up against, Captain, but you might try to explain it to your men in just those terms. If we look tough enough, the crowd will back off. If we look weak, they'll roll right over us."

Greene just grunted and saluted again, turning on his heel without waiting for the return salute. He covered the thirty or so meters to where his men were gathered in what seemed like only three strides of his muscular legs and began to bark orders and send men scurrying. In a matter of moments, some sixty infantry men had taken up positions flanking the policemen on both sides of the road. Others continued to man their machine guns and the weapons of the Bradleys, just in case things took a turn for the worse.

Chandler thought he saw the pace of the advancing crowd slacken noticeably when the additional men appeared in their bulky flak vests and with their rifles, bayonets fixed, at the ready. But then the crowd came on afresh. He could clearly make out their faces now, not enraged like those of some lynch mobs from the movies, just plain bone tired and full of fear. There was a young mother holding a small child by the hand, with a battered suitcase bound in string under her other arm. There was an elderly couple plodding forward, arm in arm, and it was difficult to tell which one was supporting the other; they both seemed so feeble. But behind the front rank, Chandler could make out more than a few younger men, all wearing similar black leather jackets. They were the ones doing most of the shouting, and he saw one of them continually prodding an older woman in front of him to keep up the pace.

But Chandler could tell that these people were not being forced to come, at least not by any agitators that might be with them. He suspected that what Morgan had said was true, that they simply had no choice and nothing to lose. That made them all very dangerous.

One of the military policemen had a bullhorn and was shouting at the crowd in passable Russian, telling them to stop, go back, go home, that they were entering the UN zone and could be fired upon if they continued. The warnings got more strident the closer they got, and Chandler saw the policeman switch the bullhorn from one hand to the other in order to wipe the sweat from his palms on his pants leg.

Then the rocks began to fly. Rocks and bottles and bits of garbage. At first they hit mainly among the policemen who were directly in the roadway, but as the range shortened, the projectiles began to strike the regular troops as well. The policemen had their tall Plexiglas shields, and they advanced a few steps to better protect the others, but the infantrymen were obliged to try to deflect the flying objects with their rifles, without much success, and one or two of them went down, blood flowing from gashes to the face.

The policemen let loose a volley of tear-gas grenades, and a terrible shout went up from the crowd. What had been meant to dishearten them had galvanized and enraged them, and the crowd began to run across the fifty remaining meters of open ground. All at once the two lines collided with an audible crash.

The policemen took the brunt of the charge with their shields, forming a solid wall across the highway, but more marchers surged up from the rear of the column and spread to either side, like flowing water encountering an obstacle, and soon the infantrymen were engaged in attempting to hold the flanks. At first it was a massive shoving match, the defenders pushing the leaders of the crowd back a few yards, but these would invariably return with two or three others, and the soldiers began to lose ground. Then the leather-jacketed men began swinging the sturdy sticks to which their signs were attached like clubs, and the policemen and soldiers replied with batons and rifle butts.

Chandler could see one young soldier trying to hold back the young mother and her child, a girl of about five with a long blond braid flapping behind her. He was trying to just fence them in with his rifle, but she kept pushing and trying to sidestep. Both shouted at each other in languages the other did not understand, and the little girl cried pitifully, grasping her mother's hand in desperation. The soldier, a boy of no more than twenty with the thick neck of a weightlifter but with a face that spoke of milk and cookies in his mother's kitchen, had tears streaming down his own face, and Chandler could just make out over the din that he wasn't shouting orders at the woman, he was only screaming, "Please! Please!" over and over again.

Then, suddenly, one of the thugs in the black leather jackets appeared and tried to grab the soldier's rifle. The soldier fought back, striking him with the rifle butt on the jaw and sending him staggering back. But the raising of the rifle butt correspondingly brought the barrel down, with its bayonet, and the point slashed across the cheek of the little girl, tracing a thin line of blood. The girl screamed and clutched at her mother. The mother screamed, dropping her suitcase and carrying the girl, running back away from the battle. The soldier just stood there, dumbly staring at the trickle of blood on his weapon.

The thug had recovered now, and rushed at the stupefied soldier again. Without a word, Chandler rushed forward himself. This was something he could understand and deal with. The thug had a firm hold of the rifle now, and the soldier was barely resisting, but Chandler decked the Russian with a punch to the jaw and stood protectively in front of the trooper, blocking a blow from another man with a sign pole and dropping him as well with a kick to the groin. In a moment Morgan was standing beside him, swinging a short tent pole taken from one of the vehicles, and Chandler noticed that the drivers from the little convoy had joined the fray as well, but they were still grossly outnumbered, and many of the soldiers, like the young man behind him, had lost heart in the battle.

Just then he heard the roar of engines and the squeal of brakes, and he turned to see several large trucks skid to a halt just behind them. Out of trucks piled dozens of tall, lanky soldiers with blue-black skin and the sky-blue UN helmets. They all had long batons and charged into the crowd with a war cry. Chandler saw from the shoulder patch of one that brushed past him that they were a company of Senegalese. They apparently had no compunctions about cracking heads, and the crowd seemed to sense this and quickly backed off. In a matter of minutes, the retreat was turned into a full-fledged rout, and the demonstrators fled the field leaving behind a pitiful debris of abandoned luggage, odd bits of clothing, and broken signs that read PLEASE LET US GO HOME in English.

The Senegalese remained formed up across the highway, just in case the marchers should decide to return, and some of the Americans paused to help their own wounded, of which there were about a dozen. The remainder of the Americans trudged back toward their vehicles, some cursing, some sobbing, and some just sullenly silent. He saw one hurl his blue helmet into the back of the APC and beat on the heavy metal door with his fists. The young soldier Chandler had been watching discreetly removed the bayonet from his rifle and let it fall into the dust as he stumbled on. A few raised accusing eyes to Chandler as they filed past, but none bothered to offer a salute, including Captain Greene, who scrambled up on top of his Bradley and sat staring fixedly at the blank wall of a building opposite him.

"I think it would be just as well if we left the company officers to manage things here, sir," Morgan was saying. "It's time we got on to your headquarters so that you can meet your staff."

Chandler didn't bother to answer but simply followed meekly, sucking at his bruised knuckles. He did notice, however, that the terrible weariness he had felt earlier seemed to have left him for the moment. The two men climbed into a different Hummer, since Morgan apparently did not choose to speak again with Elders, and Chandler did not object.

Just before the door of the Hummer slammed shut, Chandler caught a glimpse of the reporter, now accompanied by a man with a large video camera and a couple of other technicians. They must have met him at the airport, Chandler thought, and the bastard was energetic enough to follow up on the story and to come straight here. The journalist gave Chandler a hearty thumbs up signal and a crooked smile.

"Great show, Gen'ral," he shouted. "It'll make the folks back home real proud."

Go ahead and flog your blood and gore, Chandler couldn't help but think. Maybe the more people see of the horror of war, the less likely they'll be to go in for it. At that moment it really didn't matter to him what the reporter's motives might be for doing that task. He just hoped that it would have the desired effect before Brigadier General Julian Chandler broke down completely.

"This used to be really quite a beautiful city," Morgan was saying as the convoy rolled through the deserted streets. "I passed through once on one of the first delegations of foreign disarmament inspectors that they allowed in. You could get fruit, vegetables, meat, all of the things that were so scarce in Moscow, quite readily here. The skiing up in the mountains was superb, and the city was wonderfully green, quite unlike most Russian cities. Used to have a population of over a million, mostly Russians with the Kazakhs mainly living in the rural areas, but I doubt that there are a quarter million in the city now, and those mostly Kazakhs down in the western part of town. Of the Russians, only Shchernikov's boys and a few thousand poor devils that didn't get out in time are left."

Chandler was only half listening. He felt that Morgan seemed to need to talk, and Chandler didn't really want to be left alone with his thoughts right at the moment either.

They were now rolling along a street lined with ornate Victorian-style townhouses, probably the homes of the pre-Bolshevik merchant elite, Chandler thought. The ground floors of most of them had been turned into shops or restaurants, and most of these had the same ghost-town air of the rest of the city. Chandler lost himself momentarily in studying the houses with their peeling but still bright colors and elaborate cornices, but Morgan's voice droned on in his ear.

"You know that the Russians really thought they could hold on to Kazakhstan, since this was the only one of the republics where they were actually in the majority. But then the Kazakhs' Muslim birth rate took off in the 1980s, and then the revolution hit late last year, overthrowing the Russian-dominated government. Over a million Russians fled the country, along with hundreds of thousands of Ukrainians and Byelorussians whose parents had been exiled here in the thirties. There used to be nearly a million ethnic Germans here as well, but they all left when the wall came down and went to Germany. So there you have a country the size of Western Europe with a population smaller than Belgium's, and two thirds of that Muslim.

"Then came the civil war. The Russians had the edge in weaponry, mostly smuggled in from Russia proper, and the covert support from the Russian Army. But the Kazakhs had the numbers, along with support from the other Islamic republics and from Iran, so they say, and they managed to hold on to the southwestern two thirds of the country, with the Russians getting the northeast. Now it's really only this bit down here below Lake Balkhash that's still in dispute. Both sides want Alma-Ata, I mean Almaty, as their capital, for prestige purposes. The Russians under this Shchernikov fellow hold most of the city, but they're cut off from Russian lines by about a hundred miles of hostile territory, and the Kazakhs are all around them."

"And we're right in the middle," Chandler added flatly.

"Exactly," Morgan said, and they rode on in silence.

The convoy moved into the Russian section of the city, pausing at a roadblock manned by scruffy young European-looking militiamen wearing a mixture of old Red Army uniforms, more modern cammies, and assorted civilian clothes, although they all were well armed with AK-47s and RPGs. Chandler reflexively scanned the nearby rooftops and noted that the roadblock was covered by snipers and that a machine gun was set up about a hundred meters beyond it to catch anyone who might try to crash through.

Morgan handed one of the militiamen a slip of paper, which several of them studied carefully, taking their time to read every word and to look over the clearly marked UN vehicles for authenticity. They finally returned the laissez-passer, and the little column pulled up in front of the ornately columned but dingy wooden Museum of Kazakh National Instruments at one end of Panfilov Park, which now served as the temporary American Embassy.

Chandler and Morgan untangled themselves from their vehicle to see Elders off, but the diplomat had already dismounted and sprinted up the steps into the building, having paused only to gather up the case of Snickers bars that had come in for him on the relief flight. Clearly the formal introductions to the diplomatic mission would be reserved for another day, Chandler thought, but he was grateful not to have to go through with any such ceremony at this time. The burning behind his eyes had slowly returned, and he kept one hand cautiously cradling his stomach in anticipation of the renewed pain there, which he expected at any moment.

The park across the street from the Embassy must have looked better in the old days, Chandler suspected. A Russian Orthodox cathedral stood in the middle of it, the onion domes looming over a dreary landscape. Only a few bare trees remained in the park, most of the rest having been cut down for firewood, leaving a field of black stumps and frost-covered grass, and the grounds were pitted here and there with shell holes from the mortar barrages to which the city had been subjected periodically for weeks. No children were to be seen in the playground, and the swings twisted listlessly in the chill breeze.

The convoy then started up again and passed once more through the Russian lines, again submitting to a careful examination by the sentries, before arriving at the Hotel Zhetysu, a tall, down-at-the-heels structure at the very edge of the Green Belt demarcation zone in which the UNEKAZ had set up its headquarters. Most of the windows had been blown out, and the few that retained their glass sported star patterns of masking tape. A sturdy sandbag redoubt had been constructed around the main entrance, topped with a pair of machine guns and manned by grim Japanese military policemen. A row of thick metal pipes had been sunk into the asphalt of the street in a ring about ten yards from the building, a dubious protection against car bombs, which mainly ensured that the building would receive the full shrapnel effect of any explosion.

"We've gathered the unit commanders, sir," Morgan was saying as they climbed the steps. "One of the things I'm sure you're used to from Somalia is that even company commanders have a sort of diplomatic status when they're representatives of their country's contingent. But you may want to freshen up first, so I can show you to your quarters."

"I'm probably fresher now than I will ever be again," Chandler grumbled. "Let's get on with it."

The lobby of the hotel had been converted into a command center with a bank of radios lining one wall, and the reception desk was now a message facility at which several enlisted men and women worked feverishly. A dozen officers, who had been lounging on the threadbare sofas of the lobby, stood to attention when Chandler entered, and Chandler heard the unmistakable voice of a senior NCO bark out the arrival of the general. For an instant Chandler was transported back to the days when that kind of reception, the respect due to an officer, had been electric for him, ample repayment for the years at the Academy and the brutal training. But then he noticed the lack of any welcoming smiles on the faces of the other officers, and he was immediately brought back to the present. Obviously, they had been monitoring the progress of the incident on the airport road on the radio net here.

"Gentlemen," Morgan announced in a parade-field voice, "I give you our new commander, Brigadier General Julian Chandler."

The officers formed an impromptu reception line, but Chandler noted that their spontaneity just happened to work out in order of military rank. That was the military mind at work, a universal law, Chandler thought. They went from Colonel Andres Meriani, commanding the 1st Battalion of the Argentine 8th Mountain Brigade, with his neatly trimmed mustache and immaculately coiffed hair, down through the lieutenant colonels, captains, and odd lieutenants, down to the tech sergeants manning the communications gear. In each case there was a sharp salute, a firm handshake in which the junior officer tried his best to display his manhood by crushing Chandler's fingers, and a few banal words of greeting.

Chandler felt obliged to give some sort of speech to inaugurate his new command, and to fill the uncomfortable silence that followed the introductions, but nothing came to his mind. At least in Somalia he had been able to take refuge in a staff position. This had had its great pressures, and on several occasions he had been called on to lead men into combat situations, but that had been when he still felt confident enough of himself to do so. There had been a host of different national contingents in Mogadishu as well, and he had dealt with all of them, but he had not had to *command* them. And to make matters worse, several of the units, specifically the Israelis, Japanese, and South Koreans constituted their countries' first effort at contributing to UN combat missions, which added a whole new diplomatic twist to any differences of opinion that might arise.

Chandler finally screwed up enough courage to speak, although even at the moment he realized that it was more for lack of courage to remain silent that he spoke.

"I spoke with General Endicott in Frankfurt on my way here," he began uncertainly, "and he had nothing but praise for all of you and your men . . . and women." Chandler cleared his throat nervously, knowing that every person there had heard the same speech given by every new commander they had ever met. In his own time, Chandler had sometimes longed for a boss who would at least have the originality to start off with something like "I took this assignment under protest and have never had the displeasure of falling in with such a bunch of losers in my life," but he had never found one, and he didn't plan to break new ground himself.

"I had a chance to see some of the men in action myself just a little while ago, and I couldn't have been more impressed. Your men, in particular, Captain Kebe," he said, nodding to the tall Senegalese, who straightened slightly and puffed out his chest, "came to the rescue just in the nick of time, in the best tradition of the U.S. cavalry."

Chandler noticed that his comment earned him a burning look from Lieutenant Colonel Alan Peabody, the short, squat commander of the American cavalry battalion, whose men had also been at the roadblock, but he went on.

"Like some of you, I've been in a situation like this before. It's easy for soldiers to go to war, to a real war. There the job is simply to seize the objective or to die trying. But here, where the objective isn't seizable, yet the chances of dying are just as good, there is no glory, only the avoidance of pain, and even that is not always possible. It takes a special kind of courage to deal with that, day after day. We are stuck here doing a thankless job, trying to keep two groups of people apart who are determined to be at each other's throats, and both sides hate us for it. I can't promise you any relief from that. I can only promise you that I'll do my best to see that the orders we have to comply with make sense and put our men in as little danger as possible until either the political situation here sorts itself out or until we can all go home."

He could see some of the men in the back of the crowd glancing surreptitiously at each other, even though those in the front looked impassively forward, the mark of disciplined officers. This was hardly the kind of speech they had expected, or even deserved, but Chandler couldn't bring himself to say anything different. The pain in his stomach was trying to make him double over, to scream out loud, to make him go to the medics and get sent home, but he would not do that. He could master the pain, but he couldn't put on the sort of brash show military men used to hide their fears and to hearten those around them. He just couldn't do both.

"Now, if you'll excuse me," he went on after another pregnant pause. "I'm about twelve time zones out of whack, and if we want orders written with anything other than strings of random consonants, I'd better try to get some shut-eye."

Those whose military institutions went in for such things, clicked their heels smartly, and there were some mumbled words of welcome spoken in his general direction as Chandler let Morgan lead him away toward the stairway. He was also certain that he heard one or two snorts of disgust and again caught meaningful glances being passed from one officer to another.

"I'm afraid our generator isn't up to running the elevators," Morgan apologized as he led the way toward the stairway, indifferently lit through the grimy, narrow windows. "The city power hasn't been working since we arrived here."

Just before they reached the stairs, a portly man with a dusky complexion suddenly appeared before them. He was bald, with only a fringe of white hair reaching around the back of his head. He wore an olive green pullover sweater, the pseudo-military kind with the smooth patches at the elbows and on the shoulders. He extended his hand.

"I didn't want to interrupt your little speech," he said. "I am Sharad Devi, the representative of the Secretary General of the United Nations in Kazakhstan, and I expect that we will be working together quite closely in the coming weeks."

"Julian Chandler, pleased to meet you," Chandler replied, wanting very much to get on to his room. "I look forward to meeting your entire staff at your convenience."

"That was why I took the liberty of coming alone to meet you first," Devi went on. "I wanted to make clear our lines of authority when we were not in front of too many observers."

"There was a certain lack of accord between General Endicott and Mr. Devi's staff on the subject of hierarchy," Morgan explained, making no effort to hide the tension in his voice. "Mr. Devi believes that it is his staff's job to approve, or disapprove, all orders issuing from the UNEKAZ headquarters. General Endicott was of the opinion that military operations were to be run by the military command and that the UN mission was to limit itself to political affairs."

"Exactly," Devi agreed. "And since the entire mission of the UNEKAZ is a political one, there were very few instances when an action by the UNEKAZ forces could not have a political impact, which necessitated my taking part in the decision-making process. But you needn't take my word for it. We have very clear written instructions from the Secretary General. I would be happy to provide you with copies."

"I'm sure that we can work together on this," Chandler sighed, "but I would like to have copies of your instructions, just to avoid any misunderstanding."

"Of course, General. I know now that you must be tired, so I won't keep you. I look forward to seeing you tomorrow."

He turned and strolled toward the doorway, pausing at a table piled with orders and reports to leaf through them and to read one or two that caught his eye.

"You're going to have trouble with that one," Morgan said, watching him leave. "He's a twenty-year official of the UN and attached to the Secretary General like a wart, but he's also an Indian, and there have been rumors that he's rather partial to the Russians in this dispute, on orders of his own government. In either case, he gets in the way constantly."

"That won't be anything new," Chandler said wearily.

"It's worse than that," Morgan said. "They've set up communications here so that nothing, and I mean *nothing*, goes out except through the relay setup at Devi's office."

Chandler frowned. "How can that be possible? With satellite communications and all, any platoon leader can talk directly with

Washington, or London, or any other spot on earth with the right hookup. We certainly had that in Somalia."

"Exactly, sir." Morgan shook his head. "The Secretary General insisted that he couldn't have each national contingent calling home to debate UN orders, that is, *his* orders. He said there was entirely too much of that in Somalia."

"Well, he's right enough about that."

"So, his solution was to equip the entire force with 1960s-era radios for tactical use, and not to allow *any* international commo except through Mr. Devi. They even had to yank the radios out of our tanks and APCs and scrounge the inventories of every Third World army on the planet for enough working radios to equip us. Even at that, communications have been a constant balls-up. Of course, we suspect that the Ukrainians have squirreled away their own 'back-up' system for all of them to talk direct to Kiev and Moscow, but we can't prove it."

"That's insane!" Chandler growled.

"I think you're getting the picture now, sir," Morgan said cheerily.

They climbed the remaining four flights of stairs in silence, and Morgan headed down a dark central hallway.

"Didn't want to put you on the top floor," he said. "Danger from artillery fire, you know."

"But someone is quartered there, I suppose," Chandler added absently.

"Well, yes, some junior officers. For all its dreariness, this is still the nicest hotel in the UN sector, and we're all going to be subject to artillery fire at some point, after all."

"Then I'll take a room on the top floor, if it's all right," Chandler said. "The junior officers risk their lives often enough as it is. But let's make the change tomorrow, I really need to get some sleep."

"Very well, sir," Morgan said. Chandler thought he noticed the Englishman cocking his head and nodding in approval. He probably mistook resignation for bravery.

Morgan had to throw his shoulder into the warped door to force it open, and it squealed pitifully on its hinges. The room was spartan, with pale, yellowing linoleum on the floor, beginning to turn up at the corners, and only a single bed and a card table for furniture. What had been sliding glass doors had been replaced by large sheets of plywood, and one of these had been shifted to one side to reveal a narrow balcony and a thin strip of the view of the city below. The room was cold enough that Chandler's breath formed a mist in front of his face.

"Not much usable glass left in the city, I'm afraid," Morgan said. "First thing to go when high explosives start to be thrown around."

He threw Chandler's duffel bag onto the bed and stood aside as a tall, athletic man in UN uniform stepped silently into the room from the balcony.

"Lieutenant Commander Malcolm Wakeham, Royal Marines," Morgan said as the man snapped a British salute and thrust out a muscular hand for Chandler to shake. Despite the decided chill in the air, Wakeham wore no jacket and had his sleeves neatly rolled up past his elbows. In response to Chandler's raised eyebrows, Morgan went on.

"You'll have to forgive the melodrama, but it isn't widely known that Malcolm and his men are here."

"Yes, sir," the Marine continued. "You see, I have a platoon comprised of Marines and SAS commandos. We're attached to the Blues and Royals as just another batch of troopies, but it was thought that our special skills might come in handy at some point."

"Malcolm and his men have all had extensive experience doing 'operations' in Northern Ireland. The UN people remembered Somalia and how it was patently obvious that when you Americans sent in your Rangers, it was with a view to get your hands on that fellow Aideed."

"And we all know how well *that* worked out," Chandler said grimly.

"Exactly," Wakeham said. "So, it was decided that we'd just be here, doing regular infantry duties until such time as our more particular services might be needed, and thus avoid having to run the gauntlet of the journalists and risk tipping off whomever we were being called in to 'arrest.'"

"I know all about the trouble with journalists. There was one on my plane coming in, and he's already making a nuisance of himself."

"Jeff Goldman, know him quite well," Morgan said. "He's been here before and isn't very favorably inclined to our presence here."

"Who is?" Chandler heard himself ask.

The other two officers didn't reply at first.

"Secretary General Muli at the UN, I suppose," Morgan finally said, and Chandler quickly changed the subject.

"Well, I'm glad someone had this kind of foresight, Commander. I'm very pleased to have you here, and I hope that we won't be put into a situation of having to call on you."

"Actually, I'd just as soon you did, sir," Wakeham said as he headed for the door. "Bloody boring stuff, this." He saluted again and yanked the protesting door open and closed it behind him.

"Well, I'll just let you put your feet up, and we'll see you in the morning, sir," Morgan said.

Chandler just nodded and stepped out onto the balcony. It would be full winter soon. The snow line was creeping down the mountains to the south, and the thick stands of pine there were already encrusted with snow. Chandler wondered how the people here would survive.

Only a couple of civilian trucks were moving about the streets below, and he could see several long lines of people, clad in dark, heavy coats, formed up in front of different buildings up and down the street, waiting for bread, or meat, or kerosene, or some other necessity. He watched for five minutes, then ten, then fifteen, and didn't see even a sign of movement in any of the lines. Perhaps they were just lines for position when the stores opened later, or tomorrow, or the next day. Maybe they were just for practice.

Of course, he'd seen this and worse before, in Somalia. He hated to admit it, since he didn't like to think of himself as a racist, but the fact that these people were white and dressed in European style clothing, albeit hardly fashionable clothing, made it seem more personal, more tragic. In Somalia, and before that in Vietnam, there had been an alien atmosphere to the place that made the horrors that occurred there somehow alien as well. The clothes were different, the architecture of the buildings, everything made the scenes in those places look like something out of the pages of *National Geographic*, exotic places where all sorts of strange things could happen. But you could believe that these people were from Minnesota or Georgia just as easily, until they started to speak Russian. And this had been a *real* country until a few years ago. Did that mean that this sort of thing could happen just anywhere?

Chandler went back into his room and slid the plywood back into place. He dug into his bag and pulled out a pink plastic bottle and took a long drink, grimacing at the chalky taste. It didn't help.

He lay in bed a long time, staring at the ceiling. It was still broad daylight, and the plywood fit the window frame poorly, leaving the room in dim grayness. His eyes hurt, he was so tired, but his brain kept racing and would not let him sleep, even though it was after midnight as far as his body was concerned. He relived the visit to Endicott, the flight over, the fight at the roadblock, and his dismal arrival speech over and over again. He started to doze.

He felt a blast of hot air. The throbbing of helicopter rotors could be felt more than heard, and he could see the gleaming white teeth shining out from the black faces of the Somali gunmen sitting atop their "technical" armed Land Rovers and hear the clipped sound of their speech as they gossiped at their checkpoints. There was the distant chatter of small-arms fire, maybe killing civilians, or tribal fighters, or UN peacekeepers, or maybe someone was just jubilantly firing into the air. He knew he would hear one way or the other in a few minutes on the radio.

He watched the men bustling into and out of the command post, UN soldiers, journalists in their inevitable safari suits, haggard medical relief workers, and well-fed Somali bodyguards of the various bureaucrats who accompanied the mission. They were all so busy that no one seemed to have time to go pick up that boy at the traffic circle. Chandler couldn't get anyone to listen to him. He didn't want to go himself, but no one else would do it. He didn't want to see that boy's face or his mangled body again, but everyone just told him that it was his job. That's what he was being paid for

So Chandler went by himself. It was only a short walk this time. The Somalis were laughing at him as he carried the body back. It didn't weigh anything at all, because they'd taken the insides out.

But then Chandler had to deliver the boy to his mother, who lived just down the street. He knew the house.

"What did you do to my boy?" she asked. "He missed his dinner, you know, and it was his favorite. Sloppy joes. He could eat three or four at one sitting, you know. Now it's spoiled, because you really can't save that, you know."

Chandler knew. You really can't save anything.

CHAPTER 2

Sixteen American peacekeepers were injured, several seriously, in a confrontation with Russian demonstrators in the besieged city of Almaty yesterday. Graphic film footage of American soldiers beating back unarmed civilians provoked sharp debate in Congress on the administration's foreign policy. Perennial presidential candidate Ross Perot commented that letting the UN Secretary General issue orders to American troops was about as sensible as installing a gas barbecue in an ammo bunker. Russian President Balinsky denounced the action as "genocidal," and there has been a report of at least one attempted suicide in the last twenty-four hours among American troops in Almaty, although the Pentagon has declared that there was no direct connection with yesterday's incident.

CNN

ALMATY
30 October

Chandler had to straddle the toilet in order to get the bathroom door shut, and he had to shut the door in order to get at the sink and mirror. He stared at himself before he started to shave. He was certain that he hadn't had those dark rings under his eyes even two days before, and his hair, which had had its share of gray before, now almost appeared completely white, but perhaps it was just the glare of the lightbulb, which dangled precariously by a wire from the ceiling. He also noticed that his knuckles hurt as he twisted off the cap of the toothpaste tube, but it wasn't just age. He wasn't quite fifty yet, and his father was still going strong at nearly eighty. Hell, his grandfather had lived past ninety. But then, they had had rather different lives, hadn't they? His grandfather had been a farmer, and his father the manager of a supermarket, and they both had experienced the Depression—but there was a difference between only having to worry about keeping yourself and your family fed and clothed and worrying about keeping a host of strangers fed, clothed, armed, and alive when another bunch of strangers was trying to kill them. That was what wore you out.

It wasn't sunrise yet when Chandler made his way down to the ground floor and strolled out to main entrance of the hotel. A disconcerted American female staff sergeant with pale blond hair tucked up under her blue beret had said, apologizing, that breakfast would not be served until six o'clock, at least another hour away, but she'd shoved a cup of industrial waste–strength coffee into Chandler's hand unbidden. Chandler didn't actually care for coffee, certainly not black, but he thought it would be ungracious to refuse, so he pretended to sip at it until he could walk outside the building and discreetly pour the liquid into a large cement planter, which now only grew an abundant crop of cigarette butts.

Chandler reflected that he didn't do most of the things that soldiers were supposed to do. Not caring for "lifer's juice" was just one of them. He rarely swore, didn't drink or smoke, couldn't care less about sports, and even during his time in Vietnam had never felt the urge to visit any of the plethora of whorehouses, not even the clean ones. Maybe things would be easier if he *did* drink, he sometimes thought, but he was far too old to start now. On the other hand, he didn't belong to the clique of born-again Christians or the Mormons, who also abounded in officer ranks. His idea of a good time was to lie back and read Dickens, or Steinbeck, which had given him the reputation of being an intellectual, although he didn't pretend to "interpret" literature. He just liked reading stories.

Early morning was Chandler's favorite time of day, just as the night sky turned deep blue, but while the streetlights were still on, before most people had gotten up and about to spoil the day for everyone else. There were a number of men and women at work in the Almaty command center, but they were left over from the night shift, and moved with a kind of lethargy born of violating the laws of nature, which dictated that night was a time for sleep. Standing outside now in the crisp air and watching the condensation cloud of his breath melt away in front of him, Chandler felt better.

But early morning in Almaty was not like that of most cities. There were no streetlights, only the glaring security lights that surrounded the UN compound and security points he could see farther up and down the street. The rest of the city was completely dark, with only the ghostly images of the white buildings vaguely visible in the starlight. There would be none of the usual early-morning crew of paperboys or truckers delivering food to grocery stores.

Neither were there the kinds of exotic smells that he had expected to find in a city that had once been a major stop on the Silk Road used by caravans coming and going between the Far East and Europe with loads of silk and spices and other rare goods. No colorful local market days were being held now; there were only distribution points for bland UN relief supplies, when those were available. With the Kazakhs and Russians now segregated by the Green Belt, the few civilian faces he had seen in town were almost exclusively European-looking; there were no narrow-eyed peasants bringing in produce from the country on carts drawn by hairy ponies, like in the travel books. Chandler suspected that Beirut and Sarajevo had also lost much of their unique character at similar points in their own purgatories.

He walked slowly down the hotel steps to the street. He could see from the flag patches on their sleeves that South Koreans had replaced the Japanese military policemen on duty from the day before, although he admitted to himself that he would not have recognized the difference otherwise. Of course, he could when a Japanese and a Korean were side by side, but not when they were apart. He now regretted never having served in either country. They looked at him nervously as he passed through the ring of metal poles and headed off into the darkness, and one of them gestured to another, who discreetly slipped back into the building.

At the first corner he turned left, passing the TSUM, a huge Soviet-era department store. It didn't have the elaborate shop windows an American or European version would have, but then again, there probably wasn't anything inside to sell, so there wasn't any reason to try to attract customers. But when he reached the end of the building, he found a line of about a hundred silent people patiently waiting outside a door. Perhaps there had been a rumor of a shipment of shoes or blankets or toilet paper, but Chandler knew that the rare supply convoys that were getting through to the city under UN escort and the aircraft that flew in from Russia were only bringing food and medical supplies these days, and the UN distributed these goods for free. Force of habit, he assumed, or unreasoning hope.

By the time he had reached the next corner, Chandler could hear the sound of heavy boots pounding on the pavement behind him and the clatter of metal on metal. He turned to find Morgan sprinting the last twenty meters to reach him. A squad of South Koreans was keeping pace with him, dodging from doorway to doorway, half on either side of the street, their weapons at the ready; a Hummer with an automatic grenade launcher had taken up a covering position at the end of the street.

"Morning, sir," Morgan rasped, slinging his own automatic rifle and saluting. Chandler could see that he had not shaved, and the buttons on his shirt were off by one. "I see you're up bright and early. I hope you slept well." The British were so terribly polite.

"Actually, I couldn't sleep. Jet lag, I suppose, so I thought I'd get a look at the city."

"Excuse me, sir," Morgan said, making a superhuman effort to control himself, "but this really isn't advisable. We're right on the edge of the Green Belt here, and both sides like to set up snipers to try to pick each other off over our heads, and sometimes they use us for practice. We did just lose one CO, and it would be a dreadful shame if we were to lose another so soon. It might look bad on my record."

Chandler chuckled for the first time since receiving his Almaty orders. "Well, we wouldn't want that."

He turned and began to walk with Morgan back toward the hotel. "I'm sorry to have caused any trouble. I should have known better."

Morgan was silent a moment. The fact that he wasn't able to produce a quick "no problem," despite his obvious tact, was an indication to Chandler of just how seriously upset Morgan was.

"That's what we're here for," Morgan finally said, but without much conviction.

Chandler dispatched Morgan to get properly groomed for the day and spent some time studying the tactical deployment maps posted around the command center. The three UN armored cavalry battalions (British, French, and American), the Argentine mountain infantry, and the Ukrainian motor rifle battalions were stretched in a thin line around the Russian-occupied heart of the city. The American air cavalry squadron, an Egyptian artillery battery, and the Israeli combat engineer company occupied the airport several miles to the north. The Japanese, Senegalese, and South Korean military police companies were split up into small detachments to man most of the road checkpoints leading through the Green Belt. In most places the Belt was only two blocks wide, with local civilians continuing to live within that area, and it was not a deployment meant to withstand open attack by a military force, or even to prevent the passage of individuals through the lines, but only to deter major units of the opposing Russian and Kazakh forces from coming into contact.

Outside the city were scattered small Kazakh militia units. The brigades of their newly formed and blooded army were deployed mostly over a hundred miles away to the northeast, along the Lepsa River line, where they faced similar units of the Russian separatists. Patrols of both sides freely roamed the area south of Lake Balkhash. The provisional Kazakh government, in order to support its claim to Almaty as its true capital, had set up housekeeping in the modernistic Ardash Orda Concert Hall (formerly named the Palace of Lenin Concert Hall) on the southern edge of the city. The apartment blocks directly opposite the Green Belt on both sides of the line had been converted into makeshift fortresses with sandbags reinforcing apartment walls: heavy weapons had been emplaced in the windows, and communications holes had been hacked out of the interior walls of the buildings.

Inside the Green Belt was a ghost town consisting of about half of the urban area. According to reports of the UN's G-2 intelligence section, there were perhaps five thousand Russian fighters inside the city, well equipped with small arms, antitank weapons, and even some armor and artillery. They "protected" a civilian population that had shrunk to less than twenty thousand and consisted primarily of their own families. In addition to them, it was reported, the Russian militia commander, Igor Shchernikov, had prevented the departure of some thousands of other civilians, mostly women and children, with the original exodus of Russians from the Kazakh-dominated south and west of the country during the revolution. The theory was that he wanted to use them to support his own claim to Almaty as the capital of the Russian separatist state, and also to put added pressure on the UN to perform the "humanitarian" mission of helping to protect him from his Kazakh opponents. Chandler did not consider it a very promising situation.

At breakfast with Morgan, Chandler was pleased to find yoghurt available, about the only thing that would agree with his stomach these days, and it helped to soothe the burning pain for a moment. He grimaced as Morgan attacked the greasy sausages and the gooey mass of reconstituted scrambled eggs without speaking.

"You have a choice, General," Morgan announced as they stood outside the building in front of their waiting vehicles. "We use the Hummers primarily for transport, but where we're going, running right along the Line most of the way, it might be preferable to take a Bradley for better protection. The locals on both sides have been known to 'mistake' our vehicles for those of their enemies, claiming that evildoers have intentionally painted their own vehicles in UN white to slip through the lines."

"I've seen what a SAGGER missile can do to a Bradley," Chandler said, "so we might as well go with the Hummer."

They spent most of the morning passing from one UN unit to another, meeting the junior officers, and inspecting the troop deployments. After swinging around the southern end of town and passing through the Argentine, British, and French sectors, they came to the area patrolled by the Ukrainians, which guarded the key bridges over the two arms of the Malaya Alma Atinka River that bordered the city on the east, just as the broader Bolshaya Alma Atinka does on the west.

"Before we arrive at the battalion headquarters," Morgan said, "I think you'd better understand that the Ukrainians are not entirely . . . how shall I put it? . . . impartial in this conflict."

"What do you mean?"

"There was considerable argument over whether any troops from Slavic countries should be included in UNEKAZ, just as the Pakistanis were ruled out on the Muslim side. There have been a lot of accusations from the Kazakhs that the Ukrainians have allowed the Russians pretty much free rein in passing through their lines and have even supplied them with guns and ammunition."

"Of course the Kazakhs would make those kind of charges with or without basis, just because the Ukrainians are Slavs, wouldn't they?" Chandler asked.

"Perhaps," Morgan conceded, "but the suspicion was reinforced when the Ukrainian commander, Major Arkady Borysenko, with the support of both his and the Russian government, insisted that they be given this precise sector of the perimeter. General Endicott had his own doubts about this and objected, but Mr. Devi overruled him, and there it is."

"I'll have to reserve judgment on the Ukrainians until we have some evidence to go on, but I'm beginning to have my doubts about Mr. Devi already," Chandler said. "If he gets to be too much of a problem, I may have to talk to Elders at the embassy and see if we can get some U.S. government pressure on him."

"I wouldn't count on that if I were you," Morgan cautioned, shaking his head. "Elders is the only diplomat permanently stationed in Almaty. All of the other diplomatic missions to Kazakhstan work out of Moscow, because of the discomfort, to say nothing of the outright physical danger. Elders seems to have it in his head that he's carving out a brilliant career for himself here, out on what he likes to refer to as the 'frontiers of diplomacy,' and that tends to make him a little, shall we say, self-important. That would be bad enough, but he's also of the opinion that it is his destiny to 'make the UN effort here work' and that the only way to accomplish that goal is to do exactly whatever Mr. Devi and the Secretary General dictate. I know it's not my place to comment on United States government policy, but poor old Kazakhstan seems to be small enough fish in your government's opinion that this surrendering of the initiative doesn't seem to bother anyone in Washington. So I'm afraid you're on your own out here, Julian."

Chandler had learned that he could gauge Morgan's mood by whether he used his first name or his rank in addressing him. At the moment, Morgan apparently considered Chandler to be on his side.

"Well, we'll fight it as best we can, but all we can do for now is hope that it doesn't come to a showdown."

Morgan just cocked his head as if to say, "Good luck," and stared out the window.

Their Hummer and those of the security escort pulled to a halt in front of a haphazard collection of Russian-made armored personnel carriers in the parking lot of a small office building. A number of sloppily dressed soldiers were lounging about, smoking or eating food out of cans, and tossing the empty ones onto a large and growing pile of garbage next to a command track. They glanced up in a surly fashion as Chandler dismounted, but did not rise.

Several command tracks were parked close together, and a canvas tarp had been stretched between their open rear decks, forming a pavilion that sheltered Borysenko's command post. The major—a short, swarthy, rather stocky man—and his officers, at least, were a little more observant of military protocol, and not only saluted but also offered the general a hot cup of tea, which he graciously declined.

"Perhaps you could show me your dispositions, Major," Chandler said, discreetly shouldering his way past the younger officers who had, just as discreetly, formed a wall of their bodies in front of the tactical map laid out on a long table.

"Of course, General," the major said, gesturing with his eyes for the junior officers to stand aside. "Like the other perimeter units, we basically have one company patrolling and manning checkpoints on the inner ring, facing the Russians, and another facing outward toward the Kazakhs, with the third company and our mortar company grouped near my headquarters here as a reserve. We have to cover some two kilometers and more, so there are no continuous positions, just the major intersections, with the intervening space covered by roving patrols."

"And the bridges," Chandler added, tapping the map with his forefinger.

"Yes, certainly, the bridges," the major stammered. "We have a full squad permanently assigned to each."

"Wouldn't it ease your burden if we were to bring in military police squads to cover the bridges and also the inner side of the ring on the Kirova and Kalinina ulitsas that lead to them? Then your men could pull back and back them up if necessary from a concentrated center position."

"But I don't have any military police in my battalion, General."

"Not Ukrainian, but troops from the military police units attached to my headquarters, Japanese or Senegalese or South Korean."

"I'm afraid that won't—I mean, it really won't be necessary, General," Borysenko argued. "We have been doing very well by ourselves." He cast an accusing glance at Morgan, who stared him down.

"I'm sure that you have, Major," Chandler said, putting special emphasis on the Ukrainian's subordinate rank, "but I suppose if I should order a change, you'd have no trouble obeying my orders, even if you happened to disagree with them on a tactical basis."

Borysenko lowered his head and scuffed the toe of his boot against the asphalt of the parking lot. "I would have to seek the approval of the UN commissioner," he murmured without raising his head.

"You will follow my orders, Major, or I will personally place you under arrest for insubordination!" Chandler shouted. The Ukrainian officers all started at the unexpected outburst, but none more so than Morgan.

Borysenko stammered for a moment and then asked, "Are you giving me that order, General?"

"Yes," Chandler snapped.

"Then I will comply under protest . . . as soon as I have seen the order in writing, and I will reserve the right to take the matter up with Commissioner Devi at the earliest opportunity."

Chandler snatched a notebook out of the hands of one of Borysenko's staff officers and scribbled on it furiously for a moment, ripped off the sheet, and shoved it in Borysenko's face.

"There's your order, Major. I'll have the MPs here before the end of the day."

Borysenko slowly took the paper and tucked in into his breast pocket. "Exactly so, General."

Back in the Hummer en route to the American sector, Morgan shook his head. "I must say, Julian, that I'm glad to see that something can make you lose control, although I hope you don't think that the matter was ended there. Borysenko will be on the horn to everyone who will listen by now, trying to get your order reversed."

"I saw enough of that bullshit in Somalia with the Italians," Chandler said, staring out the window, rubbing his stomach nervously. "They would cut their own deals with the local warlords, using their ties from the days when Somalia was an Italian colony, to protect their troops while letting the other contingents do the fighting. I can't count on a national contingent that's got its own hidden agenda, and it's important that they understand that from the outset. What I can't understand is *why* he should be so adamant about it."

"Well, part of it is simply money," Morgan said. "We've always suspected that Borysenko accepts bribes from Shchernikov to allow shipments of weapons and ammunition through his sector after they've made their way through Kazakh territory from the north. You know how dirt poor the Russian officers are now, and the same goes for those of the new republics. But we also suspect that Borysenko's taking orders directly from Kiev, which may be in cahoots with Moscow on wanting the Russian separatist movement to succeed here. The Russians did something not too dissimilar in Georgia with the ethnic Russian Abkhazian separatists, and in Moldova—supporting a local faction with whom they can make an alliance against a local breakaway government. Why not here?"

"But you have no proof?"

"No, we're not getting any serious intelligence reporting from the CIA or MI6 or anyone. I suppose they don't want to compromise their better sources by passing information to a multinational group like ours, not knowing where it will end up. And I must say that I don't blame them."

"Hmm," Chandler nodded. He was silent a moment and then asked in a quiet voice, "You're not very impressed with me so far, are you, Randy?"

Morgan cleared his throat and inspected the toes of his boots briefly. "Well, sir, I understand that this is a difficult assignment, and a dangerous one, and I frankly got the feeling that you didn't actually volunteer for it."

"No, I didn't. Does that make a difference?"

He thought for another moment and then replied, "Well, to put it more precisely, it seemed as though you very much did not want to be here, and I think that *does* make a difference."

"I can't argue with that, Randy," Chandler said, "and you're absolutely right. I didn't want to be put in this kind of situation again, but I had my orders."

"I suspect that, in your service as in mine, there would have been dozens of officers who would have given their right arm for this command. Not much of a war, but it's the only one we've got, and all that."

"I'm sure there were, but they didn't select them. They selected me."

"And did they make a good choice, sir?"

"I suppose we'll both find that out, Randy," Chandler replied. "I can only promise you that I will very gladly die before I let you or the men down here."

The two American battalion commanders, Lieutenant Colonels Alan Peabody of the 1st Squadron, 11th Armored Cavalry, and Juan Carlos Saavedra of the air cavalry squadron received Chandler and Morgan together, and the reception was not a friendly one. They outlined the deployment of their units as had the other commanders, but then Peabody, a tobacco-chewing Texan with a shaved head, braced himself in front of Chandler to bring up his own agenda items.

"Might I ask, sir," the Texan began, staring fixedly into Chandler's eyes, "whether it is your view that it is the duty of my men to do the dirty work of those two butchers, Qasimbekai and Shchernikov, for them?"

"I beg your pardon, Colonel?"

"I'm sure that Colonel Morgan has explained the ground truth here to you, sir," he went on. "We all know that Qasimbekai must have laughed himself sick that UN troops were out there cracking the heads of Russian women and children while his men sat back and watched. And that bastard Shchernikov wanted us to do it just as bad. That way *he's* not the one who's keeping those poor slobs in the city to serve as his hostages and to feed his warped vision of himself as this little king. It's *us!* That's not what we signed up to do here, General. We came here on a humanitarian mission, escort the food shipments, keep the gunmen from murdering the innocent and all that happy-crappy. I never had a discipline problem in my unit, I swear it, before we got here, but I sure as hell got one now. What I want to know is, is that the way it's going to be from here on in?"

Saavedra, a lean, olive-skinned Latino with startling green eyes, nodded gravely in accord.

"Looks like I'm the one with the discipline problem, Colonel," Chandler said, returning Peabody's gaze firmly, and the Texan immediately dropped his eyes.

"But you're absolutely right," Chandler went on quickly. "We did just what you said we were doing, and, no, it's not at all what we, or the American government or people, thought we were being sent over here to do. But we're here, and as long as it's the policy of the American government to place us under UN orders, then we have to follow the policy the UN lays down for us. Maybe that doesn't sit well with you. I know it doesn't sit well with me, but you have to ask yourself the question then, who *is* going to do it? Are the good guys going to get along any better if we make a big enough stink to get ourselves pulled out of here? Now, if our government jerks the chain of the UN and gets the mission changed, that's another story, but that's not our job. We're just simple soldiers, and we've got to do what we're told to do, even if it isn't the kind of clear-cut military tasking that we're most comfortable with. I wish I could give you a better answer than that, but I can't."

Both of the American officers were now thoroughly fascinated with the texture of the soil under their feet.

"What I need to ask you," Chandler continued, "is whether you can buy into that or whether you're asking to be relieved."

Both men suddenly stood ramrod straight and chorused back, "No, sir!"

"Good. Then all I can do is my best to see that as many of our men make it home alive as possible and that those who do survive will be able to live with themselves. I can't promise any more than that."

Chandler then spent a few more moments discussing their supply situation and manning levels, and then he and Morgan again mounted up to continue their "parish calls."

The modernistic and still quite attractive Ardash Orda Concert Hall clinging to the southern edge of the city, which served as the seat of the provisional Kazakh government, was swarming with heavily armed, if rather scruffy, militiamen. They all had the same almond eyes and high cheekbones—not quite Asian, not quite Arab in appearance, but a cross between the two. They manned twin-barreled anti-aircraft guns on the roof, and several rusty but functional T-54 tanks were in the broad park in front of the hall. Except for the tanks, the hall reminded Chandler rather vaguely of the Kennedy Center in Washington. At the far end of the park lawn in front of the hall stood a massive granite pedestal, atop which there were a pair of bronze feet, one of which extended from a trousered leg as far up as the knee. The legacy of Vladimir Ilyich Lenin, Chandler speculated.

"You see those chaps over there with the cylindrical cloth caps?" Morgan asked, pointing to a group of bearded men gathered around a fitfully burning campfire. "If I'm not mistaken, those are Afghan mujahedin, giving the Russians a little of their own back. We believe that there are nearly ten thousand of them fighting alongside the Kazakhs. There are also a couple of battalions of Iranian Revolutionary Guards and a few hundred Hezbollah fighters from Lebanon. It's a veritable who's who of Islamic gunmen."

The UN convoy had to pass through no less than three separate checkpoints to cover the last hundred yards to approach the hall, and at each one the militiamen frowned and squinted over their safe-conduct passes and identity papers, twisting and turning them and holding them up to the light, before eventually waving them along with obvious reluctance. When they had finally run this gauntlet, they dismounted and were forced to dismiss their escort, who would await them outside the defensive perimeter of the building complex.

Bakyt Qasimbekai allowed them to wait a modest twenty minutes outside his office, which had belonged to the theater director in happier times. When they were finally shown in, he did not rise.

The office was one of the first rooms in Kazakhstan that Chandler had found reasonably attractive. It was paneled in rich, dark wood, not cheap prefabricated stuff, and an elaborate showcase was built into one wall in which were displayed a variety of silver plates and trophies, apparently the winnings of the local orchestra at regional competitions. Opposite the showcase, a huge picture window opened out onto a spectacular view of the mountains to the south, with the little cable car that ran up to a mountaintop restaurant clearly visible in the foreground. The office had obviously once belonged to a man with both artistic tastes and considerable power.

The current resident possessed only the latter. The thin fabric of the suit he wore was stretched tight over his thick biceps. His narrow eyes stared firmly straight ahead, and his broad hands and fat fingers were laid flat on the blotter atop the ornately carved and gilded desk, which had belonged to the theater director. Chandler could just picture this man sitting cross-legged on a rug in a goatskin-covered yurt, a curved bow on his back, holding court in the midst of a horde of wild steppe horsemen.

If Chandler had entertained any illusions that Qasimbekai would express any kind of gratitude for their compliance with his demands of the previous day, he was quickly disabused of the notion.

"We have still more cease-fire violations by the Russians in Almaty and nearby, and we insist that you investigate and show the world that it is the Russians who are undermining peace, and also to demonstrate to *us* that your United Nations is at least trying to be fair to both sides in conflict."

"Good morning, Mr. Qasimbekai," Chandler said, undeterred. "I have reports of numerous sniper attacks from Kazakh positions against UN peacekeepers in the past twenty-four hours, which I'm certain that you will be able to explain adequately."

The two men exchanged sheets of paper, and while Chandler read the one he had received, Qasimbekai let Chandler's drop to his desk, where it remained.

After a considerable pause, Qasimbekai looked steadily at Chandler, and when he spoke, the official hostility seemed to disappear momentarily from his voice. "I realize that you only just arrived here, General, but do you have any idea what kind of an animal you and your men are protecting behind your Green Belt?"

"I know that both sides have plenty of complaints against the other," Chandler replied.

"I make nothing up. This is not just propaganda. It has all been filmed by foreign journalists, and the bodies are still out there in shallow graves not ten miles from here, if you'd care to take a tour sometime," Qasimbekai said in an almost pleading tone. "When Russians realized that they could not rule us Kazakhs and pretend to have democracy, since we were majority in the country, they tried to set up a kind of—what do you call it?—apartheid government so only Slavs would have a voice, but we rose up and defeated them. So they decided to form their own Russian state, and steal nearly half of our country, but except in the southwest, which is almost all Kazakh, and the northeast which is almost all Russian, our peoples were all mixed together. When we were at peace, that was fine, but when they wanted to carve out their own country, it became"—he searched for the word—"inconvenient for them, and they choose to 'purify' their zone."

Qasimbekai stood and walked over to the window. "There is a small valley on the other side of that mountain," he said, pointing off to the west. They herded about two thousand of our people there and killed them like sheep. We found the bodies after the revolution."

"From what I understand, Mr. Qasimbekai," Chandler broke in, "neither side has a monopoly on killing."

"The killing was not the worst part," the Kazakh continued. "Even after three generations of socialist modernization, we still have some basic . . . well . . . traditions, and one of these is the blood feud. We can understand killing, and we know how to respond to it. What they did was much worse."

"But all that is in the past now," Chandler started to say, but Qasimbekai cut him off.

"We are a Muslim people, General Chandler," he said, still staring off toward the horizon. "The Communists tried to beat and starve it out of us, to move us off the land, to change our ways of life, but it only made our ties to Allah stronger. Do you know the most precious thing in a Muslim family?" he asked, fixing Chandler now with an intense gaze. Chandler shook his head.

"It is the honor of its women. That is what makes the father the ruler, the head of his household, that he can protect the honor of the women. If that fails, it is not like some dirty sex act you see in Western movies." He turned and spat in disgust. "The Muslim girl is ruined. Her father loses all respect for himself, and the family falls apart. Relatives and neighbors all know about it, and the community falls apart. Russians know that, so they go about and kidnap Muslim women and girls, as young as twelve years old, and held them in 'pleasure houses' for their soldiers. But they only keep them until they are certain that they are pregnant and past the time where abortion would be possible. Then they return them to their families, disgraced, brutalized, and bearing the demon seed of those monsters in their wombs. With such methods they chased nearly every Kazakh family out of the northeast, and, if it were not for the protection of our own militia, they would have done the same here south of Lake Balkhash."

Everybody has a grievance in these places, Chandler thought as Qasimbekai spoke. A brother was killed, or a father, or some other tragedy, maybe even a bona fide one. They lost the homes where their families had lived for generations, the business a father had built from nothing, a whole way of life. But the common thread in all of these places, from the Balkans to the Horn of Africa, from Central America to India, was that the solution everyone came up with, in fact the *only* solution *anyone* ever seemed to come up with, was to kill the other side, and to keep on killing until justice was achieved, or things were put back the way they had been, or set up as they should have been always. It made him sick, and more than a little tired.

And now, here were the good Americans, British, French, and others whose leaders had decided that they could just set things right with a little show of force, a few well-fed men draped in web gear with their inoffensive sky-blue berets. They could stop the killing, rebuild the cities, let the farmers get back to growing crops, and reopen the schools and churches. No trouble. He remembered the State Department officials who had resigned in protest back in '92 or '93 because the United States *wasn't* using military force to stop Serbian aggression in Bosnia. He had wondered at the time just how many bombs it would take to put a country back together.

And here was Qasimbekai, probably an old Communist party hack who made the transition from communism to nationalism with blinding speed when it became apparent which way the wind was blowing. He would wave the bloody shirt and reject all compromise, as would his Russian counterparts, until he made certain that he had a cushy job for life and all the power his ego demanded. Maybe he would never let the war die out, keep the pressure on and the emotions high forever, to make sure that his people would always need him and could never afford the risk of changing leaders when the enemy was at the gates. Chandler had seen his kind before and read of others often enough to recognize the type. His stomach hurt, and he was developing an unpleasant pressure behind his eyes.

"Mr. Qasimbekai," Chandler finally broke in, but the Kazakh immediately interrupted him.

"I can see that my name is difficult for you to pronounce correctly," he said snidely. "You may call me as Mr. Chairman. I am head of the Kazakh People's Commission which meets here in our provisional capital to provide a measure of government to the region still being disputed with the Russian enemy," he quoted from memory from some Kazakh government press release.

"Very well, Mr. Chairman," Chandler began again. "We have all heard these stories of the tragedy of your people, and we have heard just as many of the Russian men, women, and children who were killed during the revolution. None of that can ever be undone, and it would seem to me that the only rational solution for anyone is to try to find a peaceful settlement to your differences with the Russians so that those who survived these hard times can get on with their lives and so that more people will not have to suffer."

"*Stories!*" Qasimbekai screamed shrilly and took two rolling steps toward Chandler, causing Morgan to move nervously closer to the two men in case it should become necessary to rescue his commander. "You think that I have been telling you *stories* from the marketplace? *I* had a daughter, General. Her name was Jasmin, and she would have been fourteen this month, but she killed herself. She swallowed fluid for cleaning out drains, because she could not stand to give birth to a damned Russian goblin. We had told her, when she came back home, that it did not matter. I told her that I would get rid of the child myself, but she could not stand it. It took her two days to die, because we had removed all of the ways she could have found to kill herself more easily—knives, ropes. We thought we had hidden everything, but she found this fluid under the sink, and she drank it. Now, tell me about seeking peaceful resolution to *my* differences with Russians."

Tears were streaming over the fleshy olive cheeks, and the meaty fists were balled, held tight in front of his chest.

Chandler stammered for a moment. "Oh," he finally blurted out. "I didn't know."

"You did not *care* to know, General. After all, we are only slant-eyed barbarians, while Russians are blond and oh, so European now. We do not have families. Life is cheap in Asia. Is that not what you Americans always say?"

"No, not at all, but I—"

"Well, I can tell you that I have a family—*had* a family—and those godless bastards that you protect inside the city took it away from me. I was going to give you ultimatum about stopping the Russian raids across the Green Belt, but I will not do that now. I tell you just to *give* me a reason to attack. You let those motherless Russians across the line again, and we will pound the city into rubble with our artillery, and then we'll come in and finish whatever remains, and if you and your men are in the way, that will be your decision."

Back in the Hummer, Chandler held his head in his hands. His temples were throbbing, and he expected his gastric juices to burn through his shirt at any minute. If he couldn't keep these people apart, there were going to be more bodies for him to pick up, more mothers for him to talk to, and he would probably never get to sleep again.

"That man is never going to stop killing, until everyone he sees as an enemy is dead, or until he is," Chandler said.

"Just wait until you meet Shchernikov," was all that Morgan said.

They passed through the series of Kazakh checkpoints again, then through the French positions and into the Russian zone in the more heavily built-up heart of the city. At first, the guards at the corner checkpoints didn't appear all that different from those on the other side of the Green Belt, at least in their dress, weapons, and slovenly attitude, but as the convoy progressed, Chandler began to notice that the men occupied more substantially constructed positions and wore something like a uniform, a dark-light brown pattern of camouflage fatigues, and black berets. Their weapons were cleaner, his inspecting officer's eye told him, and more modern, and there were many, many more of them.

They headed down the steeply sloping Ulitsa Furmanova and turned left on Tole Be, pulling up in front of the massively ugly Government House, former seat of the republican government and current headquarters of Igor Shchernikov. It was a hulking, blocklike structure, faced in somber granite, the kind of building the Soviets had liked to demonstrate the solidity of the socialist regime. T-72 tanks in good repair were stationed at the four corners of the building, their long, 125mm guns pointed menacingly down likely avenues of approach. The Russians were obviously concerned with preventing the destruction of this headquarters as had occurred to their "White House" up the hill on Novy Polochad, nearby, during the early fighting of the revolution; the former headquarters was now well within the Kazakh zone.

"He calls himself a general," Morgan was saying, "but there is no record of him on the available lists of Soviet officers. We believe that he fought with the Serbs in Bosnia as one of the hundreds of Russian volunteers there during the civil war, so he may have just given himself the title on the basis of that. It is very likely that he picked up most of his repertoire of methods for dealing with unwanted ethnic groups in that school."

When Chandler and Morgan entered the building, they found themselves in a large, two-story foyer with a broad central staircase leading up to massive double doors on the second floor. In front of the staircase stood a long row of desks, probably looted from offices in the city, which formed a wall blocking all passage except through a narrow aisle, around which clustered a dozen of the uniformed men, all armed with automatic weapons. As they approached the barrier, a tall, athletic man with very short blond hair and a tan born of outdoor living, rather than lying on the beach, stepped into their paths.

"Good morning, gentlemen," he said. "I am Captain Lushkin of the Republican Guard Security Forces, and I must ask you to leave your personal weapons here at the desk during your visit." The man's face smiled broadly, but it seemed to Chandler that his eyes did not smile at all.

"This is outrageous," Morgan exclaimed, clutching his short Enfield assault rifle closer to his side. "UN officers have never been asked to surrender their weapons at any time by any group in Kazakhstan, especially when on an official visit of the highest level. I suspect that you have misinterpreted your orders, Captain, and I suggest that you verify them with a higher authority to avoid an incident which could be damaging to your career."

Actually, Chandler had been more than willing to surrender his Beretta, since he had never felt that it provided him with even a modicum of extra security, certainly not in the face of the real firepower possessed by Lushkin and his men. However, he suspected that Morgan was probably right in not letting Lushkin score what might be considered an important psychological point against them without a struggle.

"Oh, but I'm quite certain that that won't be necessary, Colonel Morgan," Lushkin countered. "I received the very specific orders from General Shchernikov himself not an hour ago. He was expecting your visit, and made it quite clear."

Morgan glared at Lushkin for a moment, then slowly unslung his rifle, removing the magazine and locking the bolt to the rear in proper military style, never taking his eyes from Lushkin's. Chandler flipped his pistol from its holster and slapped it on the table without bothering to unload it. Perhaps one of them will shoot himself in the foot, he thought.

They stepped between the desks, but Lushkin barred their way again.

"Excuse me, gentlemen, one final inconvenience." And he began to pat Morgan down.

The Englishman jumped back, knocking Lushkin's hands away with a deft stroke, but Chandler noticed that Lushkin recovered instantly and never actually left an opening—had it come to real blows.

"This is just too much!" Morgan shouted. "We won't put up with it."

"Very well," said Lushkin, grinning. "I will inform General Shchernikov that you refused to visit him, and he will report it to the UN Commissioner. I doubt that this will sit very well with them, but that is your decision."

"Oh, let's just cut the bullshit," Chandler finally said. "We will see Mr. Shchernikov under his terms on his turf, and we'll bring the matter up with him. You can wait here for me, Colonel." He raised his arms stiffly, and Lushkin smiled as he frisked him very carefully.

"Bloody hell," Morgan groaned, raising his own arms, and it was apparent that Lushkin took extra care in searching Morgan, but less care of how roughly he did it.

"I look forward to your next visit to our zone, Captain," Morgan growled as they turned to the stairway. "Does the expression 'body cavity' mean anything to you?"

Lushkin just smiled and cocked his head in a mock bow.

Shchernikov's office wasn't an office so much as a ballroom. It must have been some kind of reception hall in the old days and was ornately decorated in the tsarist gilt and flowery detail that had still represented style and power to their Communist descendants. It was nearly thirty meters long, painted in a deep pink with white trim, and had a row of tall windows along the outer wall. Two immense crystal chandeliers were suspended from the five-meter ceiling. A female receptionist sat at a small desk just inside the double doors of the office; Shchernikov's own gleaming black enameled table, which served as his own desk, was far down at the opposite end. The secretary was the only person in the building who did not wear brown and tan camouflage fatigues. She was wearing a rather tight-fitting silk dress and a hairstyle one saw on the wives of the astronauts in news programs of the 1960s.

As his boots echoed on the bare wood floor, Chandler suspected that Shchernikov had read somewhere that the longer the walk one forced visitors to make en route to one's desk, the greater the psychological advantage one gained over them. Chandler seemed to remember having read something about Hitler's having that idea in the design of his own office spaces.

Shchernikov's appearance seemed to comply with the mental image Chandler had built up of him over the past few days. He was rather short and powerfully built, with arms that seemed to hang

down almost to his knees. He wore the same kind of fatigues as his
men, but with the added touch of a horizontally striped T-shirt of the
Russian marines peeking out at the neck of his fatigue shirt. He had a
long, bushy mustache, the ends of which drooped past the corners of
his mouth. His features were almost Oriental, with very narrow eyes
and a flat nose, but the eyes that peeked out were a burning blue. No,
his appearance was no surprise to Chandler, but his company was.

Devi stood behind the "general's" chair, almost like a courtier,
one hand resting defensively on the back of the chair. Shchernikov
rose stiffly to greet them, and Devi made the introductions.

"We have a rather serious complaint to make, General," Morgan
began without the pretense of a greeting. "Your man downstairs
demanded our weapons and subjected both General Chandler and
myself to a body search."

Shchernikov raised his hand for silence. "I'm afraid that I've had
to take extraordinary security measures due to intelligence we have
that the Kazakhs have been planning to assassinate me. You'll have to
forgive my subordinates if they're a little excessive in their zeal to
protect me."

"He insisted that he had your specific authority," Morgan argued.

Chandler stepped in then, as Morgan was moving toward
Shchernikov, and two sturdy guards posted in the corners of the
room were also moving forward menacingly.

"Perhaps we can discuss this later," he said firmly. "There are
more pressing matters, and I'm certain the general will correct any
flaws in his security procedures."

"There certainly are more important matters to discuss," Shchernikov said, his jaw firmly set. "I have been discussing with Commissioner Devi the obvious favoritism the UN forces under your command have been showing to the Kazakhs. Now, I don't hold you
personally responsible, General," Shchernikov added, walking around
the desk and taking Chandler by the elbow in a superficially warm
manner, "but the brutal beating of innocent women and children yesterday by your troops, when all they wanted was to get to safety.
That was the kind of behavior we expect only from our enemies."

"I agree that the incident was tragic, General Shchernikov,"
Chandler replied, gently disengaging his arm from the Russian's grasp,
"but you know as well as I do that our orders about not permitting any
line crossing are very explicit, and our failure to carry them out will
only result in a breakdown of the cease-fire and a renewal of open
fighting here in the city, which would be to no one's benefit."

"At least we would know where we stood," Shchernikov argued, and he laid a meaty paw on Chandler's shoulder, having to stretch upward noticeably to do so. "What really bothers me most about this issue, General, is that we should be on the same side. I mean, you are from a civilized country, as are all of the contingents of the UN force, while these Kazakh murderers are mere animals. You should be helping us to bring them under control, to put them back 'on the reservation,' as you Americans might say of your own aboriginal people. Let them have their lands, more than two thirds of Kazakhstan, and let us have ours. It was us Russians who made this land bloom under the Virgin Lands program back in the 1950s and '60s. We built the space center at Baikonur. We built the cities and the roads and the industry. Let them go back to tending their sheep and goats and leave us in peace. You should be helping us to achieve that, but instead you take the side of the 'noble savage' and persecute us."

"You know that you are going to have to work out your differences with the Kazakhs—who seemed entirely human to me, by the way," Chandler said, twisting his body and stepping back again to separate himself from the Russian. "Our only purpose here is to encourage you to do it through negotiations and not through blood feuds."

"The general has been discussing with me a rather more immediate problem, General Chandler," Devi broke in, stepping up to the Russian's side. "It has come to my attention that you intend to post military police in the Ukrainian zone, policemen of another nationality."

Well, *that* didn't take long to work its way back," Morgan snorted.

"Actually, yes," Chandler admitted. "I plan to use military police to augment control at the bridges in the Ukrainian zone, since there have been numerous complaints about both arms and men slipping across the lines in that area, and, yes, our military police happen to be of other nationalitities."

"Complaints from the Kazakhs," Shchernikov interjected, raising his hands in frustration. "There. You see?"

"There have been no *confirmed* reports of such line crossings," Devi argued, "just allegations. The issue here, General, is a political one, not a military one. You see, the Ukrainians are the only national contingent that the Russians feel entirely confident with, and here we are sending the message that we don't trust our own men and must take their key assignment away from them and give it to another unit. I'm afraid I can't authorize that."

"I didn't ask you to, sir," Chandler said coldly. "Deployment of troops is my responsibility."

"And yet, if that deployment affects the political situation, as this does," Devi persisted, "then it becomes *my* responsibility, and it will *not* be done."

"I'll be discussing this matter with my own government, Commissioner," Chandler replied and prepared to leave.

"I already have," Devi said, picking up the receiver of the telephone on his desk. "You can ask for yourself."

He punched a speed-dial button, which surprised Chandler a little in itself, since he had not been aware that such things existed in Kazakhstan, but he was somewhat reassured when it took several tries to put the call through. Devi spoke for a moment in honey-sweet tones to someone on the other end of the line and then handed the receiver to Chandler.

"Elders here," a scratchy voice said over the accompanying rush of wind. "Is there some problem in understanding your authority, General?"

"Good morning, sir," Chandler said angrily. "Yes, there is, or at least Mr. Devi believes there is."

Chandler explained the situation, or began to, but Elders cut him off in midsentence.

"I'm fully aware of the situation, General," Elders said curtly, "and I'm afraid Mr. Devi is on firm ground there. I've been on with Washington about it, and your orders are not to interfere with the standing deployment of the Ukrainian contingent. This is obviously a diplomatic issue with which a soldier could not be fully conversant, but let it suffice to say that national interests are at stake here, and we will not antagonize the Ukrainian government over a minor question of turf. If you don't recognize Mr. Devi's authority as senior representative of the UN here, perhaps you will recognize that of the U.S. government and let this matter drop at once. I only hope that irreparable damage has not been done already by the mere fact of having made a debating point of this. Is that clear?"

"Crystal clear, sir," Chandler answered, and his hand trembled slightly as he held the receiver. "I will, of course, be confirming the instructions with my own superiors at the Pentagon."

"Feel free, General, although I hope we aren't going to have to go through this kind of 'My dad is bigger than your dad' thing every time something comes up that doesn't fit your immediate plans."

Chandler hung up the phone without further comment.

"I apologize for that, Mr. Devi," Chandler said. "Perhaps in the future, we can discuss matters of an internal UN nature alone without taking up the general's valuable time"—and without showing him how divided we are, Chandler felt like adding.

"I hope that it won't be necessary again, either in private or in company," Devi said.

"Then I guess I'll get on with my business," Chandler said, saluting casually and heading for the door with Morgan in train behind him.

"I thought that went rather well," Morgan said, shaking his head ruefully once they were back in their vehicle. "Now you get some idea of what it's like to deal with the bureaucracy here. It's not bad enough that we're getting shot at from all sides, but the striped-pants boys can't be satisfied unless our hands are firmly tied behind our backs."

"I want a meeting with Peabody, Saavedra, and the Frenchman. What's his name? De Guise? Back at headquarters after lunch. If I can't change deployments, there are still a few things I can do in my own command," Chandler said, pulling out a tactical map of the city.

It was nearly midnight when the Ukrainian armored personnel carriers rolled across the bridge over the narrow, rocky Malaya Alma Atinka River and into a grove of woods in the extensive Gorky Park, which stretched over several square kilometers along the eastern perimeter of the city. They pulled into the walled compound of what had been a caretakers' equipment complex before the civil war, and extinguished their running lights. There was nothing unusual about this movement. The Ukrainians regularly changed the guard at this outpost at about this time, and any Kazakh sentries off to the east would barely have noticed their presence.

Some forty men wearing an odd assortment of dark, ragtag clothing climbed out of the darkened vehicles and went to ground in the shadows at the base of the wall surrounding the compound, while two of their number entered the largest building of the complex, letting a blade of light briefly jab out into the darkness before closing the door behind them.

Major Borysenko saluted the shorter of the two men as he entered. "Good evening, General. Everything is ready."

Shchernikov returned the salute and followed Borysenko up a metal ladder to a trapdoor that led out onto the roof. Lushkin followed them, his face blackened with camouflage paint in fearsome patterns.

"The nearest Kazakh observation post is one hundred meters off to the right," Borysenko indicated, handing Shchernikov a night-

vision scope as the three men peered over the low parapet surrounding the roof.

"I can smell them from here," Shchernikov commented, and the
other two men chuckled quietly.

"A five-man patrol headed north about ten minutes ago," Borysenko
continued, "and they should be coming back within half an hour."

"We'll be long gone by then," Lushkin said, taking the scope from
Shchernikov and surveying the scene before him. "Besides, we are
planning a brief mortar barrage in their area to coincide with our
crossing, which should serve to make them keep their heads down.
Then, we'll head east for half a click and then turn south behind their
lines. No problem."

"I don't have to tell you how important this is, Vassily," Shchernikov said. "We have brought matters to a crucial point with our raids
against the Kazakhs, and all it will take will be one more good push to
drive them to attack the UN in full force. If we can just establish to
the world that it is the Kazakhs who are the enemies of peace, and
get the UN on our side, then we will get everything we want. We will
get arms freely from the outside, to say nothing of foreign aid, and
we will have UN troops to fight our battles for us. It all depends
upon you and your men tonight."

"You have nothing to worry about, General," Lushkin replied,
and his grin was frightening, even to the old fighter.

Shchernikov patted the larger man roughly on his shoulder, and
Lushkin smoothly slid back down the ladder and loped across the
yard to where his men were waiting. Part of the wall had been
knocked down, probably by an artillery shell, and, one by one, the
men slipped through the gap and off into the shadows beyond. They
dodged from cover to cover, using the dead ground of narrow gullies
to pass near the Kazakh outpost just as the dull thud of mortar
rounds began to rise to the south. Flares popped in the sky—designed
to ruin the Kazakhs' night vision, not to light the way—and they
made their passage without incident.

Lushkin's men were all combat veterans of Afghanistan, most
with the elite *desant* airborne troops that had borne the brunt of the
fighting against the mujahedin, and a few were former Spetsnaz
commandos. They carried standard AKM assault rifles and Dragunov
sniper rifles, all fitted with long black silencers and night-vision
scopes, and the guides of the unit wore eerie-looking goggles. They
made no noise. There was no talking, and all signals were transmitted by silent gestures or perhaps a finger snap.

Once they were through the main Kazakh positions, they moved south through the open brushland east of the river at a good pace, jogging lightly while the chill wind whipped around them in the darkness. When they came to a road with military trucks rattling by in both directions, they lined up along the berm and waited for a long space between passing vehicles, then dashed across in a body, line abreast, and into the brush on the opposite side.

Each of the four ten-man squads carried a small inflatable boat, which they prepared and used to cross back to the west bank of the eastern arm of the Malaya Alma Atinka River, keeping the boats connected with a rope to the near bank in order to haul them back for a second load of men. They then portaged the boats over the narrow strip of land between the two arms of the river and repeated the process. When all were across, they slashed the boats with their knives and proceeded even more stealthily, as they were now close to the Kazakh lines around the city again. They passed more and more darkened one-story houses and shops of what had been a working-class residential neighborhood.

Lushkin checked his compass frequently, but the lights of their target were clearly visible in the distance, since it was one of the few spots in the Kazakh zone that had a working generator. Lushkin had planned his approach well, since the Kazakh troops around the Ardash Orda Concert Hall were oriented mainly toward the west, where any Russian attack was likely to come from, not toward the eastern territory largely controlled by their own forces.

In the pale moonlight, Lushkin could see the point man holding up his hand, and the column of men silently melted into the shadows to wait. Despite the sound of the wind, Lushkin could just make out snatches of conversation in the guttural Turkic dialect of the Kazakh guards as they huddled around a small campfire. He worked his way up the line to where the point man crouched, holding up three fingers. Less than thirty meters away, he could see two men squatting by the fire, sipping coffee and talking, while a third slept in a bedroll nearby, and Lushkin designated three of his own men to move forward. Each man had a long Dragunov sniper rifle, and they took careful aim.

"Three, two, one," Lushkin said in a low voice, just loud enough for the men to hear, and the three rifles coughed simultaneously, twice each.

The two talking men pitched over onto the ground, one of them with his lifeless arm in the fire; the bedroll simply jerked. All was still again. Lushkin waved the point man forward once more.

They crept past a T-54 tank with a crewman snoring loudly on the back deck, until one of Lushkin's men slit his throat. After dispatching the rest of the crew in a similar fashion, three of the Russians took up positions at the tank's controls, in case it should be necessary to cover their escape. A dozen more of the men were deployed in a broad arc around the hall's side entrance, on which Lushkin now advanced. The metal fire door was locked, but one of the Russians pulled out a small tool kit and went to work on the lock, opening it noiselessly in seconds, and the rest of the group passed inside.

The Kazakhs had made matters simpler for Lushkin and his men by actually housing most of the members of their provisional government within the concert hall itself. This had been partly a pragmatic decision, for the availability of electricity and running water made the converted office/apartments relatively attractive living quarters, and partly a symbolic one in that it implied that the leaders of the new government worked day and night for their people. Lushkin could smell the pervasive odor of grilled shashlik, which permeated every Kazakh residence he had ever visited.

The service stairway was only fitfully lighted by bare bulbs that dangled at the landings. Lushkin deployed half a dozen of his men on each of the four floors of the building and himself on the second floor from the top, the one reported to house the senior leadership of the government. When all the men were in position, he raised his heavy combat boot and shattered the door leading off the stairwell.

Qasimbekai found himself on his feet before he realized what had awakened him. There were screams of men and women, and the sound of running feet, and now the occasional report of a gunshot or the crash of a grenade exploding within an enclosed space. He normally slept in loose-fitting clothes, mostly because of the cold, but he was grateful now as he grabbed the pistol from under his pillow and flattened himself against the wall of his room. He closed his eyes and tried to control his breathing while he steeled himself for the dash out into the corridor.

He spun around the doorway, his gun braced in both hands and found himself facing a man at the far end. For an instant, he thought that this was one of his own guards, since the clothing was decidedly Kazakh, but a wisp of blond hair straggled out from under the man's cloth cap, and Qasimbekai fired twice, just as the man brought the barrel of his smoking AKM up. The man fell back against the wall, and bullets stitched a ragged line of holes through the ceiling as his gun discharged, but Qasimbekai noticed that there was no noise other than the falling plaster. This was definitely a professional group, he thought in passing.

Almost immediately, however, he heard the pounding of heavy, booted feet coming around the corner behind the dead man and saw shadows of several men dancing on the wall, and he knew that he was outnumbered. He ducked back into his room and raced to the window.

He yanked it open and stared down at the ground three stories below. Off at the corner of the building, he saw a mob of armed men, probably from the Afghan battalion, he thought, charging in from their camp area, but a blast of canister from a tank near the building cut them down like ripe wheat. Machine guns traced deadly lines of green fire through the tents pitched in the park beyond.

The footsteps were getting closer behind him, and Qasimbekai shoved his pistol into his pocket and swung himself out the window, grasping desperately at a thin aluminum pipe that ran electrical cables to the roof. He gasped as the shoddy little nails that held the pipe began to pull out under his considerable weight. They were probably half the size they should have been, he thought idly as he desperately tried to work his way downward, some supply official's way of skimming a little off the building budget.

He went downward hand over hand, the pipe groaning with every jerk, but he knew that every foot closer to the ground meant that much less chance of injury when he did fall, as he inevitably must. He thought he could hear movement in his own room now, and the sounds of firing were almost continuous throughout the building. From the floor above, a body came crashing through a window not ten feet from him and plummeted to the ground. As it hurtled past, he recognized the bright-colored robe of the wife of one of his colleagues, and he worked his arms even faster.

About eight feet from the pavement, the pipe finally gave way with a screech of metal, and Qasimbekai hit the ground hard. He felt a burning pain in his left ankle, but he rolled quickly into some shrubbery and fumbled for his pistol. Artillery rounds were now hitting near the building, but only on the north side, and he suspected that the attackers would be using that to cover their withdrawal. Smoke rounds were also hitting nearby on all sides, and the lights around the building flickered once and then died: the generator must have been blown. Qasimbekai stayed under his bush as bullets kicked up dust all around him randomly. The Kazakh thought that he knew who had engineered this outrage—and that they had made a serious mistake when they had failed to make certain that they had killed him.

Lushkin made a quick count of heads in the shelter of the building wall and ascertained that all of his men had made it out. They must not leave anyone behind, not even the dead, and especially not the wounded. The several men who had been killed were piled on the back deck of the tank or in the interior of the old BTR-60 armored personnel carrier they had captured, and he shouted some instructions to the man sitting in the tank's cupola. The engine roared to life, and the huge vehicle rolled westward with Lushkin's infantry fanning out on either side, moving at a quick trot.

It seemed that the defenders had pulled back to regroup after their initial heavy losses during the assault, and it would take them some time to figure out where Lushkin and his men were. Lushkin's men needed only a few minutes to cover the kilometer to the UN lines, where the Ukrainians were waiting for them. Then, under cover of the fire from the Ukrainian 30mm guns, in the unlikely event that such should prove necessary, they would rush back into Russian territory and be safe once more. By the time the Kazakhs were ready to renew the battle, there would be no one left here to fight.

Lushkin grinned again as he jogged along with the rearguard. They had killed perhaps fifty people in the building, to say nothing of the more than a hundred soldiers who had certainly died in the fighting outside. He had personally seen that at least half a dozen of the key leaders had either not been present or had somehow escaped, which was just perfect. The last thing anyone wanted was for the Kazakh movement to become completely decapitated, since that would mean that there would be no attack on Alma-Ata (Lushkin did not accept the city's recent name change), and the entire mission would have been for nothing. As long as leadership remained with a fresh memory of tonight in their minds, there would be more than enough war for everyone. He glanced at the luminous dial of his watch. It was just after two o'clock, and the entire operation had taken hardly three hours, an operation that would decide the fate of his nation.

CHAPTER 3

A new era has dawned in international relations. The time is past when governments sent their armies abroad to preserve selfish goals, so-called "national interests." Our soldiers now serve the ends of furthering the goal of humanitarian aid and the building of democracy throughout the world. Some may bemoan the passing of the age of the "balance of power," but not I.

Editorial, The Washington Post

ALMATY
31 October, 0130 Hours

Lieutenant Colonel Juan Carlos Saavedra didn't normally fly missions anymore, but when General Chandler had briefed him, Peabody from the 1st of the 11th, and de Guise from the French battalion on this mission, he knew that he was the best man for the job. Not that Saavedra was the best helicopter pilot in the squadron—there were plenty of young captains and warrant officers with better vision and reflexes than his own. It was just that, given the delicacy of the assignment, he would have been dying of nerves if he had had to sit out the night back in his headquarters, ears tuned to the squawking radios, waiting for word. If everything went uneventfully tonight, he promised himself, he would let someone else have the duty tomorrow, but he had a hunch about tonight.

He banked his tiny McDonnell-Douglas AH-6F chopper to the right and swung back over the city. He had taken off nearly two hours before, meaning he had only about half an hour's fuel left, and if nothing happened soon, he would call it a night, but things were already starting to happen.

On Chandler's orders, Saavedra had filed a flight plan for Karaganda, north of Lake Balkhash, but no sooner had he left Almaty than he extinguished his running lights and returned to fly a lazy racetrack pattern over the eastern portion of the city. He was certain that, even in the pale moonlight, his matte black-painted helicopter would be no more than a hole in the night sky to anyone on the ground, and the muffled engine and rotors would not even be a whisper over the howling of the wind outside. The one good thing to come out of the civil war here, at least in Saavedra's parochial view, was that most of the aircraft and anti-air defenses and radars had been either destroyed outright in the fighting or sabotaged by the Russian technicians before they escaped to the Russian zone to the northeast, so there was little danger of detection by electronic means.

Saavedra turned his head to the right. Simultaneously the small turret mounted on the underside of the aircraft rotated in the same direction and the thermal image from its FLIR—forward-looking infrared—device projected a ghostly green image on the clear visor of his helmet. He switched to high magnification, and there they were. It was the same group he had seen cross from the Ukrainians' position to the east about an hour before, and they had been moving steadily southward since then, eventually recrossing the river heading west. Now they were approaching the Ardash Orda Concert Hall in what could only be a tactical formation. The show was about to start, and Saavedra had a front-row seat, even from nearly two kilometers away.

He lost sight of the men behind the building itself, and he was under orders to stay over the UN zone, but only moments later gun flashes erupted all around the building, both small-arms and tank fire. Then white phosphorus rounds began to strike, and it was apparent that a full-fledged battle was in progress. Mobs of men were flowing back and forth in the area near the building, but he could see some being cut down and others finally drawing away to both the north and south.

"Here they come," Saavedra said into his radio mike. "Coming up on reference point blue. Be advised, there are about four-zero men, one tank, and one APC."

"Roger," said a gravelly voice over the radio. "Remain on station to monitor. We have two Apaches en route."

There had been a brief flurry of firing as Lushkin's advance guard, supported by the tank, overran the weak cordon of Kazakh troops screening the city perimeter, but the defenders had broken and run in a matter of minutes.

Suddenly, the protective darkness evaporated as a dozen xenon searchlights illuminated the area, blinding Lushkin just as a loudspeaker began to blare a warning in heavily French-accented Russian. Through the glare, he could just make out the hulking silhouettes of the armored-car turrets upon which the searchlights were mounted.

"Remain where you are and drop your weapons," the speaker boomed. "You are surrounded and outnumbered. This is Lieutenant Colonel de Guise of the United Nations forces, and you are within the UN zone."

Lushkin noticed that the speaker didn't even make a pretense of repeating the message in Kazakh, so there could be no illusion that the UN troops had any doubts about whom they were speaking to. He cursed under his breath, but he and his men were in the middle of an open area just short of the low factory workshop buildings in which the French were sheltered. But this was supposed to be the Ukrainian zone, Lushkin cursed to himself, and hadn't they just seen a matter of hours earlier how that American general had been overruled when he tried to introduce other forces to the area?

Even as he was trying to decide on his next course of action, a second warning crackled through the crisp night air, and he could see his men turning toward him for instructions. Then he also saw the turret of the tank, which had been pointed rearward to protect against a new Kazakh attack, suddenly swing to the left, in the direction of the lights, and the machine gun mounted on the turret roof let off a long burst in that direction. That would be Petrov, he thought, not one to let himself be captured without a fight. Lushkin wasn't either, for that matter, but that was when there was an option.

Just as he suspected, before the T-54's main gun could be brought to bear, there was a flash and the sharp crack of a French 105mm gun, followed almost instantaneously by another flash and explosion as the round slammed into the T-54's chassis. At nearly the same instant a finger of fire raced out of the black sky ahead, and a Hellfire missile tore into the tank's turret, wrenching it completely free of the vehicle and tumbling it end over end in the air to land with a dull thud somewhere in the shadows.

"Drop your weapons!" the voice boomed out again, and the clatter of AKMs on the asphalt of the roadway came with what Lushkin considered almost unseemly haste.

There was a whoop of celebration in the UNEKAZ headquarters as the radio report from the French cavalry troop came in that thirty "hostiles" had been captured attempting to cross the Green Belt with no casualties on the UN side and only one "hostile" tank destroyed when the crew chose to resist. Chandler noticed that, while the men clapped each other on the back, the several young American and British female communications officers and technicians received enthusiastic hugs, some of which lasted rather longer than even the exhilaration of the moment would have justified. There was an eruption of derisive laughter when Lieutenant Colonel de Guise, who had led the mission himself, reported that the prisoners appeared to be ethnic Russians dressed in Kazakh clothing.

"You called that one right, old boy," Morgan shouted over the din, clapping Chandler on the back as Japanese military policemen, Israeli engineers, and American and British radio operators happily shook hands around the command center. "Not only did you catch old Shchernikov with his fingers in the cookie jar, but this has been the first positive action our troops have taken since they've been in this bloody country. Getting shot at day and night and not doing anything about it was hardly building morale around here, but just look at them now!"

Chandler had cheered with the others at first, but the reality of the situation was already starting to set in, and with it the dull pain at the base of his stomach.

"At least none of our men were hurt," Chandler said. "I don't have any illusions about this putting an end to the killing, but it might just make Shchernikov think twice about trying anything again, and it should also tell Qasimbekai that we're not doing the Russians' dirty work for them." He paused and took a long drink from the Styrofoam cup of milk he held, letting the cool liquid fight the burning inside him. "I just have a bad feeling about the fighting Saavedra reported around the Concert Hall. If they did anything more than shoot the place up from the outside, there's still going to be hell to pay."

Chandler gave the order for de Guise to escort the prisoners to UNEKAZ headquarters for questioning and for Saavedra to return ASAP with his own report. No, he thought to himself, things this complicated don't get solved so easily, but it does feel kind of good to be taking action again.

De Guise stood up in the turret of his AMX-10RC armored car and stared at the roadblock in front of him. Two more of the AMX-10RCs had taken up position, one on either side of his own, on the broad avenue, their long, 105mm guns pointing forward threateningly at the ragged line of trucks and civilian cars that had been placed across the avenue up ahead. Behind the barricade, which his fifteen-ton, tanklike vehicles could easily have pushed through, was the real problem: half a dozen Ukrainian BMD armored personnel carriers with their 30mm rapid-fire guns. There would be antitank missile crews placed out there somewhere as well, he knew, possibly on the upper floors of the apartment blocks that lined the avenue, and in urban fighting, armor was always at a disadvantage against well-equipped infantry.

He heard the pounding of boots and the muted clanking of gear as a squad of his own infantry hustled up to take up protective positions around and in front of the armor, and the grumble of engines as the rest of his dozen armored cars formed up for all-round defense to his rear, covering the cross streets and tucking into driveways or any other break in the line of buildings that offered some cover. He had no orders to open fire on anyone except in self-defense, and even those orders were directed toward the expected Russian and/or Kazakh fighters, not to another national contingent of UNEKAZ. Consequently, de Guise radioed in his situation and waited to hear from that pompous ass Borysenko, as he knew he would sooner or later.

Finally, the stubby figure of the Ukrainian appeared behind the line of cars in the ghostly light of the French vehicles' headlamps. Since there was no gap in the line, he was obliged to clamber over the hood of an old, burned-out Lada, and de Guise chuckled when Borysenko apparently caught his pants on a jagged bit of metal and had to struggle for a moment to free himself. Then Borysenko straightened his uniform, brushed himself off, and strode purposefully forward.

"You have no business running an ambush patrol in my zone of operations," Borysenko shouted to make himself heard over the idling vehicle engines.

"What ambush patrol?" de Guise asked, spreading his arms wide to emphasize his innocence. "I was delivering some new fire plans to UNEKAZ headquarters, and, because you seemed to be having trouble preventing armed men from crossing your sector, I thought it best to take an armed escort. Then I just happened to come across a whole platoon of fighters, with armored vehicles yet, strolling through your territory as if they were tourists on the Champs Elysées. I had just cause to fear for the safety of my men, so I occupied defensive positions and demanded that they lay down their arms. They opened fire, and I returned it, and the survivors surrendered to me."

"I don't know what kind of idiot you think I am," Borysenko said.

"Just an average one, *Major*," de Guise countered, "and I don't recall your saluting me when you came up. In *my* army that's accepted practice."

The Ukrainian did not salute, but continued. "I'm supposed to believe that you needed an entire cavalry troop to escort you, just the way the Americans ran a whole troop through here to your headquarters and back again not an hour ago, as if they owned the place."

"You may believe what you choose to believe, but I'd be careful about calling me a liar." There was a distinct edge to de Guise's voice now, all the humor gone from it.

Borysenko snorted for a moment. "I demand that you turn over your prisoners to me."

"I have orders from General Chandler to deliver them to UNEKAZ headquarters," de Guise responded, "and I intend to comply with those orders."

"They were captured in my zone, and those prisoners are rightfully mine," Borysenko shrieked.

"If *your* men had captured them, they would be *your* prisoners. I saw plenty of your men around, but none of them seemed interested in stopping the border crossing, so I took it upon myself, and now these are *my* prisoners. You're more than welcome to accompany me to visit General Chandler and make your case before him. He is my commanding officer, and I follow his orders."

"We are all under UN command here," Borysenko argued, "and the senior UN representative is Commissioner Devi. It's *his* orders that you must obey."

"I believe you're wrong there, Major," de Guise continued, his patience wearing thin. "General Chandler may have to take orders from Devi, but I, we, take our orders from Chandler. I don't have to listen to that Hindu puff pastry the way you do. Now, are you going to clear that pile of shit out of my way, or do I have to blow it up?"

Borysenko's face was red, even in the bleaching light of the headlamps, his chest bulged, and his fists trembled at his sides as he glanced back over his shoulder to his men for support, but where the French tankers and infantry grimly sighted down their weapons, the Ukrainians who could be seen were nervously milling about, evidently looking for a good place to hide until this should all blow over.

Then de Guise held his hand up to his ear, flicked the switch on his headset, and mumbled into the microphone.

"Never mind, Major," de Guise said airily. "We can leave our little discussion of the law of nations and the penetrating power of the 105mm sabot round for another time. I have new orders to return to my own zone." he hooked a thumb back over his shoulder. "This will not oblige me to demolish your attractive street decoration."

"But you are still in my zone," Borysenko blustered. "You must surrender the prisoners to me!"

"Unfortunately, your men seem to be up there," de Guise said, pointing at the barricade, "and the way is clear to my own zone behind me. So, if you care to stop me, I'm afraid that you'll have to shoot me."

Just then an Apache helicopter howled overhead, almost invisible against the dark sky. It pirouetted perhaps twenty feet above Borysenko, kicking up a tornado of dust and leaves with its powerful rotors and forcing Borysenko to grasp his beret with both hands to keep from losing it. It stayed there, wiggling its tail like an enraged scorpion and pointing its Hellfire missiles at the Ukrainian positions. From his angle, de Guise could see that one of the missile tubes was empty, and he suspected that this was not lost on Borysenko either.

The Ukrainian shouted something, but de Guise just smiled, pointing to his ear and shrugging his shoulders helplessly, and Borysenko turned on his heel and stormed off, still trying to shield his face from the storm of pebbles and debris stirred up by the helicopter overhead.

De Guise cupped the microphone to his mouth and shouted a command. The infantrymen pulled back, slowly at first, keeping their weapons trained on the barricade. Then they turned to run for their vehicles, and the armored cars slowly backed up the street until they were out of sight of the Ukrainians.

The mood in UNEKAZ headquarters was more subdued now, but still decidedly festive, with all hands fixedly listening to the shrill reports coming in from Borysenko's command track and the more droll ones coming in from the French. Chandler could see now that the Ukrainians had not been universally popular with their fellow peacekeepers in Kazakhstan. Morgan was sitting with his feet up on a footlocker, cradling a cup of coffee in both hands, and smiling to himself.

Chandler looked at his watch. "I wonder what's keeping him," he said absently.

A moment later Commissioner Devi stormed into the command center, and all talking ceased as the guards, staff, and radio men all followed him with their eyes as he headed toward Chandler.

Behind Devi at a discreet distance came a rather distraught looking Chargé d'Affaires Elders. Chandler had noticed at their first encounter that Elders was quite bald on top, which was not all that unusual for a man his age. However, Elders was evidently somewhat vain; he had let the hair on one side of his head grow to almost shoulder length and then would comb it over to camouflage the clearing at the summit. He must have used some kind of hair spray or cream to keep it in place, and this must normally have worked for him, but Chandler suspected that he and Devi had made the trip over tonight in an open vehicle, and the wind had triumphed over technology, leaving poor Mr. Elders with a sort of dorsal fin of hair, standing quite erect on top of his head, and waving every so slightly as he hurried along. It was going to be hard to keep a straight face during what promised to be a very contentious interview.

"You have directly disobeyed my orders, General," Devi said in a deceptively quiet voice.

Chandler frowned. "What orders were those, Mr. Commissioner?"

"You know perfectly well. You wanted to station other national units within the Ukrainian zone because of unconfirmed reports that armed locals were crossing the Belt in that area, and I ordered you not to."

"And I confirmed that you had no authority to do so," Elders chimed in.

"And I didn't," Chandler replied. "I have not redeployed any units at all."

"And how do you explain the firefight between a French armored column and an unidentified group of intruders *inside* the Ukrainian zone less than two hours ago?" Devi continued. "That should have been the Ukrainians' responsibility."

"I know, and it was a serious mistake, Mr. Commissioner," Chandler admitted, and Devi raised his chin slightly, sensing victory. "It should have been the Ukrainians' responsibility, but they failed to carry it out, and I plan to make a formal request to New York that Borysenko be replaced for incompetence."

Devi's nostrils flared. "That's not what I meant, and you know it. What were the French doing there at all?"

"They were escorting Lieutenant Colonel de Guise here, and they happened across the intruders that the Ukrainians had let through."

"That's not very—"

"And it's not entirely true that they're 'unidentified,'" Chandler broke in. He suspected that Devi had started running at the first word of the incident and had not heard the full report. "It turns out that they're Russians, dressed as Kazakhs, who had just conducted a violent assault on the seat of the Kazakh provisional government. We have about thirty of them in custody, and I plan to interrogate them tomorrow. De Guise was trying to bring them in just now, but Borysenko denied him passage through his zone."

Devi was obviously shaken by this revelation, and he fumbled for words. Elders was even more upset, as his mouth dropped open, and he looked to Devi for direction. Chandler took advantage of the pause to reach into his back pocket and pull out a small plastic comb, which he handed to Elders without comment. The American's eyes went wide, and he quickly turned his back and began carefully flattening and combing his hair back into place.

"That's a wild accusation, General," Devi finally said. "You have no basis for that belief, and I find your attitude not only insubordinate, but quite dangerous to the stability of the peace process in the region, and it is my intention to demand your recall immediately."

"You'll have to have us all recalled," Morgan grunted.

But Chandler just held up his hand and smiled. Saavedra was just trotting into the command center from the helicopter pad next door, waving a small black cassette box in his hand. Chandler waved him over.

"It's not a question of belief, Mr. Commissioner," Chandler said. "Although it's always your prerogative to ask for my recall at your convenience." Please, Chandler added to himself. Please, do it.

Saavedra strode directly to where a television monitor and video machine had been set up against one wall. He shoved the tape in, and a technician stepped in to punch the correct buttons. The screen popped to life, and after a brief flurry of snow, a black-and-white image appeared, like a photographic negative.

"I took the liberty of running the tape back to where it gets interesting," Saavedra said.

"What is this?" Devi asked.

"It's the tape I made off my thermal imager over the past couple of hours, Mr. Commissioner," Saavedra answered.

"From a helicopter? But there are not supposed to be any helicopter missions flown after dark . . . for safety reasons. I gave no such permission," Devi stated nervously.

"That's right," Elders stammered, his coiffure finally repaired to his satisfaction. "We have lost quite enough men through actual hostilities here without losing any more to flying accidents."

"I don't need any special authorization to conduct training, day or night," Chandler said, "or to provide immediate support to UN forces in contact with the enemy."

"That's just the point you seem unable to grasp," Devi said, the volume of his voice rising noticeably now. "There is no *enemy* here. This is not war, General. This is a peacekeeping mission, and that is why a diplomat like myself, with the strong support of my colleagues like Mr. Elders here," he added graciously, "is given overall supervisory control of the operation."

"A semantic slip, I'll admit," Chandler conceded, "but I've been to several wars, and I must say that they look remarkably like what we've got around here. Perhaps there are some nuances of the situation which escape me, but I must do my best. In any case, you're quite right to say that you have *supervisory* authority, not line command, and until ordered otherwise by my own superiors, I will continue to look out for the welfare of the troops under my command, using my own judgment."

Chandler waggled a finger in the direction of the television screen. "And as to whether or not there are any enemies around, I suggest that you watch this."

"This is where we are," Saavedra explained, pointing to a point on the eastern edge of the tactical map mounted on the wall near the television. The image was frozen on the screen and wavered slightly. "Here is the river on this side. The water is warmer than the land, so it shows up white. Here you have a bunch of Ukrainian vehicles on the road. Their engines are hot, so they show up even brighter white than the water."

He released the "pause" button, and the picture jerked forward. Then he hit "fast forward" and little figures scurried around rapidly.

"Here you see the Ukrainian vehicles crossing the bridge and heading toward this small building," Saavedra narrated. "Then this group of men dismounts, waits for a little while, and then heads south."

He followed the movement of the group of men to the Concert Hall and gave a rough account of the battle as best it could be determined from his angle.

"And then they come back toward the Belt, and that's where they run into the French, and we know the rest from there."

Devi sputtered and stretched his arms in frustration at the screen. "But how can you pretend to be able to identify that you were watching the same men during that whole time. I mean, you can hardly see their faces on this tape."

"Yes," Chandler said, smirking, "I suppose that some *other* group of men left the Ukrainian lines and went to the Concert Hall, coincidentally at the time the fighting broke out there. Then, this group of thirty or so disguised and heavily armed Russians, who must have been living with the Kazakhs in perfect harmony all this time, suddenly decided to repatriate themselves to the Russian lines at that precise moment."

"We're picking up some Kazakh radio transmissions, sir," one of the technicians called from the far end of the room.

"What are they saying?" Chandler asked, not taking his eyes from Devi.

"They're talking about an attack on their government, maybe two hundred dead all together, including a dozen members of the provisional government and their families. It's Qasimbekai himself that's on the air. He's calling for reinforcements from Dzhambul and the northeast. Says that the UN collaborated in the attack and that the time has come to take Almaty from the Russians once and for all."

"That's probably just another coincidence," Chandler said, "but I'm going to have to go and try to talk to Qasimbekai before he launches his attack, and having those prisoners in my hands is the only thing that might convince him that we weren't in cahoots with the Russians, even if the Ukrainians were."

"I demand that the prisoners be turned over to me," Devi said, trying to sound confident of his authority.

"No, I don't believe that I will, Mr. Commissioner."

"Then I'll have you relieved, General."

"That's your decision, but I have to wonder whether even the Secretary General is going to have the balls to face up to the governments of all of the member nations when the details of this incident hit the television news around the world."

"And how is that going to happen?" Devi asked slyly. "I'm sure that even you will admit that contact with the international press, to say nothing of military communications to the outside, are and should be controlled by my office." Devi smiled as he saw Chandler, Saavedra, and Morgan exchange glances. "Yes, it is my authority, and it would be disastrous for the ongoing negotiations in Geneva for word of this incident to leak out prematurely, that is, before we've had a chance to verify all of the facts of the case and present them in the most objective light possible. Therefore, I prohibit any report of this incident to be made without my personal authorization *and* coordination."

Through a great effort of will, Chandler did not ask just how long it might take for Devi and Shchernikov to fabricate the evidence they required to distort the facts, but this was made easier by his own knowledge.

"Uh-oh," Saavedra said looking at Chandler with large, sheepish eyes. "I think we're in trouble."

Devi's smile broadened. "Don't worry," he said. "I'm certain that a thorough examination of the events will demonstrate that no one here acted inappropriately."

"That's not what I meant," Saavedra continued. "You see, this tape is not the original. The recording equipment on my chopper isn't compatible with this regular VCR setup, so I had to have copies made."

"And?" Devi demanded.

"And the only people in Almaty with that kind of equipment are the newsies. I had to stop at the airport to refuel before coming here, and I ran into that guy, Goldman, at the canteen, and he offered to make copies for me."

"And you suspect that he made more than the one copy," Chandler suggested helpfully.

"Well, I couldn't say for sure," Saavedra replied, making a show of tracing circles in the dust on the floor with the toe of his boot. "But even before I got back on my bird, I saw him give something to a guy who ran like hell and got on a C-130 that was just about to take off for Novosibirsk. If that was a copy of this tape, it's probably already out of Kazakhstan by now."

"And you explained the tape to him, I suppose," Chandler said.

"Well, yes. I sort of had to in order to get him to make the copies," Saavedra shrugged.

"Then the airplane should be recalled, and Goldman and the other man should be arrested immediately," Devi stammered. "They should be brought here before they can divulge classified information which would be damaging to the UN mission in this country."

"I don't think we can do that," Chandler said, shaking his head. "That flight was a medevac carrying out some critically wounded Swedes whose jeep hit a mine yesterday. If they don't get to a real hospital soon, they're not going to make it."

"And as for arresting Goldman," Elders finally commented, "he *is* a U.S. citizen, and a journalist. Arresting him would only magnify the issue and get all of the other journalists in the hemisphere swooping down here like vultures. No, I think our best option is to issue a disclaimer as soon as possible, pointing out the nuances of the case and the fragmentary nature of the information available at the present time."

Both Devi and Chandler slowly turned their heads to look at Elders. He was standing in the middle of the room, his shoulders stooped, his hands clasping each other, and his thumbs rubbing one another vigorously. Neither man deigned to respond to his comment.

After a long moment, Devi regained his composure and turned back to Chandler. "I still demand that the Russian prisoners be turned over to me."

"Technically, they're in your custody now, sir," Morgan said. "After all, we're your troops, and you don't have any other men with guns around. And, of course, you're more than welcome to interview the prisoners yourself whenever you like."

"No, I mean I want those men brought to me, right now, right here."

"I'm afraid that won't be possible either," Chandler said with a sigh. "It seems that Major Borysenko denied Lieutenant Colonel de Guise permission to escort the prisoners through his zone of operations a short while ago, so they were transported to the French battalion headquarters, where they will be held until morning, since it's probably too dangerous to move them anymore until daylight. At that time, I'll have de Guise bring them here by the long way around the perimeter, through the British and Argentine zones, so you're more than welcome to come back and visit then."

Devi cast Chandler a glance calculated to freeze oxygen. "This doesn't end here, you know. I have my own communications link to New York, and I'll have you withdrawn immediately and then worry about getting negotiations back on track in the wake of your incredible incompetence."

Chandler just stood up stiffly and touched the edge of his beret. "Good evening, sir."

Devi turned and marched out the front door, and Elders followed after hesitating momentarily.

"Well done, General," Morgan was saying, but Chandler couldn't hear him.

His temples were throbbing and there was a definite stiffness in his left arm and shoulder. Could this be the onset of a heart attack? He knew of two classmates of his from the Point who had already died and one or two others who had had heart attacks or strokes, and they had all been in as good shape as he was—better probably. But then he realized that he had a similar stiffness in his right side as well, so it was likely due to his lack of regular exercise over the past week and not to a heart condition, at least not this time.

"I want all units on full alert until morning," he told Morgan as he moved slowly and carefully toward the stairs. "I need to get a few hours' sleep. I think that it's going to be a rather busy day."

"Yes, sir," Morgan said enthusiastically. "We'll keep an eye on things for the next few hours."

Chandler was tired. He hadn't really had a decent night's sleep for nearly a week, since he'd first received his assignment. The nightmares had come once in a while before, but now they never left him. The characters changed, the scenes, and the actual events, but the message was always the same. He knew that he wasn't up to this challenge, and he was certain that everyone else knew it as well. Morgan and the men he had recently gotten to know here in the headquarters pretended to believe in him because he was all they had, but they knew as well as he did. He was doing his best to keep his men alive and to prevent any new disasters, which would only add to his repertoire of nightmares, but it was a losing fight. Everyone else in authority in this godforsaken country seemed determined to turn it into a massive graveyard. There was no goodwill, no common middle ground, just a choice of the kind of death you wanted and who the victims were to be. He needed to get away from the crackling of the radios reporting new "incidents," the bustle of the headquarters, all the determined young men and women who were so convinced that what they were doing was making a difference to someone. He knew better, and he couldn't face it anymore.

"You know, sir," Morgan called after him. "I half expected to see Major Borysenko here with Devi and Elders. I'm surprised he didn't come to press his case."

"I'm sure that we'll see enough of the good major to satisfy us before too long," Chandler mumbled as he trudged up the dark stairway.

A thin trickle of blood ran from the corner of Borysenko's mouth, and he could taste the salty flavor on his lip. Shchernikov's blow hadn't really hurt that much, and Borysenko had gotten much worse in his days as a cadet and a junior officer in the old Red Army, but he feared that the worst was not yet over.

Shchernikov was storming about his massive office, hurling random objects—papers, glasses, books—against the walls as he screamed his rage. Half a dozen grim-looking guards who stood against the wall near the door had helped convince Borysenko to take Shchernikov's abuse stoically. As usual at these meetings, Borysenko had come alone, and he had no doubt that these men would not hesitate to kill him if he raised a hand against their chief. An explanation for his death would be looked for later.

"What the fuck were the French doing in your sector, you imbecile?" Shchernikov raved. "Why didn't you know they were there? Why didn't you warn us?"

"We didn't have any time to send a messenger," Borysenko replied meekly, "and you know that any radio or telephone contact would have been picked up by the intercept people at UNEKAZ, and how would we have explained that?"

"It would have been better than having thirty of my best men under arrest in their hands, wouldn't it?" he shrieked.

"But they won't talk, will they?"

"Of course they won't talk!"

Shchernikov stopped directly in front of Borysenko and glared up into his face. "They don't need to talk." He shoved Borysenko away from him with powerful arms in disgust. "I thought you understood that the whole point of this operation was to turn the Kazakhs against the UN, to get them to attack in a blind rage across the Belt, which would have put the UN on our side. We could have blamed the killing at the Concert Hall on some splinter radical faction within the Kazakh camp itself, and that would have worked as long as none of the attackers fell into enemy hands, alive or dead."

He grabbed Borysenko now by his lapels and pulled him close again. Borysenko let him do so without resistance.

"*My* men had done their job perfectly," Shchernikov continued, breathing heavily into Borysenko's face, and the Ukrainian reeled at the reek of liquor. "Not a prisoner, not a body left behind, but then *you* screwed things up, and now the whole world knows that the attackers were Russians and that they came from within the city through your lines. The Kazakhs may or may not believe the story, and they may end up attacking the city after all, but even that won't put the UN on *our* side. The most that's likely to happen now is that the UN will pull out all together and leave us to face the Kazakhs alone."

Borysenko knew better than to interrupt again. And ultimately there was nothing he could say. Shchernikov was right. The plan had fallen through because of the damn French, or, more precisely, because of Chandler, and there was nothing they could do about it.

"We don't have enough troops to defeat the Kazakhs by ourselves, even with the help we've gotten from Russia." Shchernikov released Borysenko and strode over to one of his tactical maps mounted on the wall. "We only have about five thousand properly trained and armed men within the city, barely enough to man the perimeter if fighting were to be renewed, and not nearly enough to face a determined assault. Our forces in the northeast will hold on to that part of the country without trouble, but we'll lose Alma-Ata and all of the land south of Lake Balkhash. Setting the Kazakhs and the UN at each other's throats was our only chance for a real victory, and now that chance is gone, and it's your fault."

"So what are you . . . what are *we* going to do about it?" Borysenko asked.

"I'll let you know if there's anything you need to be concerned about," Shchernikov snapped. "And then let's see if you can do a better job of it the next time. I can tell you this much. I didn't gain my position by letting people cross me with impunity. That American general and his friends have a great deal to learn, and I'm just the one to teach them."

Borysenko had a great deal of trouble in restraining himself from breaking into a run on the way back to his jeep.

During the siege of Paris in 1870 and at other times in their long history, the French have been able to withstand great privation if called upon to do so. They can do without luxuries, wine, and sex for limited periods in an emergency. But it is a proven fact that the French cannot survive without bread. And not just any bread either, but the baguettes to which they are addicted. French governments have been overthrown over this issue in the past.

Consequently, the French contingent had made arrangements for provision of a steady supply immediately upon their arrival in Almaty. They had located a reasonably well-equipped bakery in the Russian zone and had made an agreement with the owner under which they would supply the flour and other ingredients on a regular basis, as well as providing fuel for his ovens and electricity for his machinery and training his workers in the intricacies of producing a respectable loaf of bread. Well versed in the ways of the world, the negotiators allowed for at least a 20 percent margin in extra flour, to discourage pilferage at the bakery of their own basic requirements, besides paying the baker in foreign currency for his services.

And the arrangement had worked out remarkably well from the outset. Every morning at the crack of dawn and again in the late afternoon, a delivery van would pass through the checkpoint at the rear entrance to the large walled parking lot behind the office block the French had taken over as their headquarters. The driver of the van would drop off several hundred of the long, thin loaves, which French armored personnel carriers would then distribute to the various company command posts in the zone. It was not *good* bread by French standards, but, considering the limitations of equipment and personnel in the bakery, it was as good as could be expected and at least enough to keep body and soul together.

This morning the bread van was nearly half an hour late, and the entire French contingent was waiting impatiently. When the battered old van finally did appear, the guard at the checkpoint later commented, the driver was visibly nervous and seemed to be sweating despite the temperature being just barely above freezing. And well he might be, since the last time the delivery had been late, the driver had been handled roughly by a husky chasseur and shoved halfway down a flight of stairs. The guard checked the man's ID, even though he recognized him well enough by sight, and took the opportunity of tearing off a foot-long hunk of bread before waving the man on. Breakfast would be late, but there was no reason for the guard to suffer on that account.

The van pulled around to the loading dock at the rear of the six-story building, and a small mob of troopers gathered to "help" distribute the bread. Just then, however, the driver hopped out of the cab and began to run for the gate. The soldiers watched him go in amazement for a moment, their hands on their hips, and then one of them took the initiative to yank open the back doors of the van.

Chandler was back in Mogadishu, swatting the ever-present flies away from his face, and feeling the droplets of sweat run down the back of his neck. This time, all of the people in Mogadishu were Vietnamese, but that didn't seem to make any difference. He was on another assignment without a goal, without an end, other than a calendar date when he would be allowed to leave the place. But the great weight on his shoulders was that anything that happened prior to that date would be his fault, even though he had no control over what anyone else did.

There had been fighting in the southern part of the city, and he had called in some helicopter gunships to support his men, but someone had misunderstood him and sent a flight of B-52s instead. He saw them coming in slowly, very high up, from over the sea, and he saw the long lines of bombs start their majestic descent from the bellies of the huge aircraft. He was screaming into a telephone that there had been a mistake, that half the city would be destroyed, along with most of his troops. The person on the other end of the line, whose voice sounded rather vaguely like his ex-wife's, simply insisted in a dry tone that she had a written order in front of her with his signature on it requesting B-52s for that day. She would be glad to fax him a copy for his own records. The bombs kept falling, and he watched them come all the way to the ground, so the explosion did not surprise him when it came, but it jolted him out of bed all the same.

Chandler was breathing heavily, and his body trembled as he lay on the bed, fully dressed except for his boots. His wrinkled uniform was damp with sweat. It had been so real that he could almost imagine that the plywood covering the balcony doorway was still shaking with the shock wave of the explosion, but that was normal. He heard the same throbbing of helicopter rotors overhead as in his dream, but there really were choppers coming and going here, so that was not unusual either.

The room was weakly illuminated by the daylight that crept in underneath and around the edges of the plywood, so Chandler knew that he should be up and about, but he could not force himself to rise, shower in ice-cold water, shave, and change into a fresh uniform. Getting up would only mean dealing with new problems, and the old ones from yesterday were still unresolved. Perhaps, on the other hand, his recall orders would be waiting for him, and he could go home, not that he really had a home anymore, but at least he would be out of here. He could be dealing with personnel issues and supply and budgetary problems. That would be more to his liking, and no one would die if he made a mistake or if he should just happen to cease functioning at a given moment.

Chandler didn't know how much longer he lay there on the bed. Perhaps he even dropped off into real, dreamless sleep, but he was roughly awakened by someone pounding on the door to his room and shouting.

"General Chandler, open up please!" a high-pitched voice in the hall was calling.

Chandler stumbled to the door, leaning heavily on the right wall as he fought unsuccessfully to gain his balance. He wrenched open the door and found himself facing a wide-eyed young woman wearing first lieutenant's bars. He vaguely recognized her from the radio room.

"There's been a bombing, sir," the woman was saying. "Some kind of car bomb at the French battalion's HQ. We don't know the details, but there must have been many people killed. The blast broke windows halfway across the city. We've got Apaches on station covering the French positions, and a platoon from the quick reaction force in Blackhawks en route to reinforce them. Colonel Morgan has a chopper standing by to take him there and wants to know if you'll want to come along."

Chandler must have stared blankly at her for some time without speaking. He was hearing the words all right, or part of his brain was, and he seemed to capture their meaning in an abstract way, but he couldn't seem to make the connection between this information and what he should be doing about it. The lieutenant was still panting from having bounded up four flights of stairs and was clearly becoming concerned at the lack of response from her commander.

"Sir?" she insisted.

"Oh, yes, yes. Tell the colonel I'm coming," he finally mumbled and turned to grab his boots from the floor and his equipment harness from the table before staggering after the young woman in his stocking feet.

"It seems to have been the baker's van," Morgan was shouting over the roar of the helicopter engine as Chandler fumbled with his bootlaces. "The bloody driver, same one that always did the delivery, took off running the minute he parked by the building, and then the whole thing went up like an atom bomb."

"Did the driver get away?"

"No, fortunately, one of the perimeter guards opened up on him and took one of his legs off. I'm sure the guard did his best to kill him, but we were lucky that he fired low. The man's still alive, but probably not for long. We'll have a chance to talk to him."

"How about casualties?" Yes, Chandler said to himself. This is a good leadership type of question. The kind you must always ask in those dramatic little scenarios at the Point. Shows concern for your men and a clearness of head in a crisis, gathering data, dontcha know. It's not like you were just parroting back cliché phrases, giving yourself time to think, hoping that everything would work itself out while you were busy looking good.

"Don't know yet, maybe fifty dead, maybe a hundred. The building just collapsed. I've got the air transport troop ferrying in the Israeli engineers and their equipment to search through the rubble for survivors. I just know that it doesn't look at all good. Part of the ruins were on fire, and there's no fire department here, nor any water pressure for the hoses if there were."

"Jesus," was all Chandler could say as he looked through the open door of the chopper at the massive column of black, greasy smoke that rose up off to their right. The building looked like an anthill that had been smashed by a vicious child, with men and vehicles swarming around it just like ants desperately trying to save their eggs.

The chopper swooped down, and Chandler, Morgan, and a pair of medics were out the door before the runners hit the ground. Half a dozen French armored cars had formed a protective laager around the building, backed up now by the American aero-rifle platoon and a handful of South Koreans. In a cleared space well away from the building, more than a dozen shattered bodies were laid out in a neat row in good military fashion, and a doctor and a pair of nurses were trying to operate on a man's chest on the ground not far away. One of the nurses was sobbing uncontrollably as she held aloft the i.v. bag with one hand and smoothed the dark hair of the patient with the other. Chandler felt faint, and the image before him began to swim slightly, but he forced his feet to walk closer to the wreckage.

Chandler had visited the building only the day before, but he found nothing familiar about the scene. The building, once a modern six-story, concrete-and-glass office building, had been converted into an immense pyramid of jagged slabs of concrete, twisted steel reinforcing rods, and scattered bits of furniture and human bodies. Strangely, one wall of the building to the third floor and above still stood, with the supporting walls and floors sheared away from it; stranger yet, Chandler could see, on a segment of wall that had belonged to an office on the second floor, a fragile-looking bookshelf that still clung to the wall with its black three-ring binders neatly aligned, probably filled with all sorts of useful regulations.

A Chinook eased down and deposited a small bulldozer that had been slung underneath the large helicopter, and a stocky young man with a white yarmulke on his head sprinted to the 'dozer as soon as the cables had been dropped, revved the engine, and charged into the rubble, where lines of men were still removing blocks of cement by hand.

A French captain, his left shirtsleeve torn and a scarlet gash on his upper arm, came up and saluted Chandler. One side of his face was blackened with soot, and through the filth ran a single streak of cleaner skin, leading from his eye downward.

"Captain Gerard Martin, General, commander of the 2d Company of the Reconnaissance Regiment."

"Where's your colonel?" Chandler asked.

The captain turned to look at the pile of debris. "In there, somewhere, sir. I think most of the headquarters staff were in the building at the time. We've found a few survivors, most of them badly injured, but I fear that the rest are all . . ." His voice trailed off.

"And the prisoners," Morgan joined in. "Were they in the building as well?"

A look of cold rage came over the Frenchman's face. "I wish they had been." He pointed to a long, low building at the far end of the compound. "They were under guard in that garage over there. A representative from Shchernikov had insisted on visiting them, and we permitted it, but as soon as it was apparent that they were passing some kind of open code messages, we cut the meeting off and kicked the fellow out. When the bomb went off, they must have been ready, because they rushed their guards and killed three of them, although we got several of them in return," he added with evident pleasure. "Then some of their people on the outside must have planted a satchel charge on the outer wall of the garage and blew out a section of that, permitting them to escape in the confusion of the bombing."

Chandler was silent for a moment, his head lowered.

"What are we going to do, General?" the captain asked, his lower lip trembling slightly. "They've killed dozens of our men, and we want to make them pay. Just give us the word, General, and we'll clean out the lot of them."

"It's not as simple as that," Chandler said quietly.

"I didn't mean to suggest that it would be simple, or even easy," the captain snapped. "I just meant that it was *necessary*."

"That's quite enough, Captain," Morgan said crisply.

"No, he's absolutely right," Chandler said. "I just don't know what we're going to do yet, Captain. But I can promise you that we won't let it rest like this."

Just then two Israelis trudged by carrying a stretcher with a body covered with a bloody blanket. The captain stopped them and gently lifted a corner of the blanket.

"You were asking about my colonel, sir."

Chandler didn't know how the young man had recognized de Guise from the shattered remnant on the stretcher. The skin had been torn from half of the skull, and one eye dangled from its socket.

The teeth were exposed on one side in a kind of ghoulish grin, and the loose eye seemed to be looking at Chandler. He turned away, but he knew that he would be seeing that face again, and again.

Chandler's knees wobbled, and there was a terrible churning of burning liquid in his stomach. He wanted to go back to his room, to go back home. But he had no home, and couldn't go back to his room either. He would have to stay here and face all of the further horrors that this assignment surely had in store for him. He turned back to the captain.

"I understand that the driver of the van is still alive," he said to the Frenchman.

The Captain sneered. "The little bastard lost his leg, and I have been praying for his slow and painful death, but he is still alive, over there."

He pointed to a small maintenance shed near the main building, and Chandler and Morgan struck out for it, weaving their way through the crowds of rescue workers and stretcher bearers. Captain Martin watched them for a moment, then walked wearily back toward the wreckage alone.

The man lay on what had been a workbench, as an i.v. hanging from a low rafter fed a clear liquid into his left arm. He had fresh bandages around his chest, and his right leg was gone above the knee, the stump swathed in more bandages. A morose orderly sat in one corner of the dimly lit shed, cradling an automatic rifle and making no apparent effort to ease the suffering of the wounded man, who groaned piteously.

Morgan jerked his head toward the door, and the orderly walked sullenly outside, letting the door slam behind him.

"Who sent you to do this?" Morgan asked in passable Russian.

The man winced as he turned his head to look at them. "My family," he croaked. "They have my family."

"Who has your family?" Morgan continued.

"The Republican Guard . . . Shchernikov," he replied.

"Who built the bomb?"

"They came to me while the bread was baking and took my van. They had my wife and daughter in the back of a jeep and said that they would kill them if I didn't do what they said. They piled boxes and boxes into the van and only put in enough bread to cover them. They connected wires to the boxes, and they said that they would be watching me and that they could detonate the bomb by radio if I tried to jump from the van. They also put a microphone on the seat and said that they could hear everything I said and that they would blow me up and then kill my family if I tried to warn the guards. That's all I know, I swear it."

Morgan took Chandler aside briefly. "I've seen this sort of thing before. It was quite popular with the IRA in Northern Ireland for a while. They pick up some poor bastard with access to a target area, hold his family hostage, and make him deliver their bomb for them. I tend to believe that Shchernikov is more than capable of doing this sort of thing. From the size of the crate, I suspect that he must have had more than a quarter ton of Semtex. Shchernikov could have had that stockpiled from old Red Army stores, but he wasn't just out to make a statement with that kind of force. He wanted mass destruction."

"There's not much doubt of that," Chandler grunted. "And you don't think that this man had anything more to do with it?"

"It's not likely."

They turned back toward the man, who stared at them fixedly.

"We'll see that you're taken care of, and we'll try to find your family as well and protect them if you'll tell us just who approached you and what they said," Morgan explained.

There was no reaction from the dark eyes, which continued to gaze at them. Then Chandler noticed that the chest, which had been rising and falling spasmodically while they spoke to him, had ceased to move. Chandler threw open the door and shouted for the orderly, who walked in briskly, took the man's pulse at his neck, and just shook his head. The orderly's eyes made it clear that he would not mourn this death.

Chandler and Morgan emerged from the shed to find Devi and a small entourage crossing the open, dusty yard and inspecting the damage. While most of the UN civilian officials who followed along behind Devi were suitably appalled by the scene—one of them fell back to crouch and vomit at the sight of so much blood and the horrible stench of burned flesh that was beginning to rise from the ruins—Chandler thought that he could detect just the trace of a smile on Devi's face as he approached.

"I wish I could say that this was a surprise, General," Devi said without even the pretense of a greeting. "I'm sure you'll agree that all of this is the direct consequence of your insubordination of last night, and I assure you that my report will express exactly that opinion."

"I would not have doubted that for a moment, Mr. Commissioner," Chandler responded with a sigh. He didn't need Devi to tell him that he was responsible. His brain had been screaming it at him since he had first heard the news of the attack. "And I do accept responsibility for this. I should have ordered Colonel de Guise to shoot his way through the Ukrainians last night, if necessary. Then the prisoners he had taken would be safely out of here. That is not to say that Shchernikov might not have done exactly this anyway, just out of revenge, but it would have been less likely."

"You won't save your sorry career by attempting to blame this attack on General Shchernikov," Devi countered. "You have no evidence that he's behind it, and now even your reputed evidence that he was responsible for the killing of the Kazakh leadership looks very flimsy indeed. That was probably the work of some faction within the Kazakh movement itself, and that same group may well have been responsible for this incident."

"We have information that this attack *was* executed by Shchernikov," Chandler argued. "And as for the attack on the Concert Hall, we know that the men taken prisoner were all Russians."

"How do you know? Because they spoke Russian? Most Kazakhs speak Russian as well as their own tongue. Because some of them were blond-haired and blue-eyed? There are plenty of mercenaries about, what with the dismemberment of the USSR and the disintegration of its army. That doesn't tell you who gave the orders. And your fuzzy white-on-black film? Laughable. I only hope you have devised something a little more substantial this time for your accusations."

"We talked to the man who drove the van that carried the bomb here," Chandler said flatly. "He said that it was Shchernikov and his Republican Guard."

"I demand to speak with this man," Devi declared.

"He just died," Morgan informed him.

"How very convenient," Devi sneered. "So now we're back to having just your word for all of this. Well, it will take rather more than that, I'm afraid."

Devi stepped back a bit to reduce the upward angle from which he looked into Chandler's face.

"Now I want you to understand this very clearly. These are my direct orders. The UN units will enter a total 'force protection' mode. They will withdraw into their fortified positions, and there will be no offensive patrolling in any sector. All travel into or out of the immediate Almaty area will require my express written approval, and all use of weapons, whether defensive or not, will require prior authorization by my office. Is that clear?"

"You mean that, if our men are fired upon, they have to apply to your office for permission to return fire?" Morgan asked, his mouth dropping open.

"Exactly."

"But that would be suicidal!" Morgan exclaimed.

"No more suicidal that the policies you've already apparently been following," Devi snapped, and Chandler had to throw his own body in front of the wiry Welshman to prevent him from decking the stocky Indian. "Marvelous display of professionalism," Devi said, turning and strutting back to where his convoy of vehicles awaited

"You should have let me kill him," Morgan growled. "Combat fatigue, temporary insanity. Not a jury in the world would have convicted me."

"You may be right about that," Chandler admitted, "but I think I'm going to need you in the next few days, and I don't want to have you sitting in irons."

"So what are we going to do?" Morgan asked. "You're not planning to let that bleeding ass Shchernikov get away with this, are you?"

Why did it always have to come down to what *he* was going to do? Chandler wondered. From his earliest memories as the eldest in the too-large family of an underemployed Pennsylvania coal miner, he could never remember having been in a position where he could just "go with the flow" or leave things in someone else's hands. It was always up to him to do the deciding, and he was bone tired of it. And the decision was never easy. In fact, he could always tell what was the right thing to do by how hard it would be for him to accomplish, and this was going to be no different.

"Well, for right now, we've got some bodies to recover, and, if we're lucky, some more lives to save right here. Let's just focus on that for now." As if that weren't enough.

It was after dark by the time Chandler returned to his room. He had called a meeting of his unit commanders for very early the next morning, less Borysenko, whom he had decided to leave to his own devices for the time being, and he had requested Devi's office to authorize a secure-line call back to Alvarez at the Pentagon, which would be put through here. Besides, he needed some time by himself, away from the stench of death, to think things out. His commanders would be expecting clear instructions from him, and he didn't dare face them until he had it straight in his own mind what he wanted them to do. He had snatched a couple of yoghurts from the canteen on the way up, and he now sat absently stirring one with a plastic spoon, when there was a knock at his door.

Goldman smiled broadly and grabbed Chandler's hand and pumped it briskly as he pushed past him into the room.

"That was quite a scoop you guys gave me," Goldman said loudly as he sat down on the bed and set a small transistor radio on the table, turning it on and letting the whining strains of Central Asiatic music fill the room. "I really have to thank you."

"Excuse me," Chandler said, still standing by the open door, "but I have a rather busy schedule. I'm waiting for an important call from the States—and how did you get in here anyway?"

"I know about the call you're expecting, and that's why I've taken the liberty of calling on you without the formality of an appointment. And as for how I got in here, well, you'll find that when people get used to seeing your face, and maybe have a hope of their families seeing their smiling faces on the TV back home, they just make special allowances for you."

"I'll make a special effort to find out who that is and thank him personally," Chandler said, finally shutting the door. "Now, what do you want?"

"Let me tell you a little story, Gen'ral. I don't expect you to believe it. I hardly believe it myself, and I was there."

"Shoot."

"Well, early this year I was in Washington, looking for a hot assignment. You know that in my line of work you're only as good as your latest job, and I was just hitting a slump, but I was able to call in some chits and got named to come to Kazakhstan, but, at the same time that my boss, the producer of the international news department, is telling me about the job, he's putting on his coat and telling me that we have an appointment out at the Sheraton Hotel. You know the one, out by Tyson's Corner?"

Chandler nodded and sighed, waiting for Goldman to get to the point.

"Well, we walk into this hotel room, and who's waiting for us but Lee Cyrus, director of the good old CIA, *and* Thomas C. McClellan, the attorney general—talk about an unlikely pair. Now, I don't mind telling you that I was shocked out of my gourd. You know that the press and the agency haven't exactly gotten along well historically, and here's my editor making this clandestine introduction and telling me that taking this job has a little, shall we say, caveat attached to it. So Cyrus explains to me that the president considers Kazakhstan to have enormous potential for causing trouble for the United States, but our man in Almaty, Mr. Elders, won't allow any CIA man to work in his embassy under cover, and the secretary of state is backing him up. Well, the prez doesn't want to make a public slugfest out of it, so he and his boys talk to my boss and make this deal to have me be a sort of unofficial CIA rep. Does that blow your socks off or what?"

Chandler raised an eyebrow. "I thought that there was a legal prohibition on the CIA using journalistic cover."

"There is," Goldman agreed. "I don't work for the CIA. I'm a newsman first to last, but I did want the assignment, and this was the requirement. Evidently the rule about CIA and the media is that the agency can't get into anything that would look like they were involved in influencing American public opinion. Public opinion over-seas is fine, but not in America. So they don't write my stories, and I'm not a CIA employee. The only difference with this job is that my pal Cyrus gave me all sorts of sexy communications gear, which looks just like my regular laptop, so that I can send and receive information that's too hot for the regular telephone lines. They said that they just wanted a fresh pair of eyes on the ground and some way to commu-nicate that didn't go either through Elders or through Mr. Devi and his UN cronies. They sent McClellan along to the meeting just to prove that this wasn't some kind of off-the-wall CIA rogue operation. My producer approved because we get all sorts of juicy tips on where the hot news is going to be, classified stuff really, and I'm sure that part of it would be illegal if the other news services heard about it, and I suppose because they sold him on the fact that Elders is a big horse's ass who could get us in trouble big time if we didn't keep an eye on him."

"And what, exactly, does this all mean to me?" Chandler asked. "I mean, am I supposed to believe this and take you into my confi-dence? Frankly, Mr. Goldman, I've had my share of experiences in trusting the word of journalists, and none of them has been good."

"You don't have to believe me," Goldman said, waving his hand languidly. "When you talk to General Alvarez, you just ask him about Gomer."

Chandler did a double take. "How did you know that I was going to talk to Alvarez? One of your little sources here in headquarters?"

"Who would have known?" Goldman asked spreading his arms innocently. "That's what I'm telling you. They share info with me, and I'm here to let you know that I can get word back to them with-out anyone else knowing. You just ask them about Gomer."

"Gomer? Like in Gomer Pyle, USMC?"

"They let me pick my own code name. What do you think?"

"Perfect," Chandler said, shaking his head. "So what *do* you want from me?"

"I just wanted to pass along to you that the people in Washington figure you're just about to stick your neck out far enough to get it lopped off but that you should do what you think best. They'll back you as far as they can, but that won't be much."

"That's tremendously helpful."

"There's more. *If* you should decide to *do* something about the bombing incident, do it. And *if* you do, there's a place they want to make sure you take a look at while you're in the neighborhood."

Goldman pulled a flimsy piece of paper out of his pocket on which there was a sketched map of the city center. "Here's Government House," he said, spreading the map out on the little table as Chandler bent over it. "And just next door, to the west, is what used to be a firehouse."

"Used to be?" Chandler asked. "I've been to Government House, and the place still looks like a firehouse to me."

"That's the idea, but things are not always what they seem."

"What's in there, then?"

"We don't know for sure, but I suppose that it isn't hoses. Whatever it is, it's apparently too hot for them even to talk to you about over your secure telephone line. They said that too many people can listen in on that thing either at the Washington end or here."

"That's all you can tell me?"

"Yes, just make sure you get a good look inside. That's what they told me."

"Forgive me if I'm less than overwhelmed."

"You're forgiven," Goldman said, rising. "There's a big debate going on right now in Washington, New York, and just about everywhere else from what I gather. There's your version of what happened—When was it? Last night only? Seems like longer. And that tape tends to support your claim, but there are those who believe what Devi and Shchernikov are putting out, but those are the people who have an interest in believing them. The ones you should worry about are the 'reasonable' ones who figure that the real *truth* must lie somewhere in between. That Shchernikov's bad, but not *that* bad, and that the Kazakhs probably had something to do with all of this, and that, anyway, you and the UN forces are partly to blame for it all in any event."

Goldman grabbed Chandler's hand again and shook it roughly. "Well, it's been a real bit of heaven, but I've got my reporter thing to do. Now don't be such a stranger, Gen'ral." And in a moment he was out the door.

Chandler was still staring at the door when the phone rang.

"Your call to Washington, sir," the operator downstairs said. "Going secure now."

Chandler heard a high-pitched squeal, followed by a series of beeps and clicks, and finally Alvarez's voice on the other end. He could recognize it, but the decryption of the signal left the voice sounding like one belonging to a man who had suffered a stroke, slower and distorted. It was a hard phenomenon to get used to.

"Julian," the voice said. "I got your preliminary report. What the hell do you think you're doing out there?"

"Good to hear from you too, General," Chandler answered. Even though he and Alvarez had never been close, or even really friendly, something about hearing a voice from back home created a tremendous longing and nostalgia in him. "I suppose you've gotten the basic facts from my report."

"I'm afraid so. What was the final body count?"

"Ninety-three dead. Forty more seriously wounded. The wounded have all been medevaced out to Novosibirsk and should be on their way to Rhein-Main by now."

"Roger that," Alvarez replied. "You got any more poop on who did it?"

"Deathbed confession and common sense not good enough?"

"Not these days, son." Chandler hated to be called "son" by someone who was at most eight years his senior. "We're playing with the big boys now. I just got back from the White House. Can you believe that happy-crappy?"

"So what do they want me to do?" Chandler asked, hoping for guidance or, better yet, direct orders, which would take some of the weight off his own shoulders. "Do they want to pull me out? That's what Devi's saying he's called for."

"You bet your ass he has," Alvarez growled. "And the secretary general is backing him all the way, but the Joint Chiefs don't want to set the kind of precedent where the UN can name our unit commanders for us, and the president is riding kind of low in the polls right now, especially on foreign policy issues. Elections aren't too far away, and he's decided that it's time to rally 'round the flag and stand up for American interests. So you stay for the time being."

"*That's* how they're deciding this thing?" Chandler almost screamed into the phone. "People are dying out here, and they're making their decisions based on precedent setting and the polls."

"Wake up and smell the bullshit, compadre," Alvarez laughed. "You've worked in this building, so don't tell me that comes as a big fucking surprise to you."

"So what do they want me to *do?*" Chandler asked again.

"Exactly nothing," Alvarez replied. "It's the typical bureaucrat's decision. They think Devi's idea of going into the 'force protection' mode is perfect. Nobody gets hurt, and they get time to make a decision or, better yet, to put off making one as long as possible."

"But the Kazakhs are getting ready to come rolling right over us to get at the Russians. Shchernikov and his boys scragged half of their leadership *and* their families in the middle of a supposed cease-fire, and the Kazakhs don't see the humor in it. Our little set-to with the Russians *may* have convinced them that we weren't all in cahoots with the Russkies, but we're still standing right in the way, and I don't think that Qasimbekai is going to be any too delicate about watching which way the bullets fly, any more than Shchernikov is. What if the Kazakhs decided to plow through the Ukrainians? Are we supposed to bail them out or just sit there and watch?"

"No word on that, Julian. Just sit tight. The only word of cheer I have for you is that you have your backers here in Disney World North, and you're not going to get yanked, at least for right now."

"Is that supposed to be good news?"

"Good or not, that's all I've got," Alvarez said. "Vaya con Dios, hijo."

"Don't you have anything else to pass along?" Chandler asked, not really expecting anything.

"Oh yeah," Alvarez added. "They told me to tell you that Gomer was all right. Does that mean anything to you?"

"I suppose so. Thanks for the call."

Chandler hung up but kept his hand resting on the telephone for some time. His left knee ached, a sure sign that the weather was turning bad, probably snow, he figured. His meteorological capability was the one positive facet of the gradual deterioration of his body.

He had hoped for relief from command. He could have stood any kind of disgrace, since there was no human being whose opinion really mattered to him anymore, and he could hardly have a lower opinion of himself than he already did. But that would have been too easy. There was an invisible hand in this, steering him into the most distasteful situations possible, just to make him suffer. For a moment he almost envied de Guise. He probably didn't realize what hit him. Just *bang*, and it was all over. That would be nice.

That night Chandler got to relive Mogadishu again, but this time it was peopled with the Russian civilians from the airport road. There were still the Somali gunmen, their white teeth gleaming from their black faces, their torsos bristling with guns and ammunition belts. And he got to read the newspapers afterward this time, just as he had done when he had returned to the States, and he saw the face of the warlord who had killed the young soldier, smiling broadly in a photo on the front page, shaking the American president's hand as the official envoy to the signing of the peace agreement in New York. The caption labeled him "the voice of reason from the Horn of Africa."

CHAPTER 4

In a speech before the United Nations General Assembly today, Secretary General Justus Muli cited the recent bombing of the barracks of the French UN contingent in Almaty, Kazakhstan, as tragic proof of the folly of seeking purely military solutions to predominantly political problems. Meanwhile, demonstrators in Paris clashed with police near the Elysée palace. The demonstrators were calling for the withdrawal of French troops from UN peacekeeping missions worldwide.

CNN

ALMATY
1 November, 0230 Hours

Despite the early hour, there was no lack of focus visible on the faces of the officers gathered around the long table in the conference room where Chandler had called the meeting of his unit commanders. There was weariness there, as some of the men had not slept since the night before, and several of them had not bothered to shave in the past day or two, but all of their expressions spoke of focused determination. Each officer had a notepad and pen on the table in front of him, and they all looked to Chandler to start the meeting. Chandler stood at the head of the table with an easel behind him upon which was mounted a large-scale street map of the central portion of the city of Almaty. Chandler was pleased with their attitude. In the wee hours of the morning, he had finally decided what to do, and it appeared that they were in the mood to help him on his way.

"You have all received copies of the orders published by Commissioner Devi's office about the need to stand down, to go into what they call 'force protection' mode, and some or all of you may have received similar instructions from your own national govern-

114

ments. I know that I have," Chandler began. "But the problem I have with those orders is that they will neither bring to justice the men I know are responsible for the destruction of the French battalion's headquarters and for the bloody attack on the Kazakh provisional government, nor will they prevent the Kazakhs from launching an attack of their own on the city as soon as they are ready, probably within a couple of days. Consequently, I have come up with a plan of my own for addressing the situation. At this moment, in front of all of you, less Major Borysenko for reasons of which I think you're all aware, I can only say that I have no authority to execute the plan I have in mind, and while I take full responsibility for it, and will make that statement in writing, following my orders in this plan may cause you future problems with the UN or with your immediate superiors. I therefore ask that anyone who has reservations about this please excuse himself from the room, and I assure you that this will be no reflection on you if you do so."

The men glanced at each other, but no one made an effort to leave. Finally, Captain Sohei Kondo, commander of the Japanese military police company, rose and bowed stiffly from the neck.

"Excuse me, General, but I, for one, will require more information before I can make an intelligent decision in this matter. I believe I can guess your ultimate object, from the presence here of Captain Wakeham of the Royal Marines, our resident commando, but I would not want to make an incorrect assumption on that basis alone." He resumed his seat, and a number of heads nodded in agreement.

"Fair enough," Chandler said. "I had hoped to spare anyone unwilling to participate from the obligation of advising Commissioner Devi, or anyone else in the UN chain of command, about this operation, but Captain Kondo is entirely correct. This is a big decision. I have had all night to think it through, and it is only fair that I let you know what you are in for. If, after hearing my plan, you decide not to participate, I *ask* you, in the interests of the safety of any of your colleagues who do go with me, that you remain silent, but, in any case, I have intentionally given you very little lead time precisely to limit the effect a leak could have on our chances of success."

Chandler picked up a pointer and turned to the map. "Part of our inability to prove the involvement of Shchernikov in both of the attacks of the last twenty-four hours is due to the loss of the prisoners Colonel de Guise had captured. From what we know, they were members of the Republican Guard, Shchernikov's personal bodyguard, and I believe that right now those very men are here in

Government House with him." He slapped the pointer against the center of the map.

"What makes you think so, General?" the Argentine colonel, Andres Meriani, asked. "Could they not have been gotten out of the city by now?"

"It's possible," Chandler admitted. "It's also possible that they're being hidden somewhere else in the Russian zone, but I think this is the most likely place. I doubt that Shchernikov would have tried to get them out during daylight, and we have had the area under constant aerial surveillance since sunset, already in violation of Commissioner Devi's orders. There has been no sign of movement by a large body of men. Also, given the sensitivity of the matter, I suspect that Shchernikov would want to keep these men exactly where he could be sure of their safety, and this is the best place for that. Now, I propose that we go in there and get those raiders back."

"And your plan is to punch right through the Russian defensive positions and capture the seat of their government, which the Kazakhs have been trying to do for months without success?" asked Captain Atef Hamed, the Egyptian artillery battery commander. "I think you might be overly optimistic, if I may say so, General."

"According to our intelligence," Chandler explained, "virtually all of the Russian forces are massed on the southeast side of the city, since that's where the Kazakhs have been massing, opposite the Ukrainians, for a possible all-out assault. The rest of the perimeter seems to be covered only by screening forces. Also, we have the advantage of air-mobile troops, of which the Kazakhs have very few, so the Russians haven't worried about defending against the vertical threat very much. If the airborne troops can seize the objective, a strong armored force can punch through the thin crust of Russian resistance and pull both our men and the prisoners out on the ground."

"That seems like a great risk for the air-mobile troops, sir," Hamed insisted.

"That's what we're paid for," Wakeham snapped. "If you're not up for it, we won't expect you to come along."

"That's enough of that," Chandler said in a firm voice. "It's a perfectly valid point, and it is a calculated risk, but we learned in Somalia that, with helicopter gunship support, armor can go pretty much wherever it wants in a city like this, against this kind of threat. Armor can't hold ground, and they can't root out all resistance, but they can move, and that's all we're looking for here."

"And what will we do with the prisoners once we've got them?" Hamed asked. "Won't that just prompt Shchernikov to stage another terrorist attack?"

"If things go the way I expect, we'll nab Shchernikov himself and hold him for trial. There is, after all, a UN commission on war crimes for Kazakhstan, and there is certainly precedent enough for that from the UN efforts to arrest the warlord Aideed in Somalia."

"And we all know how well *that* worked out," Hamed countered.

"That's because we didn't catch him," Chandler replied. "Considering the noises Devi is making, and the UN's past record here, the last thing that Shchernikov will be expecting will be this kind of assault. Surprise will be with us."

"But how are we going to launch a surprise attack when there are Russian and Kazakh laborers scattered around all of our bases?" Hamed asked. "Surely Shchernikov and Qasimbekai have spies among them who report regularly on our troop movements."

"If we don't give them time to report, any information they come up with won't help. We know that unexpected moves can catch Shchernikov off-balance, which is how we captured his raiders in the first place."

"How long do we have to put this thing together?" Lt. Col. Alan Peabody asked, apparently trying to get back to the idea of planning the operation.

"The first wave goes in at 0500 hours. It will still be pitch-dark by then, but later we'll have full daylight to secure the area and extract our people."

There was a round chorus of gasps and groans from around the table.

"How the hell, excuse me, sir," Peabody objected, "are we supposed to plan and pull off an operation like this in just a couple of hours? We've got to drill the troops, gather intelligence, load the vehicles. It can't be done."

"If it can't be done in that time frame, then it can't be done at all. We'll lose surprise, *and* it will be likely that our real targets, the raiders from the Concert Hall, will have been moved to safer hiding places. It's the only chance we've got."

Chandler looked from face to face around the table. Then he returned to the map.

"Since we don't have any fixed-wing air support, and because I don't want to be using artillery within the city, I plan to use attack helicopters to neutralize the defenses first. Colonel Saavedra's

Apaches are equipped with terrain avoidance radar and can fly nape of the earth, right to the target area within less than a minute of crossing the Green Belt. Using Hellfires and their 20mm guns, they can take out the platoon of T-72s we know to be stationed at Government House plus several twin AA guns we have seen emplaced on the roofs of buildings surrounding it. Under this cover, the next wave will be Captain Wakeham's platoon mounted in Blackhawks to stage the initial assault on Government House itself, followed by a full company of infantry to help them hold their positions until the ground forces, two troops from the American Eleventh Cavalry, come in to extract them."

"Whose infantry were you planning to use?" Meriani asked, apparently guessing the answer.

"Since we've 'lost' the Ukrainians, I would like to use your mountain troops, Colonel. They're the only company-level infantry we've got now, although, if you don't choose to participate, we'll scrape something up from the infantry elements of the various cavalry units." Chandler knew that this dearth of infantry had been a weakness in the UN deployment in Almaty from the outset. The experience of Somalia and the high casualties suffered by unprotected infantry had prompted the UN to opt for the use of armored cavalry units with their high proportion of armored vehicles, which also retained a much better ground-holding capability than regular armored units equipped mainly with tanks.

Meriani smiled. "As you may know, General, in my younger days, I was a *carapintada*, one of the commandos who tried to overthrow the Alfonsin government several times. So, you will not find discipline to superior authority, especially civilian authority, as a serious deterrent to me to participation in an interesting military operation."

"Thank you, Colonel," Chandler said, bowing slightly.

Just then the French captain, Martin, stood. "General, since the murder of my colonel is part of the reason for this operation, I insist that my chasseurs be given a role in this action. Perhaps we could contribute to the ground force."

"I'm sorry, Captain, and I appreciate your feelings, but I suspect that this is just what Shchernikov will be looking for. If these people haven't learned much about democracy and freedom since the collapse of the Soviet Union, they have learned all about the blood feud. I'm certain that Shchernikov is holding back reserves facing your forces and that any movement of your troops will be spotted and reported immediately, possibly tipping him off as to the whole operation."

"Since we are breaking many of the rules of military discipline and subordination in even considering this activity," the Frenchman continued, "I cannot guarantee that I can hold my men in check, sir." He stared, unblinking, into Chandler's face, defying him to argue.

"I rather anticipated that, Captain," Chandler said, smiling. "And I do have a role for you. There is a fortified Russian position at this theater, just north of your perimeter. *After* the initial helicopter assault has begun, but *before* the American ground attack kicks off, I want two troops of your battalion to attack this position as if you were trying to force open a corridor of your own. If we're lucky, that will tie down Shchernikov's reserves in that area during the crucial time it takes for Peabody's forces to make their penetration, and by the time Shchernikov figures out that he's been had, it will be too late for him."

Martin stuck out his lower lip, considering the proposition, then nodded and sat back down.

"I also will need a section of the Israeli combat engineers to accompany the ground push, in case they run into mines or barricades that prove difficult to break through. Can we count on you, Lieutenant?" Chandler asked, turning to David Harish.

"We're from the Golani Brigade," he replied with a shrug. "We do tougher things than this for training."

"Thanks, Lieutenant," Chandler said, putting his pointer down. "Now, is there anyone who refuses to be involved in the operation? As you can see, not every unit has a direct role, but we will be on one hundred percent alert for the duration, and I can't deny that this will make all UN peacekeepers prime targets for retaliation, so if there are any objections, let's get them out in the open now."

The room was engulfed in silence. At first, each man sought to avoid the eyes of his colleagues, then they began to glance around, looking for someone to make the first move. Finally, Hamed, the Egyptian, rose slowly from his seat, looking right and left, probably in the hope that someone else would preempt him.

"I do not know whether I speak for anyone else here," Hamed began, "but I have noted that what you have avoided emphasizing, General, is the fact that joining this attack will essentially spell the end of our professional careers. If the operation were to go off flawlessly, and if we get the proof we're looking for against Shchernikov, we just might, I repeat *might*, avoid prison terms, but the stigma will remain with us for the rest of our lives. Obviously, this is less important for some than for others, and I suspect that we will have to make our own decisions on this."

"If you're that worried about your bleeding career—" Morgan started to say, but Hamed raised his hand.

"Let me finish, please. There are, of course, other considerations. We are in a unique situation in relation to our colleagues back home in our respective services. We have been offered up by our governments as a kind of sacrifice to the god of 'internationalism,' and whether we ever come home or not is only of importance in the countries where public opinion can be stirred up by such things. We have seen our rights abandoned one by one. The military has to bow to the political goals of the UN leadership, which has no responsibility for our lives and is not answerable to our wives and families if anything happens to us. We have had to sacrifice clear-cut military missions for politically acceptable, endless deployments. In Bosnia and elsewhere, our soldiers were offered up to stand for war crimes trials in front of the UN on trumped-up charges of looting or rape brought by irate local tyrants, rather than being under the jurisdiction of our own military-justice systems. What all this has proven is that, whatever country we have come from, whatever the interests our governments seek to further by sending us here, the only definite thing we have is each other. We may not have met before we got off the plane here, and our paths may never cross again, but while we are here, the only people that care about us are the men in our own peacekeeping force. The Ukrainians have violated this trust, and I pray that they will suffer the torments of eternal damnation for it. I attended training at the American artillery school at Fort Sill, and I learned a phrase from your revolution. 'If we don't hang together, we will surely hang separately.'"

The men seated around the room pounded heartily on the table and produced a chorus of gorilla grunts and hoots as Hamed sat down. Then the Japanese captain stood, bowing again stiffly.

"And as I learned when I studied military police tactics at Fort Leavenworth: *Ban-fucking-zai!*" He bowed again to another round of hoots.

Chandler smiled and raised his arms. "Great, then we've got a busy couple of hours ahead of us. I'll be out with Wakeham and Saavedra at the airport, since I'll be going in with the SAS people in the first assault."

The laughing and talking suddenly came to a stop. "Excuse me, sir," Morgan said as the officers looked at each other in disbelief. "Don't you think that you'd be better placed at headquarters monitoring the operation and coordinating it?"

"Perhaps, but I'll be going in with Wakeham, and I'll try not to get in the way," Chandler snapped. "It's not a topic for debate. It's a fact, so deal with it." He turned and walked from the room, and Morgan followed after him.

Chandler's long legs had taken him halfway down the corridor before the shorter man caught up with him.

"Julian," Morgan said, grabbing Chandler's elbow. "I know just what you're doing, and I won't have it."

"You may *think* you know what I'm doing, Colonel," Chandler replied coldly, "but I doubt that you really do, and it doesn't much matter in any case."

Chandler tried to turn and continue on his way, but the wiry Welshman spun him back around roughly.

"Oh, I know what it is all right! I've seen too much of you to think that you're playing Mr. Macho going in with the first wave like John Wayne. That's not your game. You're too professional for that. Listen, I don't know what happened to you in Somalia, but you're not going to commit suicide on *my* time with *my* men serving as spear-carriers in your grand finale."

"Fuck you, Colonel!" Chandler shouted. "Now go and do your job or get the hell out of the way and let someone else do it."

Chandler tore himself free and stormed down the hall. Was it that obvious? Chandler wondered.

Saavedra's chopper roared straight down the broad Prospect Ablai Khan at just over one hundred miles per hour through the darkness. What many people failed to appreciate about tactical helicopter pilots was that the primary difference between them and tank commanders was that tank commanders rode farther from the ground than the pilots, most of the time. The skids of Saavedra's tiny AH-6F were clearing the asphalt of the boulevard by as little as a foot or two, and he bobbed and weaved from side to side to avoid the occasional abandoned car. The looming apartment buildings on either side of the boulevard gave him a view of a narrow band of stars overhead.

So far, only a single anti-aircraft gun had attempted to engage him as he crossed into the Russian zone, but its fire had come seconds too late and served merely to mark the gun for the fire of the four Apaches that swept along in Saavedra's wake. In a matter of five more seconds, he would turn at the corner of Ulitsa Komsomolskaya, where the Government House was located, and it would be pure "rock and roll."

Through his night-vision visor, he saw several figures running toward a twin-barreled gun located in a sandbagged revetment at the next corner, and he lashed the area with a stream of tracers from his 7.62mm chain gun, bowling the figures over before he rushed past. As he tore by the dark bulk of Government House, he pulled up sharply and banked around, followed by unaimed fire from dozens of machine guns and small arms from Government House itself and several of the neighboring office buildings. He peppered the area with 2.75-inch rockets, setting off several secondary explosions and small fires as his rounds hit stored ammunition or fuel tanks.

The Apaches were in the fight now, and their Hellfire missiles tore into the tanks parked around the target building. The missiles rode into their marks as if on rails, guided by the laser target designator. It "painted" them from an invisible OH-58-D Kiowa helicopter, which orbited safely several kilometers away. Suddenly, a SAM missile arched skyward from the roof of the firehouse next door to Government House, and one of the Apaches jinked violently to avoid it, the pilot kicking out flares to distract the missile's heat-seeking warhead. The missile wavered for a moment, but then bore in on the Apache, exploding near its tail boom, and sending the craft spiraling down to the street, where it landed, hard.

Saavedra dove down into the narrow concrete canyon of the street to look for survivors, hoping he wouldn't encounter any high-tension wires strung across his path, and saw the weapons officer crawl out of the mangled cockpit. The man then turned around and reached back into the aircraft, trying to pull the pilot to safety as flames slowly began to consume the chopper from the rear.

The infantry would be coming along in thirty seconds or less, but that could be too late. Saavedra was flying alone, and his tiny craft was not designed to carry passengers.

"Buffalo flight, this is Raven One!" he screamed into his radio. "I've got one bird down, two survivors, about half a click south of the target. As soon as you drop your load, get me an evac mission in here. I'll cover, over."

"You got it, Raven One. ETA in about two minutes."

That's going to be a long fucking two minutes for those bastards, Saavedra thought to himself as he pirouetted his chopper protectively over the downed airmen. In the glaring light of the burning Apache, he could see that the gunner had succeeded in freeing the pilot from the wreckage and was hauling his inert form toward the slender protection of a doorway in a tall apartment building nearby.

Suddenly, the two men dropped to the ground, and Saavedra saw the gunner's pistol make pitifully tiny flashes as he fired at something up the street. There they were! Saavedra could just make out half a dozen dark shapes hugging the edge of the sidewalk about fifty meters away. Just as the enemy AKs began to spit green bursts at him and at the two men on the ground, Saavedra pressed the trigger of his chain gun. A long tongue of flame reached out and lashed the base of the buildings where the infantrymen were sheltering. He played the joystick left and right, hosing down the whole area, and the enemy firing stopped.

"Come on, come on!" he shouted into the radio without bothering with call signs.

"Almost there, boss," a metallic voice answered him. "Hang on."

Just then the nose of a BTR wheeled armored personnel carrier poked out from around the corner of a building down the street, along with the shadows of more infantrymen. The BTR's machine gun opened up, and the windshield on the left side of Saavedra's chopper shattered, showering him with jagged bits of Plexiglas. Saavedra returned fire, sending up a spray of sparks as his 20mm rounds spanged off the sides of the vehicle. He was also moving forward at the same time to try to shield his men, and he was rewarded by seeing the BTR burst into flames, but he immediately realized that this had been due to a Hellfire missile fired by an Apache off to his left. He turned around to look, and saw the squat shape of a Blackhawk touching down near the wreck as a crewman hopped out to help the other two airmen into the craft.

Just then, Saavedra felt a cold, burning pang in his left leg. He reached down and felt the sticky wetness on his pants leg and knew that he had been hit. Cursing loudly, but unable to hear even his own voice with the noise of the helicopter engine and the battle around him, he eased himself back into his seat and cranked up the throttle, sending the little chopper skyward like a rocket.

He called to his XO, who was flying one of the Apaches, to take over, and banked perilously between two streams of tracers reaching up from the ground. His leg had gone numb now from the knee down, making it almost impossible to work the aircraft's pedals, and he was beginning to feel light-headed. The nose of the helicopter dipped as he sped northward in the direction of the airport and safety.

Chandler sat in the edge of the doorway of the Blackhawk helicopter, his legs dangling over the side in the freezing wind as they raced toward their target, dodging between the taller buildings and hopping over the lower ones. A British SAS commando sat on either side of him, and another three sat in similar fashion in the doorway on the opposite side of the aircraft. Their harnesses were already connected to the fast rope hookup, and their assault rifles were slung over their chests. A second Blackhawk, with Wakeham aboard, kept pace with Chandler's about thirty meters to one side, and another pair followed them only a few seconds back. By using this setup, all six men in each helicopter could fast rope down simultaneously to the roof of Government House in a matter of seconds, followed closely by the second wave, putting two dozen men on the roof before the defenders could organize. A similar assault would be taking place on the fire-house next door at the same time. They would then be followed by several more relays of Blackhawks bringing in a dozen Argentine infantrymen each to help secure the targets, but it would be the commandos who would be responsible for actually seizing the structures.

Chandler could see Apaches diving and swerving all over the sky around them, blasting away with their chain guns and firing missiles at particularly resistant enemy strongholds or armored vehicles. The roof of Government House finally loomed beneath them in the pale light of the sliver of moon, which still hung in the sky above. Chandler could just make out several bodies scattered around the roof, and an anti-aircraft gun whose twin barrels were twisted at odd angles. A thin plume of white smoke issued from the front of the building, and a tank burned brightly at the near corner down on the street.

The Blackhawk had been angled forward in its approach, and it now rocked back as the pilot pulled to a halt above Government House. On this signal, Chandler and the commandos jumped from their perches, the rope running fast through their gloved hands as they slid the twenty feet to the rooftop.

Chandler landed hard and unclipped his harness. The British commandos in their mushroom-cap helmets had already secured the unoccupied roof, and one of them was attaching a plastique charge to the metal door leading down into the building. He took cover behind an air vent, and the charge blew the door off its hinges. The commando pitched a stun grenade inside and charged through the smoke with Chandler hard behind him, followed closely by several more men.

Chandler found himself in a dimly lit interior staircase with bare cement walls. The sounds of the helicopters' firing against targets on the ground floor was now reduced to a distant rumble. The first commando was braced next to a closed fire door leading off the stairwell.

When Chandler and the others were in position, he kicked the door in with a heavy boot, and they surged into a long corridor from which offices branched off on either side.

Suddenly a man sprang into the corridor firing wildly with an AKM. The commando in front of Chandler gasped as a round hurled him backward, but Chandler brought up his M-16 and cut the attacker down with a burst to the chest. As the other commandos raced along the hall, hurling grenades into each room and following them up with sprays of bullets, Chandler checked the injured man. He had caught a bullet at the base of his throat, just above his flak vest. His blue eyes stared up through Chandler's face to some image from his own past. This throat gurgled once, and he grasped weakly at Chandler's sleeve, and then he died. Another face for the repertoire, Chandler thought.

Martin's six-wheeled AMX-10RC armored car smashed through the wooden sawhorse barrier that marked the limit of the French zone and roared forward. He manned the machine gun atop the turret himself and sent long bursts at the windows where the Russians were known to have weapons emplaced in an abandoned warehouse facing the checkpoint. As he neared the street corner, he dropped down inside the turret to the gun sight and watched through the periscope as the target strongpoint came into view. He fired his first high-explosive round on the move, less concerned with total accuracy than in shaking up the defenders with a near miss. If he could buy a couple of seconds, then several more of the other armored cars would have their own 105mm guns in range, and between them they could take the building apart.

The shell hit at the second-floor level, next to a window that had obviously been fortified with cinder blocks and sandbags, and kicked up a small cloud of smoke and dust. The loader slammed a fresh round into the breech and stepped back, shouting, "Up!" to give Martin the signal that it was ready to fire again.

Suddenly an enemy armored personnel carrier opened fire from behind a low berm of earth in the center of what had been a small park. It was an old BMP-1 with a low-velocity 73mm gun, and its crew was obviously nervous, because their shot went high and wide of the mark. There was enemy armor in the area, and Martin didn't have time to change to armor-piercing ammunition to face the new threat. He fired the HE again on the move, calling for a new load. Almost simultaneously, two other French vehicles fired on the same target, and HE was more than enough to destroy the thin-skinned APC at this short range, blasting it to pieces. But where there were APCs there were likely to be tanks as well.

Martin's AMX lurched sideways as what must have been a rocket-propelled grenade slammed into the side of his turret, but the armor was thick there, and the angle must have been bad, allowing the projectile to glance off. Most of the firing was coming from the target building itself, a four-story former apartment block, and Martin called over the radio to his other vehicle commanders to deal with it first. They fired round after round in quick succession into the first floor of the structure, continuing to race from one position to another. There was no need for great accuracy now, Martin thought, just volume of fire as the high-explosive rounds tore into the supporting walls of the building.

At first, the defenders on the upper floors must have breathed a sigh of relief as the French fire seemed to be directed away from them, but then the building began to tremble, then to sag to one side. The French stopped firing for a moment as, almost as if in slow motion, the building began to slide to the right, the roof tilting downward and gradually picking up speed before the entire edifice disappeared into a massive cloud of dust and debris.

Martin smiled to himself as he searched his vision block for fresh targets.

An Abrams tank with a mine plow blade installed on its front, a wicked-looking multitoothed thing, brushed aside the twisted bodies of abandoned trucks with which the Russians had constructed a barricade across the Ulitsa Panfilova. Random bullets pinged off the thick armor of the sixty-ton monster, but the crew inside could not even hear them. The cavalry troop's mortar section had peppered the area liberally with smoke rounds, and the white, drifting columns shrouded the vehicles from all directions. While the tank-dozer widened the breach, another M-1A1 Abrams raced through the gap, followed by a dozen M-3 Bradley armored fighting vehicles.

Peabody rode with his turret in the half-open position, with the hatch cover lifted about twelve inches, allowing him a good field of vision while providing some protection against snipers and overhead artillery bursts, and he peered ahead through the smoke intently. His gunner would be using his thermal imager to identify serious targets, such as other tanks, but Peabody always felt more in control when he could look outside for himself. Claustrophobia is not a useful trait for a tanker, but Peabody always felt extremely anxious whenever he had to be "buttoned up" inside the vehicle. The closeness of fighting in a heavily built-up urban area only made the feeling worse.

With its superb suspension system and gyro-stabilized turret, the Abrams raced on at nearly forty miles per hour, up and down curbs, and back and forth over the median strip in the center of the broad boulevard as if it were moving across a billiard table. White phosphorus mortar rounds continued to strike ahead and to the sides of the armored column as it advanced, keeping it shrouded in smoke, and one round had turned a little store into a bonfire on his right. It was only a few kilometers to Government House, and resistance appeared to be light.

He came across the burning carcass of a T-72 tank, the victim of a Hellfire missile. Peabody knew that the Russians had little armor in the city, and it looked as though the chopper jockeys were going to rob him of any chance to do his thing. Just then, however, as his tank roared into an intersection, he nearly collided with a ZSU-23/4, an armored anti-aircraft vehicle, equipped with a four-barreled 23mm gun with radar guidance. The ZSU had obviously been racing to join in the fight in the defense of Government House, the tall buildings of the city center restricting its ability to target on the low-flying helicopters, and neither the driver of the ZSU nor Peabody's tank had been much concerned with the problem of cross traffic.

The two vehicles swerved violently to avoid a collision as a natural reflex of the drivers, since the huge Abrams would have rolled right over its much lighter opponent, and Peabody was hurled against the unforgiving steel of the turret ring, which knocked the wind out of him.

"Gunner, HEAT, PC!" he managed to groan into his mouthpiece, and he slammed the turret control joystick hard to the left, swinging the main gun around to bear.

"Up!" the loader replied, but the gunner would not yet have a view of the enemy, which had ended up off the left rear quarter of Peabody's tank.

Ordinarily, the ZSU would not have posed much of a threat to a main battle tank, but at this range, less than thirty meters from the Abrams's flank, a stream of 23mm armor-piercing rounds, fired at a cyclic rate of a thousand rounds per minute, could do considerable damage to the sights, antennae, engine compartment, and other external gear, to say nothing of Peabody himself. Peabody had a split second to choose whether to drop down and slam the hatch or try to get in the first shot. His instincts took over. Peabody could see the enemy turret rotating rapidly in his direction as well, and the four ugly barrels were simultaneously lowering to point directly at him.

"Jesus Christ!" he shouted involuntarily. At this distance, there was no need for any of the fancy computerized laser range-finding equipment that made the Abrams the most expensive armored fighting vehicle on earth. They would fire battlesight. "From my position!" he said, poising his index finger over the red trigger on the joystick.

The 120mm gun came around clockwise, just as the multiple barrels of the ZSU were coming around counterclockwise. The Russian commander wasn't limited to just one shot, and he pulled his trigger early. A horrible shriek came from the ZSU as a stream of green tracers reached out toward Peabody, exploding the bare limbs and trunk of a tree nearby. A fountain of shell casings shot up from the enemy turret, cascading all around. The line of tracers was just about to touch the Abrams's flank when Peabody squeezed his own trigger, and the big tank rocked slightly as the round left the tube.

Peabody dropped down inside his turret as a hail of jagged metal from the destroyed ZSU showered all around him, and he could feel the hot breath of the flames as the ammunition and fuel in the enemy vehicle ignited. He raised himself up slowly and peered over the rim of the turret. Only the lower half of the ZSU remained, engulfed in a ball of fire, and Peabody closed his eyes and tried to catch his breath a moment before ordering, "Driver, forward."

The first indication Shchernikov had that something was going on came as he was discussing with Lushkin his plans for a meeting with Commissioner Devi for the following afternoon. They had been sitting comfortably in Shchernikov's huge office, emptying a bottle of vodka that stood on his desk and tearing off chunks of black bread and sausage between gulps. Suddenly, there was a sound as if a giant were beating on the building with a ball peen hammer. Before either Shchernikov or Lushkin could react, one of the tall windows of the hall, which had been covered with plywood and reinforced with sandbags, was blown in, scattering slivers and dirt everywhere.

"The Kazakhs!" Shchernikov screamed. "How could they have gotten here?"

"It's not the Kazakhs," Lushkin shouted over the rattle of gunfire coming in now from outside. "Those are American helicopters."

"How could they do this?" Shchernikov asked as he and Lushkin ran for the shelter of an interior corridor of the building. "Devi assured me that they were restricted to their barracks, and besides that, the UN has never attacked either our forces or the Kazakhs before."

"Well, they are now," Lushkin said. "I guess if you kill enough of them, they lose their sense of humor. All that matters now is that you've got to get away from here."

Just then one of Lushkin's lieutenants came panting up, his AKM slung over his shoulder.

"Enemy soldiers landing on the roof, sir," he shouted with a note of panic in his voice. "They've knocked out our tanks on the ground and the anti-aircraft emplacements upstairs. We can't stick our noses out without those damned helicopters blowing them off."

"We don't have enough men here to deal with this," Lushkin was saying. "All of our mobile forces are down in the southern sector watching the Kazakhs and the French."

"We just had a radio call in on that too, sir," the lieutenant reported hastily. "Just before the shooting started here, the third battalion called in and said that the French were shooting up their defenses and apparently trying to move in this direction."

"They'll be wanting to link up with the heliborne forces," Lushkin said as the men jogged down a stairwell toward the basement of the building. "We've got a company of tanks positioned to stop them, so we'd better leave them just where they are and get the hell out of here in the meanwhile. They won't be able to search the city for us, our men would chew them up if they tried to go house-to-house, and they know it. Let's just let them move around if they want and just try to give them a good bloody nose. Once they start to take some casualties, Devi will be able to convince their governments to pull them back."

"I wouldn't count on Devi's influence anymore," Shchernikov said, shaking his head vigorously. "We know that he gave them a direct order, backed up by individual instructions from the home governments of each contingent, and that didn't do much good evidently. Oh, my God!" Shchernikov shouted suddenly, stopping halfway down a flight of stairs and grabbing Lushkin by the arm. "What about the firehouse?"

"I saw enemy troops on the roof over there as well, General," the lieutenant said.

"What are we going to do?" Shchernikov screamed, his already florid face turning beet red as he shook Lushkin by the shoulders.

"We'll keep our heads, first," Lushkin said, seizing Shchernikov by the arm and shaking him back. "We can't hold here *or* at the fire house right now. Once we've got the French stopped and our anti-air defenses have gotten their act together, the handful of infantry they get in here won't be able to get resupply or reinforcement either by ground or air, and we can mass as many infantry as we want to retake the place. The important thing now is to keep them from getting their hands on you, because, if they capture you, you'll be a hostage, and we won't be able to use our full force to finish them off."

Shchernikov nodded silently and allowed himself to be led into the dimly lit, damp subbasement. Lushkin and the lieutenant lifted a trapdoor in the floor, and all three men then climbed down a metal ladder into the sewer. Several other men had now appeared in the basement, some of them wounded, and they all began to file through the sewer.

Filthy water ran in the sewer up to the men's ankles as they sloshed along, using a flashlight that the lieutenant carried to guide their way. Shchernikov gave thanks to the great central planners of the old Soviet government who had gone to such great expense and effort to install these extensive underground systems of tunnels and rooms. While serving their peacetime function of a sewer system, they had also been designed with the thought of use during a war with the capitalist powers, enabling a large portion of the Soviet population to live and move in the midst of a nuclear war while their more prosperous capitalist enemies would be dying in their fine suburban homes.

One of Martin's armored cars was burning off to his right, having taken a direct hit from a T-72's 125mm gun. Ordinarily, the AMX-10RCs would not have been a match for main battle tanks, but at the limited ranges of city fighting, the maneuverability and speed of the armored cars more than made up for their lack of armor and their lighter guns. Three T-72s were also smoldering in the large industrial park in which the two forces played a deadly game of hide-and-seek, ducking and dodging behind and between buildings, or even directly through them, while infantrymen from both sides jockeyed for positions from which to fire their antitank rockets at point-blank range.

Martin glanced at his watch. He would have to keep this up for another ten or fifteen minutes. By then the Russians would have undoubtedly realized that the American thrust was the main one, but by then it would be too late for them to act on the knowledge. The target area around Government House would be secured, and he could withdraw his men back behind the line. But he was in no hurry. He was killing the enemy, and that was what he wanted to be doing.

The top floor of the Government House had been cleared, and Chandler was preparing to move to the next level. The first of the Argentine infantry had also arrived, and he noticed that they moved well, covering each other with their long FN rifles as they took control of the stairwell.

Chandler watched an Argentine and a British soldier signaling each other as they prepared to break through the door onto the next floor. Only a few years before they might have been fighting each other in the Falklands, and now they were fighting shoulder to shoulder, each wearing the same sky-blue headgear. No, he corrected himself, the Falklands was over a decade ago, and these two men were barely into their twenties, but the thought stayed with him. The two men probably didn't even speak a common language, but they had become part of something together. It was the same feeling that had come over him when his officers had agreed to this mission in defiance of the orders he knew each of them had received, just as he had received his from Elders and Devi.

It was a new phenomenon in the world, he thought, an international brotherhood of soldiers. They were not loyal to the secretary general in New York or to the UN, which were concepts that most of the men couldn't relate to. The only element of this assignment that meant anything to them was that they were part of UNEKAZ, this unit, this community of strangers in a strange land, facing the same dangers and the same handicaps. Their governments might try to impose their own agendas the way the Ukrainians had apparently successfully done with their contingent, but Chandler suspected that this would not work most of the time. For most of them, there was no longer a great enemy in the world—no Cold War, no imperialist struggles. The men's adherence to their civilian governments was mere tradition now. The real primal force of bonding would come from shared hazards and efforts. Malaysians would risk their lives to save Swedes, Nigerians to save Colombians. All they knew was that the guys in the sky-blue caps were the good guys, no matter what little flag patch they wore on their shoulders, no matter their religion or their language.

Chandler had thought, when planning the mission, to have the men replace their UN headgear with something that didn't stand out quite so much, camouflage or just about anything but sky blue. He had dropped the idea in the welter of other, more important aspects of the plan, but now he was glad that he had. He would have to get those damn white vehicles repainted, though, he reminded himself as the Argentine trooper kicked in the door and the Brit charged through firing from the hip.

There were fewer defenders on this level than on the one above, and it appeared that the defenders' main concern was to hold open one of the stairwells as an escape route down to the ground floor. Chandler could hear heavy firing and the occasional scream of a wounded man coming from the far end of the corridor where the main fighting seemed to be taking place.

Chandler ducked into an office and took the chance of peeking out of one of the shattered windows. The first American Bradleys were just pulling up, forming a defensive ring around the building and disgorging their blue-helmeted infantrymen, who charged through the splintered doors of Government House and into the firehouse next door as well. Chandler smiled. If the Russians were hoping to escape that way, it was already too late.

He followed some Argentine infantry down the corridor, now that it appeared increasingly unlikely that he would be able to find a quick and glorious death for himself today, stopping to check each office carefully. As he kicked through the scattered papers and upturned furniture and stepped over the occasional dead body, he was pleased to note that all were Russians. Just then one of the Argentines called to him. "*Mí Generál, mire usted por aquí, por favor.*"

"*Gracias.*" Chandler didn't have more than high school Spanish, but the man was waving him over and gesturing with his rifle into one of the rooms. It was a long room, laid out like a dormitory, with about a dozen beds lined up along one wall. In the far corner, huddled behind the last bed, crouched a dozen girls, all aged between about twelve and eighteen years. Half of them had the long dark hair, olive skin, and almond eyes of the Kazakhs, but the remainder were clearly Caucasian, with fair skin, and blond or chestnut hair. They all wore flimsy shifts and were trembling with cold and terror.

A young British officer had been sitting on one of the beds, trying to talk to them, and he now came back to where Chandler stood by the door. It was Captain Stephen Scott, a military intelligence specialist, who spoke excellent Russian.

"What is this, Captain?" Chandler asked. "A girls' school?"

"As near as I can determine, sir, it's one of those famous 'rape hotels' we've been hearing about, reserved for the use of Shchernikov and his Republican Guard officers. The girls are all relatives of either Kazakh officials or of influential Russians here in the city. Shchernikov was keeping them here as a means of control over their families and to ensure that the Kazakhs wouldn't level this place with their artillery . . . besides, of course, the entertainment value."

Well, Chandler thought, staring at the girls as they held each other, the stronger ones shielding the younger and weaker, Mr. Devi should be pleased. I've found at least a dozen Russians and Kazakhs who have learned to live together in peace. He wanted to capture Shchernikov very badly right now. He wasn't so concerned anymore with proving his case to the world about the bombing of the French headquarters or the attack on the Concert Hall. He had enough proof of that for himself, and it might be just as well to deal with the matter personally.

"Leave a guard on the room," he told Scott, "and see if you can't find some warmer clothing for them."

As Chandler reentered the hallway, he paused for a moment. Something was strange, wrong, but he couldn't quite identify it. Then he realized that it was the quiet. There was no more shooting inside the building, only the occasional faint burp of automatic-weapons fire from somewhere outside.

He and a small knot of British and Argentine soldiers quickly made their way to the far stairwell, where the most serious fighting had occurred. Medics were gently caring for several wounded men from both sides, and the stairs were littered with half a dozen Russian bodies. They worked their way downstairs to the main level and found Peabody prowling the main foyer, stamping his feet in disgust.

"Well, fuck me!" he shouted, waving his pistol over his head.

"Maybe later," Chandler said quietly. "What's the story?"

"The bastards are all gone!" he shrilled.

"They can't be!" Chandler shouted back.

"Well, not all of them," Peabody corrected himself. "We rounded up about twenty of them," he said, gesturing to an unhappy mob of men squatting against one wall, their hands clasped behind their heads as several American troopers watched over them. "We offed a few when we broke in here and worked our way up to meet with your men coming down from the roof, but there wasn't nearly the bag we'd expected. Then the men I'd sent down to the basement found their escape route."

"And Shchernikov?"

"Not a sign of him."

Chandler followed Peabody down another flight of stairs, and the cavalryman stood, hands on hips, over an open trapdoor in the floor.

"I sent some men down to check this out, but there are a dozen branches off this main tunnel within the first fifty yards, and we'd don't have a clue which way they went."

"No," Chandler grunted. "They'd just be able to ambush us big time if we tried to follow them down there. Shit! But get a demolitions man down here. I want those tunnels blown so that they can't use them to counterattack us in here."

"Roger, sir," Peabody said, and he passed the instructions on to an NCO nearby.

Back up on the street level, Chandler surveyed the prisoners.

"Any chance that some of these assholes were part of the original group of raiders from the Concert Hall?" he asked.

"That's what we're finding out now, sir," Peabody replied. "We brought along a couple of French troopies who had guarded them at one point to see if they could identify any of them, and it looks like they have."

Two husky UN soldiers with shaved heads under their sky-blue berets and grim expressions on their faces were sorting out the prisoners by the simple expedient of selecting those they wanted and hurling them bodily across the room.

"*Crapule!*" one of the Frenchmen grunted, planting a kick into the ribs of one of the chosen prisoners.

"Have them take it easy," Chandler cautioned. "We want those guys to be able to talk."

"They won't talk," Peabody said, shaking his head. "I had a long chat with Martin before the op, and he said that these guys knew that we wouldn't do anything to them, certainly nothing like what their boss would do to them if they did talk. The Frenchies found one guy who was still carrying a French MAS rifle, obviously a trophy he had taken when they killed their guards at the French compound. That's him over there." Peabody pointed to one of the prisoners with an angry purple welt down one side of his face. "We had trouble pulling the frogs off him."

"I don't blame them," Chandler said. "Well, anyway," he went on, gesturing toward the half dozen men the French had selected, "I want to take these guys with us when we leave. The others we'll let go, can't be loaded down lugging prisoners around with us."

Peabody shrugged his shoulders and finally holstered his pistol. Just then Wakeham strode into the room in company with the Argentine Meriani. The two men saluted Chandler.

"Sir, there's something I think you should see next door."

The four officers headed for the front door, or at least the pile of kindling that had been the door.

"There are still snipers about, sir," Wakeham was saying. "So I'm afraid we'll have to make a dash for it one at a time."

Chandler nodded. Wakeham went first, vaulting gracefully over the railing of the broad stairs down to the street and sprinting in a crouch, using the armored vehicles scattered around the small plaza in front of Government House for cover until he disappeared into a side door in the firehouse.

Chandler went next, preferring to run around the end of the railing, rather than risk the embarrassment of stumbling over it in an attempt to emulate Wakeham. But he didn't run very fast. The thought of snipers intrigued him, and he looked around at the tall apartment blocks and office buildings that loomed in every direction. He knew that his men couldn't occupy all of them, and while some of these other buildings bore the scars of recent gunfire, that would likely have only kept the enemy's head down. Any aged militiaman with a World War II–vintage rifle could conceivably pop him right here and now, and wasn't that what Chandler had been after?

But even as he thought this, his feet began to move more quickly, and he involuntarily crouched over, easing closer to the protective side of a parked Bradley. There was still something for him to do here, men he was responsible for, and he wasn't quite ready to go yet.

That was when the shot rang out, and a round clanged off the side of the Bradley, only inches from Chandler's head. He ducked down farther and began pumping his arms, covering the remaining fifty meters to the firehouse in, by his own estimation, roughly two and a half seconds.

When the four men had gathered again in the small anteroom of the firehouse, Wakeham beckoned them inside.

They stood in the large bay where the fire engines would normally have been garaged, wide enough for four large trucks side by side and nearly a hundred meters long, but there were no fire trucks, no ambulances. In their place stood three huge vehicles painted a bright army green, even taller and broader than the largest hook and ladder and over twenty meters long, their big black tires nearly the size of a man, but it was not the vehicles that caused Chandler and Peabody to gasp. It was the huge missile that each of the vehicles had mounted on its bed, still clearly bearing the red star and CCCP, the Cyrillic letters for the USSR.

"I didn't know that Shchernikov and his crowd had any SCUDS," Peabody said, whistling low. "And they talked a lot about that back at the Pentagon since those things were spread around like candy in the old Russian Army, down to the corps level. The intel people were pretty sure that the Russkies, I mean the ones from the real Russia, had taken all of them with them when they pulled out of all the Central Asian republics, not wanting to go through another Iraq thing trying to find and destroy them later. We figured that, since Russia was the only place they could really hit with them, the Russians would be real careful to pick up all the scraps."

"*Hijo de su madre,*" Meriani hissed. "Could he have bought them on the gray arms market or from some capitalist Russian army commander across the border?"

"These aren't SCUDs," Chandler almost whispered. "I wish they were."

"Then what the hell are they?" Peabody asked.

"I worked on disarmament issues for a while at the Pentagon, and had an illustrated chart posted on my office wall. I spent a lot of time twiddling my thumbs in that office and looked at that chart for hours. These things, gentlemen, are SS-25 intercontinental ballistic missiles."

"*Joder!*"

"Fuck!"

"Bloody hell!"

"Well," Peabody said brightly, "what now, Boss?"

"Look at how that slimy little bastard had these babies all polished up," Chandler said, walking slowly around one of the vehicles. "Not a spot on them. Even had this big white sidewall painted on the tires like the Soviets always liked to do for the May Day parade in Red Square. These things were his pride and joy."

"Do you suppose, sir," Wakeham asked, "that they've actually got warheads on them?"

"Dollars to doughnuts they do," Chandler replied.

"Well," Peabody insisted, "now that we're a nuclear power, what do we do with them?"

"I don't suppose you know how to take one of these things apart without making it go boom, do you?"

The three other men shook their heads, still staring up at the massive weapon.

"And I really hate to just leave them here," Chandler went on. "Soooo, I guess we'll just have to take them with us."

"Do you suppose he left the keys in them?" Peabody asked.

Lushkin and the other Republican Guard officers stood quietly out of the way as Shchernikov rampaged through the center of the command bunker located in the basement of an apartment block less than a kilometer from Government House. Lushkin thought it was almost comical how the old man's boots still squished with the piss and excrement they had waded through as he stomped around the room, hurling papers around him like confetti. But he didn't laugh or even smile, and no one else did either, because Lushkin would have killed them on the spot, even if he did appreciate the humor himself.

"How could they just drop right in on top of my headquarters and take my missiles in the middle of my own territory?" he screamed. "Where was my Guard then?"

Lushkin could have responded that they were fighting and dying for you while you were sloshing through shit, but he knew that it was a rhetorical question.

"Where are they now?" he screamed, stopping in front of a large map of the city.

"They're already on the road out to the airport, across the Green Belt," a young officer stammered, gesturing uncertainly at the map.

"Well, can't we break through them?" Shchernikov went on. "We've got tanks and artillery, and they're really just a police force, right?"

"We don't have much armor left after today," Lushkin broke in, hoping to put an end to this useless argument. "We lost over four hundred men killed and captured, nearly ten percent of our strength inside the city, and nearly all of our tanks to those damned helicopters. They may be a police force, but they have first-rate tanks and missiles, and they'd beat the shit out of us if we tried to break through." He let that sink in and then continued. "But we have a bigger problem."

"Bigger than that?" Shchernikov sneered. "Don't tell me you're worried about the men that they took prisoner."

"That's a problem, too," Lushkin said. "They can't intimidate them into talking, but what if they offered one of them a home out in the West. Can you be certain that one of those men wouldn't sing like a bird for that? But that's not what I was talking about."

"What then?" Shchernikov asked, although the possibility of one of the captured raiders being bribed into talking had obviously not occurred to him before, and his bushy eyebrows crawled down his forehead and onto his nose like two furry caterpillars as he thought about it.

"*We* may not be able to break through the UN forces to get the missiles back, because our main army is stuck up north of the Lepsa River, but the Kazakhs are still out there, and they've been massing their forces for an attack on the city. What's to stop them from over-running the UN and getting the missiles for themselves?"

"Mother of God!" Shchernikov gasped. "Do you suppose the Kazakhs know about the missiles?"

"If they didn't know before, they certainly know now. They have eyes all over the city."

The thought of the Muslims in possession of nuclear weapons made his head reel. His own plan for the weapons had simply been as a trump card to prevent his Russian brothers from abandoning him and the other ethnic Russians in Kazakhstan to their fate as they had done with the Russians living in the other Central Asian republics when those had fallen, one by one, to the Islamic fundamentalists. He had watched thousands of forlorn refugees wind their way up the dusty highways across the steppe, escaping from the south, and he had vowed not to let that happen to his own people.

Of course, the fact that *he* controlled the missiles and that this gave him almost total authority within the ethnic Russian separatist movement was secondary. What this did in fact was to guarantee that there would be a steady flow of arms and political support from Russia to the new republic they had carved out in the northeast of Kazakhstan and that Russia would welcome this state back into the fold when the time came. And the time had almost come. It had only remained to secure this final piece of real estate south of Lake Balkhash, with Alma-Ata as the capital. It would have cemented Shchernikov's position as the father of his country for all time and relegated the rump Muslim state of Kazakhstan to the subordinate status that it deserved without the industrial and cultural center of the old republic. But now all of that was in jeopardy.

"What can we do now?" he asked meekly, still staring at the map.

"Whatever we can accomplish, we can't do it from here," Lushkin said flatly. "The time has come to give up Alma-Ata, at least for the present, and join our main forces in the northeast."

"Give up my capital?"

"Just for the present," Lushkin assured him. "With yourself at the head of our main military forces, instead of those weak sisters running the provisional government in Semipalatinsk, we can come charging back across the Lepsa River and retake the missiles from the UN at our convenience, but sitting in the basement with a handful of weary militiamen around us, we can do nothing."

Shchernikov thought for a moment, his narrow eyes almost disappearing completely as he concentrated. "Perhaps you're right, Lushkin," he said finally. "And perhaps there's something we can do to improve our chances. Get Devi over here, right now!"

The missiles now were parked in a large hangar at the airport surrounded by the whole of the American armored cavalry squadron, plus the French. Chandler had advised Borysenko that the Ukrainians would have to take responsibility for the entire French zone and most of the American, but without explaining why. When Borysenko had strenuously objected, Chandler simply told him that he was redeploying the Americans and French, and if Borysenko wanted to provide some shield for his Russian friends against the Kazakhs, he had better comply. And he did. Now the Ukrainians held the eastern and southern portions of the perimeter, with the Argentines on the west and the British deployed to cover the road to the airport to the north, reinforced by the Japanese and South Korean military police companies.

Chandler strolled around the hangar watching his breath form little clouds in the cold air. The sun was just about to set, and there was a light dusting of snow on the ground, the first of the season this far down the mountain. In the horizontal rays of the sun, the mountains to the south glowed white and pink. He could just make out the Medeo sports stadium nestled in its valley above the city and the tiny cable car that ran up to it. One of the cars still dangled precariously from the cable about halfway up. Chandler had heard that there were still bodies in it from the days of the Islamic revolution that no one had bothered to get down. Why bother? he thought. There were plenty of bodies right down here; why go looking for more?

The operation against Shchernikov had not been without cost. Two Apaches and a Blackhawk had been lost and four crewmen killed, besides half a dozen more men on the ground at Government House. The French had lost eight killed and twice as many wounded in the south as the fighting had turned much more serious than Chandler had anticipated, although he now realized that he should have expected as much from the vengeful Captain Martin. Still, it had gone well enough, except for Shchernikov's escape. Chandler didn't know how the discovery of the missiles would affect things, but he could just imagine the midnight oil that would be burning in New York, Moscow, Washington, and elsewhere tonight, now that the full impact of his after-action report would be sinking in. He smiled at the thought.

He heard footsteps crunching through the snow behind him and turned to see Morgan approaching with Devi and Elders following him as quickly as their bureaucrats' legs would go. Chandler had specifically ordered that all nonmilitary vehicles be held at the entrance gate to the airport, nearly a mile away, as a security precaution, and he had listened delightedly to the screaming over the radio when Devi was forced to abandon the warmth of his Hummer. He stood now and waited for them. Devi was already yelling something, waving his arms, but the wind carried his words off toward the south, and Chandler just smiled at his mime act.

He finally picked up " . . . aggression . . . mutiny . . . World Court of International Justice . . . war crimes tribunal." Devi was yelling, and he made such an effort that, by the time he actually reached Chandler, he was out of breath and just stood there panting for a moment. Elders took over for him.

"On what authority did you conduct that bloody assault on Government House this morning, General?" Elders asked, bracing himself with his hands clasped behind his back.

"Without even informing my office," Devi gasped between breaths.

"On the basis of Security Council Resolution 1648, which empowered UNEKAZ forces to arrest individuals found responsible for the deaths of UN servicemen in Kazakhstan. According to information available to me, Shchernikov was responsible for the deaths of nearly one hundred French soldiers at their headquarters, so I chose to attempt to arrest him."

"And did you?" Elders asked, smiling slyly, since he already knew the answer.

"No, he escaped," Chandler replied, pausing to let Devi and Elders savor what they thought was a victory, "but I did happen across several of his men who were among the prisoners who escaped from the French at the time of the bombing and killed four more French soldiers in the process."

"And what proof . . . do you have . . . of that?" Devi asked as imperiously as he could between pants for air.

"Positive identification from other French soldiers who were guarding them, and the recovery of weapons stolen from the French compound at the time."

"That doesn't . . . prove anything," Devi snapped. "This city is wallowing in weapons."

"Not with serial numbers traceable to those of the French guards," Chandler countered.

Devi fumed in silence for a moment, then went on. "You directly disobeyed my orders not to leave your compounds."

"It was a simple misinterpretation, Mr. Commissioner," Chandler said coolly. "I understood that order to be based on the need for security, and, in my military opinion, the only way to ensure our security was to eliminate the threat from Shchernikov. I certainly would have advised your office, but we had reason to believe that there was a leak to the Russians from your staff."

"How dare you!" Devi screamed. "You directly disobeyed me, and you understood me very well."

"Sue me."

"I'll relieve you."

"I'll turn over command as soon as a replacement arrives."

"I'll relieve you immediately and give Morgan temporary command."

"I refuse, sir," Morgan said. "Respectfully. And if you don't mind my saying so, I think you'll find you'll get the same answer from every other officer on the force."

"I'll give command to Borysenko," Devi hissed.

"I think Borysenko knows that no one would follow him and that his chances of getting—what's the American expression?—fragged? the minute he sets foot outside the Ukrainian zone are excellent," Morgan answered.

"'Fragged?' What's this 'fragged'?" Devi asked Elders.

"It's a term from the Vietnam War, if I'm not mistaken," he replied, staring at Chandler with unconcealed terror in his eyes. "Derived from 'fragmentation grenade.' Basically means an officer getting killed by his own men, usually with a grenade tossed under his bed at night."

"Are you threatening him with murder?" Devi shrilled.

"Not in the slightest, sir," Morgan said. "It's just that Borysenko's popularity is at a rather low ebb right now, I'm afraid, what with him passing the Russians through his lines in his own vehicles and all."

"There's no proof of that," Devi insisted.

"There's enough for our men. We're not in a court of law here."

"You will be soon enough," Devi shouted, turning to face Chandler. "And you won't be in the tender hands of one of your own American military courts either. You'll be facing the UN War Crimes Tribunal, and that's *my* territory, General. I'll see to it that you suffer for this."

"I'm sure that you're not suggesting that you have a way of influencing the decision of that high court, sir," Chandler mocked him. "And might I ask what precise war crime I have committed."

"Don't worry about that," Devi said. "There will be a whole ream of papers in front of the prosecution on you."

Chandler just looked at the two diplomats with a bored expression on his face. "Doesn't anyone even want to see my new missiles?" he asked, in the tone of an aggrieved host wanting to show off his rose garden.

He turned and led the group over to the hangar where one of the huge doors stood open just wide enough for a man to enter. Elders stared at the huge missiles with his mouth hanging open, while Devi just scowled.

"Are you certain that they're nuclear missiles?" Elders stammered.

"Oh, yes, no doubt about it."

"And are they . . . *armed?*" he gulped.

"Yes. Colonel Morgan served on a disarmament inspection team recently, and he was good enough to verify that for us. These are even the new MIRVed version of the SS-25. Three warheads each, range of about ten thousand kilometers. These three could easily take out, for example, London, Bonn, and Tokyo from here," Chandler explained. "But I guess you're probably right. I should have just left them with good old Shchernikov where they'd be safe."

"Don't try to tell us that you raided Government House to recover these missiles," Devi sneered.

"No, it was a total surprise to me. Pure gravy, so to speak. Did I mention the little harem we also discovered, Russian and Kazakh girls held against their will and continually raped by Shchernikov and his friends?"

"Do you think I care about what happens to a handful of little whores?" Devi screamed. "I am a high commissioner for the United Nations, and you have obstructed my operations from the moment you arrived here, General. From this moment on I consider you to be in a state of mutiny and acting without the authorization of the United Nations, along with all of your men. What happens to you or what you do from here on in is of no concern to me." He turned on his heel and stamped off out the door of the hangar and back toward the main gate. Elders looked after him with an expression of mixed disbelief and disgust.

Devi went on for a few paces and then called back. "Elders, are you coming or not?"

"No, thank you. I'll find my own way back," he said feebly, and the three men heard Devi snort as he continued on his way, slipping now and then on the loose snow.

"What do we do now?" Elders asked timidly. Chandler and Morgan both clapped him on the back.

MOSCOW
1 November, 1500 Hours

"This is very bad, worse than I had ever imagined," President Balinsky was saying as he shook his head of bushy white hair. The members of his cabinet sat around the table in the Kremlin conference room examining the latest reports from Kazakhstan and from the Russian embassies overseas. "We have had to admit to the world that we *lost* three ICBMs and nine nuclear warheads and that they were in the hands of a 'warlord' in the midst of a civil war."

"Shchernikov is not a 'warlord,'" Marshal Malyshev growled. "He is a Russian patriot, and that is a very scarce commodity these days. I can't say that I blame him for taking those missiles as a guarantee of our not abandoning him."

"I was certainly reassured," Foreign Minister Gostev broke in, "to learn that the SVRR and the military had been aware for some time where the missing ICBMs were located, even if they couldn't bring themselves to share this information with the Foreign Ministry or any other branch of government—"

"Would it have made you any happier to know?" Malyshev asked, raising his eyebrows quizzically.

"No, especially since *I* haven't forgotten that this Russian *patriot* killed several hundred other Russian patriots in order to get his hands on the missiles in the first place. The man's a butcher and a maniac, and we should all be down on our knees in thanks that the weapons have been taken away from him. God only knows what he might have done with them."

Balinsky might be president of the newly democratic Russia, but he had been raised as a Communist, and to hear so much talk of God in the very halls of the Kremlin made the hairs on the back of his neck rise up. "I think that thanks to anyone might be a little premature, Mikhail Petrovich," Balinsky said. "The missiles might be out of Shchernikov's hands, but they are still deep inside Kazakh territory with two hostile armies between us and them."

"Well, let's go in and get them out," Gostev declared. "I'm sure the UN will turn them over to us, so all it will take will be for us to fly some aircraft in there, under escort if necessary, and remove the warheads and other vital parts. I assume that we don't need to recover the transporters or the booster rockets themselves."

"We could, but we won't," Malyshev stated flatly.

"And why not?" the diminutive Gostev asked, turning to look the burly marshal full in the face.

"Because we have been formally notified by the provisional governments of both the Kazakhs and the ethnic Russians that the entry of any Russian aircraft or military forces into their territory will be regarded as an act of war. Now, I'm not particularly convinced about the ethnic Russians. I suppose they just wanted to make a statement, but the Kazakhs certainly meant business, and it's their territory we'd actually need to enter."

"I know that the Russian Army isn't what it used to be," Gostev sneered, "but I should have thought that it could still take on the Kazakhs with some chance of success."

Malyshev lolled back in his chair, folding his hands over his expansive stomach. "Oh, I suppose we could go in and get the missiles without too much bother . . . but we won't, and I'll tell you why. If we did, that would be the outbreak of a real war, Afghanistan on a scale ten times larger and right on our borders. It would be Islam against the infidels, and all of the Central Asian republics would probably jump in on the Kazakhs' side, along with Iran and Afghanistan. We've got thousands of miles of border with them, and much of our oil reserves are located near it. They could bleed us white with guerrilla tactics, and we could never completely win. That's even ignoring the fact that the Chinese, if they ever got their own act together, would probably be only too happy to jump in along with them, and, no, the Russian Army isn't up to that right at the moment."

"So you're just going to sit here and do nothing?" Gostev asked, appalled.

"That's my plan," Malyshev smiled. "If the Russians get the missiles back, well, we'll tell them that fun's fun, but they have to give them back to us now, and they will, in exchange for some more conventional weaponry, but I can tell you right now that the army will not attack our fellow Russians in Kazakhstan. Even if I ordered such a thing, which I won't, no one would obey me. If the Kazakhs manage to get the missiles, we'll send in the air force and blast the whole area off the face of the map. Even a long war with the rag-heads would be better than letting them have nuclear weapons. But in the meanwhile, we are not about to stick our necks out on this matter."

Gostev turned to the president. "And this is your opinion as well?"

"It doesn't matter whether it is or not," Malyshev announced. Balinsky winced but made no comment. "The army has stepped in twice to save this government from overthrow, not counting all the times they saved old Yeltsin's ass. We'll continue to do that only because we figure that any alternative to the 'democratic process' is going to be worse for everyone. But we'll pick our own foreign wars, thank you very much. You've gutted the military to provide your peace dividend, and this is it, so enjoy it." He turned to Balinsky to emphasize his point. "You can replace me anytime you like, but if you push the military on this matter, you'll be the one sweeping the streets to earn your black bread and vodka."

Balinsky hung his head and avoided eye contact with any of the cabinet members. "Yes, I think that Marshal Malyshev is quite right. Prudence is what is called for at the moment. I'm issuing instructions that there will be no military action taken on this mat-ter, and that we will not permit any further UN support for their military forces within Kazakhstan to originate in or pass through Russian territory."

"So, we just sit here and hope for the best?" Gostev sighed.

"I guess you could say that," Balinsky replied.

ALMATY
1 November, 1900 Hours

It had taken even longer to establish the secure line to Washington this time, and Chandler was doing push-ups in his room while he waited for the call. He had gotten out of the habit of doing much in the way of exercising lately, and only his lack of appetite had kept him from putting on weight. But his slowness during the day's fighting had convinced him that he had better do something about it now. Besides, he felt a need for exercise, to feel his muscles burn and respond to his demands. It was a kind of pain that felt good for a change. He was between sets and mopping his sweat with a towel when the phone finally rang. Devi must have finally decided that Washington might be able to talk some sense into him, Chandler surmised.

"I hear you've had a busy day, little man," Alvarez was saying.

"Well, it's been rewarding. What's the word from Washington? I know what we can expect from the UN: nada."

"It took some doing to get the president to pay attention to the issue," Alvarez explained. "It seems he's got a big vote coming up in Congress on the new tax package, and he's been working the Hill real hard, what with the election not that far off and him being down in the polls and all. His advisers tell him that he needs a victory in Congress to enhance his image and that, with his limited experience in international affairs, he's more likely to screw up than score big if he gets involved in your business. Besides, since it's a UN operation, they're thinking it would be a relatively easy write-off if things go to hell in a handbasket."

"Are you trying to tell me that we're forgotten out here?" Chandler shouted into the phone, more to make himself heard over the static than because he was upset. Actually, he had expected something like this all along.

"Not forgotten, certainly," Alvarez said. "The military has been raising holy hell about this with anyone who will listen, and we do have our friends in Congress, but they're mostly interested in posturing for the elections themselves, so there's no big rush to get anything done right now. But it's more basic than that. No matter what they decide to do here, the Russians have closed their borders to UN military missions. Had you heard that?"

"Oh, yeah. We focused on that right away out here."

"Well, there's literally no way for us to get there from here except by going through either Russian territory, China, or the other Central Asian republics, and nobody's opening the door. So, short of shooting our way in, there's not much we can do."

"I can read a map as well as anybody," Chandler commented. "What I want to know is what's being done to get the Russians to change their minds."

"Oh, the State Department boys are trying to club them a little with the threat to cut off economic aid, and the British and French are doing the same, but the Russians say that they're not going to war themselves with the Kazakhs and they're not going to let anyone run a war from their territory, so there. All they're willing to give us is that any UN forces that make it onto their territory will be well-received and repatriated to their home countries immediately. The president finally settled on creating a blue ribbon commission to study the situation."

"That's comforting. So, what you're telling me is that we're on our own. No air support, no resupply, no evacuation?"

"That's about the size of it for now."

"Has it occurred to anyone that I might be tempted to *buy* my way out of here by giving up these damned missiles?" Chandler hated these secure lines, since he knew that the distortion in his voice caused by the encryption and decryption would lose the deadly undertone he was trying to inject into his speech, but he hoped that his message would get across anyway.

"In fact, that very thing came up at the National Security Council meeting I attended earlier today," Alvarez said. "I forget who said it. The Sec State, I think. But, anyway, I told him that I knew you better than that."

"I wonder if you do," Chandler said flatly. "Listen. I think we're going to be out of touch for a while, at least on this link, since I know Devi will pull the plug, and we don't have any other commo gear that will let us reach you."

"I think I know what you have in mind, Julian. It's a damn shame they wouldn't let us give you some of this state-of-the-art commo gear, but since you've got all those damn foreigners running around, I guess we couldn't, not that communications with us have done you a whole damn lot of good anyway."

"Precisely."

"Good luck, *hijo*," Alvarez said, and the line went dead.

Chandler took a quick, very cold shower and put on a clean set of fatigues. When he arrived in the conference room downstairs, all of his unit commanders (less Borysenko, of course) were seated around the table. The murmur of their conversation came to an abrupt halt when Chandler entered the room.

"I just got off the line with Washington," Chandler began as he took his seat at the head of the table. "And it looks like what we anticipated has come to pass. We're on our own."

There was a round of groans and the shaking of heads around the room.

"What the devil do they expect us to do out here on our own?" Saavedra asked, banging the head of his cane on the table. He was seated at one of the corners so that he could rest his heavily bandaged leg on an empty chair to one side.

"I don't know or care what anyone else expects from us," Chandler replied. "I only know these basic facts: A, The Russian government has cut us off from the outside world. They won't come and get us, and they won't let anyone else do it either, but they've also committed themselves to taking us in if we reach their territory. B, We've got three ICBMs that I don't want to see fall into the hands of either of these two gangs of killers. They could probably be disassembled or destroyed, given time, but we don't have either the time to do it or the technical know-how, and I sure don't want to go screwing around inside a nuclear warhead with a pair of pliers. I also don't think that these two gangs are just going to sit by and wait. They'll come after the brass ring as soon as they're ready. And C, we've got nearly four thousand men and women here, not counting the Ukrainians"—this brought forth a chorus of growls and hoots—"whom we're responsible for and whose job here is definitely finished. It's time to go home, gentlemen."

"You don't mean—" Peabody exclaimed.

"Just how far is it to the Russian border?" Chandler asked.

"I've escorted the convoy from Novosibirsk via Semipalatinsk," Kondo, the Japanese captain offered. "It was about one thousand kilometers from the border to Almaty via the M3 highway."

"Aren't you overlooking the detail, sir," Peabody objected, "that the M3 runs right through the main front line of the Kazakh and Russian separatist armies and that either or both of them might object to our going that way?"

"I'm aware of that, Colonel."

"Now," Peabody went on. "I'll be the first to admit that neither the Kazakhs nor the Russians are anything to write home about when it comes to modern hardware, and they don't even have all that many troops, but we've only got the equivalent of a cavalry regiment with limited fuel and ammunition, and you're asking us to move six hundred miles through completely hostile territory with no air support, no resupply, and fight and beat two whole armies on the way? If you don't mind, sir, I'm going to call my broker and tell him to put all my money in Kazakh war bonds."

There was some nervous laughter at this, but it was clear that the other men shared Peabody's opinion about their chances.

"You're right about the main rival armies being east of Lake Balkhash along the Lepsa River line. That's why we're going around the other side where the truce has been in effect for weeks. According to our intelligence, they've both only got token forces there, and no armor to speak of."

"But that route's fifty percent farther at least," Saavedra noted.

"And both sides can certainly shift forces fast if they have to," Peabody added.

"Not if we move quickly enough. Neither side can move as fast as we can. The main thing is that we can pull an end run by going up the M2 highway through Karaganda, then get out either through Semipalatinsk or Pavlodar to the border. Driving time alone, at the rate I expect we'll end up traveling, could be a little more than twenty-four hours, although I'm sure that it will take us longer than that. But the sooner we get the hell out of Dodge and put some miles behind us, the better our chances are of getting through eventually."

"That's an awful long shot, sir," Peabody said. "Will the road net be able to handle the traffic, especially the SS-25s? They're not exactly off-road vehicles."

"Over most of the route the terrain is a flat plain, so we can get around any road obstructions easily enough. There are a few rivers, which might pose a problem, but if we move fast enough, we should be able to take the bridges intact, and the main highway bridges are all easily capable of handling all our vehicles. If we do get stopped along the way, we'll just be back in the position we're in here, just a lot closer to the border and safey. It's a chance we'll have to take," Chandler responded. "Certainly no longer a shot than sitting here and waiting for the UN Security Council to get its shit together to come and rescue us? Anybody got any other bright ideas? I'm open to suggestions."

Chandler looked around the table, from face to face, and there were no more comments.

"Good, then. I want a full logistical plan worked up by 0700. The priority will be to get the people and the missiles out. Everything else is expendable. Equipment is only worth something if it contributes to that mission, otherwise we can do without it. Let the taxpayers send me the bill."

Some of the men shook their heads in doubt, but they all furiously took notes.

"We're not going to bother to tell Washington, London, or anybody else about this, particularly not any of the civilian officials here in Almaty. They have entirely too-close 'contacts' with one side or the other among the locals. Let's keep this as our little secret," he added. "Now," he said loudly, clapping his hands together and rubbing them vigorously, "what's for dinner at the mess hall."

"It's steak night, thanks to our Argentine colleagues," Morgan said, and Meriani took a slight bow. "But I'm sure the cook can whip up anything else you might like, sir."

"I haven't had a good steak in ages," Chandler said, slamming his palms on the table as he rose. "And it looks like we'll all be needing our strength over the next few days.

Morgan just raised his eyebrows and followed him off toward the dining room.

CHAPTER 5

Meetings went on late into the night at UN headquarters in New York in the wake of reports of a mutiny by UN peacekeeping troops in Kazakhstan yesterday. While a strict news blackout has been imposed on reports coming out of the former Soviet republic, it appears that the UN troops engaged in fighting against Russian separatist forces they believed responsible for the earlier car bombing of the barracks of the French UN contingent. Sharad Devi, chief UN representative in Almaty, has reported that some of the troops, including American Brigadier General Julian Chandler, have refused to obey orders, although spokesmen for the Pentagon have denied the charge. The Russian government, meanwhile, has curtailed all air traffic with Kazakhstan and sealed its borders. Informed sources here in New York claim that the UN plans to withdraw all peacekeepers from the Central Asian country in the near future, which could cause a new outbreak of fighting in the simmering Kazakh civil war. A spokesperson from the White House stated today that U.S. forces are *not* involved in any mutinous action and that recent incidents do not pose a security threat to our troops serving with the UN.

CNN

ALMATY
2 November, 0630 hours

While most of the single officers and enlisted men at Fort Lewis, Washington, lived for the weekend and made the roads leading off the base a veritable deathtrap between five and six o'clock Friday afternoon, Chandler actually preferred to hang around, unless he had scored a hot date with some coed from the university, which was a rather rare occurrence. With the married officers all off with their families, the Bachelor Officers' Quarters and the base as a whole was like a ghost town. He enjoyed walking around the vast base, checking out what movie would be playing at the theater that evening, shooting pool at the rec center without having to wait for a table. Since he didn't drink, he avoided what crowd there was at the officers' or NCO clubs and could enjoy the fresh pine-scented air and the view of Mount Rainier.

Chandler was taking one of these walks now, eating chocolate chip cookies out of a paper bag and sipping a Coke as he went. He was at peace with himself and glad to be a soldier, living in the insular, brotherly world of men in uniform. He thought it strange that Morgan should be there, since he knew that Morgan was British, and was some years younger than he in any case. He was thinking that Morgan should have been at Sandhurst or wherever the British officers trained, but Morgan approached him and laid a hand on his shoulder.

"Sir," Morgan was saying, shaking him gently. "I'm sorry to wake you."

Chandler blinked and tried to look at his watch, able to get only one eye open at a time.

"Jeez, it's nearly 0630," he mumbled. "I was out like a light. I don't even remember my head hitting the pillow. I haven't slept like that since . . . well, since I can't remember when. Thanks for waking me, Randy."

"I would have let you sleep a while longer, Julian, but there's a problem . . . I think."

"You think there's a problem, or you think that what there is, is a problem?" Chandler rubbed his fists in his eyes and rolled his feet to the floor.

"They're gone, sir."

"What? The missiles?" Chandler shouted, jumping to his feet.

"No, not the missiles. Just everyone else in the bloody city is all."

"What?"

"The Russians, sir. All of the Russians. Shchernikov and all his troops and, it seems, the civilians as well. Our troops were in a tight defensive posture in their positions, as we instructed them, so as not to give the Russians an easy target if they decided to try to get even with us, and it appears that during the night the Russians just packed up and left town through the Ukrainian sector, taking Borysenko and his men with them, I might add."

"Well, where the hell are they now?"

"We sent up some reconnaissance flights. They weren't hard to find. It looks like the lot of them moved directly north to Lake Balkhash rather than trying to make it directly to their own lines along the M3 highway. We've spotted dozens of boats either along the shore or coming down from the Russian side to the north. They're loading everyone and everything on board like a sort of mini-Dunkirk."

"And what are the Kazakhs doing about it?"

"Not much, it seems. Of course, the force they were gathering to hit the city with is down well to the southwest, far from the scene, and it looks as though the Russians along the Lepsa River staged a demonstration attack to pin the Kazakh units there. But even so, I would say that the Kazakhs made no effort to stop them. Why should they? What they really wanted all along was the city, and now it's theirs for free. No point in looking a gift horse in the mouth."

"Maybe, but I would have thought that the Kazakhs would have jumped at the chance to catch the Russians strung out on the road to even up the score a little bit. It makes me worry. Maybe the Kazakhs are saving themselves for something bigger."

"If that's the case, I suspect that we'll find out soon enough, sir," Morgan went on. "Qasimbekai has *announced* that he will visit you at 1100 hours this morning out at the airport perimeter gate. I suspect that he knows all about our little find at the firehouse and will be offering to take the missiles off our hands."

"He can kiss my butt," Chandler grunted as he headed for the bathroom.

"I doubt that that will be part of his proposal," Morgan said under his breath once the bathroom door was shut.

The unit commanders were again gathered in the conference room when Chandler and Morgan came downstairs. Each of them had a pile of papers and maps before him and the look of not having gotten much sleep the night before. The map of Almaty that usually stood on the easel near Chandler's seat had been replaced by a larger-scale one of eastern Kazakhstan.

"Good morning, gentlemen," Chandler said brightly. "I suppose you've had plenty of time to work out that little problem I set before you last night."

This was greeted with a round of groans, and Morgan stepped up to the map board.

"At least we came up with a full appreciation of the magnitude of the undertaking."

"I'd prefer we avoid the use of the word 'undertaking,' if you don't mind," Chandler chuckled. "It sets the wrong tone." The other officers laughed politely but with a certain nervousness in their voices.

Morgan took out his pointer. "The first thing to keep in mind is that our force will contain somewhere in the neighborhood of eight hundred vehicles. Assuming a standard tactical dispersal along the route of march of fifty meters between vehicles, that would make the entire column some fifty kilometers long from tip to tail. That would be very hard either to control or protect, so we managed to trim that slightly. Since there won't be any traffic going the other way on the highway, we'll alternate vehicles, one along the right berm, one along the left, and staggered every twenty-five meters. Also, we will have considerable forces out to the flanks for protection, so the column itself will be reduced to some twenty kilometers at most."

"So far, so good," Chandler said. "How about fuel?"

"That's going to be a problem. We've only got a limited carrying capacity, so we're eliminating some vehicles, but even that won't solve our problem. Unfortunately, these armored vehicles were designed with a serious appetite for gasoline, which was based on the assumption that one would have access to resupply from the rear. Since we don't have a rear or any resupply, we've got to carry it all with us."

"Can we make it?" Chandler asked.

"Not with what we've got. The only chance we have is what Colonel Saavedra came up with." Morgan nodded to Saavedra, who rose painfully to his feet with the help of his cane.

"We've been doing aerial reconnaissance all along of the opposing forces, and we dug up some satellite photographs that showed that the Kazakhs have established a sizable supply depot here at Chiganak at the southern tip of Lake Balkhash," he reached over and tapped the map, "for their forces to the north. We can't be sure what's there, but it looks like the place is still in use, and we assume that there would be fuel stores, at least since our sigint people have reported no complaints from the Kazakhs up toward Karaganda of fuel shortages. That's just a guess, but it's our best shot. I don't know if you're much of a student of military history, but the German General Erwin von Rommel, you know, the 'Desert Fox,' was able to cover the ground he did in North Africa during World War Two with the supplies his recon forces were able to steal from the British. No offense," Saavedra added with a nod to Morgan.

"None taken."

"So what are we going to do about it?" Chandler asked. "That's got to be over three hundred kilometers. We have to assume that the

Kazakhs will figure out where we're going by then. Wouldn't they have time either to pull the stuff out or destroy it before we could get there? Remember," Chandler added, "they don't have to wipe us out to get what they want. All they have to do is *stop* us. Sooner or later we'll run out of fuel, food, and ammunition, and they'll just come in and take the missiles at their leisure."

"We thought of that, sir," Saavedra went on, "and it ties in to my other problem. Our helicopters give us great mobility, but we can't run them without a fixed base with refueling, rearming, and repair facilities. We've got that here now, but once we move out, my birds won't last long."

"So what's your solution?"

Saavedra explained his plan to the group in detail for getting to Chiganak, and Chandler nodded in consent.

"Do you have any current intelligence on how strong the Kazakhs are at Chiganak?" he asked.

"Well, *current* intelligence, no," Saavedra admitted. "But, as of last week, we estimated that there was only a militia company on the ground."

"That could have changed a lot in a week."

"Yeah—like the rest of this operation is a sure thing," Peabody snorted. "It doesn't sound to me like we've got all that much of a choice, sir."

"I think you're probably right," Chandler conceded. "But what are we going to do about your choppers after we abandon the airport? They're only good for a few hours' flying time, and we'll be on the road a lot longer than that."

"We plan to load up the transports with any wounded or unessentials we can carry and fly them out to Novosibirsk across the border once we've gotten as much use out of them as we can. We'll dedicate some of the fuel capacity for the Apaches and just leapfrog them up the highway to keep their air cover for us as long as they continue to run. That's not the way they were designed to operate, and I expect attrition to be pretty high, but we're figuring them all as a write-off, so whatever use we get out of them in the meanwhile will be pure gravy."

Chandler could tell that, despite his cavalier mention of the loss of his aircraft, this was affecting Saavedra deeply, like an artilleryman abandoning his guns. He was glad that this was Saavedra's plan. Chandler had actually come up with a similar solution, but he would not have wanted to have had to suggest it to Saavedra himself.

"Sounds acceptable. Now, how do we stand on ammunition?"

"That's less good," Morgan admitted. "As you know, Mr. Devi didn't allow us to stockpile much in the way of munitions, and in this respect, he might have been right. You know that the Ukrainians were busily engaged in selling weapons and ammunition to the Russians, and there were cases of others doing the same during the course of the UN presence here. Then our little exercise of yesterday used up a great deal, so we're down to a little more than one basic load of ammo for the armored fighting vehicles and Apaches and very little artillery and mortar ammunition indeed. In fact, that's where we're weakest, just one battery of real artillery, and we know that both the Russians and Kazakhs are well equipped with big guns, since the Russians produced that cannon the way McDonald's produces hamburgers."

"Not much we can do about that," Chandler said. "I suppose that there's a chance that we'll pick up some ammunition as well at Chiganak."

"Maybe small arms, but I doubt that there will be any larger-caliber stuff that will be usable for our weapons."

"Is there any *good* news?"

"Well, the one really good piece of news is that we don't anticipate any air threat. If either side had a real air force, they could eat us alive out there on the open steppe. Our anti-air defenses are almost nonexistent, since those units were dropped as being unnecessary for this mission. All we've got are the hand-held variety of missiles, such as American Stingers or British Blowpipes, that sort of thing. Fortunately, when the revolution occurred here, most of the air force pilots were ethnic Russians, and they flew their planes off to Russia proper or destroyed them on the ground before escaping. Each side has perhaps a handful of old MiG-21s and some helicopters, but nothing major, and I doubt that they'll even risk what little they have against us."

"I hope you're right, Randy," Chandler said. "The important thing to remember when the men are getting the vehicles ready is that we take the bare minimum of material, just fuel and ammunition, as much of that as we can carry, and any spare parts which might be necessary for quick repairs. Any vehicles that have mechanical problems, we leave behind now. We won't waste fuel and time loading up trucks that end up left by the side of the road. There'll be enough of that despite our best efforts. Don't worry about trying to save equipment. Between the tanks and armored recovery vehicles, we can deal with any vehicles that get bogged."

"I'm still worried about water crossings, sir," Morgan said.

"Actually, there are only a couple on the route, minor streams really, since it's almost a desert anyway, and the Russians, bless their hearts, had built any number of concrete fording points, even if the bridges are out. The only one we've really got to worry about is the Irtysh, but that's up by Pavlodar, almost at the border, and I doubt that they'll be in a position to stop us if we get that far. Still, we just don't have a choice in the matter."

"I think we've got the idea, sir," Morgan assured him.

"Our first step will be to pull everyone in to the area around the airport. We'll stage out of here."

"When do we leave?" Morgan asked.

"I want to leave the city about 1400 hours."

"That doesn't give us much time."

"It doesn't give our enemies much time either. That's the idea."

The airport was a beehive of activity during the morning as mechanics frantically disassembled, cleaned, repaired, and reassembled trucks, Hummers, armored vehicles, and helicopters, stripping down all inessential gear and filling all available space with fuel cans and boxes of ammunition. Chandler and Morgan strolled through the base on the way to the perimeter gate, watching the men work as the outlying units pulled into the base and took up defensive positions.

"It may be a final surge of energy before the end," Morgan was saying, "but I haven't seen the men work like this since we've been here, sir."

"Their lives are on the line. I think it was Samuel Johnson who said something to the effect that 'there's nothing like a death sentence to focus your attention.'"

"Oh, I think it's simpler than that," Morgan said as they saw a squad of South Koreans helping Egyptian artillerymen break open crates of artillery rounds and store them in their self-propelled pieces and Japanese and Argentines chatting happily and unintelligibly as they cleaned their rifles. "Things were grim here before. There were occasional deaths and always the tension of possible violence just around the corner without the men having any control over it, nothing to *do* about it. There were frequent fights between units, over nothing at all, really, and little or no cooperation. There was also a growing drug problem. I'd caught men more than once smoking hashish on duty, and even heroin was making its way up from Afghanistan in some quantity. If anything, the danger now is worse than it was before. We've taken very serious casualties, and we're about to set off on a march of imposing proportions through very hostile territory indeed. We've been betrayed by our colleagues and abandoned by our own governments, and yet everyone seems happy as clams."

"I suspect that it's not the size or the danger of the task that either makes the men, makes us all either pull together or hunker down, it's knowing what the damn task is," Chandler said. "It may be a long way to Novosibirsk, but they all know that it's a fixed number of miles, and when they get there they'll be finished. They'll have done what they set out to do, to deliver those missiles and get out with their skins. That's very different from serving a fixed term as part of an unending struggle. You did your own time and kept your head down, just like we did in Vietnam or your folks still do in Northern Ireland. It's hard to motivate yourself for that."

They reached the gate and waited next to the small guardhouse, squinting against the cold wind, which was just starting to carry stray snowflakes and bits of ice, which stung their faces. A column of Russian-made GAZ jeeps pulled up to the gate, guarded by an armored personnel carrier, their tires crunching loudly on the snow and gravel at the edge of the roadway.

Qasimbekai got out, followed by several other Kazakhs. Chandler noticed that where previously Qasimbekai had always taken pains to wear a business suit, however poorly tailored, to emphasize his role as civilian government official, he now wore a set of camouflage fatigues, as did his officers. They all had the broad, olive faces and narrow eyes of their people, and Chandler imagined them riding up on shaggy ponies with bows slung over their backs, demanding surrender in the name of the Great Khan. Chandler could see that protocol was not going to be a major issue of the meeting.

"We have eyes inside the city, you know. We know what you took from the firehouse, and we want it," Qasimbekai stated flatly.

"You know that we can't give them to you," Chandler replied. "Wouldn't you be more comfortable if we talked inside the guardhouse?" he added, making a sweeping gesture toward the small building from which Senegalese guards watched warily.

"This is our land, and we are not afraid of its weather," Qasimbekai snorted. "We want the missiles, and, if you will not turn them over to us, we will take them from you. We know that you plan to leave here, and we will find you on the road if you will not be reasonable now. Any loss of life will be on your head, not mine."

"We will take no action against your forces unless you force us to do so," Chandler said, but even as he said it he wondered how honest he was being. Had they not just left a planning session for the seizure of the Kazakh supply depot at Chiganak? Well, by the end of this, with gross insubordination, war crimes, international piracy, and God only knew what other charges they could bring against him, perhaps "lack of candor" wasn't so bad. "All we want to do is evacuate your country. You now have control of your capital, which is what you said was your main demand, so you should be happy with that. The Russians massacred your leadership, and *we* captured them, and our men paid a price in blood for that. We have proven our good faith."

Qasimbekai smiled cruelly. "That brings us to our second demand. We know that you have as prisoners in your camp several Russian pigs who attacked the Ardash Orda Concert Hall. We demand that they be turned over to us for trial. They committed a crime against humanity in our country. They will be tried by our courts."

"I cannot do that either. They will be tried by a United Nations court for war crimes, murder, or whatever you like, and your government will be represented there, but I am not going to turn those men over to you for execution."

"Let me make this very clear for you, General," the Kazakh said without emotion. "We cannot let you take missiles out of our territory, because we know that your route will take you over Lepsa River into land of Shchernikov and his butchers, and we will not allow missiles to fall into their hands. *That* is something we will die to prevent." The Kazakhs began to move apart slightly, spreading to either side of Chandler and Morgan, causing the hairs on the back of Chandler's neck to bristle. Two of the Senegalese guards moved casually out from the guardhouse, facing down the Kazakhs and fingering their rifles menacingly.

"The missiles have been in their hands for some time, and nothing came of it," Chandler said, "but we don't intend to let Shchernikov have them, either."

"Nothing came of it," Qasimbekai spat. "Why do you think that we did not just crush the Russians with our artillery and storm this place all of these months? We knew of the missiles, and our only hope was to starve them out, or to come to negotiated settlement. We hoped that, with Almaty in our hands, the Russian government in Moscow would simply get their missiles back, and all would be ended, but if we tried to take the city, Shchernikov was mad enough to use them, even if he did not know how to aim them. And as for the prisoners, I cannot believe that your men will be willing to die to protect the same animals that destroyed your French barracks."

"What we choose to die for is no concern of yours," Chandler snapped. "If you want the missiles *or* the prisoners, you know where to find them. Come and get them."

Chandler turned on his heel, and Morgan followed him. When they had gone a few paces, he half turned and shouted over the wind, "There was something else we found at the Government House that some of my men were willing to die for."

He waved at the guards. They opened the guardhouse door, and out came six young Kazakh girls, carefully bundled in army overcoats. They ran up to Qasimbekai and his men, jabbering in shrill voices, and his officers gathered around, talking quickly and gesturing wildly. Qasimbekai looked up at Chandler with an expression of bewilderment. It seemed as if he were about to say something, but he bit his lip and simply led the girls back toward the vehicles. It was not until the small column had disappeared in the distance that the guards returned to the warmth of their building.

By nightfall, the work had progressed considerably. Long lines of white-painted trucks were lined up along the airport runway, some loaded with fuel drums, others with crates of food, ammunition, and spare parts. The three cavalry squadrons held the perimeter of the base, with the Argentine infantry and the military police, artillery, engineer, and medical and support units occupying the center. The cooks had laid on a tremendous banquet, Chandler having decided that what the men carried in their bellies would not have to be stored and transported separately. There was baked and boiled ham, the last of the Argentine steaks, roast beef, mounds of rice and potatoes, and tables groaning under loads of cakes, puddings, and hundreds of dozens of cookies. The mess halls had set up an "open house" to serve anyone who came around from any unit, and the men made a progressive dinner out of it, sampling the fare at each tent or building before staggering back to their billets with bloated stomachs. There was only minor griping about the lack of beer or other stronger refreshments, but even at that the men seemed to realize that this was a night they'd better still be alert for.

Chandler was finishing a huge plate of scrambled eggs mixed with chopped tomatoes and onions, his second, in the British hall, when a South Korean policeman came looking for him.

"There are people at the gate, sir," the policeman said in labored English. "Many people."

"What do they want?" Morgan asked through a mouthful of beef.

"You'd better come, sir," was all they could get out of him.

It was hard for Chandler to drag himself away from the warmth of the mess hall into the brisk night air, but, he thought, a little walk might help settle the load and make room for some desert.

When their Hummer arrived at the main gate, Chandler found himself facing Captain Greene, whom he had met first at the airport road battle, what seemed like years before.

"It's like déjà vu all over again, General," Greene said with a growl in his voice. "Look."

He pointed out beyond the chain-link fence and concertina wire to where the perimeter spotlights barely illuminated a ghostly crowd of people. They stood silently, alone or in small groups, clad in tattered overcoats or wrapped in blankets, some empty-handed, and some carrying luggage or pushing baby carriages loaded with packages.

"They started showing up about an hour ago," Greene said. Chandler could tell that the captain was ill at ease. "They didn't try to come in. Didn't even say anything to anybody, as a matter of fact. They're just standing there. We yelled at them over the bullhorn to go back to their homes, but they won't leave either."

"Who are they?" Morgan asked.

"All Russians, by the look of them. Mostly old folks, women, and kids. None of Shchernikov's thugs this time. We calculate that there's over a thousand of them, that we can see."

"I'd better see what they want," Chandler said calmly.

"No, sir," Morgan objected. "I'll go. My Russian is better than yours."

"You can come if you like, but I'm going out there," Chandler replied and, without waiting for more arguments, strode out to the gate, waving to the South Korean policemen to open it for him. Morgan hustled along behind him, and Greene signaled his men silently to cover them with their weapons.

In the center of the roadway stood an elderly couple. The man was tall and slender, probably over seventy, but he held his head quite erect. He was dressed in a dark suit and overcoat, both of which had probably been rather elegant in their day, but that day had been a long time ago. The woman was barely half his height and about the same age. She clung to his arm for support and pressed herself against him to shield herself from the cold. At her side was a small paper bag with twisted-paper carrying straps; a bundle of very old books could be seen peeking out the top.

"I am General Chandler, commander of the UN forces here. What can I do for you?"

"My name is Dr. Ilya Restrepov, and this is my wife, Lara," the man said, in heavily accented but correct English, bowing graciously. "I am . . . or was, professor of anthropology at the university in Alma-Ata until it was closed down. And we have come to you for protection."

"Why didn't you leave with General Shchernikov?" Chandler asked. "I was under the impression that the city had been completely evacuated."

"*General* Shchernikov, as you call him," the doctor said with a sneer, "would not let us leave months ago when we tried. It seemed to serve his purpose to have a certain civilian population in the city. And it seemed to work. After all, it brought the UN here, did it not? But we were not friends of Shchernikov, and he did not see fit to use his valuable transport to take us away with him when he left, and he would not even be slowed down by letting us walk with him. He must have been afraid that his agreement with the Kazakhs would be short-lived and wanted to get as far away from here, as quickly as he could. He did not tell us about the planned evacuation, and you may have heard the shooting when some of us tried to follow him.

"And now, here we are," he went on. "We have suffered months of shelling and starvation while Shchernikov has committed his barbarities against innocent Kazakh civilians. Now he has left us alone and unprotected, although Shchernikov's kind of protection included his men looting our meager stores of food, raping our women, and beating or killing anyone who objected. I am certain that the Kazakhs have their own Shchernikovs who will not bother to make any distinction between him and us, and who will take their vengeance on us for all of Shchernikov's wrongs."

"And what do you expect us to be able to do?" Morgan joined in.

"We know that you are leaving too. Everyone knows."

Chandler looked at Morgan and rolled his eyes. So much for security and the element of surprise.

"We want to go with you," Restrepov continued. "We will walk beside you if you let us. We will follow you in any case."

"You wouldn't be able to keep up with our vehicles any better than you could with Shchernikov's. In an hour you would be all alone on the steppe and at the mercy of the Kazakhs," Chandler argued. "How would that improve your situation?"

"The Kazakhs will come and kill us here. There is no doubt of that. At least on the open road they might be too busy dealing with you to worry about us. You see, we really have no choice. At least we trust that you will not shoot us the way Shchernikov did."

"Then I suppose we'll have to take you with us," Chandler said, shrugging his shoulders.

"Are you out of your mind . . . sir?" Morgan gasped. "There are hundreds of them. Where are we going to find the transport? We have barely enough working vehicles for our own men and a minimum of supplies. How can we do it? And what if there's fighting? Don't forget our *cargo*. We're going to be like a magnet drawing enemy attacks from every side. And now we'll be tied down protecting an immobile mob of civilians, and we'll be cut to pieces. And have you given any thought to the idea that this might be some kind of Trojan horse set up by Shchernikov? Even if these people aren't armed, they could cripple our defense if they wanted to during an attack. It's insane."

"I couldn't live with myself if we left them here, and I just don't believe that this is part of some devious plot by Shchernikov," Chandler said calmly. "The doctor is quite right. The Kazakhs would kill them all, or close enough to it. I'm willing to risk my life to try to save them, and that's all there is to it."

Morgan bowed his head for a moment in thought. "Well, we won't really need much food. Either we'll get where we're going in two or three days or we'll all be dead anyway. And we could save a few more trucks that had some minor mechanical faults. I suppose we'll find room somehow."

Chandler grinned and clapped Morgan on the back. Then he turned to Captain Greene, who had been listening uneasily from a few paces away.

"Get some more men down here and do a quick search of the people as they come in. No weapons and no luggage that they couldn't carry on their laps. At first light we'll go into the city to make a quick sweep looking for stragglers. It looks as though the Kazakhs are waiting until we leave to occupy the city, so we have some time."

Greene nodded. "It's a good thing, too, sir. If you'd ordered me to beat these people back again, well . . . I don't know what I would have done." Chandler just winked at him.

"Doctor," Chandler said, taking his hand. "You and your people are welcome. We'll make room for you all in our vehicles, and we will protect you as best we can until we get into Russian territory. In the meanwhile, we have quite a bit of food still to get rid of, and we'd be pleased if you'd join us for dinner."

The doctor blinked in disbelief for an instant, and then closed his eyes in relief, continuing to grip Chandler's hand firmly while his wife buried her face against her husband's chest and sobbed noisily. He then turned and called to the people standing nearby and relayed Chandler's message, which was answered with cheers and screams of joy. Slowly, hesitantly, the people made their way up to the gate as the American and South Korean soldiers waved them forward.

Chandler gently and discreetly patted down the doctor and his wife and peeked into the bag she carried.

"They are old books on the peoples of the steppes," the doctor explained, shrugging his shoulders helplessly. "I suppose it is foolish to carry such worthless things with us when we have had to leave behind everything else we ever owned, but I just could not bear to leave them behind."

Chandler took the old gentleman by the arm and led him toward the airport terminal buildings. He wondered what he would take with him if he had to put his most valuable possessions in a shopping bag and abandon the rest. But since his divorce, he really couldn't think of a single thing that he owned or anyone that he knew that he couldn't walk away from without concern. In fact, about the only thing he had now that had not been issued by the army was his wedding band, which he still wore and which he now rubbed absentmindedly. In that way, he supposed, he was a poorer man than this elderly refugee, which made it seem all the more worthwhile for Chandler to try to save him.

"Have you been able to communicate with your wife at all since you've been in country, sir?" Morgan asked.

"Oh, no," Chandler stammered, looking down at his ring. "Actually, I'm divorced, or separated. I'm not sure what level the legal paperwork has reached yet."

"Sorry to bring it up."

"If I might say," Restrepov's wife chimed in, "and I do not have the pleasure of having met your lovely wife, sir, but I do not think that papers will keep your wife from watching television news every night and worrying very much about you."

"Perhaps not," Chandler sighed. "This used to be the hardest part of being an army wife for her, and Lord knows I put her through it often enough. Then, when I finally did come home, I thought perma-

nently, we found outselves arguing about every little thing about running our home." Chandler paused briefly when he said the word
"home," as he felt the wind almost knocked out of him by the
thought of what he had lost. He no longer had a "home," anywhere.
"I tried to avoid problems by figuring out what subjects to avoid, but
I guess that ended up leaving not much to talk about at all, and then
she started complaining about the silence."

"Women are curious animals, sir, and no denying it," Morgan said.

"Not curious at all, sirs," Mrs. Restrepov continued. "Very simple.
I was a nurse at hospital in city these past months. When a patient
would stop speaking, this was a bad sign, and we would try anything
to get him talking again. Sometimes argument is easiest thing to start,
but any sign of life is good. I believe your wife saw your marriage the
same way. Argument was like pounding on chest of dying man. Looks
like fighting, but has different purpose. When she got no reaction,
she pulled sheet up as we did so often."

"Maybe I will give her a call," Chandler said. "That is, *when* we
get a chance to call anyone."

Chandler had sent his driver back to pass the word to the various
mess halls to expect a new wave of diners, and by the time he had
arrived at Restrepov's stately pace, the soldiers had cleared away
from the tables and were standing around the fringes of the room,
watching curiously. At first Chandler felt a certain resentment on the
part of the soldiers, and fear on the part of the dazed and apprehen-
sive Russians as they filed into the hall. After all, the only serious
fighting the troops had engaged in recently had been against the
Russians. But the large percentage of children soon eliminated all
reserve, and husky troopers were carting trayloads of cakes and sand-
wiches around the room and handing out canned soft drinks and car-
tons of milk. Chandler saw one muscular American soldier whom he
vaguely recognized sitting with a little girl with one pale cheek covered by a blood-stained bandage, cutting a steak into bite-sized pieces
for her and pouring her milk as the girl's mother warily kept one eye
on them, between bites of a thick ham sandwich.

"This is never going to work, you know," someone said from behind
Chandler as he sat watching the Restrepovs eat bowls of steaming
soup. He turned to find Elders standing there, shaking his head.

"Aren't you going to stay and greet the new government?" he
asked.

"No, I think the time has come to turn mother's picture to the
wall and head for the border. There are only half a dozen of us on the

embassy staff, and we've got three bullet-proof Blazers with plenty of our own fuel, so, if you don't mind, we'd like to join you on your little trek."

"We may need your extra seating capacity at that," Chandler said. "What do you suppose Mr. Devi is saying about all of this?"

"I don't have to suppose much at all," Elders replied. "He's been on the line with New York almost constantly since our session out here earlier, and the secretary general is trying to put pressure on Washington, which, in turn, is passed down to me. But I've come to the conclusion that this is a losing battle, and I'd rather not be associated with either Mr. Devi or the people he represents any more, no matter how fashionable they might be right now down at Foggy Bottom."

"What about the big career?"

Elders just folded his arms. "I went into the Foreign Service to serve my country, and I thought I'd serve myself at the same time. I had my degree from Georgetown, and I knew everything. The trouble was that I didn't know anything else." He chuckled to himself quietly. "I never wanted to be a soldier, an officer, because I knew that I could never make decisions that would cost people their lives, but I just realized that that is just what I've been doing here, and I haven't been doing a very good job—"

Suddenly, Elders cut off and the loud buzz of conversation in the hall stopped as the diners heard a horrible rattling, whirling noise followed by a shattering explosion. The fluorescent lights in the hall flickered and swung from side to side, and a fine dust dropped from the ceiling. There were no screams, however. The people had been through too many shellings for this to affect them unduly. Chandler was amazed to see men and women, even the youngest children, simply gather up their plates in a very businesslike way and retire under the tables to continue their meals. While the shells continued to fall, conversation soon resumed as before.

"You were right, General," Peabody said as he came jogging in from outside.

Chandler and Morgan followed him to the doorway where they took cover behind a wall of sandbags and watched the high-explosive and white phosphorus rounds hit up and down the runway where the line of trucks had been parked just before sunset. Chandler had waited until after dark and then quietly had the trucks moved, without lights, to scattered, hidden positions within the darkened base.

"I thought so," Chandler said. "You see, the Kazakhs aren't out to kill us all, just to lame us. They don't have the muscle to come in here and take the missiles yet. Their forces are mostly still well to the northeast. They probably figured that if they could knock out a significant portion of our transport, we'd never be able to make the move, and they could close the ring around us at their leisure."

The Egyptian artillery was already putting out a lively return fire, and two pairs of Apaches howled off into the night sky. Soon they could hear the scream of rockets and the chatter of the helicopters' guns, and the shelling stopped.

"There," Chandler concluded. "Just a battery or two. Can't blame a guy for trying, I guess, but this does take a load off my mind."

"How's that?" Peabody asked.

"Well, apart from the odd sniper attack over the past months, the only real fighting we've done has been against Shchernikov's people. I was a little reticent about what could be construed as an unprovoked attack against the Kazakh base at Chiganak. But now they've fired the first shot, and we're good to go."

"But we *were* going to hit Chiganak anyway, right?"

"Oh, yeah, but now I feel better about it. Do you suppose that there's any of that strawberry shortcake left?"

CHAPTER 6

THE M3 HIGHWAY NORTH OF ALMATY
3 November, 1730 Hours

Greene's estimate of the number of Russian refugees had turned out to be rather on the conservative side. In the course of the night hundreds more drifted toward the airport, and a sweep of the now truly deserted city by squads of American and British cavalrymen brought in even more until more than two thousand bedraggled, shivering, and terrified men, women, and children had been gathered within the UN perimeter. While the medical staff tended to their wounded, of which there were quite a few, and the cooks gladly distributed the perishable food that they would have had to leave behind in any case, Chandler and Morgan were left with the task of finding room for them all aboard the available transport.

It had taken all night and most of the morning to make additional room on the existing trucks, primarily by discarding food, communications gear, and engineering equipment, which the column would just have to do without. Even personal gear and clothing had been largely abandoned to find space for a few additional passengers. A dozen deuce-and-a-half trucks that had been slated for destruction as surplus had been reprieved at the last second and pressed back into service, and the search for further refugees had also uncovered a windfall of six large city buses in running order, which were provided with fuel and added to the convoy.

Chandler had had considerable experience conducting road marches during his career, but this monstrous column now contained over one thousand vehicles, in addition to some eighty helicopters that would also be involved in the move. The men and women in the column came from nearly a dozen different countries with different cultures, spoke about half as many different languages, and had been trained in different operating procedures in their armed forces. They would be facing two hostile armies that, if not well equipped, could be fanatical in their pursuit of victory over their enemies, and Chandler's little command was now the sworn enemy of both sides. To make matters worse, the sprinkling of snow that had dusted the city off and on for the past couple of days had turned into a driving snowstorm, not the classic ones typical of the legendary Siberian winter, since it was still only late autumn, but quite enough to obscure the drivers' vision and make exposed skin burn with the cold.

One troop of American armored cavalry led the parade out of the air base in the midafternoon, driving north along the M3 highway. The British squadron screened the right flank, running on a parallel course over the open, flat steppe that at least served to facilitate cross-country movement and prevented the column from being totally tied to the roads. Another American troop screened the left flank, and the third was held in reserve behind the lead unit. The reduced French squadron would be the rearguard, while the body of the column would be formed by the supply trucks, the artillery, engineer, and support units, and the all-important SS-25 TELs, under the immediate protection of the three military police companies.

Chandler and Morgan sat on the hood of Chandler's Hummer in the gathering darkness of the fall afternoon several miles north of the airport on the four-lane M3 highway at its intersection with the narrower P10 bypass. The P10 branched off to the southwest, forming an arc around Almaty, and intersected with the northwest-running M2, which led toward Chiganak. While the lead elements of the American armored cavalry were already some eight miles to the north massed along the Ili River, the body of the column had yet to reach the P10 turnoff, and the rearguard had yet to depart the airport.

"Aerial reconnaissance reports things are largely unchanged," Morgan was saying. "The Kazakhs are dug in across the highway north of the Ili River in nearly division strength, mostly infantry, but with about a battalion of tanks and plenty of artillery. With Lake Kapchagayskoe covering their left flank, there would be no way for us to get north except by going straight through them."

"And to the west?" Chandler asked.

"So far, so good. It looks as though word has gotten out that we're trying to bull our way through by the direct route, and they don't appear to have reinforced Chiganak or sent any other units out that way. And behind us, they're only just starting to send skirmishers into the outskirts of the city."

"Then I think it's time to make our move. They don't have much in the way of high-tech vision equipment, and the last clear view any observers will have had of us will have confirmed our northerly direction of march." Chandler could feel the electric excitement in his veins as he raised his radio microphone to his lips. It was a tremendous gamble, but he felt a sense of power, as if this enormous snake of vehicles and men were part of his own body, its combined horsepower and firepower responding to his will as would his arm or his leg. He gave the prearranged code message. "All stations, please acknowledge radio check." While each station on the radio net did acknowledge and report the clarity with which it was receiving his signal, the message meant a good deal more.

Peabody heard the message over his radio headset as he stood in the turret of his M-1 tank, which accompanied the cavalry troop that formed the left-flank guard of the column. He dropped down inside and quickly switched channels on the radio and blared out his orders to the troop commander, again disguised by an open code.

"I see unidentified vehicles moving off to your left," he said, trying to keep the nervousness out of his voice. "Investigate and report."

"Roger that," the voice crackled in reply.

The nine tanks and fifteen Bradleys of the troop suddenly did a simultaneous pirouette to the left and raced westward on the two-lane P10 highway. An Abrams led the way and the other units were stretched out behind along the road. Prudence would have dictated setting out flank guards, but Peabody knew that speed was their best protection now, and the quicker he could get to Chiganak, the better the unit's chances of survival would be. He would have to take the chance of some losses if the enemy sprang an ambush on him now, because he also knew that, behind him, the long, unwieldy column would be making the surprise turn west off the M3 and following in his wake. The cavalry troop, which had been the advance guard, would automatically become the right flank guard and eventually the rearguard, following along behind once the entire column had moved off to the west. He had debated whether to accompany this spearhead unit or stay back with that troop, since they would be the ones to catch hell from the Kazakhs once they realized what the UN forces were up to, but his cavalryman's blood had demanded that he be in the lead, and besides, Chandler and Morgan had volunteered to watch over the rear. His heart raced along with the engine of his tank and they bumped onto the road and followed the troop toward Chiganak.

By Peabody's calculations, they had to cover just over three hundred kilometers, in the dark, through territory nominally controlled by the enemy. At the maximum speed of the column, which had been optimistically set at thirty miles an hour, even if they didn't run into any resistance, it would take them at least seven or eight hours to reach Chiganak, and probably a couple more to secure the place. They had reason to hope that the Kazakhs wouldn't realize their change of direction for a couple of hours, maybe not even until morning, when they would realize that no UN attack on their Ili River positions had occurred. But Peabody could be mistaken. There could be some ragtag platoon of militia out there on the road with a radio, which could hardly miss the passage of almost a thousand heavy vehicles on an otherwise deserted highway. And that same platoon might have a few antitank missiles, enough to force Peabody's men to deploy to deal with them. Or maybe there would be a minefield that would have to be cleared. All that would take time, and as soon as the Kazakhs realized that they had been hoodwinked, they would come down like a ton of bricks on the rearguard; even a very good company can't hold out long against even a very bad division. It was just a matter of physics. It was definitely going to be a long night.

SOUTH OF CHIGANAK
3 November, 0000 Hours

Saavedra resented having to ride as a passenger in the left seat of this Blackhawk, but he had to admit that his wound made it impossible for him to pilot an aircraft on such a mission. He had even overheard a couple of comments made, supposedly out of his earshot, that it was about time that the "old man" stepped aside and let the squadron's pilots do the flying and limited himself to command. But it still made him uncomfortable, and he had to consciously restrain himself from grabbing at the controls when the young warrant officer pilot made a move different from what Saavedra would have done himself. That had done nothing to improve his mood, but he was buoyed somewhat by the knowledge that his unit's part in the operation was key. If he failed, this whole damn force, with all of its armor and firepower, wasn't going to get anywhere. Even if he succeeded, they only had an outside chance, but without him, they were dead meat.

His own twenty Blackhawks plus a pair of French Super Puma helicopter transports were now whipping along, flying nape of the earth, as they swung in a wide arc southwest of the M2 highway to come in on Chiganak from the south. Between them they carried the squadron's own aero-rifle company, plus another full company of Argentine infantrymen, nearly three hundred men in all. They were escorted by some two dozen Apaches, half as many armed OH-58 observation choppers, and a couple of British Lynxes that happened to be caught in Almaty when the crisis occurred.

On paper it sounded rather cut-and-dried, Saavedra thought as he used a small penlight to examine one more time the map strapped to his thigh. They would swoop in on the almost undefended (he hoped) supply depot at Chiganak and take the place, and the infantry would dig in while the Blackhawks raced back to the airport once more to load up their mechanics and the most vital tools and spare parts, plus the last of the Argentine infantry security force at the base. They would hit Chiganak probably within an hour of when the main column made its massive westward turn at approximately 0000 hours. They had already been airborne for over an hour, and hopefully the column would turn before the Kazakhs got any inkling of what was afoot. Even if the Kazakhs did see the move and jump to the right conclusion instantly, the difference for the initial assault on Chiganak would be marginal, since reconnaissance didn't report any anti-aircraft defenses to speak of and only a small guard force.

However, that left at least four or five long hours, and probably more like six or eight, *after* the enemy had been fully alerted by the seizure of Chiganak that the UN infantry would be out there, all alone, waiting for the main column to join up. If the Kazakhs had a company of tanks stashed somewhere nearby, which was always possible, and could scrape up a few hundred infantry to go with them, the Argentines and his own infantry would be sucking wind for quite a while. Saavedra *really* wished that he could be at the controls on this one.

THE M2 HIGHWAY WEST OF ALMATY
3 November, 0000 Hours

Captain Martin also received the radio net check message and screamed over the intercom to his driver to move out. With a single troop of a dozen of the big AMX-10RC armored cars, a dozen armed jeeps, and three VAB wheeled APCs crammed with infantry, Martin had ostensibly been conducting a final security patrol off to the southwest of the airport; he made sure to keep in frequent radio contact about his location and progress, for the benefit of anyone who might be listening. The "go" signal had just *happened* to find him several miles northwest of Almaty on the M2 highway, which put him substantially closer to Chiganak than the main column, which would have to come down the P10 and turn onto the M2 long after Martin had passed the junction.

Furthermore, his wheeled vehicles could move at over fifty miles per hour, if he didn't take any special precautions, which he didn't plan to do. This would cut his driving time to the supply depot to perhaps four hours—*if* everything went smoothly. That difference in time could make the difference between survival and destruction for the heliborne forces. His priority was to tear up the highway to Chiganak and to hunker down with the infantry there until the main body arrived. Martin would be out on his own, for better or worse, since he could count on no help himself for his small force. While he would have preferred to be fighting Russians at this point rather than Kazakhs, his blood was up, and any fight was better than none at all.

SOUTH OF CHIGANAK, NEAR KHANTAU

Mahmud Kabrak lay back on the impromptu bed of spare blankets that had been made up for him in the back of his GAZ jeep. It was still early evening, but it was now totally dark, and there was nothing much that he could accomplish on a road march, so he might as well get some rest.

He thought back to his days of running guns into his native Afghanistan across the border from Peshawar; those endless miles he walked over high mountain passes, the bitter cold, and the ever-present threat of a sudden attack by Soviet or Afghan government aircraft or by Soviet troops brought in by helicopter. But that was a long time ago. The Soviet-backed government in Kabul had fallen, and his faction of mujahedin had gone on to compete in the still-smoldering battle for domination of the ruins of the nation.

When Kabrak had ridden into Kabul aboard a captured armored personnel carrier that was still emblazoned with the white aircraft and parachute emblem of the Soviet airborne forces, he had thought that things would go back to the way they were when he was a medical student at the university, but they didn't. The city was just a burned-out shell—not that it had exactly been Paris before the war.

Most of the people he had known were either dead or had fled to Pakistan or Iran, and ten years of fighting had dulled his taste for medicine. He found that it was much easier to blow people up than to try to piece them back together. So he had stayed on in the new army and was now commander of the 9th Division, the spearhead of the Islamic fundamentalist group within the new Afghan government.

Consequently, it had not come as a surprise to him that his division was selected to become an Afghan "expeditionary force" to help their Muslim coreligionists in Kazakhstan. He had already fought in Tajikistan on a more covert basis. This time his government had decided that since it was likely that a peace treaty would soon be signed between the Kazakhs and the Russian separatists, it would give them more influence with the Kazakh government if Afghan support were more substantial, especially since it looked as though there wouldn't be any more serious fighting. The Russian abandonment of Almaty just the day before seemed to confirm that view. His division had been diverted in Bishkek northward from their goal of Almaty and was now on the P140 highway, approaching the town of Khantau, about sixty miles south of Chiganak. There they would turn northwest onto the M2, to bolster the Kazakh lines west of Lake Balkhash.

Kabrak's long years as a guerrilla fighter had instilled in him the habit of secure movement. That was why his division moved only by night, taking cover during the day from possible aerial observation.

It wasn't much of a division, by Western standards at least. Kabrak had about four thousand men, less than a full-strength Western brigade, but they were all mounted on vehicles, making his virtually the only fully motorized division in the Afghan Army. He also boasted a full battalion of thirty venerable T-54 tanks and two batteries of towed 122mm artillery; also, one of his infantry battalions was equipped with BTR-60 APCs. This sort of unit wouldn't have lasted long on a "conventional battlefield" against a modern army, but for Kazakhstan it was a formidable force indeed.

Kabrak turned over and hacked loudly, trying to make himself more comfortable. He was disappointed that he wouldn't be able to participate in the looting of the Russian civilians of Almaty, but at least he wasn't walking this time. At his division's current leisurely rate of advance, they would reach Chiganak to refuel in less than three hours, and his aide would wake him then for dinner, and there would likely be the usual boring round of speeches by local politicians and mullahs. In the meanwhile, he might as well get some sleep.

NORTH OF THE ILI RIVER

Qasimbekai scanned the horizon with the night-vision scope his
Iranian military adviser had provided him with. Qasimbekai resented
the man's pompous know-it-all attitude, but he had little choice but
to listen to him. Although Qasimbekai had served two years in the
Red Army and had even seen combat in Afghanistan, like most non-
Slavs in the old Soviet military system he had been relegated to
unskilled tasks, rising only to be a sergeant of a construction platoon
whose task was to repair the roads and bridges the mujahedin were
constantly destroying. Consequently, neither Qasimbekai nor most of
the officers in the new Kazakh army had much experience of manag-
ing large units in combat. Still, while he recognized that the Iranian
had long years of experience fighting the Iraqis, he was also aware
that the Iranians had not done particularly well in that long war, and
he would have felt much more confident with, well, he couldn't
think offhand of any Islamic nation's army that had done exception-
ally well in the past couple of decades, but he would rather have had
someone else all the same.

Qasimbekai could just make out what the Iranian had identified
for him as American armored personnel carriers, the advance guard,
no doubt of their column, now sheltering in narrow depressions in
the open grassland beyond the small, muddy river. The Iranian had
said that the Americans would have spotted the Kazakh positions, or
guessed where they would be, and would be waiting for their combat
elements to join up before attempting a crossing of the narrow Ili
River. It was easily fordable, and the Kazakhs had left standing the
highway bridge that spanned it, but it would still pose some tactical
problems in terms of deployment. *That* was the sort of thing
Qasimbekai resented, that attitude that "you wouldn't understand
the details, so don't worry your head about them, but we *military*
men speak a common language and understand each other." It left a
sour taste in his mouth just to think about it.

But he had to admit that the positions the Iranian had laid out for
the Kazakh forces looked very solid. The tanks each had two or three
alternate firing positions behind protective berms; the antitank guns
and missiles could cover any approach for miles, from the lake on
their left to the sand desert on their right that stretched along the
southern side of the Ili all the way up to Lake Balkhash, making movement of mechanized ground forces from there virtually impossible.
They had even scattered extensive minefields along the north bank of

the Ili River, both to channel the attackers into the defending guns' sights and to disable their vehicles in the killing zone.

The Iranian, with complete self-confidence, had predicted that the enemy would hit them with armor and helicopters first to force a breakthrough. They had several precious ZSU-23/4 anti-aircraft tanks positioned behind the front lines and had handed out dozens of SA-7 shoulder-fired missiles to deal with the air threat. They were both confident that the few enemy tanks could be destroyed at the river. Just in case, Qasimbekai had also coerced the Kazakh High Command in Dzhambul into stationing a squadron of twelve Mi-24 gunships nearby at Taldy-Kurgan to the north, along with several Mi-8 transports with additional infantry to deal with any possible enemy penetrations of the line. Then, they had a company of tanks and a battalion of mechanized infantry in readiness on the right flank prepared to ford the river and slam into the demoralized enemy ranks and seize the SS-25s before they could be damaged or destroyed. The only handicap for Qasimbekai's forces would be that they daren't use their substantial superiority in artillery to smash the enemy for fear of hitting the prized missiles.

All things considered, however, Qasimbekai had reason to be contented. There was no way in the world that the enemy could get through this position. Qasimbekai might have to take constant advice from an Iranian, but he was still the nominal commander of this army, which would make his country a nuclear power within the next twenty-four hours. His people would know how to reward him for that kind of service. He was already something of a hero for surviving the attack on the Ardash Orda Concert Hall, and he had taken no small share of the credit for the Russian abandonment of Almaty. With this one last achievement under his belt, he might just have to get used to the idea of being the new president. Yes, he thought he might be able to handle that.

SOUTH OF THE ILI RIVER

Chandler glanced at his watch nervously every few seconds as he supervised the Israeli engineers frantically laying mines behind the tissue-thin line held by the single troop of American cavalry facing the Ili River. The choppers should be hitting Chiganak any moment now—or shouldn't they have done it already? his fevered mind asked him. So far there was no sign that the Kazakhs had noticed the main column's divergence, but then the last of the trucks had only just made the turn off the M3. Even when the attack on Chiganak went in, it still might not immediately tip their hand to the Kazakhs, who might figure that it was some kind of diversion and wait for a few more precious hours before they came boiling across the Ili River, where they would outnumber the Americans perhaps one hundred to one.

Of course, the Americans had far superior weapons, including a pair of Apaches Chandler had taken from the Chiganak attack force, a dispersion of forces that would be considered a cardinal military sin if he failed. But if he succeeded, the Americans would be able to give the attackers a severe bloody nose at long range, then retire a couple of miles. The minefields would slow the pursuing Kazakhs down, but then it would be "Katy, bar the door!"

The one advantage Chandler had was that the Kazakhs would have to come across right here and follow generally the route of the column. They couldn't cut off the UN column closer to Lake Balkhash because there were no other crossings of the Ili River closer to the lake; even if they could get across, they wouldn't get far because of the broad sand sea south of the river, through which no sizable mechanized force could travel.

For the first fifty or so miles on the M2, however—the part the column was still crawling down—it ran parallel to and only about ten miles west of the M3. The two roads were separated by open, flat ground, which meant that the Kazakhs could quickly catch the column until its tail safely crossed the narrow Kurty River, a tributary of the Ili, and the road veered westward. The column would not cross the Kurty for at least another hour.

With Chandler's delaying tactics, even the slow-moving column would be able to outpace its pursuers, but only if there was no resistance on the other end. Even the time it would take to refuel the vehicles—if he reminded himself, they were fortunate enough to capture Chiganak and find sufficient fuel stores there—would be paid for in the rearguard's blood. And if a substantial Kazakh force got ahead of the column, it could use the same tactics that Chandler was planning to use here. With his vehicles burning irreeplaceable fuel and Kazakh forces rapidly converging, time was entirely on the enemy's side. He pulled up his sleeve to look at his watch again. It was 0000 hours.

"I suspect that they'll tell us over the radio when they attack Chiganak, Julian," Morgan mumbled as he pored over a fire plan.

Chandler just sighed.

NEAR THE KURTY RIVER

Bakyt wrestled with his conscience as he debated whether or not to wake Yerik and tell him about the trucks. Bakyt was only fifteen, and Yerik was not only twice his age but had even served in the old army, the Soviet one, and he (justly) considered it degrading to be placed on the isolated outpost with a mere boy like Bakyt when real fighting men were in such short supply elsewhere on the front. He often took out his frustration on Bakyt and cuffed him about the ears for any perceived disrespect or act of sheer ignorance on the boy's part, which Bakyt was only too ready to admit he committed with discouraging frequency. In his calmer moments, Yerik had explained to him that this was simply the way of the old army, with the senior conscripts pounding the newer ones, just as he had suffered during his first year of army life. The difference now, Yerik never failed to mention, was that in the old Soviet army, he had taken additional abuse from the Slavs for being a Kazakh, and he pointed out that Bakyt should be grateful to Allah that he would never have to suffer this indignity. Bakyt was surely grateful for this, although he had a suspicion that Yerik felt that Bakyt should undergo additional beatings to make up for this otherwise "soft" version of the military experience.

For over an hour dozens, maybe hundreds, of trucks and tanks had been rolling past their tiny hilltop outpost just north of the M2 highway near the town of Akchi. Bakyt had long since lost count of them, but he had never even imagined that there were so many trucks in the entire world, and most of them were painted white like those of the UN. He could see for miles over the otherwise flat, barren terrain, and there was no sign of other Kazakh forces besides him and Yerik anywhere in the area.

Bakyt thought that someone should report this, but he had been soundly thrashed earlier that same day for wanting to call on their radio to report that a pair of helicopters was overflying their position. Yerik had pointed out that the battery in the radio was the only one they had left, and to waste it on such nonsense was criminal. Moreover, he told Bakyt that the enemy could hear every word they said on the radio, something Bakyt had never even considered, and the enemy helicopters would also be able to tell where the radio transmission came from and swoop down and bake them alive with fire dropped from the sky. He certainly didn't want that, and this huge army passing before him could obviously do even more damage than a pair of helicopters.

No, it would be better to wait. If Yerik awoke, he would see the trucks and know what to do about them. Or, more likely, since Yerik was a notoriously sound sleeper, someone else would spot the column, someone with more authority, and report it if it were necessary. Bakyt nodded to himself and slapped his face to keep from falling asleep. Yerik would hit him far harder if he caught him doing that.

CHIGANAK

Chiganak wasn't much of a town. In fact, it had barely enough drab little one- and two-story cinder-block buildings to justify having a name at all. It was almost lost in the emptiness of the barren country. There were plenty of electric lights burning in Chiganak, however, a sure sign, Saavedra thought, that it was a supply depot. They had fuel to spare for their generators, and supply people don't like to suffer any inconveniences if they can help it.

He'd just done a quick orbit of the depot, which was half a click outside of the town itself. He'd spotted a couple of obsolete anti-aircraft weapons, a couple of small armored cars, and some halfheartedly prepared infantry positions, about enough for a weak company, and that was it. There might be more enemy troops in the town, but by the time they could get into the fight, it would be over, and his men and choppers would cut them down as they came rolling in.

"Blue team, go, go, go!" he shouted into his radio mike.

An instant later, fingers of fire reached out from several points in the night sky as 30mm cannon lashed the enemy positions. One of the armored cars exploded in a ball of fire, and he could see the dark forms of men flopping out of the anti-aircraft positions and then lying still on the ground.

Even before the preparatory fire began, the Blackhawks were sliding in and dropping off their passengers in clusters on all sides of the depot. Saavedra watched the groups of men through his night-vision goggles as they rushed the enemy perimeter. Tiny pinpoints of light flared up as they cleared the shallow trenches of defenders. His own aircraft swung in low and disgorged its dozen Argentine infantrymen and then rose to hover above the town. The remaining Blackhawks were already on their way back to the airbase at Almaty, there to refuel one last time and to bring out their mechanics and the last of the infantry guards at the base.

"Target clear," the simple message came over the radio.

"And reference point orange?" Saavedra asked, referring to the town itself.

"We've been through it and no sign of hostiles," the voice answered.

"Roger that. Back in a flash," he said with more good humor than he really felt.

"We'll be here."

That was the easy part, Saavedra thought.

NORTH OF THE ILI RIVER

About ten minutes later, an aide handed Qasimbekai a radio message. He read it and frowned. He debated just not telling the Iranian about it, since it didn't seem vital at the moment. After all, the UN troops would undoubtedly come charging across the river to break through his front at any instant, and anything that happened on any other part of the front was definitely a sideshow. In fact, if he *did* show this to the Iranian, it would imply that he didn't recognize this basic military fact and expose him to another one of those condescending sneers; he would be humiliated in front of his officers while the Iranian explained it to him. Then no amount of his own protestations that this was exactly what he had been thinking himself would solve the problem, since no one would believe him anyway.

Qasimbekai looked over the American positions again and then folded the note and stuck it in his shirt pocket. Someone had attacked the base at Chiganak, at the southern tip of Lake Balkhash, and all transmissions from there had ceased suddenly. That wasn't far from the Russian zone, so maybe it was some kind of raid by the Russians. It didn't matter. Chiganak was two hundred miles away, and the missiles were right out there, just over the horizon, and nothing else mattered.

NORTH OF KHANTAU

Kabrak slept soundly in the back of the jeep. He kicked at the major who tugged at his pants leg. The major was former regular Afghan Army and had deserted to the mujahedin only when the Russians were already withdrawing. A prudent man, but not one you could trust very much.

The major tugged again. "General," he was saying. "We just picked up a message on the radio about an enemy attack on Chiganak."

"The Russians?" Kabrak grumbled.

"Whoever it was, it sounds like they took the place."

This man had heard enough of his own garrisons go under to recognize the sound, Kabrak thought ungraciously. "Tell the recon unit to pick up speed and get out well ahead of us. I don't want to be surprised by whatever we find there. Put out a company of tanks in advance and put out flank guards as well. How long until we get there?"

"About an hour, with the main body of the division."

"Good. If they've taken the place, we'll hit them before they're able to consolidate. Make sure the recon people report back as soon as they find out what's going on. And get on the radio to the damn Kazakhs," he added as an afterthought. "See if they know what the hell is happening in their own backyard."

There was no point trying to go back to sleep now, so Kabrak took a long pull at his canteen, rubbed some of the water on his face, and began to lace up his boots. Back to work, he thought.

CHIGANAK

Meriani had formed his men in a tight defensive ring around the supply depot. The Americans were far better equipped than his own men, with their Javelin antitank missiles and a pair of tripod-mounted TOW missile launchers, and he positioned them in three small platoons around the perimeter, interspersed with his own men. He'd also set out small ambush parties about two klicks both north and south on the M2 highway and on the P140, which ran due south toward the town of Khantau. These would both give him advance warning of the approach of any sizable enemy forces and, he hoped, engage them with small-arms fire and with their Carl Gustav antitank rockets, forcing them to deploy early and thus buy some time for the relief forces to arrive.

There had been very few casualties in his capture of the depot: only about a dozen enemy killed or wounded and two of his own men nicked by shrapnel from a Kazakh grenade. He had captured about fifty men who were now docilely sitting in a small garage under guard, while the remainder of the defenders had simply scampered off into the darkness, most of them leaving their weapons behind.

Meriani was very much concerned about his place in his country's history at that moment. He was aware that the only "press play" that the Argentine military ever got was when they overthrew the government, arrested and/or killed civilian opposition leaders, as during the long "dirty war" against the Montoneros, or when they got their butts thoroughly kicked by the British on the Malvinas, which the British called the Falklands. Meriani had been only a lieutenant at the time of the Malvinas War and had spent the campaign watching the Chilean border for an expected offensive from that quarter in support of the British, an offensive that never came. He had also had no part in the suppression of dissidents in the "dirty war," although he had joined the commandos in several attempts to overthrow the civilian Alfonsin government because of its blatant leftism and anti-military attitude. He recognized very well the disdain with which the professional military men in the UN force viewed the Argentine military. He had even overheard some of the older British NCOs, who had been in the Malvinas, talk about the frightened, undernourished Argentine prisoners, conscripts who had told their captors that the British interrogator was the first officer of either side they had seen in days, while their own officers rested comfortably in the warmth of commandeered Port Stanley houses. Well, Meriani was out to prove that Argentines could fight.

Meriani was proud of the way his men had performed in the capture of Government House and here at Chiganak thus far. They had fulfilled their missions perfectly. A couple of the men had been killed in Almaty, but their countrymen would be naming plazas and streets after them for decades, just as if they had been football stars in the World Cup.

He was just wondering what they would name after him in his hometown of Mendoza in the wine-growing region on the eastern slopes of the Andes, when the muffled radio message came in from the outpost to the south that an armored column was approaching rapidly from Khantau. Those would not be friends, he figured, and he rushed out to check on the defenses one more time.

NEAR THE KURTY RIVER

"You idiot!" Yerik screamed, while at the same time trying to keep his voice to a hoarse whisper. He took another swipe at Bakyt's head with his broad, callused hand. "What the devil do you think they put on this godforsaken hill for? You expected the Prophet to be coming down the road, and we were to let people know so that they could have hot tea ready for him?"

The tail of the long column of trucks was just now crossing the narrow bridge over the Kurty River: huge American five-ton trucks, snoutless Volvos, and even a couple of city buses from Almaty, interspersed with tanks, armored personnel carriers, and small-wheeled armored cars that buzzed about the flanks of the column like angry bees.

Yerik paused as he crouched over the radio. Clearly, he was considering how to report the passage of the column without having to explain why he and his young charge had not reported the movement an hour ago when, according to Bakyt, the first vehicles had passed this point.

"This is Post Ten," Yerik began, once he had raised their company headquarters, which was located miles to the south in the town of Kopa. "Listen, I was out on patrol, and I have just returned to my position. A large number of enemy vehicles has just passed, headed northwest on the M2 toward Chiganak."

This was answered with a stream of curses that, fortunately, was lost to Bakyt in the static of the poor connection. Finally, the speaker calmed down enough to inform Yerik that this column had already just been reported by the garrison of the town of Kolshengel, nearly forty miles farther along the M2, which had just been overrun by what must be the advance guard of that same column.

Bakyt couldn't make out the rest of what was said over the radio, but he could see Yerik cringing, even at this distance, from the voice of the company commander, as he meekly described what he had seen of the enemy vehicles. Bakyt closed his eyes and wished that he were somewhere else as he anticipated the blows he had coming just as soon as Yerik finished on the radio.

NORTH OF THE ILI RIVER

The Iranian was running his fingers through his greasy black hair in frustration as he sought to control his rage and concentrated instead on studying the map before him. Qasimbekai stood erect, his chin thrust out, and mentally dared this foreigner to say something disrespectful. All right, he had made a mistake. The enemy was heading around the far side of Lake Balkhash and was not coming this way after all. But he was certain that the Iranian would have come to the same conclusion as he had, and it was only with the benefit of hindsight that this Persian fop would be able to say how clear the evidence had been and how he would have acted differently if only he had known. If this son of an unknown father dared to say anything, Qasimbekai swore that he would shoot him through the head with his own pistol.

But the Iranian did manage to control himself, albeit with some effort, and instead of railing against Qasimbekai, set about in a professional manner to repair the situation.

"We must break across the river and get a pursuit started immediately," he was saying. "It appears that they've already eliminated all serious opposition in front of them along the M2. Our only chance is to keep hard on their heels and hope that the Afghan division is close enough to cut them off from in front. Once we get them stopped and forced to deploy, we can bring up our heavy forces and deal with them at our leisure. Out in the open like that, unless they're totally mad, they'll quickly see that their gamble hasn't paid off and will surrender easily. If not, we'll just cut them to pieces."

"But it will take time to get our forces concentrated," Qasimbekai argued. "They're spread out for miles in small groups all along the Ili River line."

"We'll use our reserve force for the moment," the Iranian replied, with barely concealed impatience. "Plus the tanks right here near the highway. These enemy vehicles we can see here must only be a screen in any case. We'll blast them with artillery and punch right through them. We know that the UN was weak in heavy armor, and they won't be able to hold us. In the meanwhile, we'll send those helicopter units, the Hind gunships, and the company of airborne infantry in transports from Taldy-Kurgan cross country to jump ahead of them and hit the column on the march. They'll be able to pick their targets, even in the dark, and avoid hitting the missile carriers. If we can disable some vehicles and block the road at some choke point, even for an hour or two, that will give us valuable time to trap the whole batch."

Qasimbekai nodded and gestured to his aides to give the indicated orders. This could still work out. There would be no mention later of his mistake, just as long as they eventually captured the missiles, and there was still an excellent chance of that.

ALMATY

The last of the Apaches was just completing its refueling and taking off from Almaty airport under Saavedra's frenzied supervision when the call came in from Meriani that the enemy was on the way. Even at their best flying time, it would take the Apaches over an hour to get back to Chiganak. At almost the same moment, the Israeli radar unit they had installed on one of the rare high points near the Ili River line reported over a dozen contacts, enemy aircraft heading southwest from Taldy-Kurgan. They must be helicopters: Saavedra pulled off a troop of seven Apaches and their accompanying four OH-58 observation choppers to deal with that threat. He had sent another four Apaches on a special mission to carry out a preemptive strike against enemy fighter aircraft in Chimkent, which left him with only ten for the protection of Chiganak—if they got there in time even for that. Things were coming undone very quickly.

Demolition charges were going off all over the base now as the rearguard destroyed any military equipment they couldn't take with them. More disturbing was the rattle of small-arms fire that now came through clearly on the frigid night air from the southern perimeter of the base. Even muffled as it was by the lightly falling snow, the sound was growing louder as the last protective screen of infantry retreated quickly to the choppers whose rotors were already turning.

Saavedra saw a squad of Argentines with their long FN rifles jogging toward him in a crouched position. Now and again one of them would stop and let off a short burst into the swirling snow to slow the pursuing Kazakhs, while two of his comrades helped a third with an obviously wounded leg. By his own order, Saavedra's Blackhawk was the last to leave the base, and he sat in the copilot's seat urging the men on as the waist gunner now joined in, firing over the heads of the crouching men with his machine gun. One by one they piled into the back of the helicopter. Saavedra could now see shadowy figures beginning to materialize in the mist behind them. The chopper's gun sent a stream of tracers out into the distance, and one or two of the figures dropped, but the others grew darker and larger as they approached. Then there was a sharp "ping!" and a delicate star pattern appeared on the Plexiglas of the windscreen next to Saavedra's face.

"Go!" the gunner screamed over the intercom, and the Blackhawk lifted off, angling to the right to add as much distance as quickly as possible between them and the Kazakhs, while Saavedra could see the legs of the last infantryman flailing frantically in the air as he was pulled aboard at the last second. Jesus! Saavedra thought. I wonder what I would have to do to get myself a desk job somewhere.

CHIGANAK

There was a flash and a resultant explosion in the distance as Meriani watched through his binoculars. A Carl Gustav rocket had found its mark as the UN outpost opened fire on the advancing enemy column. He could see the black shape of a small armored car silhouetted in the flame of its own burning fuel; a ring of blinking lights crowned the small, round, wind-eroded hilltop where the outpost was stationed. But these were answered by dozens, then seemingly hundreds, of other, greenish lights all along the base of the hill nearest the road. There were augmented by the brighter flash of tank guns and of what must have been mortar shells hitting the hilltop. More ominously, Meriani could make out the dark shapes of enemy tanks rolling straight up the road, ignoring the little battle going on around the hill and heading straight for Chiganak. The road was a pure black ribbon against the ghostly paler gray of the scrub-covered plain. He knew that the enemy forces, which obviously dwarfed his own, would be in contact with his main defensive line in a matter of minutes, and there was no sign of relief in sight.

Enemy smoke rounds began impacting in front of the UN positions, and Meriani was relieved to see that although the enemy clearly had artillery support, they had not chosen simply to flatten him with cannon fire, probably in the interests of preserving the supplies in the depot for themselves. His own single mortar was gamely popping out rounds, special antitank munitions designed to seek out the weak upper armor of enemy vehicles, but he had only perhaps a dozen such rounds, and these were expended in less than a minute, although he did see several tanks or APCs suddenly flare up and burn on the open ground out in front of him.

But more tanks kept coming, and between them he could see hundreds of infantrymen on foot, running forward and firing their weapons from the hip. He hoped his raw Argentine troops wouldn't get what was known as "tank panic" and simply turn and run from the forty-ton behemoths that were bearing down on them. The rising crescendo of fire from his own lines told him that they were holding. TOW missiles reached out to swat enemy tanks at a distance, and the shorter-range Carl Gustavs added to the din. His men had also found one of the enemy 23mm anti-aircraft guns in working order, its crew dead around it, and the fiery spears of tracers tore through the night, knocking out the lighter vehicles and shredding unfortunate infantrymen like paper. The pair of tiny OH-58 helicopters that had remained with Meriani to provide some support darted back and forth overhead, strafing the lighter vehicles with 20mm cannon fire after their missiles had been expended.

But the enemy tanks continued to advance, and Meriani could see that they were firing directly into the first line of entrenchments, sweeping the defenders away with point-blank machine-gun fire. Then an enemy machine gun found its mark, lopping the tail boom off one of the helicopters and sending it plunging down in a flaming ball to the ground. Meriani had committed all of his reserves, and they were simply not enough.

OVER CHIMKENT AIRPORT

Lieutenant Todd Kopeki had seen Chimkent airport before, and on a normal night, you would have had trouble finding it in the dark. But tonight, even though the place was lit up like a Christmas tree, you certainly wouldn't mistake it for Rhein-Main airbase in Germany.

Kopeki's OH-58 hovered just below a rocky, razor-backed ridge-line several kilometers from the airport, but he was able to observe the entire scene—without being seen—with the large bulbous periscope that extended up through the center post of the chopper's rotor. He watched as four aged MiG-21 fighters were wheeled from their hangars. It wasn't much of an air force by modern standards, but even these obsolete aircraft could wreak havoc among the slow-moving vehicles of the UN convoy. They wouldn't be able to attack until dawn, since they weren't equipped for night operations, but Kopeki couldn't wait until then to act.

"You've got an SA-6 near the east end of the runway, and another on a knoll to the northeast, plus half a dozen flak guns scattered around the airport buildings," he said into his radio. "And I make four Fishbeds on the tarmac."

"Roger," four Apache pilots said in turn.

A moment later the Apaches popped up from behind the same ridgeline and launched Hellfire missiles at the anti-aircraft missile launchers and their radars. One of the SAMs was able to get off a shot, but the missile ran wild when the launcher was destroyed by the Hellfire. The flak guns opened fire, hosing the sky with green and yellow tracers, but the Apaches merely dropped back down below the ridgeline and side-slipped to new firing positions. They each rose up twice more, loosing missiles at the aircraft on the run-way, even as the ground crews frantically tried to roll them back into their protected revetments, but each one was shattered by a missile that was designed to penetrate tank armor and had little trouble with thin titanium and aluminum skins. For good measure, the Apaches kept firing until each had expended all eight of its missiles and dozens of smaller 2.75-inch rockets, destroying transports, fuel tanks, and finally the control tower itself. Then the black-painted helicopters banked gracefully and swept up a shallow gully toward Chiganak to the north.

SOUTH OF THE ILI RIVER

As Chandler watched the horizon, it was suddenly illuminated by dozens of dancing light flashes, like static electricity coming off a fuzzy sweater in a darkened bedroom.

"Holy shit! That's torn it!" he shouted, long before the rumble of the distant enemy artillery reached his ears. He was shouting into the radio for his own meager pair of mortars and lone Egyptian self-propelled gun to return fire, but the gunners had also seen the flashes, and he could hear the popping of the mortars even as he spoke. At the same instant, the few vehicles he had allowed to move forward of the low ridge toward the Ili River now slammed into reverse and backed into the defensive positions dug for them by the Israeli bulldozers.

Chandler dropped down inside the turret of his Bradley and clanged the hatch shut behind him as the enemy shells began to crash all around him. It was unlikely that the Kazakhs possessed any modern anti-armor rounds for their artillery, at least according to Goldman's CIA sources. "Unlikely" was not a very reassuring word at a time like this, however, and it seemed as if the Bradley and the piece of real estate it stood on were being lifted into orbit by the erupting shells.

The big M-1 tanks were ignoring the barrage altogether and were running up to their covered firing positions, blasting away at targets Chandler could not see, and then pulling back before the enemy could return fire. The shelling was starting to slacken now, and most of it had fallen short, hitting on the forward slopes of the ridge where the Kazakhs evidently assumed the main UN forces to be. But the unavoidable sense of relief that the end of the continuous thunder brought also meant to Chandler that the enemy ground forces would now be coming forward. He ordered the driver of his Bradley to move up to the ridge so that he could get a better look.

The vehicle's gunner had swung the TOW missile launcher from its stored position on the left side of the turret to the raised position above it, and Chandler was able to look through the sighting mechanism without exposing the body of the vehicle above the crest of the ridge. He could see a T-54 tank burning on the bridge over the Ili, and several others scattered about in the open and spouting smoke and flame. The Abramses were doing good work, but there were too few of them, and several enemy tanks were already across the river, as were over a dozen APCs, with many more armored vehicles rushing across the bridge or fording the shallow river to either flank.

The Bradley's gunner sighted a TOW on one of the tanks and fired. Chandler watched as the missile bobbed and weaved over the intervening terrain, always staying at the crosshairs of the sight until it impacted on the tank's turret, and the enemy vehicle disappeared in a cloud of smoke. But a return shot threw up a geyser of earth directly in front of the Bradley, and they backed down the slope.

Chandler scanned right and left and saw that two of his own tanks were out of action, along with three Bradleys. They had made the enemy pay a high price for the crossing, but it was time to beat a retreat.

"Pull back to Line Orange," he shouted into the radio headset, and the unit commanders acknowledged one by one.

Chandler paused to pick up a pair of wounded crewmen who had escaped from their wrecked tank and then followed the other vehicles through the gap in the Israelis' minefield and swung to the west. Instead of following the M3 highway due south toward Almaty, they would go overland directly to the M2.

Sporadic enemy shelling continued to chase them, but they successfully broke contact and passed through the delaying position set up by the second troop of American cavalry about three miles to the west. Chandler now attached himself to this group to await the new Kazakh onslaught.

THE M2 HIGHWAY WEST OF THE KURTY RIVER

Driving the Blazer, Elders leaned far over the steering wheel and peered through the windscreen at the tiny red light on the tail of the truck ahead. His own headlights were covered with heavy tape, leaving only a square the size of a matchbook that allowed a derisory beam to escape, which was totally swallowed up by the swirling snow and darkness within a matter of a few feet. He kept glancing down at the speedometer, careful to keep at the prescribed twenty-five miles per hour, and then looking up quickly, for the column had been jerking and stopping frequently since they left the airbase hours ago. His knuckles were as white as the plastic covering on the steering wheel.

Goldman sat next to him, a map open on his lap, and rubbed enthusiastically on the windshield with a rag when it became foggy. His cameraman, a red-haired veteran of Central America and Yugoslavia, was sound asleep and snoring loudly, even as his head banged against the window support. He shared the rear seat with an elderly Russian couple who smiled idiotically and gave Goldman a reassuring "thumbs up" sign whenever he looked back at them.

Suddenly, the truck in front of them burst into flames. Elders swerved to avoid it, bouncing off the narrow asphalt strip of the road and fishtailing in the loose gravel before recovering control, but did not slow down, per Chandler's orders. Goldman pressed his hand up against the frigid glass of the window as if to reach out to the men who must still be inside the burning truck's cab, and he thought he could see the dark silhouette of a man hunched over the wheel inside the inferno. At least, he thought, it had been a supply truck, and not one of the ones filled with refugees or one of their precious fuel tankers—which would have meant that Goldman would almost certainly have been fried himself.

A second later he heard a terrifying howling, and the snow was mixed with flying dust and pebbles as the white underbelly of a helicopter zoomed over the column and banked away. He recognized the fat shape and stubby wings as those of a Russian Hind gunship, of which he had seen all too many during a dangerous trek with Afghan guerrillas through the Khyber Pass some years ago. He knew that there would be another Hind right behind this one, as they executed their "wheel of death" over the column, since the Russian pilots preferred hitting their targets at close range, like World War II dive-bombers, rather than by means of standoff weapons, like their American counterparts. They worked in pairs, orbiting over their target and hitting it again and again on each fresh approach. He'd interviewed enough scarred Afghan survivors of such attacks to recognize the tactics.

Off to the left of the column Goldman saw a small armored vehicle, probably British, by its shape, with a man standing upright on its back deck aiming a bazooka-like weapon skyward. There was a flash out of the back and the front of the weapon simultaneously, and a tiny rocket streaked off in pursuit of the Hind, which was dropping a string of flares in an effort to divert the heat-seeking warhead. Goldman watched, fascinated, as the bulky helicopter banked to left and right and the pinpoint of light that was the missile's exhaust flame tracked it exactly until it finally exploded against the chopper's side. But the Hind did not bear the nickname "flying tank" for nothing, and the aircraft merely shuddered and then lumbered back off to the north trailing a plume of black, greasy smoke.

Shit! Goldman thought to himself. If that was the best they could do against the Hinds, then the column was dead meat, unless the Kazakhs had only one such beast. But by now they had passed several other burning vehicles, and Goldman knew that this wasn't true. He hoped that his journalistic credentials would carry some weight with the Kazakhs when they were all herded into a concentration camp. Just then a huge fireball appeared in the sky overhead, followed quickly by the sight of the unmistakable humpbacked fuselage of a Hind crashing to earth not twenty meters from the side of the highway. Goldman looked quickly skyward and could see the fiery trails of missiles and bright lines of tracers crisscrossing between the low clouds. He didn't know who was up there, but he was glad for it.

"I hope you got some of that on film," he shouted over his shoulder to his cameraman, but when he turned around, he found the man sprawled across the laps of the Russian couple, a thin trickle of blood dripping from the corner of his mouth. Then he noticed the neat, round hole in both the glass and the mylar protective covering of the side window and the corresponding hole just above the cameraman's right ear. The old Russian woman smoothed his hair and rocked him gently, possibly remembering some child or grandchild who had also died in her arms. They both gave Goldman the same inane smile, but with less enthusiasm than before, and the old man still gave him the "thumbs up" sign. Goldman wondered what that meant now, perhaps just that the old man himself was still alive.

NORTH OF THE ILI RIVER

"What the hell is happening?" Qasimbekai screamed as the Iranian hunched over near the speaker of a radio, listening intently to the raspy, disjointed bits of conversation coming in from the helicopter sortie.

Instead of replying, the Iranian imperiously held up his hand and continued to frown pensively at the speaker. His dark, bushy eyebrows and beard and his black eyes gave him a sinister appearance, and Qasimbekai was momentarily cowed into silence, but then he recovered and grabbed the Iranian by the shoulder.

"What is this?" he shouted over the crackle of the radios. "Have they stopped the column or not?"

Most of the Hind pilots were Iranian or Afghan mercenaries, or "volunteer," and had been jabbering away in Farsi, which Qasimbekai could not understand. He knew that they had sighted and opened the attack upon the UN column, but then all sorts of conflicting messages had started to come in, some of them cut off in midsentence, the callers breaking into each other's transmissions with frantic calls for help. That much he could understand, but he didn't know why.

The Iranian looked at Qasimbekai with infuriating calmness. It seemed that the more frustrated the Kazakh became, the more in command the Iranian appeared to be.

"It would seem that our heliborne force has been jumped by a number of American helicopters armed with Stingers or some other kind of anti-aircraft missile. They hit our force from behind and wiped out the troop transports first, with the infantry still aboard, then went after the Hinds. The pilots claimed to have downed at least two American copters, but more than half of our aircraft have been lost, and the rest are retiring to their base with my concurrence."

"*Your* concurrence?" Qasimbekai shrieked. "*Your* concurrence? Who are you to concur? I am the commander here, and stopping that column is more important than a handful of helicopters. Order them to turn back immediately and renew the attack."

"There would be no point in such a sacrifice," the Iranian said evenly. "They have destroyed a few enemy vehicles, but the ground there is quite flat, and the column can easily go around any obstruction. Without the infantry to set up a blocking position, the only thing you will accomplish is to run the risk of one of the ICBM vehicles getting hit by mistake, and, might I add, that such a mistake would be quite easy to make when the Hind pilot is busy fending off attacks by enemy helicopters that are more maneuverable and more modern than his own."

Qasimbekai tore at his hair and bit back his tears of rage and frustration. It had all seemed so close within his grasp, and now it was all coming apart. First, the commander of the ground attack had decided his losses had been too great in taking the enemy positions south of the Ili River and had insisted on "regrouping" before he continued his advance. The Iranian had concurred with that too, but Qasimbekai had recognized this as a mere pretext for trying to sit out the battle while the enemy slipped away unhindered. He had had the commander shot, but now even his replacement was dragging his feet, calling for engineers to clear an enemy minefield in which he had lost several tanks already. Meanwhile, even the enemy rearguard forces had now peacefully withdrawn over the Kurty River. Even if his own units were to start moving now—which it did not appear that they were about to do—they were more than an hour behind the rearmost enemy vehicle, probably more. There had been a mysterious air attack on the airfield at Chimkent, eliminating that part of his own plan, and now the helicopters were gone too.

Now it all depended upon the Afghan division, which was reportedly closing in on Chiganak. If they could slam shut the front door to the UN column, then even his timorous commanders would be able to close in from the rear and finally deliver him his missiles. In the meanwhile, he must keep up the pressure and not let anyone count on the other guy to save the day for him.

M2 HIGHWAY SOUTHEAST OF CHIGANAK

Volley fire had gone out of style more than a century ago, Captain Martin knew, but it did have a certain panache to it. After his wild ride along the M2 with no running lights through the utter blackness of night on the steppe, Martin's vehicles were now drawn up line abreast less than a kilometer from dozens of Russian-made tanks and APCs, which were closing in on the ring of fire surrounding the depot at Chiganak. Martin had avoided the towns along the highway by bouncing across broken ground to the south of the main road, but it had paid off. He had arrived on target and unobserved.

He scanned his line of ten AMX-10RCs with the long-barreled 105mm guns and the VAB personnel carriers with Milan missile launchers mounted on the roof. They were hull-down in shallow dips in the gravelly, barren ground, only their turrets showing. When the last vehicle pulled into place and the gunner confirmed a lock on his target, Martin gave the order.

"Fire, fire, fire!"

"What the hell was that?" Kabrak shouted. He was monitoring the progress of the battle from the hood of his jeep, parked among a handful of stunted trees near the edge of the highway, when he saw what looked like a sheet of flame reach out and smash an entire mechanized company on the right flank of his assault. Individual enemy guns continued to fire, and the toll among his own forces continued to mount alarmingly. He could see ten or more tanks burning, besides those he had already lost, and even more APCs, most of them, he knew, still carrying their infantry squads.

The bulk of his armored force was gutted, and all he had left were infantry mounted in unprotected trucks. Protected or not, they would have to move as far forward as possible before dismounting, or the foot soldiers would take too long to reach the objective. He knew from his scouts that strong enemy armored forces were hurrying up the M2 highway from the east, and these unseen assailants must be a vanguard of that force. Kabrak ordered up another battalion of infantry to reinforce the attack on the depot, where his men were already falling back in disorder, and a second to hit the new enemy force on its left flank from the south.

The big Russian trucks belched smoke as they pulled out of the gullies in which they had taken shelter, their engines groaning in protest as they picked up speed. He could see the dozens of cloth-swathed heads and the barrels of the rifles of the infantrymen crammed in the backs of the trucks, some of them shouting prayers to Allah over the noise of the motors.

"Perhaps we should pull back and re-form for a combined-arms attack," the major was saying into Kabrak's ear, but Kabrak waved him away in disgust. That was the kind of attitude that had cost the Babrak Karmal government and its Soviet masters the war in Afghanistan. To pull back would now mean crossing that open ground again, and paying once more the horrible price they had already paid. They were within hand-grenade range of the objective now. If they could just fend off this one last desperate attack by the enemy, which was precisely designed to distract them from their true goal, they could both take the town and destroy the enemy in detail. Men like the major would never understand the expression Kabrak had learned as a medical student in France many, many years ago. *"Qui ose, vaincra!"* He who dares, wins.

Despite the havoc his initial assault had caused in the enemy ranks, Martin was hard-pressed now by at least half a dozen T-54s that had gotten into hull-down positions and begun to return fire in an orderly fashion. He had lost two armored cars and an APC, and he could make out more enemy vehicles coming in his direction. Martin had managed to slip half a dozen jeeps, with about thirty infantry and a few missile launchers, into Chiganak to bolster the defenses, but he was in an exposed position here, and his AMX-10RCs were not meant to stand toe-to-toe with main battle tanks. They didn't have the armor. He was just about to pull back a few hundred yards to better ground when the first Hellfire missile whooshed over his head and neatly lifted the turret off a T-54 and flung it haphazardly to one side.

CHIGARAK DEPOT

Meriani had run out of ammunition for his assault rifle and was firing wildly with his pistol now. He put two rounds into the chest of a bearded man who leaped over the low wall of sandbags near his command post. An American lay dead next to him; Meriani took the man's M-16 and continued to fire as grenades burst all around him.

The defenders had been pushed back to the buildings of the compound itself. A corrugated metal storage shed to his right was on fire, but some of his men continued to fight from inside it as burning embers from the roof rained down on them.

Another Afghan vaulted over the wall, but a burly black American flattened him with a butt stroke of his rifle, and an Argentine pinned him to the ground with his bayonet. The two men then stood back to back, their matching sky-blue berets touching, and fired at other attackers until they were both cut down by a shower of shrapnel from a grenade.

More Afghans were coming over the wall, and the defenders were about to fall back again, when the line of enemy infantry disappeared in a series of quick explosions. Meriani turned around and saw a French trooper firing a 40mm automatic grenade launcher from the back of a jeep over Meriani's head into the enemy as a dozen French infantrymen charged forward firing from the hip. The Afghans began to waver and to pull back from the wall.

Like shooting fish in a barrel, Saavedra thought. The Apaches had to pick their targets, using missiles only for identified tanks and turning their 30mm guns on softer prey. The great and wise planners of the UNEKAZ mission had foreseen little need for anti-armor weaponry and felt more reason to fear that such sophisticated equipment might lead to its falling into hostile hands. They had consequently kept TOW and Hellfire missile reserves at perilously low levels throughout the UN peacekeeping mission.

However, 30mm rounds did a fine job on APCs and an even better one on the scores of simple trucks the enemy was using to transport the infantry to the front line. Saavedra watched through his
night scope as the ground around one big ZIL truck erupted in hundreds of tiny volcanoes and large chunks of the truck flew off in odd
directions. He could only imagine what the rounds were doing to the
close-packed human flesh in the back of the trucks; even in the heat
of battle, it made him cringe a little.

From his lofty position, Saavedra had a panoramic view of the
battlefield, arching from Chiganak at the southern end of Lake
Balkhash to the northern reaches of the lake, down past the M2 and
the position of Martin's troop, past the little hill where Meriani's outpost had made its stand. He could perceive a visible shudder in the
enemy line when his gunships opened up. At first they simply
stopped advancing and were slaughtered in place, an occasional
stream of tracers would arc skyward, or a SA-7 missile would jump
up ineffectually trying to fight back, but then the enemy line would
buckle backward upon itself. Then it broke. Vehicles turned sharply
around, some of them tipping over as the drivers panicked and
headed for the rear at speed, plowing through scattered infantrymen
who happened to be in the way. Still the choppers lashed them with
cannon and rocket fire, and many crews simply abandoned their vehicles intact and ran for the hills. He could see their tiny glowing figures in his thermal imager, and he was glad that he had never been on
the receiving end of such an attack.

SOUTHWEST OF CHIGANAK

Kabrak screamed at the commander of an artillery battery set up
next to the clump of gnarled trees—rare in this terrain—to open fire
on the depot. If they could not have the fuel and supplies there, at
least they could deny them to the enemy. He screamed into one
radio microphone after another, piling abuse on his commanders,
insisting that they hold their ground or continue their attacks.

At least he could not fault the major for cowardice. The man had
grabbed the 12.7mm machine gun mounted on the back of a jeep and
was firing wildly at the enemy helicopters swooping and diving all
around them. It was futile, but at least the man was no coward,
Kabrak thought. The helicopters only seemed to be breathing down
their necks; they were mostly two or more kilometers away, and
mere machine guns would not reach them. He had seen only one

small copter go down so far, despite the thousands of rounds the Afghans had thrown at them.

Kabrak took a deep breath and reconsidered. It was over. His primary responsibility now was to return the division back to his country before it ceased to exist as a fighting unit. As men who had taken cover straggled in, he was pretty sure that his overall losses, other than the vehicles—which he could see clearly burning all around—would probably turn out to be lighter than they appeared at present. He must pull his men out of this meatgrinder quickly. He issued the orders, and he noticed that the major seemed to move a little faster in complying with them than he had when the orders were to continue the attack. But that was all right. The man could fight, and there would be other battles. There would always be other battles, Kabrak mused.

He saw a series of flashes near one of the guns of the artillery battery nearby. The gun was flipped up into the air, over and over. The flashes peppered the ground, walking right over one gun after another. Then they hit the jeeps of his escort and made the major disappear not ten meters away. They just kept on coming.

THE M2 HIGHWAY NEAR THE KURTY RIVER

Chandler had waited with the rearguard by the Kurty River for over two hours, and there had been no sign of enemy pursuit. As the sky began to lighten, he left Morgan in charge of the rearguard, which was now free to follow the column farther along the M2 to the northwest. The two troops would leapfrog each other about a kilometer at a time until they could be sure that the Kazakhs were not in pursuit. Chandler jumped into a Hummer to catch up with the main body. He passed the burned-out trucks and APCs and the victims of the enemy air attack; he saw the skeletons of the Hinds nearby as well, and the latter sight did nothing to lighten his grim mood.

As he neared Chiganak, he found long lines of trucks waiting at the several refueling points that had been set up. During the layover, people had dismounted and were scattered about eating MREs, Russian civilians and troops of all contingents mixed together haphazardly. Off to one side of the highway, near the tip of Lake Balkhash, Saavedra's helicopters were clustered, receiving quick repairs and getting their tanks topped off, while several Apaches cruised protectively overhead. Some of the aircraft, too battered to be airworthy, had already been torched by their crews, and thin wisps of smoke rose from their cadavers into the clear cold air.

Off to the left was the wreckage of the Afghan division; charred tanks and APCs and dead bodies were strewn across the flat ground like the toys of some evil giant child that have not been put away. He could also see a small Israeli skip loader digging a grave for the defenders who had fallen as well. He closed his eyes at the dimensions of the hole. Peabody, Martin, Saavedra, Meriani, and the other unit commanders were waiting for Chandler at the small building that was Meriani's command post.

"How does it look?" Chandler asked.

"What's left of the Afghan division hasn't stopped moving south all night," Saavedra said. "I don't think we'll have any more trouble with them, and there aren't any significant Kazakh formations between us and the demarcation line of the Russian separatist zone past Chiganak."

"And our losses?"

Meriani flipped open a notebook. "We lost over one hundred killed here in Chiganak alone. The French lost about twenty and Saavedra about the same, plus whatever hits the column and the rearguard took on the way up here. We calculate about two hundred forty killed in action and about twice as many wounded among our troops and a few scattered wounded among the refugees, which leaves us with just under twenty-five hundred effectives. As soon as the Blackhawks are fueled up, we'll be able to load all of the seriously wounded on them and the OH-58s and fly them out to Novosibirsk. Not having the choppers anymore will hurt us, but we can't really operate them from here on out anyway. We'll retain a few of the Apaches for cover as long as they'll run, and as long as weather permits. There's a nasty storm coming down from the north. But we don't think that Shchernikov's people will bother the departing Blackhawks, even if they could, although they'll never let them back in. All things considered, we're not in bad shape, considering the opposition we faced."

"But we're not home free yet," Chandler grumbled. "There's no sign that the Kazakhs behind us are trying to catch up either, but we still have to get through the Russians. They're better armed, and we're a lot weaker than we were a day ago. That, and the fact that we don't have any special surprises we can pull on them. It's got to be 'Hey diddle diddle, right up the middle,' and that's not going to be easy."

"Well, at least we've got full gas tanks, and we're about a third of the way there," Peabody said, puffing out his chest. "I don't know about you guys, but I'd ride with these boys right into the jaws of

hell with a smile on my face after what we went through last night."
He grabbed Kondo roughly by the back of his collar and shook him
good-naturedly.

There was a commotion outside, and Chandler stepped out to
investigate. The men along the perimeter wall, Senegalese military
policemen, were talking loudly and pointing off to the south.
Chandler walked forward and saw a ragged line of infantry wearily
trudging up the gentle slope toward the depot, half a dozen of them
in all, carrying long FN rifles and wearing badly soiled sky-blue
berets.

"Escobar!" Meriani shouted and vaulted the wall, rushing down to
embrace the leading infantryman, who was limping badly, but who
stood erect, carrying his weapon at high port. "They're from the hilltop outpost to the south, the ones who took on the Afghans first," he
shouted back to the others. "By God, I thought you were all dead."

"Very close," Escobar, a young, lanky lieutenant, replied. "They
overran us completely, except for a few of us up on the crest. Then,
when the fighting really started down here, they lost interest in us.
We still lost four more men during the night to shelling, but we had a
fabulous view of the battle."

Escobar smiled wanly, and Meriani reached around to support
him as he helped him toward the aid station. The Senegalese sergeant
barked something to his men and they stood at attention and presented arms as the Argentines slogged by, but their broad smiles
showed through their smudged and scarred faces.

Chandler nodded. "So far, so good. Now let's get topped up and
back on the road before the enemy really gets mad at us."

NORTH OF THE ILI RIVER

It took three men to wrestle Qasimbekai to the ground and to take
away his pistol. The Iranian was still leaning against the wall of the
command post, staring in amazement at the gaping hole in his chest
and trying to staunch the flow of blood with his hand.

"Place that man under arrest!" Qasimbekai screamed as they tied
his hands behind his back with some packing cord. "It was his incompetence that cost us this battle, and I'll have his head."

"We will leave that up to the Kazakh Provisional Government,"
one of his senior officers said in a calm voice as the Iranian slumped
to the floor. There was little doubt among the officers present that
Qasimbekai was just as responsible for the failure as the Iranian, but

the Iranian had made no friends with his abrasive attitude. The officers were taking this action, now that it was clear that the missiles had escaped their grasp, not out of any sense of indignation at the summary execution of the Iranian, but because the murder had made it easier to place the blame for the defeat on Qasimbekai's shoulders an obviously unbalanced man. The fact that his removal would open up promotion possibilities for all of them was also at the back of their minds. Qasimbekai was dragged from the room still screaming about treachery and issuing orders to everyone within earshot.

NORTH OF LAKE BALKHASH

Shchernikov's convoy was making good time as it moved along the M11 highway toward Karaganda. He was a little disappointed with the forces the Russian Provisional Government of Kazakhstan had provided him, but they should be more than sufficient for his purposes. Although he had lost all of his own vehicles before crossing the lake by boat, he still had about two thousand fanatically loyal infantry, which were now mounted on trucks obtained from Semipalatinsk, and he also had a full regiment of over a hundred T-72 tanks and a regiment of mechanized infantry, in addition to engineers, anti-aircraft units, and artillery.

He had been following the battles between the UN troops and the Kazakhs with great amusement on the radio. He was not surprised that the UN had been able to blow through the Kazakhs like a bullet through paper. It was, after all, a largely European force against Asiatics. Things would be different when the the bulk of the Russian separatist forces faced them—not just a handful of besieged fighters who were also defending against the Kazakhs on all sides, but a fully equipped field army sitting astride the UN troops' route of march. *Then* they would get a taste of what NATO would have gotten if the Red Army had ever boiled across the border between the two Germanies.

CHAPTER 7

Longshoremen on both coasts have now joined a wildcat boycott of all shipping to and from the former Soviet Union in protest over the refusal of the Russian government to allow American or other military forces to use its territory to reach the UN contingent reportedly fighting its way out of Kazakhstan. The President, who has been actively campaigning for his party's candidates for the upcoming congressional elections, has stated his intention of creating a blue ribbon commission to study the problem and has promised a quick solution to the crisis. Meanwhile, the *Washington Post* has published a story, complete with satellite photographs obtained from a clandestine source in NPIC, which showed evidence of the UN column trying to fight toward the Russian border. The story also contains reports that the UN troops had reacted to threats of attack by either Kazakh or ethnic Russian forces, or both, contradicting statements from the UN Secretary General that a mutiny by the contingent's commander, American Brigadier General Julian Chandler, had occurred. UN officials have continued to refuse all direct communications with the peacekeepers, claiming that all communication links have been disabled by General Chandler's troops.

CNN

SOUTH OF KARAGANDA
5 November, 0600 Hours

Chandler sat with Morgan on the hood of his Hummer, the freezing metal biting right through his fatigue pants and long underwear. The mountainous gray clouds were moving down fast from the north, and he had to brush the stray snowflakes from the lenses of his binoculars to watch the long lines of trucks and APCs arrive. The column was much smaller now than when they had left Almaty. Of course there had been some losses in combat on the way to Chiganak. Mainly, though, the number of vehicles and the fuel and supplies they required had been significantly cut by dropping off their Russian refugee riders at the town of Balkhash, the first sizable settlement north of the demarcation line. But there were still several hundred vehicles, and they churned the white snow into a gray muck where they maneuvered off the paved highway.

Chandler couldn't help but smile when he thought back to their leave-taking from the refugees. It seemed that each contingent of soldiers had "adopted" some of the Russians, and there was much sobbing and hugging and the shouting of mutually unintelligible promises and prayers back and forth as the sky-blue berets had mounted up on their vehicles in Balkhash. A delegation of Russians, led by Dr. Restrepov, had even presented themselves to Chandler and had suggested that they be taken along in the hopes of dissuading their countrymen from firing on the convoy. Restrepov had pointed out that he had considerable experience in the role of human shield, and he wouldn't mind serving this function of his own volition for a change.

Chandler thanked the old man profusely, finding it hard to speak for the knot in his throat, but pointed out that Shchernikov had never had many scruples about firing on civilians, his own or anyone else's, and that their sacrifice would probably be without benefit. Restrepov was obliged to agree , but he was so insistent on being given the chance that Chandler was forced to accept the continued presence of about one hundred of his former passengers, all men now, as possible go-betweens for future dealings with Shchernikov. Chandler planned to take the men a little farther up the road and drop them off if real combat seemed likely.

Chandler surveyed the scene through his binoculars in the growing daylight. He could see the American vehicles deployed in a rough arc stretching to either side of the main highway up ahead, with the British covering both flanks, and the French now taking up positions in the rear to provide for all-around defense. In the center were massed the transport trucks, fuel tankers, and command vehicles, with the vital SS-25 TELs huddled together at the base of the hill upon which Chandler sat, closely guarded by the Japanese military police company.

The lights of Karaganda had been visible for some time in the distance while it was still dark, but now that the sun was rising, only a brown smudge on the horizon betrayed the presence of a large formerly Soviet city. The rolling fields all around the city were covered with a smooth blanket of snow broken only by dark clumps of pine forests, which now finally began to break up the monotony of the open country through which the column had passed. But it was what he could see in the foreground, closer than Karaganda, that gave Chandler cause to worry. Across the black ribbon of highway, three great trenches like the claw marks of a huge tiger had been gouged out of the frozen ground. He estimated that they must each be at least ten meters wide and half a kilometer long. While he did have a single armored vehicle–launched bridge with the column, that would do for only one of the trenches, and in any event they would be well covered by direct and indirect fire.

In itself, this was not insurmountable, since the stripped-down column was quite capable of going overland, even through the snow, which was not overly deep yet, but he could see the burned hull of a British armored car that had tried to probe around the flank of the barrier and had discovered a minefield.

And beyond this, he could make out dozens of prepared defensive positions, and he knew from flights by the handful of functioning copters that Saavedra had left that most of those positions were indeed occupied by modern tanks, far more than he had at his disposal.

"It was all going so well," he said casually without removing the glasses from his eyes. "I mean, after the battle for Chiganak, the Kazakhs left us alone, and then we crossed into Russian territory with no problems, not even sniper fire. We're more than halfway home, but now I don't see how we can get any farther. There's no way that we can punch through the Russians. They outnumber us and outgun us, and all they have to do is screw us around until we run out of gas, and we're dead."

Morgan just sighed. "It's supposed to be the coldest November on record," he said absently.

"What?"

"The weather. It gets cold here in late autumn, but I've been listening to the radio reports from Omsk and points north, and they've got a full-scale blizzard going. That's what those clouds are that are headed our way."

"Thank you, Willard Scott," Chandler growled.

"Who?"

"A disgustingly upbeat American weatherman on television. Never mind. But to get back to the subject of our impending deaths for just a moment, do you have any brilliant suggestions?"

"No word, I suppose, from the UN in Novosibirsk or from official channels?"

"The Russians are jamming our frequencies. I suspect that the UN is still there, just sitting, but I can't see them doing anything to help us out at this point. I'm sure that Devi poisoned that well quite thoroughly. They probably see us as some sort of rogue elephant, crazed soldiers running around with nuclear weapons. Devi has probably painted Shchernikov as the good guy in this. According to Goldman's sources in Washington, Moscow was putting tremendous pressure on the Indian government for Devi to favor Shchernikov, all completely under the table, and the secretary general's desire to run things here just played into their hands very conveniently. Goldman is off now trying to establish contact with his own commo gear, but I don't expect anything to come of that, even if he can get through to someone."

"And the American government? Can't they do anything?"

"Not out here," Chandler said, shaking his head. "The UN still has forces in Semipalatinsk that were escorting the relief convoys through Kazakhstan, and I suppose the air units that enforced the no-fly zone are still there as well, but if Moscow won't permit passage of U.S. forces, which they won't, how could the Americans get to us? We're smack dab in the middle of the world's biggest continent. No carriers cruising off the coast can do us any good this time. No, my friend, I'm afraid we're totally on our own."

"Well, in that case, I don't see what we have to lose," Morgan said.

"What we have to lose by what? We're dug in here with Russians blocking the road in front of us, and probably more cutting off the road behind us. When they're good and ready, they'll just charge forward and cut us down, unless we surrender first. Shchernikov keeps threatening on every radio channel that if we destroy any 'captured equipment,' meaning the missiles, of course, he won't take any prisoners. Not that that would stop us if we knew how to disable the missiles permanently without running the risk of having them go off in our faces."

"Actually, the reason that I brought up the weather just now was related to this," Morgan replied. "I was just thinking that we have far more vehicles at this point than we absolutely need to transport the men we've got left or the fuel we'd need to reach the border."

"Yes, I suppose we could get rid of quite a few. What of it?"

"Well, the Russians have the road itself blocked, but the land off to the northeast is almost perfectly flat, and our vehicles all have excellent off-road capacity; even the SS-25s could do it."

"So we just sidestep the Russians? But they'll just move back in front of us. They've even got highways all over to move on and would have no trouble at all keeping ahead of us, to say nothing of the damage they could do by hitting our flanks as we moved, picking our vehicles off out in the open. There's no way we could get through."

"That's supposing that the Russians knew that we'd gone around them."

"Oh, and what exactly are we going to do? Tell them to close their eyes and count to a hundred? They're right over there, damn it!" Chandler said acidly, waving at the dark blotches of upturned earth on the white landscape in the distance.

"I was thinking of this blizzard. Perhaps, if it's as bad as it appears, we could move off under cover of that."

"It might look bad to us, but these people are fucking Siberians, for Christ's sake! This is probably shirtsleeve weather for them."

"I don't think so," Morgan argued. "They're only human, and we know that these ethnic Russian forces are not all that disciplined. For many of them, their hometown is right behind them, Karaganda—don't you think that some of them will be taking the opportunity to shelter in a nice warm building? And we also know that they're very short on thermal imagers for tanks and whatnot. They don't have state-of-the-art stuff at all. We can see in a blizzard, but they can't."

"You're serious, aren't you?" Chandler asked, stiffly hopping down from the hood of the vehicle.

"It was just a thought at first," Morgan replied, "but the more I think about it, the more I think that we really don't have any other option. It's either stay here and be taken after all we've been through, or give it a go."

"But what about minefields? We know that they've lain some, and under the snow, we'd never be able to find them. And, if we try to use our mine-clearing charges and other equipment, that would give away any surreptitious move we would be trying to make, wouldn't it?"

"The Russians have only had a couple of days to do what they've done, extract their forces from Almaty and collect them here in front of us. They've obviously expended great effort digging those ditches across the highway, through frozen ground, and I doubt that they've been able to surround us completely. If we were to head due east for even a few klicks, we'll find the P49 secondary highway, which heads up to Pavlodar, and from there it's just over a hundred kilometers to the border."

"But from here to Pavlodar is still a good four hundred kilometers, and all the Russians have to do is pull back straight up the M-Eleven to Pavlodar. If we're on some country road, probably wading through three feet of snow, there's no way that we'd get there ahead of them. We'd end up in the same situation just a little farther on and a little weaker."

"And if we got a good head start on them? What if we were gone for twelve hours before they realized it. Even if we can only do ten miles an hour, we'd be halfway there, and the going for them on the highway won't be much better than it will be for us. Listen, we know that all of their available forces are concentrated either right here in front or in back of us, or back down on the Lepsa River, facing the Kazakhs in case they get any ideas. And maybe, if we got a lot closer to the border, even Moscow might feel obligated to step in and help us get their damned missiles back for them."

"Why don't you wish for a million dollars for me, while you're at it?" Chandler laughed, shaking his head as the two men walked through the snow to the one-room log cottage, or *izba*, where Chandler had set up a temporary command post in a small farming commune. The temperature, which had not risen above freezing for days, was dropping fast now, and Chandler could feel the thick snowflakes sticking to his eyelashes. The clouds were dropping and seemed now almost to be touching the ground, cutting visibility to less than a kilometer. "So, how would you propose that we sneak twenty-five hundred men and about two hundred vehicles out of here without anyone noticing?"

Inside the dark, smoky, windowless *izba* stood the unit commanders and, Chandler was surprised to see, Professor Restrepov.

"I took the liberty of inviting the good doctor to our meeting, because I think he might be able to be of assistance to us. I've also taken the liberty of discussing my plan with the other unit commanders before I raised it with you. I wanted a sanity check, and I think it just might work."

"Well?" Chandler said, hands on his hips. "I'm open to suggestions."

"Not to be overly optimistic," Lieutenant Harish, the Israeli engineer, began, "but I think we would have about one chance in a thousand."

"I don't like it," Peabody grumbled. "If we're going to buy it, I'd rather do it right here and get it over with. No point in running off through the snow and getting all cold and everything first, and *then* dying anyway."

"I do detect a note of sanity," Chandler admitted as he leaned over the map spread out on a low table, the only piece of furniture in the room.

"Peabody is just upset, because he'd have to give up some of his tanks," Morgan argued. "I've worked this out with some precision, if you'd care to listen."

"Shoot," Chandler said.

"Listen. With typical foresight, the British squadron's transport section consists of two dozen of those Swedish Hagglunds all-terrain vehicles. With those, we can carry enough fuel for all of our vehicles, and we cut ammunition to what each vehicle can carry with it. If we need more than that, we're out of luck anyway. Then, if we cozy up a bit, we can fit all of our men into the running armored personnel carriers, the American Bradleys, British Spartans, and the French VABs, which all have good cross-country capability, and a few Hummers. And for firepower, we keep the French AMX-10RCs and four American M-1s. Everything else we leave in place, in plain sight for the Russians to view."

"I don't understand why we would have to leave a good ten functioning tanks behind," Peabody pouted. "If we get into a fight, you'd sure wish we had them."

"If we get into a serious fight," Morgan replied, "it will be with a tank regiment, and ten tanks more or less won't make the difference. The M-1A1 Abramses guzzle too much gas and don't carry enough people. The same with the British armored cars and all of the support vehicles and command tracks."

"But what we take and what we leave doesn't answer the question of how we're supposed to get whatever force we decide upon out of here without the Russians catching on," Chandler insisted. "They're barely three klicks away. Even if this storm is as bad as you say, and even if they don't have equipment for seeing through it, the minute the snow stops, they'll see that we're gone, and the chase will be on."

"That's where Dr. Restrepov comes in," Morgan said, wagging a finger in the air. "I have suggested, and the good doctor has agreed enthusiastically, that he and his countrymen, our 'hostages,' will run the vehicles we leave behind, driving them around, keeping some fires going, as it were, to give Shchernikov and his people the idea that we're still here, so that even if the Russians are watching us with thermal imagers, they'll see enough activity." Restrepov, who was obviously straining to keep up with the English, nodded his head vigorously. "The storm will cover our tracks as we leave, and if we can just avoid contact ourselves with anyone on the road, even after the snow stops, they might be able to carry on the deception for a few more crucial hours. As I said before, if we can move out steadily for ten or twelve hours before the Russians figure out where we've gone, we'll have a lead that they won't be able to make up easily."

"And they won't be alone," Saavedra said, waving his cane over his head. "I've still got six Apaches and six OH-58s left in running order. During the storm, nobody's aircraft are going to be up. As soon as the ceiling lifts, we'll be up and around, giving even more of an impression of life, and we can also carry about twenty of our own armored vehicle crewmen who can help move things around, and we can keep up a lively chatter on the radio for Shchernikov's boys to listen to. Then, either when the Russkies start coming or when you all give us the word, we'll pop away at Shchernikov a little and then hightail it up to where you are. I suspect we'll have to be abandoning our birds at some point, but I suppose I could swallow my pride enough to ride out on the ground."

"That's easy for you to say," Peabody said. "Most of your choppers already flew out. You won't be leaving the best part of your command on the field *and* in running order. That's the kind of thing the Iraqis do, not Americans."

"They do it when it's a question of saving their men's lives," Chandler snapped. He knew now that his one goal was to get as many of the men out as possible. The message they had received that the Blackhawks with the wounded had landed safely at Novosibirsk had lifted a tremendous weight from Chandler's shoulders. Now there seemed to be a possibility, however remote, of getting everyone else out as well. "There are some simple, basic facts here that we can't lose sight of. We're *not* going to let Shchernikov get his hands on these missiles again. He's certifiably nuts, and the world is just flat lucky that he didn't decide to pop off one of these babies while he had them. The other is that Shchernikov is more than capable of killing every one of us to try to get the missiles or of massacring us if we somehow were able to disable them. If we stay here, our only option is to fight to the death, and I don't even want to think about what being a prisoner in Shchernikov's hands would be like for any of our men. I don't think this end run has a ghost of a chance of coming off as easily as Colonel Morgan has laid it out, but I didn't really think we'd get this far, either. I say, let's try it."

There was a general, albeit reluctant nodding of heads around the room. Even Peabody finally just folded his arms closely and grunted, "Oh, what the fuck. I'm in."

"The one thing that still concerns me," Chandler said, turning to Restrepov, "is what Shchernikov might do to you and your people if he believes that you aided us in our escape."

The doctor smiled patiently and put a long, white hand on Chandler's shoulder. "General, you are a good man, and I can understand how these things are hard for you to comprehend. My friends and I could have died at any time in the past several years. Shchernikov could decide to kill us whenever he chooses, whether we do anything that would provoke him or not. You and your men, on the other hand, have risked your own lives to save us and our families. We owe you a debt that we would like to try to repay, and this is a good way to do so. However, I cannot say that our willingness to do this thing for you is from entirely altruistic motives. We have a selfish purpose as well. It has occurred to us that, if you are successful in getting those hellish missiles out of Shchernikov's hands, his power here will be broken. He will then be responsible both for the loss of Alma-Ata to the Kazakhs and for losing the missiles, after undoubtedly stealing them from the Russian government. No one will want anything to do with him, and there are other men among the Russian separatists who would enjoy cutting him down to size. Perhaps those who replace him will be less evil. They could hardly be worse, but it would give us all great joy to eliminate his power in any case. If doing this entails some risk, so be it. The game is worth the candle, as you say in English."

Chandler just nodded and shook the old man's hand. He remembered it as being rather weak, when they first met, but now there seemed to be a new strength in the grip of the long, flexible fingers.

"Very well," Chandler said, "if there are no other objections, let's get on it. We'll want to have the men loaded in the selected vehicles and ready to move when the weather closes in."

The men looked at each other for a moment, then all moved toward the door.

Shchernikov wiped the last crumbs of lunch from his mouth and peered through the infrared scope set up in the steeple of a church in a small farming village south of Karaganda. The driving snow outside made the sky and ground one solid wall of white, and even the green-ish image on the scope was obscured as drifts of snow began to pile up around the UN vehicles in the distance, masking their thermal signature.

"This is the worst storm I've seen this time of year," he said to the officers standing behind him. "I wonder if this isn't a signal from God."

"In what way?" Colonel Stepan Kurikin, commander of the 25th Guards Tank Regiment, asked. Kurikin was a former officer of the regular Russian Army who had been "detached" to the ethnic Russian service in Kazakhstan, and he had little use for Shchernikov or the undisciplined gunmen who formed his entourage. While some of them might have had combat experience in Afghanistan, most of them had little in their backgrounds other than the killing of unarmed civilians. Still, Kurikin recognized that even these scum were ultimately doing a service for Russia itself, securing for her a huge territory with immense natural resources and helping to halt Russia's rapid slide from superpower status to that of a fragmented Third World country. He would fight for them, but he wouldn't take any shit from them, he repeated to himself.

"I mean that this might be the opportunity we've been waiting for to recapture the missiles," Shchernikov stated flatly.

"In this storm?" Kurikin asked. "You can't see ten yards ahead of you outside. Any attack would become totally disorganized in five minutes, and we'd be involved in a nasty knife fight at point-blank range where our superior armament and numbers wouldn't be able to tell. If we just hold the enemy where they are, they'll burn up the little fuel they've got left in a matter of days, and if they try to break through our lines, we'll pick them off without any risk to our own troops. To go looking for trouble now would be to court disaster. It's the only way you *could* lose this battle."

"Thank you, *Colonel*," Shchernikov sneered, emphasizing the junior man's rank. "From your limited point of view, you're perfectly right, of course. But *I* must look at things from a broader perspective. We know from Mr. Devi," Shchernikov nodded to the short, stocky figure who stood at the back of the crowd of officers and who bowed slightly in return, "that there is tremendous public pressure on the governments whose troops are in the UN forces to do something to rescue them. This pressure has been transferred to the UN, and, although Secretary General Muli has done wonders to attempt to divert public anger away from us and toward General Chandler, whom he has painted as a maniac running his own private war, he has not been totally successful. The news reports which have continued to filter out from that reporter Goldman have done us tremendous damage, and the interviews with those wounded UN soldiers who were evacuated did us no good, either, with their stories."

"We should have destroyed those helicopters like I suggested," Lushkin interjected. "Then there wouldn't have been any interviews with wounded soldiers."

"How stupid do you think people are, Lushkin?" Kurikin shouted. "I don't care what kind of weak story you might have cooked up to blame such a barbarous act on the Kazakhs. No one would have been fooled for an instant, and the pressure on us would have been ten times as great. Not even Moscow could have afforded to have been identified with us."

"What's done is done," Shchernikov said imperiously, raising a hand for silence. "And I'm glad that you're starting to think in political terms, Colonel. But my point is that every day that passes is to the advantage of the enemy. If our supporters in Moscow knuckle under to blackmail from the West, the game will be up in ten minutes. But if we can get our hands on those missiles, we'll be back in control again."

"*You'll* be back in control," Kurikin mumbled.

"Do you have a problem with that, Colonel?" Shchernikov growled, and Lushkin took a menacing step forward, as did one of Kurikin's lieutenants, and the officers in the cramped room began to divide into two hostile camps. Shchernikov put a pudgy hand on Lushkin's broad chest. "I'm sure I don't have to remind you that you are under my orders here, and if you don't think you can comply with them, we can simply have you reassigned."

Kurikin glared at Lushkin over Shchernikov's head. "That won't be necessary . . . General."

"Good. Then let's think this through. The UN forces have been moving and fighting for days without rest, and they were already worn out from the regular daily pressure they were under in Alma-Ata when they started. We know that they must be low on ammunition and fuel. All it will take will be for us to demonstrate to them that resistance is futile, and they will cave in quickly. This storm which poses problems for us is even worse for them, because each defensive position will be largely cut off from the others, and junior officers will have to be making decisions on their own. If we can just crack the hard crust of their resistance, they'll fall like a house of cards. I guarantee it. These men are *peacekeepers*, not warriors. They're here to prevent fighting, not to conquer. What kind of motivation can that be for a fighting man?"

"Ask the Kazakhs," Kurikin said.

"We're not Kazakhs," Shchernikov reminded him. "And the UN has taken its losses as well. They're still a long way from their goal, and now they've been stalled here for more than half a day. They've lost their momentum, and their morale must be in the toilet. I tell you that now is the time to strike!"

"It will take time to concentrate our forces," Kurikin mumbled, lowering his head.

"How long?"

"Twenty-four hours."

"I'll give you eight, and not a second more."

"Exactly so . . . General," Kurikin said, giving a halfhearted salute. He smiled inwardly at the frown that always appeared on Shchernikov's face when he paused before addressing the little Napoleon with his "rank."

"The storm was playing hell with my communications," Goldman said, as he and Elders sat shivering in the back of a Hummer with Chandler and Morgan. "I was able to get out the message of your planned move, and I got a kind of electronic handshake to indicate receipt, but when they tried to respond a few minutes later, all I got was gobbledygook."

"Not that I expected much more than that, even with perfect communications," Chandler laughed. "We've been on our own for so long that I've kind of gotten used to it." He turned to Morgan, who had just joined them and was still brushing snow off his coat. "Are we ready to go?"

"As ready as we'll ever be. It's going to be very cramped, and the fuel is just barely going to be enough. If we start losing vehicles mired in the snow or with mechanical breakdowns, we're going to be in trouble."

"Well, we're not leaving anyone behind except Saavedra's detachment, and I don't expect that we'll discover oil in the next few minutes, so I guess that will have to do."

"Something just occurred to me," Elders joined in. "Suppose that the Russians hit us *before* the weather improves enough for the choppers to fly? Tanks can roll in all kinds of weather. Then how are Saavedra and his men going to get away?"

Chandler and Morgan looked at each other. "That's right!" Chandler declared. "We've been planning things all on our own and forgetting that Shchernikov might have his own agenda without consulting us."

"They say that there's no such thing as bad luck," Goldman commented, "only other people's plans we didn't consider."

"Actually, I *did* consider that," Morgan said. "And I talked with Saavedra about it. He's got twenty-four men altogether, and I've left him two running Bradleys, just in case. I told him that he'd have no head start, and the Russians would already be as mad as hornets, but he insisted that the people who wrote the manuals with the design limits of the helicopter never had the incentive of a T-72 bearing down on them. He said that if the Russians come, he'll fly, weather or no weather."

Chandler was silent for a long moment. This put things in a different light. As long as his forces were working together it was all right, even if they were fighting against long odds, even though there had been casualties, lots of casualties. But there was something different about the thought of turning his back and leaving men behind to face this kind of danger alone, something that made the pain in his stomach growl to life again, and he suddenly realized that he hadn't had the pain for days—and he hadn't missed it.

"The one advantage they'll have," Morgan went on, seeing his chief's indecision, "is that Shchernikov will want to get on after us immediately once he realizes we're gone. He's not going to waste time chasing after small fish."

"Maybe he'll want to have a chat with a small fish or two, to find out the details of our plan," Goldman suggested, and Morgan shot him a nasty look, making the reporter wince.

"Shchernikov's the kind of man who would let even his main goal escape him, just to get revenge," Chandler said, talking to himself. "I don't want to think about how he'd treat anyone who fell into his hands alive if we escape him."

"Listen to me, sir!" Morgan shouted, grabbing Chandler roughly by the shoulder and shaking him. "Don't back out on us now! Saavedra and all the men with him could have died just as easily at Chiganak, but they didn't. We might any one of us die in the next couple of days. There are no guarantees for anyone, and Saavedra knows that. It's what he and the other volunteers are willing to do that will give us even the slim chance that we've got. It was their decision, and you can't make it for them, sir."

Chandler remained silent, rubbing his stomach gently. "I suppose not," he finally said. "Let's go."

"I'm sorry, sir," Morgan said, tugging lightly at Chandler's uniform as if to straighten out any wrinkles he might have made, although several days of riding and fighting had left the uniform in less than parade-ground shape. "I had no right to do that."

"Yes, you did, Randy," Chandler replied, shaking his head. "I was the one who was out of line."

Wakeham had taken part in many Royal Marines exercises above the Arctic Circle in Norway in which they practiced getting NATO reinforcement of their flank in the event of a major war with the old Soviet Union. Since they never did that sort of training when the weather was nice, this made him the column's closest thing to a cold weather expert. He had given briefings to the vehicle drivers and had planned out their route using the best maps available.

They would travel in a tight phalanx of nearly two hundred vehicles, in three long columns running only some ten meters apart, with about the same distance between vehicles to limit the chances of anyone getting lost in the storm. All of the vehicles would drive with their lights on, since they would only be visible for a few meters during the storm and present little danger of being spotted by the Russians. The APCs and tanks with thermal sights would be scattered throughout the column to augment the visual guidance of the vehicle commanders, who would ride exposed in their open hatches. The men would rotate frequently to keep anyone from freezing to death. Chandler and Morgan hoped that this formation, and the Global Positioning Satellite locator system each vehicle carried, would eliminate the need for radio communication and still prevent straggling.

Saavedra leaned out of the hatch in the roof of his Hummer to shake Chandler's hand as the latter did the same from his own, the two vehicles parked side to side at the edge of the long column.

"Good luck, Julian."

"I think we'll all need it, Juan Carlos," Chandler replied. "Now remember, I'd rather you run if things get dicey here. Once the game's up, it's up, and there won't be any point in adding to the butcher's bill by screwing around here."

"Race you home, Julian," Saavedra said, giving Chandler's hand one final shake and then shouting down to his driver, who wheeled away into the swirling snow.

Chandler's own Hummer pulled into position just behind the strange Swedish transport that Wakeham was using to ride point. It was a very small-tracked vehicle connected to a separate tracked trailerlike affair with a large hinge in the middle. It looked to Chandler like a larger but stubby version of an HO-scale diesel loco-motive he'd had as a kid where the trailer was one of the cars. Chandler raised a small red-and-green pennant and waved it high over his head. Wakeham waved his in return, and Chandler turned to see the other commanders of the column repeating the signal. He could only see about three vehicles back, about twenty-five meters, just far enough to make out the hulking form of the first of the huge SS-25 TELs, tucked into the center row of the column.

2100 Hours

The four remaining guns of the Egyptian captain Atef Hamed's bat-tery of self-propelled 155mm pieces were all loaded and carefully registered on the crossroad the Russians would most likely pass through as they concentrated for an assault on the UN position. Hamed was alone in the M-109's turret with the gun's lanyard in his hand, and three of his men, who had remained behind with him, were likewise holding the lanyards of three other pieces. One M-109 stood hub to hub with Hamed's, and the other pair was several hun-dred yards away. His plan was to fire the four rounds almost simulta-neously when the order came to fire. Then, the man from the other gun would join him and the two of them would load and fire his gun as long as possible with the ammunition standing in the ready racks, as would the two men on one of the other guns. They would be firing largely blind, and it would be unlikely that they would seriously hin-der a Russian advance. But the main point was to make as much noise as possible, to convince the Russians that the entire force was still present. Nearly all of the fuel had been drained from the tanks of the big M-109s, so they would not be able to displace to avoid Russian counterbattery fire, and Hamed did not hold out much chance of having time to get off all of the rounds he had prepared.

Saavedra had posted a scout close to the Russian lines, and Hamed had just received word on his field phone that he had picked up the noise of many tank engines approaching. The storm had abated only slightly, and visibility was limited to perhaps one hundred meters, but Hamed still frequently looked out from the turret hatchway to try to get a view of something, anything. No matter how often he wiped the snow off his goggles, it all looked white to him; since the sun had set, a couple of hours before, it was a white veil before a dark backdrop.

Hamed's field phone rang, and Saavedra's voice came over it.

"Fire your pattern!"

Hamed yanked the lanyard, and the turret rocked with the recoil of the big gun. Now Yasuf leaped into the turret with him to help load the next round. They placed the correct number of powder bags into the tube before slamming the breech closed. The gun barked a second, and then a third time. By now the first round, one of their few SADARM anti-armor rounds, would be suspended from a parachute high above the ground, rotating in the wind and searching the ground with its tiny radar for any large metal object—like a tank. When it found one, a rocket motor would ignite, propelling the warhead down onto the thinner top armor of the target.

But now he was firing simple high explosive, just for effect, and he could feel the ground begin to shake from the eruption of near misses by enemy artillery. Their radars would have analyzed the trajectory of his incoming rounds and plotted his position, and he could hear the shells walking their way toward him. He and Yasuf worked feverishly, heaving the heavy rounds into the tube and firing until the ready racks were empty.

"That's it!" he shouted, and the two men dove through the open back hatch of the turret, landing up to their knees in snow and wading heavily away from the piece.

Hamed looked to his left and saw the other gun illuminated for an instant as it fired a round, but almost simultaneously it was transformed into a ball of fire as an enemy round found its mark. He did not have to worry about survivors, he thought. He and Yasuf were still surrounded by geysers of snow and earth as the enemy barrage continued to rain down on them. They found a spot where the snow was less deep and broke into a run to the jeep they had left parked nearby. For a terrifying instant, the motor of the jeep groaned and strained as Hamed leaned on the starter, but it finally caught, and they wheeled away just as both of their guns were destroyed by a deluge of enemy shells.

The jeep fishtailed repeatedly as Hamed tried to stay on what he assumed was the road and tried to keep his orientation, looking for the pad where Saavedra's helicopters would be. He had the headlights on, since he doubted that the enemy could see him unless they were close enough to spit on him in any case. Not that they were doing him much good. He cursed the snow and the cold and the darkness until he just barely made out the tiny red light on the nose of one of the choppers. Then he praised Allah and drove like mad.

Greene saw the shape of three tanks loom up in his thermal imager almost simultaneously, one directly in the crosshairs of the sight. The gun was already loaded, and he merely shouted, "On the way!" and pulled the trigger. Then he dropped down from the commander's position, yelling for the driver to move his Abrams to the next position. He grabbed a new round, slammed it into the tube, and closed the breech. He jumped back to his sights and lined up the next shot.

He could see the flames from the first tank as soon as the driver pulled them back up to the crest of the low ridge behind which they were sheltering. He scanned for the other two enemy tanks, but there were now at least half a dozen, all firing in his direction. He saw a flash as one of his two other Abramses, which he was fielding with two-man crews instead of the regulation four, took a carefully aimed shot and accounted for one of the enemy. But the enemy tanks were racing forward too quickly. They were less than a kilometer away now, and they were followed by swarms of armored personnel carriers.

Greene fired again and scored another hit, but then one of his Abramses exploded off to his right as it tried to back down from the ridge. He watched as the top hatch flew open and a figure clambered out onto the back deck. A second explosion within the tank hurled the figure to the ground, but the man scrambled to his feet and slogged through the snow, turning to look back as the Abrams was engulfed in flames. Greene shouted orders to his driver, and they skewed to a halt in front of the man, who dragged himself wearily up the front glacis of Greene's tank and eased himself into the loader's hatch, which Greene held open for him.

"Jesus!" the man groaned. "Thanks, Captain."

"No way Henderson got out of there," Greene said, "but I could sure use a loader in here."

"You got it, boss." The man slammed a fresh round into the chamber, pausing an instant to wipe his eyes roughly with his sleeves.

Something was definitely wrong, Kurikin thought as he steered his tank toward the last known position of the missiles. He had had the feeling for some time that afternoon, even though their sensors showed plenty of activity within the UN perimeter on the rare occasions when their sensors were able to overcome the intense cold and the blowing snow. Vehicles were driving back and forth, the buildings radiated heat, and their radio intercept stations showed a normal level of intra-unit chatter. Still, the place had seemed to lack the kind of *life* that the base camp of a brigade-size unit has.

Now, as they pushed through the enemy front lines, there was some resistance, but far too little: a few rounds of artillery fire, very easily suppressed, and now just a handful of enemy tanks exchanging fire with his advance elements. Then, nothing. He had taken some losses, certainly, but nothing compared to the meatgrinder that the Kazakhs had gone through at the Ili River. Russian intelligence satellites had monitored that engagement with great interest, and eventually, if somewhat unreliably, had passed the information on from Moscow to the Russian separatists in Kazakhstan. This was not the same sort of fight at all. Not that he was complaining. Perhaps the enemy had used almost all of its ammunition. Perhaps some of these national contingents had unilaterally decided to give up the battle. But he had a bad feeling about it.

Just then the snow suddenly cleared a bit, and his gunner called his attention to two American tanks that were making a run for it, pursued by over a dozen Russian ones. The Americans were firing on the move, over their back decks, but far more slowly than was the American standard. One of Kurikin's tanks took a hit, but they stopped one of the Americans as well, first knocking off a tread to immobilize it, then pouring several rounds into the stationary vehicle at rapidly closing range. But now the other American had dropped into a gully and was gone from sight.

Kurikin was listening intently to the radio messages coming in from his accompanying infantry, who were busily blowing up UN trucks with the lighter guns of their APCs and searching the buildings they overran.

"No UN prisoners so far at all," one crackling voice announced, "just Russian civilians. Say they're from Alma-Ata. Over."

"How'd they get here? Over," the unit commander came back.

"They say the UN soldiers brought them. Saved them from the Kazakhs when Shchernikov left them, over."

Kurikin almost choked when he heard that. That fucking Shchernikov, the great general, really had run off and left our people to the Kazakhs?

"How many have you got? Over."

"We've picked up maybe a dozen. They say that there are about a hundred here, but over two thousand were dropped off back in the town of Balkhash. Over."

Kurikin hadn't heard anything about that, and he doubted that anyone else on this side of the demarcation line had either. If it was true, then Shchernikov had used his control over the provisional government to get the information suppressed. Overlooking some stragglers in a city you have to abandon might be one thing, but it was obvious that Shchernikov had cut and run with his cronies, leaving the civilians to fend for themselves—and the UN, the *enemy*, had had to step in and save them.

"Get off the damn radio, you imbeciles!" a gruff voice broke into the transmission. Kurikin thought he recognized it as belonging to Shchernikov's watchdog, Lushkin. "Bring those prisoners into headquarters for questioning, and don't talk to them in the meanwhile. Those are direct orders from the high command."

Naturally, Kurikin mused. If they have information that would be embarrassing for Shchernikov, the chances of their living through "questioning" would be very slim indeed.

"Now what about the missiles?" Lushkin asked. Kurikin noticed that this "soldier" didn't seem to know anything about radio procedures, no "over" at the end of a transmission.

"No sign of them," the unit commander replied. "And not half of the vehicles we saw move in here are anywhere to be found. Most of the ones that are here are trucks that have been disabled, and there are a few running ones that the Russian civilians were driving around. Over."

"This is Brickbat," Kurikin broke in, "and I can confirm that. Very few vehicles. Very little resistance. I think that the enemy has pulled out except for a small rearguard. Over."

"What?" a new voice screamed. Kurikin knew that it must be Shchernikov. "Which way did they go?"

"This is Brickbat. There are at least two feet of fresh snow on the ground. I don't think we're going to find any tracks out here, sir. Over," Kurikin said with a broad smile on his face.

"Well, get after them, you idiot. Find out where they went . . . no, wait. There's only one way they could have gone, northeast toward the border. Kurikin, pull back to Karaganda and head northeast to Pavlodar immediately."

"We'll need to refuel before we can move that far, sir, over."

"There's no time for that. They're getting away!"

"Our tanks will run out of gas halfway to Paulodar if we don't refuel, and the facilities in Karaganda will permit us to accomplish the refueling much faster than we could do out on the road in this weather, over."

"If those bastards get away with our missiles, it will be your fault, Kurikin!" Shchernikov raged.

"Exactly so, General."

Saavedra didn't like the noise the rotor of his OH-58 Kiowa was making, creaking and groaning as it turned laboriously over his head. Despite the best efforts of the handful of men he had kept with him to run the engines frequently and wrap them against the cold and wind, only two of the two Apaches and four of the OH-58s responded when the time finally came to start up for real as the Russians over-ran the base perimeter. The wind had died down slightly now, and Saavedra hoped that, if they could just get airborne, they could rise above the worst of it and get away.

The Apaches each carried a crew of two and had no room for passengers, being designed as trim fighter aircraft, so he sent those aloft first, watching as they were buffeted and rocked until they disappeared into the dense cloud cover. The smaller OH-58s could carry a total of four people, five in a pinch counting the pilot. But Saavedra's already had two Apache crewmen huddling in the rear, as did the other working Kiowa. Only six more could be evacuated. He found himself consciously trying to avoid praying for heavy casualties among the ground pounders, although he might soon be faced with the awkward decision of either leaving someone behind or overloading his aircraft to the point where no one would get away. He knew that there were a total of twenty men, apart from the departing Apache crews, in the stay-behind force. There was no way that they would all fit.

The first men Saavedra saw were Hamed and his other artillery-man, who ditched their jeep about fifty meters away and struggled to the choppers, bending low under the slowly turning rotors. Hamed sent his man to the other bird, and climbed in next to Saavedra.

"I lost two," he said flatly.

Saavedra only nodded. That left a total of eighteen to lift. He waved to the other pilot and jerked his thumb skyward. There were already four men aboard that Kiowa, and he doubted that the small choppers could lift even that many in this wind and with ice sure to build up on all surfaces. The other pilot hesitated for a moment, then nodded, revving his engine and raising the craft a few feet off the ground. He then tipped the nose downward and moved off horizontally, gaining altitude very gradually.

Suddenly there was a snapping sound clearly audible above the whistle of the wind and the whine of Saavedra's own engine, and a yellow flash shot across the nose of the rising Kiowa, then another. Jesus! Saavedra thought to himself, they're here already.

The third shot, or more likely a burst from a 30mm gun, tore through the body of the Kiowa, which was about ten meters from the ground now. The rounds ripped huge chunks from the fuselage, and the craft careened over at a sharp angle, plunging sideways into the side of an equipment shed and exploding instantly.

Saavedra was debating whether to try to take off or wait—the enemy, which had been well beyond visual range in the storm, might not notice him for a few more precious seconds. Just then a huge white form roared across Saavedra's field of vision, firing its main gun into the whiteness. The tank's shot was followed by a brilliant ball of orange flame off in the distance, then the tank fishtailed to a halt, its turret turning slowly as the gunner scanned for new targets.

Then the hatches on the tank flew open and three men piled out and raced for Saavedra's chopper. Greene pressed his snow encrusted face up against Saavedra's side window.

"I've got three here, and five KIA out there." Then Greene looked at the apparently full chopper and looked around for more. "Where the hell is everybody?"

"This is all there is, partner. I can take one more man inside, and the other two will have to strap on to those external seats mounted on the skids."

"Holy Christ!" Greene whistled. "That's going to be awful breezy, isn't it?"

"I don't know if I can get this pig up in the air at all, so it's economy supersaver class, or you're walking."

Greene nodded and pushed one of his men through the door, where he sat on the laps of the two pilots in the rear, while Greene and his driver strapped themselves onto the skids.

Saavedra saw ghostly forms moving out in the blowing snow. He had extinguished all running lights, but they would see him soon, if they hadn't already. He gunned the engine and yanked the stick over, trying to put distance between himself and the enemy even as the rotors clawed at the frigid air for altitude.

They were firing at him, but it was only rifles so far, and he heard the distinct ping of rounds striking the aircraft. Fortunately, the ground on this side dropped away slightly, and Saavedra was able to get a running start, picking up ground speed before he had to try to gain height. He ducked behind a low farm building to shield him from the enemy infantry and then slowly rose into the overcast sky.

The stick felt like a broom handle with a giant on the other end trying to wrench it from his grasp. He narrowly avoided a stand of snow-laden pines, but the tiny aircraft finally rose to high enough to be completely surrounded by unbroken whiteness. It was going to be a long ride.

NEAR ROUTE P49, NORTHEAST OF KARAGANDA
5 November, 2200 Hours

Things had not gone at all as planned. Of course, Chandler knew that road marches always fell behind schedule, no matter how routine they were, no matter how carefully planned, even on the training fields of Fort Lewis. So it was not really a surprise that they would have trouble keeping to schedule plowing across country, through enemy territory in a blizzard. Still, he had hoped that his goals were realistic enough. He had calculated an advance of perhaps ten to fifteen miles per hour, just a good steady jogging speed, but he had also hoped for at least a twelve-hour head start before the Russians realized he was gone.

Chandler had heard the radio messages from Greene and Saavedra about the Russian attack, which had begun half an hour before, barely eight hours after the column had set off. He had hoped they would have covered at least a hundred miles by that time, but he reckoned they had done perhaps sixty. They had crossed the major east-west leg of the M11 highway northeast of Karaganda and were now rolling through sparsely wooded country roughly halfway between the northern leg of the M11, which linked Karaganda and Pavlodar, and the narrower Route P49 to the east, which paralleled the M11. Chandler and Wakeham figured that, since the roads were no clearer of snow than the fields, they would at least avoid the towns that clung to the highways in this vast open region, thus not giving the enemy warning of their movement and bypassing any local militia that might be stationed there.

But the going was tough. They had already lost several vehicles either to mechanical problems or from becoming stuck in some undetected ditch. Naturally, each stoppage had brought the entire column to a grinding halt and had entailed at least a few minutes' effort to extract the trapped vehicle, sometimes with success, or to offload men and supplies and to distribute them among the other, increasingly crowded vehicles.

Now that they knew that the Russians had overrun the base and would be hot on their trail at any moment, Chandler had ordered an increase of speed to eighteen miles per hour, with orders not to waste time trying to salvage trapped vehicles, except for the SS-25 TELs, of course. They would also cut over to Route P49 in the hope that there would at least be less chance of a vehicle crashing through the crust of ice on a snow-covered pond.

When the men no longer fit inside the remaining transports, they would ride on top, taking turns with those inside to avoid frostbite. They only had about two hundred fifty miles to go—maybe twelve to fourteen hours—*if* they could keep to this new schedule. Even as Chandler thought this, however, he had to ask himself how they could hope to move faster now if they had been falling behind when they were still relatively fresh. The snow was still falling heavily. Chandler sat in his Hummer and peered into the cottony distance, straining to keep the taillight of Wakeham's vehicle in sight, watching for soft spots in front of them, signaling to the driver to go left, right, speed up, or slow down, and trying to keep from freezing to death.

CHAPTER 8

THE M11 HIGHWAY SOUTHWEST OF PAVLODAR
6 November, 1000 hours

In Russia, people have learned not to expect miracles, or even efficiency, from government. In the midst of Siberia, during a civil war, one can become downright resigned to the lack of public services, and the residents consequently know how to get about even in a blizzard.

Kurikin's column was able to keep quite handily to the schedule he had set for it. He had tanks equipped with mine plows leading the column, echeloned right and using their heavy blades to push away the worst drifts of snow as they rolled unperturbed northward at a stately twenty miles per hour. The refueling stop in Karaganda had given the bulk of his men time to get a few hours' sleep and to pull some much needed maintenance on their vehicles, as well as to replace the ammunition they had expended. And to bury their dead, he added to himself.

The worst of the storm had passed, and although there was still a low cloud cover, which would prevent any significant air support from the Russian separatists' modest air force, observation planes with sensing equipment had easily pinpointed the location of the enemy column. The lead elements of Kurikin's own force were already passing through Pavlodar, making the right turn onto the M3 highway toward the southeast, and Semipalatinsk. There they would patrol the M3, which ran along the northern bank of the frozen Irtysh River. The UN forces would be attempting to cross this line soon, their last barrier before the border with Russia proper, and Kurikin would intercept them there and recapture the missiles. With any luck, the UN would see that there was no point in further resistance. The vehicles Kurikin's men had discovered abandoned south of

Karaganda showed that the enemy had very few fighting vehicles, making this now more of a police action than a military operation. That suited Kurikin just fine.

NEAR THE VILLAGE OF DJANAKSHIMAN
6 November, 1230 Hours

Where Route P49 bent from its northeasterly course to due north to intersect the M11 highway, Chandler redirected the column once more, to the northeast. He followed a narrow country road, or more likely, the general track of it, for the road was under more than a foot of snow and was completely invisible. This road would lead them straight to the Russian border, crossing the River Irtysh about thirty miles ahead, halfway between Pavlodar and Semipalatinsk, the two largest Russian cities in the region. This crossing point was about midway between the two cities—and the armed units that might be located in them.

The column had covered nearly a hundred miles in the past twelve hours, still far below Chandler's hoped-for rate of march, but it was now a straight shot to the border. Even at this rate, in less than twelve hours they would be in safety. If the Russians had had even half the problems Chandler had encountered, there was no way their main forces could get in front of his column. Coming up from Karaganda by the main highway, they had to cover nearly double the distance. Chandler's information was that the enemy didn't have sizable units in either Pavlodar or Semipalatinsk—or at least nothing that even the reduced fighting capability of the UN forces couldn't handle out in the open—so if that information was reliable, they had almost made it.

Chandler's Hummer stood to one side for a moment as he watched the column crawl past. They had by now lost one fifth of the nearly two hundred vehicles with which they had started the march from Karaganda; infantrymen were huddled, shivering, on the top decks of the APCs, their helmets and field jackets covered with a crust of snow and ice. Even though the snow had stopped some time before, the temperature hovered just below zero degrees Fahrenheit, and a biting wind swept down from the north. Chandler, who had experienced his share of cold winters back in Pennsylvania, could not stop his teeth from chattering, and he could hardly remember ever having been too warm in his life, although he knew he must have been at some point. The Senegalese suffered especially, and Chandler was gratified to learn that the South Koreans and Japanese had volunteered to take their turns riding topside. It was quite a little army he had, Chandler marveled to himself. It was almost a shame that it would soon either die or be disbanded.

He reached down inside the Hummer and tapped his driver on the shoulder and felt the man jerk awake. Most of them had been awake for over forty-eight hours now, straining nerves, eyes, and muscles to keep moving through the storm, and they were reaching the end of their stamina. The Hummer moved out, spewing snow to both sides in waves as it paralleled the column, making its way back up toward the head. They were trying to follow the road now, a very narrow one, so they had reverted to single file, apart from some small scouting units Chandler had put out to the flanks to take advantage of the improved visibility. The entire cavalcade stretched for nearly three kilometers.

As they moved, Chandler noticed that they were finally getting into more and more frequent heavy stands of trees, silent and shrouded with snow, with mists hanging mysteriously in their branches. It was a sign that they were at last leaving the featureless, bare steppe country and approaching their goal. The River Irtysh was the formal geographical boundary of the steppe. Just a few miles beyond that, Russia!

Chandler's vehicle slipped in behind Wakeham's once more, and Chandler dropped down inside the cab to warm up for a moment. The heater was blasting warm air, but, since they had to keep the roof hatch open, it was fighting a losing battle against the cold. Elders and Goldman were huddled together in the back, along with several infantrymen, making a virtue of the cramped quarters at least to share body warmth. Chandler pulled off his frosted goggles, leaned back against a duffel bag, and closed his eyes, just for a second.

Despite having been stationed in Germany for two years with V Corps near Nuremberg, Chandler had never learned to speak German. It had made him feel alien, even though most Germans seemed to speak passable English and the place was crawling with American servicemen. He had spent several weeks on patrol with the 11th Cavalry up along the East German border and had been brought back to Nuremberg for the Thanksgiving holidays to rest. Unfortunately, his wife's father had just passed away, and she had rushed home for the funeral. Since Chandler never got along with her family, and since they really couldn't afford the trip, he had stayed behind, and was staying at a hotel run exclusively for American servicemen, right across from the entrance to the old walled city itself.

Winter in Germany was a magical time, and he especially loved the open-air markets that were held in the open squares; booths were set up selling all sorts of Christmas ornaments, toys, crafts, and, of course, food. Chandler had spent most of the evening elbowing his way through the crowds, munching hard rolls stuffed with bratwurst and sipping the hot, spiced wine they sold, even though he normally never drank, when he suddenly had a craving for some pastry. He found a place, but the crowd around it was three-deep, and he couldn't quite get through. The harder he pushed forward, the farther back he seemed to get, and he could see that the booths were beginning to close their shutters for the night. When he finally worked his way up to the counter, the girl behind it just smiled, shrugged, and closed up shop, and the departing customers jostled him out of their way. The girl looked very much as his wife had when they had first met, years before, in high school.

"General," Elders was saying as he shook Chandler by the shoulder. "Captain Wakeham's calling from up front."

Chandler opened his eyes and looked around in embarrassment. The Hummer was stopped in a line of trees at the top of a slight hill, and the small red brake light of Wakeham's vehicle shone through the front windscreen. Chandler pulled himself up through the roof hatch and saw Wakeham pointing down the hill and smiling.

A small village consisting of perhaps fifty low, sturdily constructed houses and farm buildings clustered along the edge of a river that was about two hundred meters across and had large chunks of ice floating sluggishly down it. A narrow concrete bridge spanned the river, and dirty tire tracks led up the opposite bank and disappeared into the trees beyond.

"The town is Spunik, sir," Wakeham called back to him from the roof of his own vehicle, "and that's the Irtysh."

Chandler shook the cobwebs out of his head. They were perhaps fifty miles from the border now, just a few more hours, if they hurried. And no sign of enemy forces. The streets of the village were deserted, but blue smoke rose from some of the chimneys.

"Let's get some scouts across, Captain," Chandler shouted, as he pulled out his map and laid it flat in front of him. "The M3 angles away from the river a little on the opposite side, so we should be able to get everyone across without running into any casual traffic on the highway. Then we can make our dash for the border."

"Yes, sir," Wakeham said energetically, and he stood up taller and waved at the column.

Half a dozen Hummers and a pair of Bradleys peeled laboriously out of the column and through the banks of snow on either side, passing Chandler and moving quickly down into the village. Meanwhile, Peabody's three tanks took up overwatching positions in the treeline. One of the Bradleys discharged a squad of infantry, and more soldiers climbed out of the Hummers and quickly checked through the houses in the village, running from door to door. A tall Japanese policeman ran out into the open and gave Chandler the all-clear signal. Chandler let out his breath in a rush.

Two of the Hummers now rolled across the bridge, followed by one of the Bradleys, and Chandler caught his breath again as he saw the bridge visibly shiver under the weight of the APC. The Bradley weighed only about thirteen tons, maybe a little more with about twenty infantrymen crammed on board, but one of his tanks weighed at least four times that. More important, Chandler didn't know how much an SS-25 weighed, but it was certainly a lot more than a Bradley. He quickly rationalized as best he could to put a positive spin on the situation: Now the Bradley had been moving fairly quickly, and one of the Hummers had also still been on the bridge. And, of course, the bridge hadn't collapsed, so, perhaps, if they took it very slowly and sent one vehicle over at a time, there would be no trouble. It would take a little longer, but they would make it.

"Did you see that, sir?" Wakeham called back. "I don't like the look of that bridge."

They had abandoned their bridging unit back at Karaganda, but even that would not have been able to span a river this wide, and the floating blocks of ice would prevent even their amphibious vehicles from fording the river.

"Yes, but I think we can make it. Besides," Chandler added, "it's the only bridge we've got."

"We could try farther upstream, sir," Wakeham suggested. "The map shows a larger bridge at Chagan."

"That's another fifty miles," Chandler countered, "and very close to Semipalatinsk. Whatever shortcomings this bridge has, at least it doesn't seem to be defended. It will have to do."

Wakeham nodded and turned back to see the commander of the Bradley standing atop his vehicle near the tree line on the opposite bank, waving a pennant as the signal to move forward. While it was almost certain that the Russians knew just where the column was by this time, Chandler thought, there was no reason to give them a precise fix by using the radio. He waved back and jumped down from the Hummer.

Chandler waded through the deep snow over to where Peabody's tank sat. Peabody leaned down from the turret.

"I don't like the look of that bridge," Peabody said in greeting.

"Nobody does. We're going to have to take it very slow, and bring your tanks over last, since they're the heaviest."

"No problem, but what about those big honkers?" Peabody jerked a thumb at the first of the SS-25s in the column, which was just visible about two hundred yards back. "They're not built out of feathers, either."

"We'll have to do our best."

Engineer Lieutenant Harish was already down at the bridge examining its supports when Chandler arrived in his Hummer. He was already waving the smaller vehicles across, one at a time, and a file of infantry trudged alongside to establish a secure bridgehead on the far bank.

"I would say twenty to twenty-five tons capacity, maximum," Harish said, leaning on one of the concrete supports and feeling its vibration as a Hummer rolled over above him.

"But the M-1s weigh nearly sixty," Chandler pleaded.

"You can try it, if you like, but I'd wear my swim trunks."

"Do you think the missile carriers can make it?"

Harish looked at him with his dark, sad eyes. "It will be very close, but we don't have much choice."

"Isn't there anything you can do to reinforce the bridge?"

"Not in the time we've got or without materials and tools. If we had twelve hours or so, I could probably get what I need by dismantling some of the houses here, but I don't think we've got that long, do you?"

"No, I suppose we don't."

"Very cheap construction," Harish mumbled, almost to himself. "They've probably been putting trucks across this for years well over its load capacity. It will likely fall down on its own soon."

"That's very reassuring."

For the next two hours, the lighter vehicles were fed across the bridge with painful slowness. Meanwhile Harish's men and some American and British mechanics were busily stripping the SS-25 TELs of everything that seemed superfluous, to decrease their weight. Radios, tool kits, even the metal panels over engine compartments, were pulled off and either cast aside or transported separately over the river until there was nothing left that they dared to touch. Other men were busily sweeping snow and chipping ice from the bridge itself, anything to save what might be the vital pound or two.

Finally, everyone and everything was across the river except for the tanks; a platoon of Bradleys, which would form the rearguard; an armored recovery vehicle, which was very nearly as heavy as one of the tanks; and the three TELs. Some of the Russian civilians had let their curiosity overcome their fear, and they now stood in groups of two or three, shaking their heads in doubt as the first of the massive vehicles inched its way onto the span.

The huge tires rubbed up against the low curbs on either side of the roadway, and Harish stood in the middle of the bridge, guiding the driver. He held his hands up and waved the TEL forward, sometimes indicating a slight angle to the right or left; then he would step back a pace, almost seeming to pull the beast across with his own muscles.

The snow crunched under the giant black tires as they turned, ever so slowly. Harish stepped back gingerly, as if it were his steps that might collapse the bridge and not the weight of the missile transport.

At first things seemed to be going well enough. The bridge groaned pitifully as one pair of wheels after another put their weight on it, but it held, and Harish had almost reached the midpoint himself, looking back over his shoulder nervously to see how much farther he had to go. Step by step, he backed over the bridge, and the TEL followed him like a recalcitrant dog. Then the entire TEL was on the span itself. Chandler, standing near the northern end of the bridge with Morgan and Meriani, could see the structure wobble; Harish had trouble keeping his feet as he moved backward, but he kept going.

"We've got to go through this *three* times?" Goldman asked, coming up to the group. All three glared at him angrily, and he said no more.

Now Harish was on firm ground. Chandler saw the muscles in his face loosen as he looked to either side and saw that the river was past. He waved the TEL forward again, and Chandler saw the smile on the driver's face as well. The snow crunched again under the tires as they turned, just a little faster than they had before, and the bridge groaned again, but this time the groan turned into a high-pitched shriek, and the nose of the TEL began to wiggle sideways. The smile disappeared from the driver's face, and Harish clapped his hands together over his head, the signal to stop, but it was too late. With a sharp snap, a section of the bridge under the front wheels of the TEL gave way, dropping at an angle; the nose of the vehicle itself smashed into the road, its two front tires suspended in air, the rear ones still on the bridge, and the entire thing wedged firmly in place.

Harish immediately began shouting to the driver of the armored recovery vehicle, basically a tank chassis without the gun turret and with an assortment of winches and pulleys used for extracting other heavy vehicles from such situations. As the ARV positioned itself at the far end of the bridge, Harish turned to the commanders, none of whom had been able to find words to speak yet.

"If I can connect some cables together and hook them onto the rear of the TEL," Harish explained. "Maybe we can pull it back out of this hole and off the bridge."

"But you don't have anything that would be able to repair this broken span, do you?" Chandler asked.

"No," Harish admitted. "The entire structure is much weakened now. In fact, we'll be very lucky if we do manage to extract this TEL to the other side."

"Then what?" Chandler asked of anyone with an answer.

"Perhaps we can run the TELs east along the river to the bridge at Chagan after all," Morgan suggested. "We still have Peabody's tanks and APCs to escort them, and we can keep pace along this side of the river."

"And practically all the way to Semipalatinsk?" Chandler countered. "The Russians would be all over us, and three tanks and APCs aren't going to be enough to protect the missiles with most of us on this side of the river." He slammed the heel of his hand against his forehead. "It's my own stupid fault. I should have tried to move the missiles across as soon as we had a viable bridgehead. Then at least we wouldn't be divided by the damn river, and we'd have time to figure things out."

"Frankly, sir," Morgan said, "you shouldn't blame yourself. If the Russians do catch us out, our entire force, reduced as it is, isn't going to be enough to protect the missiles. If the TELs couldn't make it across the bridge, we were going to be in trouble whether they went first, last, or anywhere in the column."

"*Merde!*" another voice grunted from behind them. They turned to find Martin standing there, staring at the trapped missile carrier. "I thought *I* was coming with bad news, but this is much worse."

"What bad news?" Chandler and Morgan asked together.

"I was out with the scouts about three kilometers west along the M3 highway, and we spotted enemy reconnaissance vehicles coming down the road from Pavlodar, supported by a platoon of tanks, and when I arrived here, one of my lieutenants had just come up from the scouts from out toward Semipalatinsk, and there are armored vehicles coming that way as well."

The news galvanized Chandler into action. "No point in worrying about radio silence anymore," he shouted as he ran for his Hummer. "Get Peabody and warn him, tell him to get into the best defensive position he can, and send a company of infantry back across the bridge to support him. He's got to cover his own back, but to lend us fire support if he can. Have Harish do what he can to pull that monster out of its hole, but I also want the TELs wired with explosives."

Morgan looked at Chandler in horror. "And what do you think will happen to those nuclear warheads in such an explosion?"

"Frankly, Randy, I don't know," Chandler admitted as he climbed into his Hummer. "I always understood that a nuclear detonation is really kind of difficult to arrange. We don't believe that the warheads themselves have been primed to detonate, and maybe we will just manage to destroy the usable hardware. But, if there is going to be a nuclear explosion, this is about as good a spot as any for it, fifty miles from the nearest city. All I know for sure is that we can't let that butcher Shchernikov get his hands on the missiles again. He'll use them for sure, and the result will undoubtedly be worse than anything that could happen here."

Chandler's Hummer roared off, following Martin's jeep toward where the defensive line had been established in a tight semicircle around the bridgehead, about a kilometer across. He turned in his seat and saw Morgan explaining his orders to Harish and saw the Israeli cover his face with his hands before slowly heading back down to the riverbank.

Kurikin's reconnaissance troop had reported locating the UN forces a few minutes earlier. As the rest of his regiment moved up the road toward them, the recon troops spread out to either side, to determine the form of the UN positions. He had caught Chandler trying to get his troops across the river. It couldn't have worked out better. The UN force was helpless, and there would be no point in their offering any resistance now.

Kurikin's GAZ jeep raced along the M3 toward the front of his column, weaving dangerously between the moving tanks and APCs, fishtailing on the packed snow. Kurikin held on to the edge of the windscreen with one hand and to the base of his seat with the other, trying to keep from being thrown completely out of the speeding vehicle; he had to get to the point of contact with the enemy first. Immediately upon receipt of the message from the scouts, Kurikin had ordered all radios in the regiment shut down—turned off, not just on radio silence—so he couldn't very well receive any orders, and thus couldn't be accused of disobeying them. Kurikin figured that Shchernikov would order an immediate, bloody, and totally unnecessary attack on the UN troops, but if Kurikin himself could only open a parlay with the enemy commander, he was certain that he could convince the man to surrender to avoid further loss of life. Shchernikov didn't want to avoid killing, he thrived on it, and if he could eliminate all of the witnesses to his atrocities in Almaty, so much the better. Kurikin had to prevent this. His standing orders were to find and fix the enemy, and he was doing that. Kurikin estimated that, since no helicopters would fly in this weather, he would have an hour at most before the evil little dwarf would be able to get up to the front and take command. If he were lucky, an hour would be enough.

The American Bradleys, with their 25mm guns and TOW launchers—although few TOW missiles remained—were now the most powerful elements of the UN force's arsenal, and were spaced along the perimeter Chandler had set up around the bridgehead. The French and British cavalrymen, who had lost most of their vehicles, along with the Argentine, Japanese, and Senegalese military police, were placed as infantry, while the South Koreans were sent to reinforce Peabody on the south side of the river. The Egyptian artillerymen were helping Harish's engineers to attempt to extract the TEL from the bridge. A few Milan antitank missile launchers also remained, and the machine guns of the armored personnel carriers were also incorporated into the defense, but Chandler knew that the line was hopelessly thin and that it would not stand up against a determined assault by enemy tanks and infantry.

Chandler lay in the snow next to Morgan and a pair of Argentine infantrymen who manned a small Carl Gustav antitank rocket. He saw a Russian tank company, deployed on both sides of the M3 highway, coming from Pavlodar. Obviously, this was the source of greatest danger, since the vehicles reported by Martin to be coming up from Semipalatinsk had not appeared yet. Just the enemy troops Chandler could see from here would be more than a match for his forces.

Harish gave a final, and really unnecessary, tug on the heavy steel cable that connected the trapped TEL to the recovery vehicle. They had had to attach several cables to cover the distance between the rear end of the TEL and the closest point on the bridge where it was safe for the recovery vehicle to approach, and Harish didn't like it. The strain on even one cable doubled over, which was the prescribed method for such towing, would have been dangerous enough, but to have a single cable, with tenuous points of connection, pulling that weight was just asking for trouble. But he didn't have a choice, so he jogged a few steps to one side and raised his hand so that both the driver of the TEL, who would try to use the rear wheels to help back out, and the recovery vehicle driver could see him.

He brought his hand down dramatically, and the ARV belched diesel fumes and took up the slack in the cable, inching backward away from the river. At the same time, the TEL driver revved his engine, and two of his tires began spinning on the slick snow and ice of the bridge. Then, slowly, almost imperceptibly, the nose of the TEL eased away from the jagged edge of the broken roadway. Harish made a fist and pumped it up and down, and the ARV gunned its engine louder. The wheels of the TEL were starting to take a bite now, and there was a groan of metal as the cab of the TEL pulled free and straightened out.

Suddenly the air was filled with a high-pitched twanging sound, like the plucking of some massive steel guitar. With a tremendous crack and a whirring noise, the cable snapped and lashed out like a huge whip. Harish clapped his hands together over his head and screamed for the men who were idly watching the effort to take cover. Harish dropped to the ground as the cable lashed over his head, neatly severing a small tree next to him; then it lay coiling and twitching on the ground for a moment, like a wounded snake. Harish raised his head and saw the TEL wedged more tightly into the gap in the bridge than ever.

Kurikin could see the enemy positions clearly. They had not had time to dig in or to put out any significant camouflage. He smiled to himself at how easy this should be. He had just received a report from one of his scouts who had infiltrated along the southern bank of the river and had sighted the TEL trapped in the middle of the damaged bridge. The UN forces were completely trapped. They would either surrender or attempt to run, and in either case, he would have the missiles in his grasp. Even if they tried to fight, it wouldn't last more than a few minutes.

He gave his men a few more precious minutes to extend their line down to the river to the south and on the northern flank as far as the road the UN forces were undoubtedly planning to take north-eastward to the border. If they tried to escape to the east, there was nowhere for them to go but Semipalatinsk, where small but adequate Russian forces would easily contain them until Kurikin could catch up with them.

Kurikin took a long tent pole with a white camouflage parka tied to one end. Raising it high over his head, he walked down the center of the highway in the direction of the enemy lines. It was a very long hundred meters. Kurikin could sense *everything* about him, the crisp cold of the air, the delicate pine scent of the woods, even the quiet whirring of the turret of the enemy APC as it turned to track targets and the click of rifle bolts as they chambered rounds undoubtedly meant for him.

Finally, a tall man with graying hair stood up, still covered with snow from lying on the ground. He wore the sky-blue UN beret and had an American flag patch on his shoulder. He walked out a few paces from his lines and met Kurikin in the middle of the roadway.

"You must be General Chandler," Kurikin said, extending his hand. "I am Colonel Kurikin, commander of the 25th Tank Regiment of the Republican Guard. You have given us quite a chase."

Chandler smiled broadly. At first Kurikin thought that it was in response to his simple compliment, although he had meant it sin-cerely enough. But he had rather expected the man to be haggard and at least a little frightened. He must have known that he was beaten, and he certainly had no reason to know that Kurikin didn't plan to deal with them as harshly as Shchernikov could be expected to do. Perhaps he was just glad that it was all over.

"That's right, Colonel," Chandler said, "and I'm afraid that I'm going to have to ask what are the intentions of your forces."

Kurikin was taken aback. "Excuse me, sir, but this is *my* country, and *you* are the foreigners. I will take my forces where I please, and I do not have to give accounts to you. I think you know that I have come to demand in the name of the Russian Provisional Government the surrender of the missiles you have in your possession. I guarantee you that your men will have safe conduct to the Russian border."

"I can imagine what a safe-conduct pass from General Shchernikov is worth. I've seen some of his handiwork, thank you."

"It is I who offer you the safe conduct. General Shchernikov is not here at the moment, and I give you my personal word that no harm will come to you or any of your men. You may even take your arms and equipment with you. All we want are the missiles, and you will be free to go. I should add that I safeguarded the Russian civilians you left back at Karaganda over Shchernikov's objections."

"I don't believe I'll be able to accept your offer, Colonel," Chandler said, standing with his feet apart and his hands behind his back, rocking onto the balls of his feet. "Instead, I have a counteroffer for you. I want some engineer vehicles to help me get the missiles across the river. I believe you have some floating bridges which would serve the purpose. I am also demanding, in the name of the War Crimes Tribunal of the United Nations, the surrender of General Shchernikov for trial for genocide and acts of terrorism."

Chandler kept the smile on his face. Even if the game was lost, there was no point in giving this bastard the satisfaction of seeing him crawl. He had come to the decision to surrender. They had fought the good fight, trying to save the world, and the world had abandoned them. Now it would be up to someone else to get thermonuclear weapons out of the hands of this madman. Chandler wasn't going to watch any more of his men die trying to do it for them. The most he could do at this point was to play out his bluff and hold out for the best possible terms for his men. At least the fight that his men had put up would serve to keep the Russians at a respectful distance and encourage them to get them out of the way rather than to seek further trouble with them.

Kurikin couldn't help but let out a bark of laughter. "Are you out of your mind? I don't mind a little show of military machismo, but I can't believe that you truly understand just how desperate your situation is. We both know that you don't have the weapons to stop my regiment if we choose to cut right through you and *take* the missiles. I'm just trying to avoid needless bloodshed on both sides. But what you *really* don't appreciate is that you'd be much better off dealing with me than with the general. Now, I won't tell anyone of your ridiculous demand to arrest him. That won't do either of us any good, but you must realize that the man is certifiably insane, and I'm telling you that my troops and I are all that stands between you and his desire for revenge. I'll protect you, but I've got to have the missiles in my power to do it. That's what we all really want, and the missiles are going to buy the lives of your men. Surely that's worth it."

Chandler heard footsteps in the snow behind him and saw Morgan approaching with a pair of unfamiliar UN officers, one of whom wore a Canadian shoulder patch and the other one a patch from Brazil. More surprisingly, he saw Saavedra hobbling along with the aid of his cane. Morgan looked like the cat who had eaten the canary, and Saavedra winked openly at Chandler, and the two UN officers just nodded politely.

"Permit me to introduce my executive officer, Colonel Morgan," Chandler said, not knowing what else to say in the circumstances. "Colonel Kurikin."

"Good day to you, sir," Morgan said, bowing stiffly, "and these are Colonels Saavedra, Ferguson, and Pineiros. They've just arrived with a contingent of UN forces from Semipalatinsk, as you may already be aware."

From the look on Kurikin's face, it was obvious that he was very much *not* aware, and Chandler stared intently at Morgan, showing the whites all the way around his eyes, trying to force an explanation. Kurikin winced at the unexpected cost of shutting down all of his column's radios during his approach march.

"It seems," Morgan went on, "that our colleagues in Semipalatinsk, a Canadian, a Brazilian, and an Italian Alpini battalion, mistook the road to the Russian frontier and headed this way instead, shortly after the arrival of Colonel Saavedra, who flew there yesterday from Karaganda in his helicopter. The authorities of your provisional government don't appear to have had the strength of conviction necessary to oppose their move by force of arms, and so we now have two additional battalions here. The Italians are now reinforcing our positions on the other side of the river. I'm sure, Colonel Kurikin, that you'll want to take this new information into consideration before making a decision on your course of action."

Kurikin looked from one smug face to another in confusion. Just then a voice called to him from his own lines.

"Colonel, General Shchernikov is here and wants to speak with you."

"I'll bet he does," Chandler said. "You'd better go."

Kurikin turned and started to walk away, but then turned back and said in a low voice, "Just remember what I tried to do for you. Just remember that."

Chandler waited until he and the other officers were back in the safety of the woods, where he now found a pair of Canadian Leopard II tanks positioned in support of his Bradleys. Then he grabbed Ferguson's hand and pumped it vigorously.

"I can't remember when I've been more glad to see anyone," he said, shaking hands with Pineiros and Saavedra in turn. "Now, what the hell are you doing here?"

"When Saavedra here crash-landed at our base in Semipalatinsk, Mr. Devi was just ordering us to get our tails out of Kazakhstan. We'd only gotten bits and pieces of the story of what you all were up to, mostly from the Blackhawk pilots and wounded you sent out earlier, and, well, we just couldn't quite bring ourselves to leaving you behind. We saddled up for the move, but instead of heading north to the border, we just pulled a left turn and headed west up this way. The Russians really didn't have the muscle in Semipalatinsk to stop us, but I'm surprised that this fellow apparently didn't expect us."

"It wasn't a crash landing," Saavedra muttered.

"Oh, I suppose that the rotor blades are supposed to dig into the ground like that," Ferguson said.

"It was a controlled descent. There's a difference," Saavedra insisted, "but I was lucky to get there in any condition."

"So, what now?" Chandler asked.

"I've got a company of Swedish engineers with all their equipment, and they're now trying to pull that hog off the bridge. We can just move it down to Semipalatinsk. I left another battalion of Finns there to watch our backs, but it didn't look like the Russians there were really in the mood to do anything. It's just this asshole Shchernikov who's causing all the trouble, and his star certainly seems to be on the wane."

"Well, let's book up," Saavedra said, "before they change their minds."

"What kind of imbecile are you?" Shchernikov screamed into Kurikin's face. "You could have gone through them like a hot knife through butter before their reinforcements arrived, but you were busy *negotiating* on your own, and you missed the opportunity. Now we've got to fight them all together."

Kurikin didn't flinch at Shchernikov's assault. While Lushkin stood next to the general, half a dozen of Kurikin's own officers surrounded them and let Kurikin see in their eyes that they were with him.

"They say that they've got three fresh UN battalions with them now, possibly more."

"What of it?" Shchernikov shouted. "That's what you have tanks for. Go in there and get them!"

"We have about sixty functional tanks and two motor rifle battalions. That isn't enough to take on a total of five or six enemy battalions in defensive positions. Unless you can call up more troops, we aren't going to attack at all."

"You know that there aren't any more troops, you coward!" Shchernikov shrieked. "Even if we had more, they wouldn't be enough for you, because you haven't got the balls for a fight. I'm going to have you shot for cowardice in the face of the enemy! Lushkin!"

Lushkin took a step toward Kurikin, but he stopped quickly when he felt the cold metal of a gun barrel at the back of his neck.

"You call *me* a coward?" Kurikin said, shoving the shorter man back forcefully. "*I* didn't abandon Alma-Ata without a shot. *I* didn't leave two thousand of our people behind for the Kazakhs to massacre. If it weren't for those men on the other side of the clearing, those people would all be dead now, because *you* were so fucking busy being the great warlord. Well, they demanded we surrender you to a war crimes tribunal, and I think we might just do that!"

Shchernikov hadn't drawn his sidearm to do anything other than kill the odd prisoner in many months, and his reactions were slow. By the time he had the pistol clear of its holster, his body had been penetrated by half a dozen bullets from several different directions. Lushkin watched his former leader collapse to the floor with equanimity, just stepping back a bit as Shchernikov grasped feebly at the leg of his pants.

CHAPTER 9

NOVOSIBIRSK
8 November, 1400 Hours

When Chandler woke up, his feet were propped up on his duffel bag and he couldn't remember what he had dreamed. It was the first time in a long while that that had happened. He only knew that it was something peaceful, and he felt good and rested for a change.

The long lines of huge American C-5B transports clogged the taxiway like rush-hour traffic back in Washington, and air force transports or chartered airliners from other nations were also present in force, their cargo ramps and passenger stairways feeding swarms of heavily laden men and women into the bellies of the aircraft in a steady stream. Chandler watched them through the tall windows of the airport terminal in front of him as dozens of soldiers in sky-blue berets milled back and forth, talking happily. His own flight would be leaving soon, but at least it would be a passenger version of the C-5A, with a seat for him in the upper deck "officers' country" with accommodations at least approximating business class on a commercial airline. He could see the other officers gathering to make their final farewells.

Saavedra was hobbling along on his cane, together with Hamed and Greene, and they were apparently giving Peabody the details of their escape from Karaganda, with Saavedra acting out the piloting of the helicopter using his cane as a make-believe joystick, and Hamed using the flat of his hand to describe the banking and bucking of their flight. And Peabody was swaggering noticeably, since he had ultimately been able to drive out of Kazakhstan in his own tank. Meriani, Kondo, Harish, and the others were also congregating. Morgan, who had been dozing next to Chandler, dragged himself to his feet, smacking his mouth and rubbing his head.

"It's going to be a long flight home," Morgan said, trying to flex his stiff muscles.

"Not as long as the road here, I hope," Peabody said, and the others chuckled.

Chandler stood erect and raised a Styrofoam cup of cold coffee in a mock toast. "I won't give you a long speech," he began.

"Believing that we've already suffered enough," Saavedra added, then looking quickly over his shoulder as if to try to catch whoever had said that.

Chandler just raised an eyebrow and continued. "*But*, I have to give you a few parting words. I don't know what our respective governments will say when we get home, whether we'll be received as heroes or be punished as mutineers, but there can't be much doubt in any of our own minds that we did the right thing. Those damned missiles have been turned over to the Russian government, and they were dismantled under international supervision even while we were getting here to the airport. And it even looks like the new governments in Kazakhstan, both for the Kazakhs and for the Russian separatists, seem more willing to come to terms, now that they're free of the influence of Qasimbekai and Shchernikov. The latest word is that Colonel Kurikin has seized power on the Russian side and has named our old friend, Professor Restrepov, as the chief negotiator with the Kazakhs and the UN, a very good sign indeed. I don't expect that this will be the end of their troubles. There are still thousands of refugees on both sides of the line with revenge in their hearts, but at least we seem to have bought some time for their governments to organize and settle down, and perhaps, since the memories of those two gentlemen Shchernikov and Qasimbekai are now held in some disfavor, maybe the policies they pushed will also be abandoned."

"I can tell you something about how you'll be received back home," Goldman said as he and Elders came up behind Chandler.

"Yes," Elders broke in. "Of course, the fact that those Russian prisoners you brought out, the ones who had been in on Shchernikov's raid on the Concert Hall, spilled their guts as soon as they found out about his death certainly helped your position, proving that what you had been saying and doing all along were right, and Devi was dead wrong. The administration may not know much about foreign policy, but they can read opinion poll results with the best of them, and Goldman's stories have created quite a little whiplash of public feeling against having our boys serving under the UN flag, at least where American interests aren't actually at stake. It even caused such a reaction in the UN itself that the General Assembly and then the Security Council both voted to restrict the authority for the dispatch and direction of armed troops to the Security Council, taking it away from Secretary General Muli. They also reinstated what was really part of the UN Charter, the policy of noninterference in the internal affairs of member states, no matter how noble the purpose seems to be. That should cut down on the number of cases where we've got troops involved as well. All in all, not a bad day's work."

"All I can add to that," Chandler said, after a round of cheers died down among the officers, "is that I'm more than proud to have served with you all. You are tough sons of bitches and damn good men into the bargain. Thanks for everything."

There was the usual round of handshaking and promises to write and offers of a place to stay, "if ever you're in town," which none of the men really anticipated would be fulfilled. But, at that moment, of course, they all meant them most sincerely.

"I don't know about y'all," Peabody said when they had finished, "but I'm emotionally drained and I think they just called our flight to the States via Frankfurt. So let's get the hell out of here."

As the Americans struggled through the crowd and out onto the tarmac, Chandler found himself walking next to Goldman.

"So, Jeff," Chandler said, using the reporter's given name for the first time that he could remember, "do you have in mind a brilliant new career as a spy?"

"No way, José," Goldman replied, shaking his head. "I think the very first plane in brought this guy straight from Langley, trenchcoat and all, and his only message was that he had to take away my little commo set, and, by the way, your country expresses its deep gratitude for your contribution, etc., etc." Goldman had lowered his voice to emphasize the pomposity of the little speech. "No, when I do something, I want to see that byline right up there on the top of the front page. No more of this serving in the shadows for me."

"Well, if you can stand any more gratitude, I'll toss in my own. I've been on the line with Alvarez, you know, the general at Central Command back in Washington, and he says that your last message did get through. It was your heads-up that let our people put enough pressure on the Russians to eventually get us out of there."

"Well, that's good to hear, Gen'ral."

They approached the passenger stairs of the massive green aircraft, and Goldman took Chandler's hand once more. "I'm sitting in the back with the proletariat, so I'll be seeing you." And before

Chandler could reply, the reporter had loped off and inserted himself into a line of grumbling, complaining troopers at the ramp.

"It looks as though I'll be riding with you," Elders said, struggling a bit to catch up to Chandler.

"And what does your future look like back home?" Chandler asked.

"I don't know what anyone else has planned for me, probably a job with significant rank and no responsibility."

"I know how that works," Chandler agreed.

"But I think I've had about enough of this. I've got a doctorate, and I think I'll test the waters for a teaching position somewhere, maybe Kansas, somewhere as far from an international border as I can get."

"You did your best in a tough job," Chandler said, without much conviction.

"I'd like to believe that, but I don't, any more than you do," Elders said, shaking his head. The wind ruffled his short hair—he had apparently decided to eliminate the comb-over at some point during their exodus from Almaty. "I was running a career back there, and I forgot for a minute that what I was doing really made a difference in people's lives, even made a difference as to whether they survived or not. I don't want that kind of responsibility anymore. I guess I'm not cut out for it, not like you."

Chandler laughed out loud. "It's going to be a long trip, and I've got an interesting story to tell you about my ability to deal with responsibility." Chandler wrapped an arm around Elders's shoulders and led him up the stairs into the airplane.

ABOUT THE AUTHOR

ALEXANDER M. GRACE is a veteran of nearly twenty years in the Foreign Service and a former officer in the U.S. Army Reserve. This is his third novel.